PROJECT ONION

The Melville Consulting Series

Happy reading!

Karen

Karen Stensgaard

Project Onion is a novel and a work of fiction. Names, characters, places, and incidents are used fictitiously and not intended to disparage any company's products or services. Any similarity to living or dead persons, events, or locales is coincidental.

Copyright © 2021 by Karen Stensgaard

Karen Stensgaard
Sandefur Metz Publishing Company
554 N. 18th St.
Philadelphia, PA 19130

ISBN 9780999219751 (ebook)
ISBN 9780999219744 (paperback)

Other Books by Karen Stensgaard:

The Aquamarine Sea Series:
~ *AQUAVIT*
~ *BLUENESS*

~ DEDICATION ~

To anyone who struggles with doing something brave;
To my cats, Lucy and Cosette, masters at balancing
work-life-sleep; and
To Dad, this book's first reader and a devoted fan.

~ THE ONION ~

One of the world's most widely consumed vegetables can
be deadly if eaten by cats, dogs, and many other animals.

Like onions, people are multi-layered. If someone
says, "You know your onions," it means you know a lot.
You're clever!

Onion in street slang means an ounce of a drug. An onion
of coke refers to an ounce of cocaine.

~ INSPIRATION ~

"Life is like an onion. You peel it off one layer at a time, and sometimes you weep."
Carl Sandburg, American Poet, 1878 - 1967

"People like us, who believe in physics, know that the distinction between past, present and future is only a stubbornly persistent illusion."
Albert Einstein, German-American Physicist, 1879 - 1955

"We cannot live only for ourselves. A thousand fibers connect us with our fellow men."
Herman Melville, American Novelist and Poet, 1819 – 1891

PROJECT ONION

Chapter 1 ~ *Just Do It*

"What's so special about Fridays, and why do they make you feel so great?" I stared at the hazelnut coffee in my mug for an answer. This existential question was too early for my half-asleep brain to crack, so I sipped more caffeine.

Today was just another workday, but it was loaded with so much anticipation, especially with a three-day weekend ahead. Tonight I had dinner plans at a fancy restaurant with my boyfriend and his work buddies. I couldn't bear to jinx things by overthinking it.

My unwanted blues and nervousness, shadowing me for months, had faded some. This first week back to the old work grind had gone surprisingly well, and the early morning rush wasn't so bad.

I lifted my mug and made a silly toast to my big brother Keith. He smiled back from an old photo. "You'd be so proud of your little sis. Vengeance shall be ours, eventually." If only I could call to tell him my fantastic news.

My phone alarm sounded with John Lennon's optimistic song "Imagine," reminding me to leave. I gulped the rest of my coffee, cringing at the gritty aftertaste of coffee grounds from my sloppy preparation. After I rinsed out my mug, I drank some of New York City's tasty bargain-priced tap water.

Living alone inside my apartment, without even a pet, took getting used to. So sometimes, I chatted with Giuseppe, my gargoyle, perched on the kitchen shelf. "Keep an eye on the place while I'm gone, buddy. And scare off any evil spirits."

Giuseppe's stony eyes glared from a vigilant, crouched position with his mighty wings folded tightly against his chest. I sighed. Sure, I'd rather stay home, but someone had to get a job and pay the bills. Or both of us would lose our high-cost perch.

Once I moved past the first month with this new job, I will spend more time with my old friends. I even planned to get a real live roommate that purrs.

Running late, I hustled down four flights of stairs inside my apartment building. I pressed against the building's front door to exit when a woman said, "Kat, wait up!"

I froze, irritated at the delay, and whispered under my breath, "Hell's bells and buckets of blood." I picked up that odd tiresome slang from a witty sailor on my seven-month voyage, and it wouldn't leave my memory bank.

Turning around, I saw Abby, my neighbor down the hall, who used to be my closest friend. Usually, I was happy to see her, but not now. "Hey. Sorry, I'm in a hurry. New job and all."

She grinned. "Headed to the subway?"

"Yeah." I opened the door, prepared to say a quick goodbye outside.

Abby asked, "The one at 66th and Broadway?"

"Yep." Not being a morning person, I preferred to commute solo. Another less convenient subway line was next to the park on Central Park West. Except I would be late and ruin all my extra effort this week to make a winning first impression. We strolled toward Broadway.

Abby was one of those annoyingly cheerful and chatty morning types. "I'm riding that subway too. So I'll walk with you. What a beautiful Friday to go to New Jersey. I hope this weather holds for a while."

The warm rays from the sun improved my mood. For the beginning of November, this was one of those unusually exquisite fall days. We were lucky *Sunna*, the Nordic Goddess of the Sun, still lingered here.

"Why New Jersey?"

"Looking at an apartment. You get so much more for your money there."

"But Abby, you can't leave Manhattan." And me, I wanted to add.

"Never hurts to look. It's so much more affordable." Abby sounded stressed. "I hate to bring up terrible news. Did you hear about Nathan in 8B?"

"Nathan? Not sure I know him."

"You talked to him at the rooftop party before you left on your bucket-list cruise."

Interrupted by a roar above our heads, we looked up to observe a noisy jet flying east toward the Hudson River. The plane's destination was most likely Newark airport in New Jersey. Despite being more than eight thousand feet over Manhattan, planes still made me nervous. Even if they lost engine power at that altitude, commercial jets could glide for hundreds of miles.

Abby and I stopped briefly to watch the plane disappear from view. An invisible bond existed among New Yorkers who had experienced that fateful day almost twenty years ago.

Jackson Chow, my new boss who was a former CIA operative, shared some essential tips during my impromptu training yesterday. His message was bleak. "Don't count on Homeland Security or anyone else who investigates terrorists." Overly cynical, but with his extensive industry contacts, he'd know.

I was tempted to share with Abby what Jackson told me. But this would only cause panic or invite unwanted questions about him and my job.

While we waited to cross busy Columbus Avenue, taxicabs, cars, and bikes flew by as if they were on an urgent mission to save the world. After a seven-month cruise from Copenhagen to Hong Kong and a trip to Texas and the West Coast, I was still adapting to my old life in nonstop Manhattan.

I refused to let irrational fear or worries consume me. Instead, I refocused on Abby and our mutual neighbor Nathan. "Now, I remember. The fortyish quiet guy who worked in publishing. What happened?"

"He died."

"He did? How?"

"Heard he committed suicide."

The word suicide hit home painfully. I stopped walking and touched Abby's shoulder. "Oh, how terrible. Maybe it was an accident."

"Well, if you call slitting your wrists and bleeding out in

your bathtub an accident."

"Such a shame." My stomach ached at what must be a suicide.

"Tell me about it. Nathan lost his job about six months back. He told me he had to downsize and sell his apartment. Publishing sucks. No one reads anything longer than a 280-character tweet."

"Yeah, I know. So sad."

Abby began walking again, and I followed her down the stairs into the subway station. My new position was tenuous, with my paycheck based on customer demand and what they agreed to pay. Approaching fifty and the ugly midpoint in life had made it more challenging to land a new job this time around. All this trying to please had pushed my stress level out to some undiscovered planet.

Abby and I passed through the turnstiles to wait for the next downtown train.

She took out a tissue, dabbed her eyes, and blew her nose. "Nathan had some drug issues."

"He did?" I felt a sharp stabbing wound deep in my chest. The inescapable dependence on deadly narcotics claimed another victim, ruined a life, and devastated a family. "I think I told you my brother died years ago. Not suicide but an accidental overdose. The pain never disappears."

Abby wiped away a tear with the back of her hand.

I would never forget the exact date and time my dad told me my brother Keith was lost forever from an overdose. My biggest regret was that I should have done more to prevent it.

"Nathan's problems might have been solvable." These final acts of giving in and giving up ignited something inside of me. I wanted to slap Nathan and Keith to toughen them up and face whatever problems they had. Unfortunately, life wasn't all smiles and way-to-go moments.

"Hey, I'm with you. It's the damn drug dealers. I wish someone would lock them up forever."

I nodded, thinking about how important my work was this week.

Abby stared at me. "Since you got home from your long

voyage, you've been so different. All closed up and a loner. I miss the old Kat."

I unbuttoned my jacket and peeked at my shirt. After a silly Kat Jensen physical inspection, I tried to prove I was still the same. "Yep, she's still all here."

I forced a laugh, but Abby didn't smile. "Sorry, Abby. I know you haven't seen me much recently. Settling back in has been hard. The job search took over my life. Soon things will be like before. Please don't move to New Jersey."

Nathan's suicide troubled me. I had been forced to shut down my struggling consulting business a year ago. My nest egg had shrunk from paying bills while I was unemployed for a year. I had faced plenty of despair but never considered suicide.

An incoming subway screeched to a stop, and we lined up with the crowd. The rush-hour train was packed, so we squeezed into the car's narrow aisle between the filled seats.

Today, in memory of poor Nathan, I would try harder to adapt to their unique work culture. Working for a small investigative company run by a former spy, with a lawyer and an ex-NYPD detective as colleagues, was unusual.

I was accustomed to working with Wall Street traders and businesspeople at global banks and big-name companies. All boasted about their services with costly marketing and publicity support teams. My new firm, Melville Consulting, intentionally stayed off the grid, and client projects had secretive names.

"How's the new job?" Abby paused, eager for details I couldn't give.

I was under a strict nondisclosure agreement and had a paranoid boss. To not let anything slip, I had decided to say virtually nothing about my job. But Abby was my closest friend and trustworthy, so I could share some vague details. "So far, okay. My first week and getting used to the old grind."

"What do you do exactly?" Abby asked.

"About the same as before. Internal auditing is similar to what an investigative journalist does. Digging in, finding issues, and reporting them with suggestions to fix them. So, my job usually covers a wide range of different projects. This week was more forensic accounting. I analyzed financial records and crunched numbers."

The client's name on my first assignment was strictly off-limits. The pre-assigned codename 'Project Onion' told me nothing. Even if I figured it out, I had signed those pesky nondisclosure documents, promising not to breathe a word.

"Sounds pretty dull." Abby's opinion was not uncommon.

"Can be. Like anything else."

Except this week was more like a game called follow the drug money. I had traced the flow of dollars and foreign currencies from one account to another as if solving a complicated numerical jigsaw puzzle. My in-depth analysis, propelled by my twenty years of auditing, delved deep into the logistics of money movement.

She smiled. "I'm glad you found something. You seemed so stressed out."

"Yeah, it was incredibly hard this time around. Getting older and better at your job didn't help."

My hard-earned nest egg was gone, so I was desperate to find a job to avoid downsizing and moving. Jackson's enthusiastic job offer was a welcome ego boost. I'd spent weeks waiting around and hearing so many prospective employers turn me down.

I sighed. "One week down with another twenty years to go." Please let this job last at least two years. The job interviews and being scrutinized from head to toe in an uncomfortable business suit were awful.

"You and me both." Abby grinned, understanding what I meant.

To afford pricey New York City, single women without a ton of money often had to work until they dropped dead or got tossed out.

She looked wistful. "At least we're getting together Tuesday. Don't forget our girls' night out with Darlene. You've already canceled twice."

"I'll be there. Even if something happens, I'll hobble in

with a broken leg."

"Oh, Kat. Please don't break anything. Just show up for once."

"I will. I promise."

The doors opened for her stop at 42nd Street and Times Square. We exchanged a quick hug goodbye.

She whispered, "Be careful," and disappeared into the mass exodus.

I pushed my way back inside the crowded subway car. Abby's parting comment was weird and unlike her. At first, I assumed this referred to my lame joke about breaking my leg. However, I must always be prepared. Anything could happen at any time.

Inside the heated car, I loosened my cashmere scarf and noticed a small hole. "Darn moths," I said to the invisible, hungry critters. Buying anything new and nonessential had to wait.

At last, the subway pulled into my stop, Christopher Street, in the historic, hip West Village. I gathered up my belongings and some determination for day five at Melville Consulting.

Jackson, the founder of the company, was a fan of the author Herman Melville. He even used Ahab, the name of the ship's captain in *Moby-Dick,* as the code word to enter the office's front door.

To anyone who might be spying on me inside the half-empty station, I warned, "Moby Dick, here I come.

Chapter 2 ~ The Waiting Game

"I'm tired of trying to see the good in people." Anita Garcia's voice echoed from her temporary hiding place inside the closet. My chatty work colleague had inspirational quotes from her hero Oprah pinned all over her desk's bulletin board.

"Oh, you two. Enough. You're scaring Kat." Shantelle Nkosi, another colleague in our four-person investigation company, sat on the floor next to me and squeezed my hand. Sadly, her flowery perfume had lost the battle against the musky smell of dust down here.

I struggled to be brave. But hiding with Shantelle under the office's conference table was abnormal. I should have known Jackson would do something weird like this and escaped an hour ago when he gave me a chance.

But no, I was striving to be more of a team player, adapting to whatever culture this diverse workgroup represented. Heck, Nathan, this was your fault. Your suicide over not having a job made me hesitate when I had the opportunity to leave. But I couldn't blame the dead. If Nathan were still alive, he might regret his suicide attempt.

Now, after just one week on the job, I was bonding by hiding with them. My boss Jackson, a former CIA spy, and Anita, an ex-NYPD detective, were probably used to this.

"How long are we going to be here?" I released Shantelle's hand and shifted my aching legs while pulling up my skirt to cross them. Not a ladylike position, but this was the least of my worries. Shantelle was one of the dumb reasons I stayed. If a lawyer could stay and witness this arrest, I could too.

"Not long. Maybe five minutes," Jackson said.

Jackson and Anita had handguns and customized night vision goggles. They had assured me this was all precautionary with our brave men and women in blue on their way. If they were late, Jackson would temporarily detain him.

"Didn't you say this Puerto Rican drug lord has a weird nickname?" With so many foreign shell companies, pseudonyms, and account numbers, I had lost track. His name was long, like so many Spanish names. Although his name didn't roll off my tongue, I was ready to roll it from my memory bank.

I was coated in a layer of sweat and wiped the accumulation from my face. This didn't help much since sweat continued to slide down my back. My elegant silk shirt was stained and likely ruined.

"Yeah, El Rey. So many months, and now we've trapped him. Is that coming through, Esteban Miguel Rodriguez?" Anita piped up from the storage closet with the door open.

"El Rey as in the king?" I was curious but didn't want any new information to lead to my demise.

I pulled at my shirt, trapped under a bulletproof vest that I couldn't take off. According to my work gang, this was standard equipment and available for a few hundred dollars online at Walmart. Later I should google bulletproof suits and helmets, and if they exist, buy one of each. But only if I don't quit first. My plan to give this job thirty days was way too optimistic.

"Yeah, the Puerto Rican drug king. Now he's dead broke. Brilliant work, Kat. You nailed the operation's twisted account setup." Jackson's voice was chipper, so at least I had done something right this week.

"Thanks. They sure went to a lot of trouble to conceal it." I had struggled all week to prove my worth as their first-ever forensic auditor. Our secret client had sent us reams of documentation to sift through. The wire transfers had codes indicating which financial institution, so it was only a matter of unwinding the data piecemeal and tracking it.

The wires flowed to accounts domiciled mainly in the Caribbean. I loved the challenge of a game. Once I traced the transfers from one account to another, it led to El Rey's banks in the United States. That part of the job was enjoyable. Jackson's daring CIA undercover background had been my main concern, and hiding like this was never part of the deal.

"I figured he'd go to the ATM this morning to pull money out for the big weekend. I wish I could have seen his face when the bank told him his account was frozen," Jackson said.

Entertaining to witness for about a second until he figured it out and exploded.

"Any plans for the long weekend, Kat?" Jackson asked.

Monday happened to be Veterans Day, a federal holiday, but not for Wall Street employees. In a group vote yesterday, we opted to take the day off.

"Nope. Why?" As soon as I said this, I regretted it. I should have made up something important for my weekend to-do list. I had tentative plans to go to Connecticut with Charlie, my unrelenting boyfriend, on Sunday. After this ordeal today, I wanted to back out and stay home.

As soon as this ended, I was getting the hell out of here. I'm not hiding in the dark or helping him chase a criminal around town. This whole cloak-and-dagger spy stuff and dodging bullets brought back memories of working on an investigation with Jackson years ago in Hong Kong.

These crazy situations were what I had declined to do if I joined his investigation firm. Jackson had agreed and promised that it wasn't a problem. But here I was in a dangerous position and trapped until the police showed up.

"You wore a skirt today. I told you this is a 'jeans-and-T-shirt' operation," he said.

I tried to stretch my aching back and legs. In the dark, my skirt flopped around, showing more than it should. "Someone forgot to tell me I'd be sitting on a dirty floor for half an hour waiting for an angry drug king to show up." Next week, if there was such a thing, I'd set them straight by wearing my *Don't Mess with Texas Women* T-shirt.

No one said anything. Possibly to avoid being bombarded with another biting quip from me, the grump. The silence was unnerving. "I dressed up to meet a friend for dinner if I get out of here."

"You'll be out of here way early. Shantelle, when our man is arrested, take Kat to the roof and show her the fire escape stairwell."

"Appreciate the early start to my ruined weekend," I said.

"You can't say this isn't exciting," Jackson said.

I didn't bother explaining that I had experienced way too much excitement lately. Now I craved dullness and being a homebody who got her thrills from a movie or novel.

"We're putting away a power-hungry murderer and drug trafficker. El Rey's evaded arrest for years. So be proud of yourself, Kat. You helped do this." Shantelle patted my shoulder in thanks. She had the expertise and pleasure of doing the company's legal filings and court work.

I was proud despite not knowing the purpose of the complicated account mess when I unraveled it. But why did we need to suit up and hide? This stakeout ruined the entire week, and my presence here was so unnecessary. Like in one of those corporate team-building exercises, I was stuck.

"You should buy a rug to put under this table for next time." After years as an internal auditor, recommendations gurgled out of me like the spring water fueling the Jack Daniel's Distillery in Lynchburg, Tennessee.

"Go for it," Jackson said. "Something colorful that doesn't show dirt. We don't hire snoopy cleaning crews."

Yeah, I wonder why. "Get a red one to roll out when your drug cartel kingpin drops by again."

"Nah. This is a one-time deal. Where he's going, there won't be any carpets."

Did Jackson mean dead or in jail? I didn't want an answer.

Shantelle said, "We have plenty of evidence. With his account activity as proof, more than enough to keep him behind bars."

"On second thought, don't bother with the carpet. I better find another more secure office tomorrow," Jackson said.

Shantelle and Anita groaned but didn't complain. Changing offices was sensible. Who would want to go through this ordeal again?

"New codename?" Shantelle, experienced at triple crossing t's and dotting i's in legal documents, followed up on the details.

"How's *Pequod?*" Jackson tossed out another *Moby-Dick*-inspired codeword.

"What's a pea-quad?" Anita repeated the unusual word

slowly.

"Oh my God," I blurted out. "The name of the whaling ship in *Moby-Dick*. What's with this weird fixation on Herman Melville?"

Jackson said, "That book's a masterpiece. The best novel ever written. Not my fault colleges fall way short in their required reading lists. Read it this weekend with your extra day off. That's an order!" But he chuckled, and we knew he was only teasing.

"Sorry, but I have no interest in reading about hunting and killing defenseless animals," Shantelle said.

"Not quite so defenseless. That whale took a major bite out of Captain Ahab." Jackson never gave up quickly.

"Well, he deserved it." I patted Shantelle's knee in agreement. I had seen some whale ships and met whalers. Whaling was a brutal, disgusting business.

"I started that book on my Kindle. Stopped when I saw how dang long it was. There ought to be a law with book police to enforce a three hundred-page limit. That Moby Dick was not at all who, or what I expected." Anita giggled.

All this talk about *Moby-Dick* and Melville was a feeble attempt to distract us from worrying about El Rey.

Shantelle, as usual, steered the conversation away from sex. "Have you read it, Kat?"

"Nope. But I heard all about it when I was at sea." The second mate on board the ship brought along the three-volume British version, titled *The Whale*.

"On that infamous voyage around the world?" Jackson teased.

"Only halfway. Sometimes not much else to do but read."

"What happens when you go off the grid. I'd load up my iPad with fifty books and be set to go."

I was tempted to say, "Best of luck, recharging without any electricity onboard." But I didn't want to argue with the head honcho or invite more questions.

The conversation died off, and I shifted again to keep my legs from cramping.

Anita broke the silence. "Hey, Kat, I'm going to target

practice tomorrow afternoon with some of my old buddies from the force. Want to come along?"

"Target as in shooting guns?" She most likely wore a small hidden pistol under her clothes all the time.

"Well, it ain't bows and arrows." Anita snickered.

"Thanks, but I'm busy. I have a resignation letter to write for Monday."

"Monday is a holiday." Shantelle was always precise and punctual.

"Okay, I have an extra day. For Tuesday."

"Ah, come on, Kat. You promised me a month. Isn't chasing and catching the bad dudes thrilling?" Jackson's voice boomed with the others echoing their support.

"Maybe to you but —"

Loud car brakes screeched outside, interrupting me, and I dug my nails into my thick vest.

"Shush! It's the cops. But it might be El Rey. Ready, Anita?" Jackson growled like an angry dog.

"Yo, what I know for sure," Anita said.

Despite my racing heartbeat, I smirked, hearing Anita whisper Oprah's catchphrase from the monthly *O* magazines piled on her desk. This week the monthly magazine's colorful pages were a welcome diversion after staring at row upon row of numbers and computer files.

Shantelle took my arm and pulled me to the closet. At the same time, Anita got into position by the doorway across from Jackson. I considered sprinting for the window to jump, but we were on the third floor. The fire escape was on the other side of the office and required passing the front door.

I reached up to cover my mouth and stay as quiet as possible. But my elbow bumped up against something in the closet. I reached for the glass vase, but it slipped through my fingers and fell to the ground. The glass shattered into what might have been a million pieces, and the noise pierced the air.

"Sorry," I whispered so quietly that I almost didn't hear it. Shantelle's flower vase and our hiding place were both ruined.

Someone banged on our office's front door so hard I feared it might get knocked down. Would the police hammer away like this without identifying themselves? My heart pounded. In a few minutes, whoever it was would enter our conference room and find us.

A man screamed, "Jackson, *pendejo!*" along with a string of other Spanish words I didn't understand. Naturally, the cops didn't arrive in time.

Sometimes I might agree that Jackson could be an asshole, except for how that man said it. My employer of a mere five days might be history soon. Lifeless, like Ahab and most of the crew from the *Pequod*. They ended up at the bottom of the ocean. Jackson had picked terrible code words.

El Rey, or whoever it was, continued banging on the door, and splintering noises increased. A man yelled, "I know you're in there hiding, you idiot Chinaman. It's all over. Start praying." The attack continued, and our old wooden door wouldn't last much longer.

Another man yelled in Spanish. I was able to translate some of it, including, "You're a dead man!" If they were ready to kill Jackson, we didn't stand a chance, even with guns.

I prayed but not to a god most people believe in. My wish was for the men in blue and the familiar Manhattan sound of sirens. Anita had called them, and they knew all about this. Why in the hell weren't they here by now?

Chapter 3 ~ *What Would Dorothy Do*

Whoever invented the hot shower deserved a gold medal, millions of dollars, and whatever else they wanted. Steamy hot water pelted my back without mercy. I coated my brush with a Tahitian coconut scrub to extend my moments of ecstasy. How I managed seven months on a ship without hot showers and modern plumbing was beyond me.

If I knew who to thank for my daily shower, I would hug them. The creator belongs right up there with famous inventors like Thomas Edison, Alexander Graham Bell, and Steve Jobs. They deserved gifts and some of my delightful herbal bath gels, nutty scrubs, and quality loofas.

I sang along with Freddie Mercury to Queen's classic hit "Bohemian Rhapsody," blaring from my radio. It was a too-long, offbeat number that became a surprise hit and always would be in my book of music. Good old Freddie, the underdog turned top dog.

Climbing out of the shower, I recited my mantra. "I will adjust to life here and now." I had repeated this almost daily during the past year, especially during the dangerous voyage to Hong Kong.

I grabbed a bath towel and dried off in a hurry, swearing to never take the immense pleasure of a modern bathroom for granted. The shower idea likely came from a time-pressured woman like me, who didn't have time for a soak in a bathtub.

Crazy Jackson Chow! Who did he think he was? Captain Ahab chasing Moby Dick, the whale, for biting off his leg? Or Ishmael, the sole surviving crew member, when the ship sunk?

At least shots weren't fired, the door didn't get knocked down, and the police arrived in the nick of time. They blamed the screw-up on poor coordination with the D.E.A.'s agent-in-charge. Both of those organizations could benefit from a thorough internal audit review of their interagency procedures. Just not by yours truly. At least El Rey was arrested and carted off to jail. I never planned to see him or his accounts again.

Luckily, I didn't observe a thing since I'd stayed hidden in the closet until it was over. I had curled up into a tight ball in the corner. Later, I was coaxed out when each of my colleagues, including Jackson, promised me the coast was not just clear but completely secure.

All these reminders about ships and life at sea didn't benefit my mental or physical health. The day's ordeal had involved moving around on the floor on my knees. I stood in front of the full-length mirror inside my bedroom, looking for bruises, scrapes, or cuts. Luckily, no new injuries were detected. My body was colorless and pale but injury-free. At least on the surface, except for an unwanted souvenir from my not-so-grand voyage.

A three-inch braided band of misery, wrapped around my left arm between my elbow and shoulder, glared at me. A lousy reminder that came with me after a stopover in Indonesia. I kept this attention-grabbing, intricately designed tattoo well hidden. Now, with November's cooler weather and wearing long sleeves, it was easier to do.

Mom had been horrified when she saw it a few months ago in Texas. She obtained a referral to a specialized tattoo-removing dermatologist, but he confirmed what I expected. In that impersonal chairside manner, he had said, "Old-style tattoos made with thorns and that kind of ink are nearly impossible to remove. Best to not even try."

Resigned to being disfigured, I gave it the usual scratch without a hint of affection. The only plus, from the smug, tattoo-adverse doctor, was that it wasn't cancerous.

With a loud sigh, I pulled on my jeans, but they were uncomfortably snug. My lack of willpower among plentiful food and all-too-frequent alcoholic, calorie-loaded drinks was the culprit. New York bagels and ice cream, what I'd missed the most, weren't helping either.

"Gym tomorrow, 9 a.m. sharp." I stared down at my belly and repeated this out loud for more sticking power. Despite my too-tight jeans, I preferred this outfit to the dressy dinner-date clothes I'd worn to work today.

After seven months at sea and three months traveling around in the United States to reconnect with my parents and friends, I had expected too much too soon. Working a regular day job after a year off was a significant adjustment.

I was lucky to have a job. Unemployed women approaching their fifties and working in the finance business had a tough time. My situation was far from a position of strength, and in fact, no position at all. At least I wouldn't go extinct like the endangered Amur leopard. But this situation was so unfair, and I wanted to scream.

Explaining how I took a year off for no real reason made job-hunting challenging. Few women would go solo on a seven-month cruise from Copenhagen to Hong Kong. Some interviewers viewed my bucket-list vacation as daring, and in a weird way, admirable. But this didn't bode well when they sought stability and professionalism.

The part they didn't buy into was taking months to slack off, including a road trip from Texas to the West Coast. My main excuse was to visit friends and family and readjust to life back in the good old U.S. of A. But this was difficult to justify during serious, competitive job discussions. Job interviewers didn't understand how a once-in-a-lifetime trip was a worthwhile use of my time or how it enhanced my audit and managerial skills.

I liked Jackson, Anita, and Shantelle, and the work was fascinating and meaningful. Shantelle lived with her longtime boyfriend, and Anita lived alone like me. Jackson wouldn't say, but I couldn't picture him committing to what he'd classify as optional.

Frequent last-minute business trips and the long hours for this kind of profession didn't help build relationships or families. The four of us were so different, but we had quickly eased into a comfortable work-team relationship. So ideal, it would be hard to replicate.

Jackson was the only one I'd known before joining his company. We met on a Hong Kong money-laundering investigation when I was employed by one of the largest global banks. Then I left to start a consulting business that didn't make enough money to stay afloat.

Before I went on the cruise last year, he'd offered me a job since he needed a CPA. I was still unsure exactly what he did then and now. This week confirmed he intended to keep it that way. He was a major smart-ass, yet an all-around good guy who got me out of some tight spots in Hong Kong.

I wandered into the living room and kitchen to get a bottle of sparkling water and looked for my purse and cell phone to call Charlie. The least I could do was apologize.

Carrying a gun and being Jane Bond was never one of my fantasies. Hiding in the shadows and staying under the radar, like a law-abiding Catwoman, was more my style. We were just plain lucky when the police showed up right before our demise. I refuse to be a sitting duck, and I'm way too old to hide under conference room tables.

I found my shoulder bag on the couch and pulled out my cell phone. Unexpectedly, tears spilled down my cheeks, and I checked to see if Giuseppe had noticed. At least he didn't stare directly at me.

I grabbed a tissue off the side table and dropped my cell phone on my lap. "Don't be a crybaby!" I counseled the only human inside my apartment while drying my face. To think about something else, I started the movie *The Wizard of Oz*, recorded the previous night.

But I couldn't focus, with my work situation bouncing against the soft walls of my brain. Maybe I needed a complete change in careers and should find something entirely different. However, that meant going to the bottom of the pay scale, and with my current financial issues, it wasn't an option.

Surprisingly, it wasn't difficult to adapt to working for someone again and not be responsible and the leader-in-charge. Being an independent contractor gave me some degree of control. Talented internal auditors have that innate skill to question everyone and everything, not merely numbers. Digging in and looking for why and not just how. These past five days had honed my rusty analytical skills.

Being productive and accomplishing something again

tasted better than devouring containers of Ben & Jerry's ice cream. At some point, I had to stop relying on eating their Americone Dream flavor and start living it.

Another company, unthreatened by irate, murderous criminals, was bound to hire me. I sniffled one last time and picked up my phone to return Charlie's call, determined to be more optimistic. After all, what else was there in life?

My cell phone buzzed that Charlie was calling again. He deserved an answer, so I paused my video in the middle of the dance down the yellow brick road with the munchkins.

"Kat, where are you? We agreed on 6:30 at Nobu Downtown. I hope you aren't at the one in Midtown."

"Nope. I'm really sorry. I can't make it tonight." I should have texted him to take the easy way out.

He responded with some cuss words, including shit, to express his disappointment and then apologized. "Can't or won't?"

"Both, I guess."

Charlie waited on the other end, and I visualized his face filled with frustration. Repeatedly, I had told him to move on. Charlie was one of those annoying types who would have rejected boarding a spare lifeboat. He would have gone down on the *Titanic*, optimistically insisting a rescue would arrive in time.

"Kat, I thought you were up for this. An enjoyable and expensive meal out with some of my team. Even my senior manager and his wife are here and eager to meet you."

"I had a rough day at work. I can't go anywhere now."

"But we spoke last night. You said it was going fine, better than expected."

"Well, the unexpected happened. I'm quitting next week."

"That bad, huh?" Charlie sighed, echoing my feeling of despair.

"Worse." He deserved more, but I couldn't tell him much. "I got sick and threw up."

"At home?" His voice softened in concern.

"No, at work. So humiliating. I vomited into a half-empty box of copy paper. Ruined about four packages."

He chuckled. "Doesn't sound like you. My environmentalist tries to save trees."

I tried to smile, but it hurt. "Today was truly awful." But right after I threw up, Shantelle had given me a wet paper towel to clean up and a cup of water.

"Was it something you ate?"

"Maybe." Our African takeout for lunch was unusual, but this was a reaction to pure, uncontrolled stress. While at sea in dangerous situations, I sometimes vomited.

"I'm sorry, Kat. You were so upbeat about starting something new. A promising challenge."

"I decided boring is more my style."

"Nah. Not you."

I bit my lip and blinked to keep the tears from falling.

"So, what are you doing now?"

I paused, not wanting to confess my evening's diversionary TV lineup. Charlie would scold me again.

"Let me guess. Watching *Little Women* or *Doctor Zhivago*? Or what's the third?"

"*The King and I.* Nope."

I used to enjoy *Gone with the Wind,* with the sassy, kickass Scarlett O'Hara. She survived the Civil War in a nineteenth-century man's world. But the slavery bothered me so much that I stopped watching it.

"What then?"

"*The Wizard of Oz.* I like Dorothy. She's brave. Saves Toto and manages things."

"At least that's a new one. You know I love a good flick. But you should stop hiding behind those old movies. You watch the same ones over and over. There's a glut of modern-day flicks out there to see. How about it?"

"Next week." I had repeated that last week and the week before, and I hoped he wouldn't harp on it.

After I hung up, I wandered to the kitchen and nodded a polite greeting to the gargoyle. Giuseppe focused on monitoring me in addition to the usual kitchen and living room. His patina and skin color transitioned from a grim grayish-green shade to an attractive deep purple in the evening.

I found a stray ginger beer inside the refrigerator. From the freezer, I grabbed an ice-cold washrag and wandered to the living room, taking the beer with me. With the soothing rag over my forehead and eyes, I stretched under a blanket on the sofa.

Secure in the knowledge that Giuseppe was on guard duty, my exhausted body sunk into the sofa. Eventually, I drifted off to what I hoped was a safer, saner place.

Chapter 4 ~ Treeby Therapy

While propped up on my elbows on the sofa, the damp rag fell on the floor. I shook off the unpleasant memories from my summertime road trip when I had tried to tell my parents and a girlfriend the truth about my unusual voyage.

After finishing my lukewarm ginger beer while humming "Somewhere Over the Rainbow," I padded off to the kitchen to scrounge around for food. I hung on the refrigerator door, relishing the cold air against my face while staring into an almost empty white void.

A box of microwave popcorn packets sat on the kitchen counter, but I couldn't handle their salty aftertaste anymore. Last time, they brought back the terrible memory of an emergency night swim off Timor Island in Southeast Asia when I swallowed way too much saltwater.

I considered throwing out the popcorn, but I was proud to be unofficially participating in the Swedish-led zero-waste movement. The average American tossed out over two hundred pounds of food annually, and developing countries only threw out twenty pounds. After those trying months at sea with such limited resources, I had learned not to waste anything.

A diet filled with more vegetables and quality leftovers was my current plan. I pulled a jar of olive relish from the fridge, sniffed it for freshness, and grabbed a bag of tortillas from the freezer. A microwaved olive quesadilla minus the cheese was edible but dull.

I frowned at Giuseppe. "Can't you bother to bring anything to eat into this house?" His food choices would be gross insects.

Tomorrow morning, I will do what Dorothy would have done for her Aunt Em. Go grocery shopping and gather more options for better quesadillas. Stock up with real food like a normal person. Something healthy to reduce the size of my tummy now pressed against the kitchen counter.

A Mexican beer or a Spanish red wine would be superb,

but my alcoholic drink options were nonexistent. A stiff drink is what I needed, and after this hellish week, what I deserved. And the wine store was almost next door, so easy to do.

I grabbed a jacket to cover my ratty T-shirt, doubling as my nightshirt. Unstoppable, I ignored my reliable peephole and opened the door to venture back into the wilds of Manhattan.

"Wait just a New York minute!" I announced inside the deserted hallway, surprised at a much better idea. So fabulous, I hopped in the air from sheer happiness. My uncontrolled jump was welcome under the circumstances. At the bitter end of this dreadful day, life was finally looking up.

I marched in double-time to the end of the hall and knocked on Abby's door. I envisioned how thrilled she would be, welcoming me with open arms. Enthusiastically, I knocked, waited, put my ear against her door to listen for her footsteps, and waited some more.

Her absence smashed my plans to bits. Abby must still be in New Jersey, already signing legal documents to buy the large and cheap replacement home she mentioned this morning.

Resigned to losing her in a few months, I trudged toward the stairwell. The elevator door opened, and as if by magic, the person I most wanted to see in the entire world stepped out.

"Abby, you're back. I just knocked on your door." I hugged her. She grinned, and I dogged her steps to her apartment. "You didn't sign up to buy an apartment in New Jersey today, did you?"

"Oh, no. Not my kind of place to live after all. You know me too well."

"I knew it!" I couldn't help yelling. "We will figure this out. We must stay here. Together."

She smiled and unlocked her front door. "What are you doing home tonight?"

"Nothing. I canceled my date with Charlie."

"You did? Why?"

"A rough day at work, and besides, I'm seeing him Sunday

night. He's probably having a better time alone with his colleagues and work friends." That dinner was guaranteed to be aggravating with all those smart-ass ultra-wealthy guys from his private equity management team.

She opened her door, and Treeby, her Siamese cat, peeked out. I scooped her up and kissed her irresistible furry head. "She looks adorable and just the same."

"Nothing much changed here, but you."

I nodded and trailed behind as we passed through her creamy-beige-colored apartment to the bedroom. I put Treeby on her bed, kicked off my shoes, and without waiting for an invite, stretched out on her bed, staring at the ceiling. Her bedroom was so calm and unfussy, restful like a spa. Maybe I should redo my African cheetah animal-style bedroom.

Treeby climbed on my stomach and acted eager for a back rub. "She's purring, Abby."

"They do that when they're happy." Abby sat on the bed, pulled off her high heels, and sorted through some paperwork inside her briefcase.

"Pure honesty. Too bad people don't send signals like that. When things settle down, I'm going to adopt another cat. Maybe two. Some cat sisters who need rescuing." I kept petting Treeby, appreciating some cat companionship.

Abby smiled. "Great idea." She climbed into her bed and lay next to me, staring up at the ceiling too.

"Want to catch a movie tonight like the good old days?" There went my plan to finish *The Wizard of Oz* with a glass or two of wine. But this was a healthier, better option, spending quality time with Abby.

"Sorry. I can't. I have a client meeting in about an hour. You could join us, but we are going over co-op apartments and condos on the market. All terribly overpriced."

"How about a movie on Monday night? If I get home in time from Charlie's mystery destination."

Treeby moved between us, taking advantage of being surrounded by two cat lovers. Abby and I rolled on our sides, facing each other.

"Sure. I told Darlene we're still on for Tuesday. She's

dying to get all the juicy details about your cruise. She insists you must have met some hot seamen on board. They convinced you to ride the waves for five extra months."

Inwardly cringing at her suggestion, I stopped petting Treeby, stared at the ceiling, and closed my eyes. That was the last thing I wanted to talk about. The cruise was supposed to be two months, then three months with stops at the ports of call.

After a few weeks at sea, I learned that timetable required racing and sailing nonstop. I almost jumped overboard in despair. Sticking it out and arriving in Hong Kong on that ship was my only way home. But it took seven long months.

Abby touched my arm to get my attention. "Are you okay? You looked sick for a second. Your face's still pale."

Thinking you might die three hours ago would tend to do something like that. Followed closely by haunting memories of a long voyage where peculiar disasters struck in practically every port of call.

"I'm fine."

Abby didn't look convinced.

"Really. First week back at work, so I'm tired." I wanted to delay telling her my depressing news about being back in the dreaded job-search mode again. Technically, I was still employed.

"I can imagine. So altogether, after your big cruise, you've only been home in New York City for what? Two months?"

"Yeah, about that. And not that much fun sending out resumes and doing interviews."

"Well, now you can relax. Enjoy your overnighter with Charlie. Did I tell you what a gentleman he was while you were gone?"

"You did."

But she didn't listen and continued lecturing me for what felt like the fiftieth time. "We went out every month or so for coffee. Charlie was so worried, especially when no one heard from you for months. He kept calling to ask about you. He didn't date anyone else, as far I know. Hard to believe with any guy, much less a handsome and successful one like that."

I forced a smile. My boyfriend refused to consider or allow the word "quitting" into his vocabulary.

"I've got to get ready and change clothes." Abby stood and stripped out of her business suit, tossing her underwear on the floor. She apologized, but it was her bedroom, and I was the intruder.

I pulled Treeby over to rub my face against her soft fur and not embarrass Abby. When I looked up, she had put on some lacy black lingerie that even matched. "Looks like your meeting might turn into something more."

From inside the closet she yelled, "Yeah, but he's broke like me. He lost a bid on an excellent place. The co-op board argued his financials were too weak. So many want all-cash deals now. Studio apartments go for half a million. It's crazy."

She exited her closet in a dressy shirt and designer jeans.

"Who needs money when you have love?" I countered, optimistic about her prospects for a romantic evening. If she was dressing up this much, he must be worth it.

"New Yorkers, that's who."

"Is Darlene still doing that Tinder-swiping dating routine?"

"Not so much. She's down to just dating two guys."

"Only two? They must be terrific. Before I left, she switched them daily like underwear."

"Yeah, she sure did. She ran into some issues but won't mind if I tell you."

I sat up, leaning against her pillows, ready for the scoop. Treeby walked off, likely uninterested in hearing about romantic entanglements. Abby fumbled around inside her jewelry box and sat on the edge of her bed. She put on her earrings, and I helped latch her necklace.

"She still keeps pushing me to use online dating sites, so it wasn't that bad. She had a scare and got roughed up a tad."

"Oh, my God. Not Darlene!"

"Yeah, she said she had a bad vibe after her intro-drink-in-public routine. But her date was incredibly charming and attractive. She went to his place and got tied up for a long time. He was into some sick *Fifty Shades of Grey* control games. You know, Darlene. She likes her freedom."

"Poor girl. Scary world. Must trust your gut." I patted my stomach, thanking it for the times it came through with useful intel and warnings.

"Yeah, or not do such crazy stuff so often." Abby picked up her phone, scrolled through it, and insisted I take it. "Some photos from her birthday a few months ago. Look through them while I freshen up my makeup."

I flipped through the photos on her phone. Darlene and Abby looked happy, but I didn't recognize anyone else. "Looks fun." Her photos made me realize how much I'd missed.

She called back from the bathroom. "You would have liked it. Scroll back to my photos from last year. There are some photos of your surprise goodbye party."

I found last year, November 2016, and stared at my face. So innocent and unsuspecting. If only I knew then what I know now. Nevertheless, there was no going back.

Charlie was captured perfectly. He was super friendly at parties and the ultimate Mr. Entertainer. Matteo, the Italian hunk now back home in Italy, who I dated for what seemed like only a few hours in bed, looked gorgeous. So many friends showed up to say farewell and brought gifts. People I needed to reach out to again and on my to-do list for when I got in better financial and mental shape.

I put Abby's phone down, feeling guilty about not reaching out to my friends. Months ago, when I'd returned, I sent an email around to say I was home. Invites had poured in, but I was either not up to see them or out of town.

With the ban on all social media sites mandated by my boss, it was harder to keep in touch. I clicked on the photo app to see them once more. The app's configuration displayed Abby's earliest photos first.

Her phone was new when we made the pre-Halloween weekend jaunt with Axel to Philadelphia, and these popped up first. We had gone to Philly's annual haunted house at the massive penitentiary and visited the art museum.

I stared at Axel. My husband had his customary smirk but looked so happy and healthy before cancer took its toll.

Abby asked, "Didn't you get some photos from your cruise? I know you couldn't take your cell phone along."

How to sidestep lying? "I have a few. Remember, though, they had those reenactment rules. We were dressed in old-timey clothes. The photos are blurry and not in color."

"Cool. Bring them to the restaurant on Tuesday."

"All right, will do." I got up and stood outside the bathroom, watching her finish her makeup.

If I could open up, she could too. "I found out the truth about Axel. How he planned to leave me before his cancer diagnosis and move back to Denmark. You knew, didn't you?"

"What?" She dropped her lip gloss tube in the sink.

"Axel's brother told me at our ash-scattering ceremony in Denmark. Opportune timing, since it was the exact same day I boarded the ship. If my sister-in-law hadn't forced him to tell me, I would still be the grief-stricken wife. She never liked Axel and wanted me to move on."

"I'm sorry, Kat. I'll tell you everything. How about a glass of wine first?"

I marched behind her to the kitchen, refusing another delay, and sat behind the nearby dining table. Abby switched on the radio. Billy Joel's classic song, "Scenes from an Italian Restaurant," played.

She took a bottle of white from the fridge and placed it on the table in front of me. "Bought your favorite, a French Viognier, when you came home to celebrate. It's been chilling ever since."

I couldn't be bought off with white wine, not even a Viognier. "Why didn't you tell me, Abby?" My voice, high-pitched and tight, was unrecognizable to me.

She poured me a glass of Viognier and a Cabernet Franc for herself. Slowly, she lowered herself into the chair across from me. "I wanted to. Axel convinced me it was better for me to stay quiet. I didn't know until after he was sick, and he'd given up his plans."

"But still. Axel was dead for over a year before I left."

"I know. It was wrong. The longer I waited, the harder it was. I felt terrible about it. Still do. Please forgive me." Her eyes narrowed, and she looked pained. Her voice dropped to a whisper. "Axel asked me to help him. Pia came here to see him."

I choked on the Viognier, thinking about what went on inside our home, which was still my apartment.

"It's not what you're thinking. Pia came over merely to say goodbye. When Axel was so sick at home during those last few weeks."

"But lots of people came over. I wouldn't have stopped her."

"I know, but he wanted to be alone with her. You had that big proposal with the bank later that week. You even told me how critical it was to save your business. Axel argued that if I told you, it would throw you off track."

The big proposal I didn't win. A miserable three-hour meeting in which five anxious J.P. Hamlin execs grilled me for solutions to some tricky compliance issues in their broker-dealer trading company. I gave them options, and they ran with one without hiring me. As usual, they brought in a big-name firm for appearances and to impress the regulators.

Abby finished her glass and refilled both our glasses. "I was going to tell you the day you left for Copenhagen. Except when I came over with your gifts, Charlie was at your place making breakfast and naked under your apron. You were both so happy. I just couldn't do it."

She plodded into the living room and pulled an envelope out of a cabinet. "Axel said you were bound to find out. When you did, I was to give you this."

She slid across the table a white envelope with Kat scrawled on it in his unique style of writing. He wrote in all capitals, like the Peanuts comic strip. No one else I knew wrote like that.

I held the envelope, shocked to hear from him so many years later.

Abby returned to her bedroom, giving me some much-needed privacy. The radio switched to the song "Fix You" by the British band Coldplay. The lyrics reminded me of how not long afterward, I was at sea with strangers. By necessity, I had to fix myself emotionally.

After wondering what I did wrong, I ripped open the envelope. Axel's explanations were bittersweet. In his abbreviated all-cap style, he apologized. He hoped I wouldn't hate him forever but didn't expect or deserve forgiveness. He didn't think his cancer was God's punishment but purely lousy luck since he remained an atheist to his last breath. Axel closed by wishing me a happy and healthy life.

Long prose didn't fit Axel's style. I never got romantic love letters. His emails were like texts, with few words and incomplete sentences, and his all-cap style hurt my eyes. More than once, his email responses consisted of a lone question mark. Axel always preferred to chat on the phone, while I was the opposite. Phone calls and voice mail messages were inefficient compared to texts or emails.

Abby reappeared and scanned my face. "How are you? I'm afraid I must leave soon to make my meeting."

I shared Axel's short letter with her, and she read it. Her physical reaction was like mine. She sighed, disappointed he didn't provide a more sincere apology.

I hated to return to my apartment with the memories of our life together tainted. I tried to shrug this off. If another well-paying job doesn't come along soon, my only option was to sell it.

Outside, on Columbus Avenue, Abby gave me a hug farewell and apologized again. "A weight has been lifted off my shoulders. But I'm truly sorry. Now it's been transferred to you."

"I'm fine. Been over Axel for a while. Time dulled the pain. Now I understand why you didn't tell me."

She looked surprised, but I was past blaming her or anyone else for Axel's actions.

"But Abby, if anything like this happens again, with Charlie or someone else, promise me you will tell me. I'm the type who'd rather know than not know."

She gazed out at the street as if afraid.

"Abby, is there something else?"

"Yes, but this is a pleasant surprise. You'll find out this weekend. Personally, I'd love it."

I frowned, unhappy with more secrets.

"I promised a special someone not to say anything." She winked at me.

This must concern Charlie. "Okay. Monday night, when I'm home, I'm coming over. You must tell me then."

"Absolutely. I want a recap covering the entire weekend. By then, you'll know."

We waited for a taxicab on the same corner where this morning we'd watched the plane fly overhead. So much had happened in between. Abby put her hand up to flag down a cab but stopped.

"This is weird. But it might help you." Abby tensed up, and I wasn't ready for another bombshell message from the past. "I took a class on screenwriting, just for fun. You know how we love movies."

I nodded. We had seen hundreds together.

"Well, in class, we take stories apart. When we don't like the endings, we change them. Make them better. So, I started doing that with my life. You can too."

"What endings?"

"Well, like with Axel. Let's imagine he didn't die. Say Axel did leave and even moved back to Denmark. Got together with what's her name."

"That bitch, Pia," I mumbled.

"Exactly. Assume Axel did all this. But it didn't work out, and he came crawling back. Dog paddling to New York City across the Atlantic."

I couldn't help but laugh at that image.

"See! Don't you feel better already? You can reimagine your past. Move past the hurt. Get rid of the pain. Devise your own happy ending and move on."

Rethinking the entire voyage and making it better had never occurred to me. I smiled at Abby. "That's an amazing idea."

"What's stopping you? Who says it all has to be one hundred percent true? You aren't writing a memoir. Let yourself off the it-must-be-true requirement. Just do it!"

Abby eyed her watch, and I knew she had to go. She raised her hand, and a taxicab slammed to a stop within seconds. We hugged goodbye. Her suggestion had so much potential. I could rewrite my old painful memories to something better and more upbeat.

A sign plastered on the window of the corner liquor store announced a two-hour South African wine tasting. I could remake some of the bad memories from Cape Town as Abby had suggested.

I'd finish *The Wizard of Oz* and a bottle of sweet wine from Africa. But this never ended well. I'd crash into dreamland but wake up thirsty at 2 a.m. and feel hungover the next day. I was a social drinker and wanted to keep it that way. Besides, I was committed to my early morning appointment with the dumbbells at the gym tomorrow.

Instead of the wine tasting, I crossed Columbus Avenue toward Broadway, hurrying toward the local megaplex movie theatre with at least a dozen movies. I was determined to sit through an entire show, alone in the dark, with a living and breathing crowd.

~ ~ ~

Something happens after seeing a sad movie, especially one based on actual events. A film can magically lighten your load and make whatever miserable situation you were faced with less significant. A transformation from utter devastation to ho-hum. As if a switch snapped on with light and fresh air illuminating what was once dark and deadly.

An experienced partner at a global consulting firm had once lectured a group of us who were bitching about a difficult client. He'd said, "At least we aren't dodging bullets." Years ago, he'd spent time in the military and seen conflict but never talked much about it. His perspective silenced our petty complaints.

The film, *Dunkirk,* based on the tragically true World War II story about the evacuation of British troops trapped on the coast of France, did likewise. My hands shook so much I could barely buy the ticket after seeing the movie poster. So many ships of all shapes and sizes were launched to save as many soldiers as possible. These vessels were mainly modern and from the twentieth century, but facing my fears was beneficial self-help therapy.

As I walked home from the theatre, I congratulated myself. My newly acquired ship phobia might be behind me, and that film put my life-or-death problems in perspective. My issues somehow shrunk from the size of wine barrels filling an underground cave in the Loire Valley to grains of sand on the blood-stained French beaches.

Back at home and a few pounds lighter after the day's stress, the film, and skipping dinner, I listened to a voicemail from Charlie. He jabbered on about some free opera tickets he'd received from his manager. Presumably, his boss felt sorry for Charlie since he was stuck with a loser girlfriend like me.

Transformed to a more upbeat mood since I wasn't facing Nazis or a real war, I called Charlie back. I apologized for not attending his company dinner and accepted his invitation for a night at the opera tomorrow.

With my worries submerged into some hidden area of my brain, the only reason I could foresee canceling would be the start of World War III.

Chapter 5 ~ Bronx Bound

"I don't think so. Guns aren't my thing."

Shantelle meant well, but how much longer could I say no in a polite manner? Not that I had anything to do until the opera date this evening with Charlie. However, I was anti-guns, and going to target practice with a former cop was too weird.

"Oh, Kat. I understand one hundred percent. You don't have to shoot or anything. And they are legal handguns, not anything crazy like AK-47s. Just say hi to Anita and be there. She —"

Over the phone, a man's voice in the background interrupted us. I stared at Giuseppe, and our eyes met. He won the contest again since I blinked first.

"Are you still there?" Shantelle asked when she returned to the phone. "Sorry, my boyfriend had to tell me something. Anita needs some friends. Normal girlfriends like you."

"Me?" I swallowed hard. At least part of it was true.

"Normal as in someone who doesn't carry a badge. She feels guilty about teasing you during the week for being a newbie. Especially now that you want to quit."

"It wasn't her fault. It was the situation."

"Well, whatever you decide. You might enjoy doing something different. Anita doesn't warm up to that many people, and she likes your feisty attitude. We all do."

I liked playing verbal ping-pong with Anita. What would it hurt? How could anything terrible happen at a casual target practice with a former NYPD detective? Plenty. Remember yesterday when they didn't show up in time, you fool.

During my mental debate, Shantelle continued nudging me. "I would come too, but I'm busy with the move and the paperwork for our new office. Jackson gave you the new address, right?"

"Yep. Tuesday morning I'll be there. Why don't I help you unpack at the new office today? Then you could hang out with Anita." I refused to set foot back at our West Village location. That entire neighborhood was under a three-month minimum no-visit rule.

"Nice of you to offer, but Jackson and I can handle this. We keep our offices tidy and lean, so there's not much to move. If you spend time with Anita today, it would be a huge personal favor."

"Well, I guess I could call her. But I'm not touching those guns." I picked up a notepad and jotted down Anita's cell phone number.

"Don't be shocked if you change your mind. I did. It can be quite empowering."

After we hung up, I considered what my former self, the old Kat Jensen, would do. She'd stay home, search online for another miserable job, or rearrange her messy closet. But doing something sensible never had a chance if an adventure was waiting.

"Look over there." I pointed to the TV to temporarily distract Giuseppe while I called Anita.

~ ~ ~

"Okay, Kat. You ready?"

I nodded and bit my lip to prevent repeating my quirky sailor swear words in front of them. This was almost fake, only practice, and there would be no blood. I had memorized the instructor's security briefing, the advice from two current cops, and helpful hints from my colleague Anita.

Oversized headphones blocked most of the noise, and special protective eyewear rested on my nose. I spread my feet a foot apart and picked up the surprisingly lightweight handgun with both hands. I aimed at the sheet of paper, a silhouette of half a person, in the distance.

"Go ahead, make my day, scum-bucket punk." I stared at the target, visualizing evil and unrelenting people that frightened me, like El Rey. Thankfully, his face was as blank as this white sheet since I hid inside the closet and avoided him. Freezing up again like yesterday, my finger refused to pull the trigger.

Readjusting to put some muscle behind it, I hesitated, ready to back out. However, this was merely an exercise. I recalled the soldiers in *Dunkirk*. Always better to be trained and prepared. Survival required being ready for anything at any time.

Now it would be Anita and her buddies turn to jump when I pulled the trigger and forced the first bullet out. Zeroed in on the distant paper target, I couldn't glance over my shoulder to observe their reaction. But it was doubtful Anita and her two regularly gun-toting buddies would be bothered. Police officers and the other pro-gun NRA types hanging out here must be accustomed to gunshots.

I shot the remaining bullets transfixed by the target at the other end and put my firearm down. My heart pounded almost to a breaking point even though my life wasn't at risk. All the watching and waiting had built an agitated hornet's nest of adrenaline. After it was over, a cold streak of sweat slid down my backbone.

When my bullet-ridden target was handed over, Anita seized it. "Fantastic for a rookie."

I mumbled my thanks. They had assumed this was my first time to shoot a gun, and I lacked the courage to explain that they were dead wrong.

After our target practice concluded, we transitioned over to the best part of my day so far. Over Mexican beers with Anita and my new NYPD pals, Frankie and César, at a nearby dive bar in the Bronx, I could finally relax and joke around. After shooting a few thin white paper criminals in the heart and few other unmentionable places, this was what they usually did to take the edge off.

Frankie and César were entertaining, and out of uniform, they blended in. Some of the locals stared at us but in a curious, unthreatening manner.

Frankie said, "Kat, you should sign up and take more classes. Great untapped skill there."

"Thanks, but I'm somewhat overloaded at the moment." I wanted to be polite, but I had no interest in practicing or doing a repeat performance.

Frankie sipped his beer. "Getting a concealed-carry license, if you want one, is near impossible. Unless you have political clout or a godfather with connections."

"All it takes is tons of money." Anita grimaced and slammed her beer down on the table. "Shit, you can buy anything if the price is right."

The three experienced police officers made brief eye contact with each other and sipped their drinks but mercifully didn't elaborate. To avoid hearing anything that might endanger my life, I would resort to sticking fingers in my ears.

"She'd be wicked standing by with a shotgun. Right, Anita?" César teased, but after seeing my horrified face, he said, "Just joking around."

César left to buy Mexican snacks from a food truck parked next door. When he returned, bags of tacos covered our table. He bought a wide assortment, including *birria de chivo* with goat meat, *carnitas* with pork, and *chorizo con pappas,* a blend of sausage and potatoes. They even had veggie and cheese tacos for my green plant-based diet.

But I couldn't resist and tried them all. While we munched on the freshly made tacos, Frankie asked Anita, "What's this all about? Bringing down El Rey?"

She surveyed the people near us inside the bar and tilted in. "Yeah. We did it. The narco boss man is in jail and then prison if all goes right. Jackson went a little *loco* on Friday." She waved in the air for emphasis.

"Hell. Anyone would be crazy. That complete sack of ..." Frankie grimaced and ran his finger along a scratch on our wooden table. "Not sure I believe it, but some say he even killed a cop."

"I for one believe it. Bodies never found and no closure for families." Anita clinked her beer bottle against mine. "Kat's the one who did it. She followed the money like a zombie cat bat-killer."

"A zombie what?" I asked.

"Nothing. Just made it up." She smirked.

"Yeah, Anita has her own lingo." César snickered but looked uncomfortable.

I nodded, but I would never kill a bat unless it was rabid or threatening me.

She took a bite of her taco and continued, undeterred. "We froze the bad boy's accounts, and he went ape shit."

She had some red salsa and cilantro stuck between her teeth, so I pointed it out. She winked and cleared it away.

"No one likes being broke all of a sudden. Been there. I know." After losing my wallet last year, I always carried emergency cash hidden inside my purse.

Frankie looked wistful and asked César, "Apart from the inedible green meatless ones, how much do I owe you for the tacos? Next time we're doing New York's finest, pizza."

I reached for my wallet to contribute, but he waved us off.

"How about lunch with the 'ladies who lunch'? Office still in the West Village?" César asked.

"No, we moved to —"

Anita interrupted me. "What Kat means is we transferred to a new locale. Keeping it quiet."

César pursed his lips and looked disappointed.

Anita cleared her throat and leaned in again, speaking low. "Okay, *amigos*. I'll level with you both since I trust y'all with my life. Someone tipped off El Rey. He left where he was supposed to be for the takedown. He found our office, and someone delayed the NYPD. You tell me. Strange coincidence, huh?"

Frankie frowned and rapped the table in anger. "We'll investigate. Discreetly, of course."

Anita nodded and appeared relieved. I had a strange inkling she had wanted to tell them this all along. "Sure thing. I know the drill. Don't rat out a buddy. Keep your fat ass covered."

We all laughed at this image. César's backside would fit this description, but Frankie didn't have a spare inch to pinch.

Happy-go-lucky music, "La Bamba" by Los Lobos, started, and we sang along softly at first, our volume rising as we warmed up and drank more beer. By the third chorus, we were screaming out the lyrics, "*Yo no soy marinero, soy capitán*," which meant I'm no sailor, I'm a captain.

When the music ended, I strolled over to the jukebox and found some coins at the bottom of my handbag. I punched in the numbers for Ricky Martin's "Livin' la Vida Loca," Santana's "Smooth," and Enrique Iglesias's "Bailando."

I picked up my phone and noticed the time. "Damn. Sorry, *amigos*. Got to run. This was fun, but I'm meeting my boyfriend tonight. Last night I stood him up."

"Naughty girl." Frankie, the younger guy, winked to tease me. "One dance first. Ricky's finest! He may not be Sinatra, but he'll do in a pinch." He reached for my hand and led me to a corner, carving out a temporary dance floor.

He wiggled and took my hand to twirl me around into a salsa-jitterbug combo while grinning nonstop.

Back at the table, Frankie rubbed my shoulder, leaning his face so close I felt his warm breath. "Join us again sometime. We do this every month."

"You can turn into a pro shot and give Tony a run for his money." César winked at Anita.

"Tony? Who's —"

Frankie interrupted me. "Just an old joke among us boys."

Anita looked away, and César grimaced as if this was a stupid joke.

"Come on, guys ... and gals. We're good, right?" Frankie said.

"Yeah," Anita said, shaking her head at her two friends. "I knew with the two of you the cat would escape and trap the canary."

"Private joke, huh?" I was used to tired cat jokes with my nickname. I finished my beer and stood around, listening to my song selections.

"Yeah, I'll tell you later." Anita punched them on the shoulder while I gave them rapid-fire hugs. Genuine police officers for friends couldn't help but come in handy.

Anita walked with me toward the nearby Gun Hill Road station, appropriately named since it was almost next door to the shooting range. The Bronx was so different. Like another world from Manhattan, but usually not as scary as most people thought. Although at night, it was another story.

I hugged Anita goodbye to avoid a friendly punch on my shoulder, even if it was a light tap. "See you Tuesday."

"Are you still quitting?"

"I don't know. I really like the group, and the work is okay, but not the stress. I can't handle another Friday like that."

"Friday was *bizarro*. Believe me, it's usually Dullsville around the office. Jackson was dying to arrest that guy, and our client waited years for this. I really hope you change your mind."

"Well, I'll think about it."

"Please do. Why don't I give you a lift? Should be faster than the subway."

An express train took over an hour, and the wait could be another twenty minutes or longer, so I accepted Anita's offer.

"I'm parked over there." She waved toward a small parking lot. "I guess Shantelle and Jackson didn't tell you about me. My situation."

I shook my head, and she started walking away at a fast clip. I ran to catch up and touched her back, worried it was something serious like an incurable disease.

Anita twirled around in her high-heeled boots and stared at me. "I'm trans. I used to be called Tony, short for Antonio. The patron saint of the poor and lost. Was going to stick to Toni but with an *i*. Except, a new me deserved a new name. Now I'm Anita. Sometimes my old friends call me both."

She walked ahead while I stood still, astonished and unsure of what to do or say. Anita wasn't big or tall like most men, and she liked girly things, including the Oprah magazine and bright colors. She wore heavy makeup like some of my Latina friends in San Antonio.

Anita strolled back to where I stood. "Trans as in the T in LGBTQ+."

"I know what you mean. Sorry. I was just surprised and relieved. I thought it was something like cancer."

"Cancer? Hell, no. You still want a lift?" She motioned to the subway stop, my other option, as if embarrassed and uncertain.

I touched her arm to reassure her. "Sure do. You know, it's great about being trans. I'm glad you told me and proud of you, Anita."

She smiled, showing her white teeth against bronze lipstick, and chuckled. "Not a fun thing to explain. Some women get turned off or weird."

"Well, it's all fine by me. You should be happy in whatever sex or way you want to be. That transgender actress Laverne Cox is amazing."

Anita nodded. "Got trendy. But still a ton of prejudice out there."

"Don't let that bother you. Too many people fear anything different. Isn't it getting better now? More mainstream?"

"Yeah, that is one thing I know for sure. Still, way too many bad memories." Her eyes got misty, and she took out her mirror to inspect her thick black mascara. I could have told her she looked terrific.

"And Kat, don't stress. I just want new friends who like the new me." She opened her arms, moving her hips slightly. She showed off her silky shirt, clinging to what must be new breasts and curves she didn't have to conceal anymore.

"You look fantastic, *chica.*" Her lingo was uninhibited, and some Spanish words had moved into my vocabulary. "Next weekend, maybe we can do something else besides shooting. Go shopping or to a museum."

Excitedly, she grabbed my hand. "Shopping! Jackson complained how I need some blah business suits for client meetings. I'm so intimated inside those high-class shops. After years in a uniform or nondescript clothes to hide my identity, I love wearing color."

She was wearing a lime green silky shirt that might glow in the dark. All week she had worn hot pinks, sunny yellows, and florescent purples. Her go-to shades reminded me of bright highlighter pens that stained my hands.

"Sure, we can do that. I'll take you to my favorite discount outlets that sell suits. I need new clothes too." My unimaginative black sweater and jeans outfit warranted an upgrade.

My phone rang, ruining this unique bonding moment, but I had to take it. "Charlie, I'm in the Bronx but on my way.

Hold on. Anita, what's our ETA?"

"Less than an hour if traffic is light."

After I told Charlie, I glanced up. Anita stood next to a motorcycle wearing a helmet and handed me a second one.

"Wow." I had expected a car and slipped her helmet over my hair. "You are jam-packed full of surprises, Anita."

The helmet hid her expression. She ignited the engine, and I climbed on behind her. I yelled above the noise, "What a wild and crazy day!"

She screamed back, "Effing fabulous! Hold tight, *chica*."

As instructed, I wrapped my arms around her waist, and we zipped out of the parking lot toward Manhattan.

When we reached 68th Street and my apartment, Anita's motorbike zoomed up on the sidewalk under the green awning over the entrance.

Charlie, dressed in an expensive suit but without a key to my apartment, stood right there waiting. He moved out of the way and glared at us.

"Is that the guy, your *hombre?*" Anita nodded toward Charlie.

"Yeah. My Prince Charming." I giggled as I climbed off her motorcycle and delivered my warrior-riding helmet with a flourish. Compared to Frankie and César, Charlie was so stiff. I shook out my hair while thanking Anita. I was fifteen minutes early, so Charlie had no reason to complain.

After realizing it was me, Charlie walked up to us, and I introduced them. He stared at Anita, but she didn't bother to take off her helmet and revved the engine, showing off.

I said *adios* and thanked her again for the fabulous day. Charlie shook his head as if in shock at seeing me with a motorcycle mama.

Anita zoomed off and disappeared down the street toward Central Park. Reluctantly, I turned and smiled at Charlie, determined to be optimistic. A date tonight at the nearby world-class opera was filled with promise, and Charlie could be so charming.

Chapter 6 ~ A Dramatic Date

Charlie trotted behind me, obedient as a hungry dog, and I unlocked the door to my apartment building.

Inside the elevator, his dreaded interrogation began. "Who was that again?"

"A friend from work."

"At the new consulting job that you're quitting?"

"Yeah." Doubts were creeping back in.

"I can see why."

I rolled my eyes. Charlie's job at his private equity fund was all about appearances and way too conservative for me.

"I like Anita a lot. She isn't why. The people there are great." I bit my lip in regret. Jackson would disapprove of identifying Anita. In his world, confidentiality ruled supreme. Whenever in doubt, don't say anything.

"So what's the problem?"

The elevator doors opened, and I hesitated. "Charlie, I don't have time for all this. If you want me to be ready to go."

"Fine. Sorry. I was only curious." He looked concerned and checked his watch. "Plenty of time."

I nodded and grinned, wanting our date to go well.

Charlie followed me into my apartment. "Riding around the city on a motorcycle is risky. You must admit she is unusual."

"And so am I." He should know this by now. I walked toward my bedroom to change for our date.

He trailed along, but I couldn't bear to undress in front of him. He had seen every inch of me before I left on my cruise, but not my new addition. The tribal tattoo armband from the pirate-infested Dutch East Indies, now called Indonesia, would scare him away.

Over the past few months, we'd gone on some dates. When I didn't let Charlie stay over, he had teased me about my imaginative range of excuses.

"Make yourself at home. Why don't you grab a beer and put on some music or something?" I pointed him to the fridge, proud of restocking it this morning.

Music from our favorite classic rock radio station began, and Charlie sang along to "All of My Love" by Led Zeppelin. My Wall Street guy was such a talented musician.

I didn't lock my bedroom door but selected a dressy long sleeve shirt and velvet skirt and switched from my casual sweater and jeans in a flash. By the time he reappeared with a couple of beers, I was slipping on black suede boots.

"Shoot. I missed out again." He grinned and held up two beers. Naturally, I took the offbeat ginger beer and left him with the traditional Brooklyn lager.

"Missed what?"

"The transformation." He clinked his beer bottle against mine. "Cheers."

At first, I thought he was referring to Anita, but he meant me. "Nothing much to it."

He put his beer down, kissed me, and tucked some of my loose hair behind my ear. "Now you know that's not true, Kat."

He took my elbow in a friendly gesture escorting me across the living room to the front door. Regrettably, his hand landed on the horrible tattoo hidden under my shirt. I grimaced and pulled my arm away.

If we stayed together, Charlie was bound to see it and ask questions that would be so hard to answer. How would I conceal it during our night away? I didn't want to lie or lose him, so my gut instinct made me push him away.

~ ~ ~

The Lincoln Center Metropolitan Opera House was world-class, and we had center orchestra seats. I was excited until I saw the program for *The Flying Dutchman* by the German composer Richard Wagner.

I swallowed hard at the reminder and regretted not finding out which opera we'd be seeing before saying yes. This was the last opera I saw about a year ago in Lisbon, Portugal, with the ship's captain. The story involved a ship captain, a love triangle, a sinking ship, and worst of all, death. All tragic events I had experienced during my seven-month voyage.

Frequent reminders didn't allow for distance and perspective. These bad memories were like digital photos that should be transferred off my phone to a Zip drive. Still out there and available but not easily seen.

Gazing around the theater, I was convinced that this performance would be different. Remembering the movie *Dunkirk* and how they faced much worse convinced me I could handle this.

Charlie patted my leg and scanned the opera house, looking pleased. The Saturday night crowd and our stellar location were exhilarating.

Behind me, a man spoke Spanish to his date. I couldn't help but turn around to peek at him. My attempts to translate his rapid Spanish failed miserably, but his voice sounded familiar. If only I had gotten a glimpse of El Rey ... but then he'd have seen me too.

The likelihood our drug kingpin was at the opera tonight and seated behind me was crazy. El Rey was locked up inside a jail. But could this be a friend, or an employee, sent to do his dirty work?

Charlie asked me what was wrong and squeezed my hand, but I couldn't say a word. The lights dimmed, and my chance to slip out without disturbing the long row of people before the aisle went dark as well.

I sat in my plush seat, uneasy during the entire first act. Somehow, I made it to the intermission and bounded to the restroom. I was eager to escape sitting in front of a possible drug kingpin and across from the stage with painful reminders from my clipper ship voyage.

Charlie waited at a lobby bar with two glasses of champagne and handed me one. "You look sad, Kat."

"Just tired. I'm going home after I finish this champagne. I hope you don't mind."

"Now? Before the next act? Oh, Kat. Please stay. You can sleep late tomorrow. I won't pick you up until 10 a.m."

I shook my head and swallowed the last drop of champagne. After putting the glass on a nearby counter, I kissed his cheek. "I don't deserve you."

I hurried against the crowd, being summoned back into the theater, and out the front doors. As I approached the large fountain in the plaza, Charlie called my name, and I turned around.

When he caught up to me, he looked concerned. "Wait up. I'll walk you home."

"I'm fine walking home alone. Stay and see the rest. I saw that opera last year."

"You did? On the ship, you saw an opera?"

"In Lisbon. It reminded me of the ship and everyone on board. Sometimes I miss them."

"Wait! You were in Lisbon, Portugal, and couldn't be bothered to send any of us an email or make a collect phone call?"

"Charlie, how many times do I have to explain and apologize? I would have contacted you, but I couldn't."

"The ship that cuts you off from civilization in a major city. I just don't get it."

"I know you don't, and I wish it made more sense." I hustled across Broadway before the traffic light changed, but he was right on my heels.

"Well, I still don't believe it. Not with you. You wouldn't go along with something asinine like that."

I ignored him, but he grabbed my arm, demanding an answer.

I pulled away in anger. "Like right this moment, I am without a choice."

He let go, and I rubbed my aching arm.

Charlie apologized. "You're upset. Let's stop for a coffee."

Reluctantly, I accompanied him to a café near my home. Already, my sense of well-being improved with some distance from the opera and the bad memories it conjured up.

He suggested I grab some seats while he ordered our drinks. I started to request a specific coffee, but he said, "I know what you like. Same as last week?"

I nodded and smiled. Charlie was so attentive and returned with my seasonal favorite, a pumpkin spice latte. He got his usual, an unadventurous plain black coffee. I sipped my coffee with some regret. The caffeine would keep me awake for hours.

He glanced at his steaming coffee, waiting for it to cool down, and then at me. "So, did all the passengers go to the opera together and play make-believe?"

"No, I went with the captain." I looked away. Remembering him that night made my eyes mist up.

"Oh, yes. The mysterious captain. Kat, if you feel so strongly about him, you should invite him to visit. I really want to meet him."

"Invite him here?" I asked in surprise.

"Yeah. The captain can stay at my place if that works for you. That's what I'd prefer."

"Well, I can't. Even if I wanted to."

"And why not? Is he still off the grid?"

"No, not exactly."

"Well, why don't you at least ask him?"

"I would, but I can't." To end this, I tried to stay emotionless. "He's dead."

Everyone I met then had to be dead. My decision to leave them behind in the 1860s and return home to the modern-day was agonizing but necessary.

At first, I was ecstatic to be back in my comfortable life and see my family and friends. But after the initial excitement of being back home wore off, I faced the facts. I would never be able to communicate with anyone from that long, arduous voyage.

Daily, I wondered about my friends and what had happened after I disembarked in Hong Kong. I ached for just a few words or a letter from any of them. But this was impossible.

Charlie's green laser-focused eyes narrowed. He sat back, knocking over his coffee. The blackish pool spread and ran toward the table's edge and his expensive suit.

I grabbed a handful of napkins and threw them down to stop the stubborn flow.

When we got the spill under control, I grabbed the

opportunity to exit. "I'm exhausted and going home. Thank you for the coffee, the opera, and tonight."

Perhaps, he would stop asking all these badgering questions. I wanted to tell him everything, but I had said too much already. He was sensible like my dad, so he'd never believe me, and I couldn't face the anger or denials again. Charlie's childhood experiences with Native Americans and Wyoming's mysticism that he sometimes bragged about didn't come close.

I smoothed his brown hair with my hand, kissed him farewell on the cheek, and retreated to my Upper West Side cave to lick my invisible wounds alone.

Chapter 7 ~ Onboard a Tesla

In the morning, Charlie texted that he was downstairs waiting. I grabbed my old-fashioned traveling carpetbag, a useful souvenir from the voyage, and hurried downstairs.

A flashy red car was double-parked nearby, but I ignored it and scanned the streets for the usual sports utility vehicle that Charlie preferred to rent.

"Yo, Kat." Charlie rolled down the window of the fiery sports car and waved to get my attention.

I crossed the street to his side of the car. "What's this?"

"My buddy's car, but we can borrow it for the weekend." A car vacated a parking spot, and Charlie slid his vehicle into that lucky opening before it was gone. He jumped out while I stared at the bright cherry-colored car.

"What do you think?" He opened the door for me. "Beautiful, huh? It's brand new. A Tesla roadster."

I stood still in awe while contemplating the red-hot fireball.

"Hop in, Kat. In exchange for letting my friend park at my building's garage, I get to use it. But I might buy one. Still mulling it over and want to test out the Jaguar E-type Zero first."

"Well, this car is really extreme." I hesitated at the idea of riding around inside a car from the rich-and-famous playbook.

He patted the car fondly. "I'm sitting pretty. I paid the divorce settlement off, so money isn't an issue now."

I bit my lip and frowned, filled with envy. If only I had that problem. My hard-earned savings were about gone, and I got nothing but bills when Axel died. Young and foolish, we didn't bother buying life insurance. Unexpected expenses that the insurance company declined to pay and losing investments had taken their toll.

"Kat, can't you be happy for me for once?"

"Sure. I'm thrilled." To forget about my money and job woes, I made a silly grin. "Pop the trunk."

"Trunk?"

"You know. A place for my bag?" I swung my carpetbag around to show him.

"I'll handle that. Get comfy in this amazing flying machine." Charlie took my bag and tossed it in the back seat.

I climbed inside and buckled my seatbelt, overwhelmed by the new car scent. He ran around and hopped behind the wheel like a kid with a brand-new birthday gift.

Before he started the car, I received a slobbery kiss. "Would you rather drive?"

"Me? No. Absolutely not." Even with insurance, any possible dent would cost a fortune to repair.

"You'll enjoy this. I promise." He guided the car that screamed "stare at me and drool" to everyone we passed in the direction of Central Park. "This model isn't officially available until 2020. My friend has connections. He got it as part of an early Tesla testing program."

"Hope it was thoroughly tested and not a lemon."

"Come on, Kat. This model has record-setting acceleration, range, and performance." He cut across the Upper West Side to the highway along the Hudson River.

"Seems so extravagant."

"Yeah, it is. But I've wanted a car since I moved here. I work hard and deserve it."

"Taxis and car services with an occasional rental car is all we need. Haven't you heard about Zipcars?"

"But with a car of our own, we could easily go places. Make our own memories filled with new exciting adventures together."

I gazed out the window as we traveled north toward the Bronx, unsure if I was up for more adventures.

Charlie continued on with the sales pitch. "Fastest production car ever. Up to a hundred miles per hour in about four seconds."

"But why? You can't do that anyway. You'll get an expensive speeding ticket."

He shrugged off my negative waves. "And it has three electric motors. Much better for the environment. Aren't you happy about that?"

"Nope, but thanks for the warning. I'll keep my Uber app ready in case you run out of juice."

Charlie switched on the radio, and "American Girl" surrounded us. We both loved classic rock.

"I always thought Tom Petty's lyrics described you. The desire to explore. Your wanderlust."

"Not anymore. I've relinquished that role to younger American girls. I'm ready to stay home and grow old." A boring life, but I had seen enough of the wild world, and traveling was too expensive.

I still loved this song. "American Girl" was Tom Petty's final number in his last performance at the Hollywood Bowl before he died from an overdose. Opioids, with some other prescriptions, struck again.

"But what about our Wyoming trip in a few weeks? My family is so excited to finally meet you."

"Traveling around the good old U.S. of A is fine." A few months ago, in a moment of weakness, I had consented to go. My concerns still loomed about meeting his parents and witnessing their disappointment with me as their son's new girlfriend.

"Going overseas with all the security precautions is a major hassle now." He tapped his fingers in time to the song's strong guitar riff.

Traveling anywhere could be a pain, remembering mechanical problems on my recent drive from Texas to the West Coast.

"You'll love it in the summer with the glass roof off. This little baby can go fast."

"Speed won't help unless it can fly or jump over traffic." I had experienced those massive summer weekend traffic jams in and out of Manhattan. A slowpoke commuter train was often faster. "What does a car like this cost?"

"The base is two hundred grand. But this is the premium edition, so slightly more."

I bit my lip in shock. For that price, it should fly.

~ ~ ~

An hour later, our flaming-red car had cooled to a crawl

trapped in the heavy traffic. At least on a train, you could walk around. The only plus riding in his car was the music. The speakers blasting the 1970s song "Crazy on You" were perfectly tuned, as expected with the car's extravagant price tag.

Charlie usually sang along, but now he turned the volume so low I could barely hear it.

I stared out the window as the city gave way to the burbs. "Something wrong with the car?"

"Nah. I can't listen to this one."

"Why not?" This song was one of the best from the band Heart.

"Yeah, well. I used to like it." He adjusted his sunglasses and contemplated me for a second. "A number at my ill-fated wedding reception. Her favorite."

"How's she doing being single again?"

"From what I heard, better than she deserves. She got married a few weeks after the divorce."

Ouch, that must have hurt. Unlike me, Charlie may never stop hating his ex.

Billy Joel's "Big Shot" started. Charlie turned the volume back up, singing along. He qualified for that select group of top-earning big shots on Wall Street. But he didn't let it go to his head.

After this overnighter, I would decide if we should break up. It was unfair to string Charlie along. Axel reminded me of a character from a novel. My life with him was like a book with happy and sad parts, but now I was reading something else. Dating Charlie might only be a short story.

Charlie stopped singing. "Are you okay?"

"Yeah, you know. I'm a city person." This overnighter was an inconvenient delay before restarting my job search.

"Right. Well, this is a short jaunt. You'll be back soon."

"For twenty-four hours, I can handle it." I smiled and joked with him. "I won't melt or anything."

"So last night, about the opera. I must ask you something."

"What?"

"The opera with the captain. Sounds serious. Were you in love with him?"

I stared at the car's bumper in front of us, not wanting to memorize the license plate numbers or lie. "I was for a while."

"I expected that. But no more?"

"No."

"How did he die?"

I paused, wondering. I hoped from old age, but I didn't know.

Charlie said, "Never mind, I don't want the answer to that. What about others from the ship? I get it that you miss them. Don't you want to invite some over here to visit?"

"Yes, but I can't."

"Why not?"

"Please stop with all these questions, Charlie. You don't want to know."

"I do. We must work through this to build a life together."

I contemplated what to say, but any explanation would make me sound insane.

"I know they stay off the grid. In Lisbon, of all places, they ignored the internet and telephones." Charlie's tone said it all. He'd never believe me.

"Well, they are busy. Always a lot of work to do on a sailing ship."

"Weird. Like a mountain guy I heard about back home in Wyoming. He lived in a primitive shack and used an outhouse and candles. Nothing modern. He was completely wacko."

Life was primitive on the old barebones and unrenovated clipper ship built in the 1850s, but not by choice.

"Kat, I just want you to be happy. If you prefer to find that ship and your friends again, I understand. But first, give us a chance. Not just for my sake. For Abby and your friends here. We all care about you so much." He looked away and blinked several times.

After a few commercial interruptions, the Beatles' "Let it Be" serenaded us. "I know. I'm trying. I just need more time."

"But you've been home for five months and are still so distant. I can't figure you out. What you want. If you even like having me around."

"I like you, Charlie." I patted his arm. "A lot, or I wouldn't be here. Can we just do what Paul McCartney is singing about? Let it be for now?"

He reached for my hand and gave me a weak unconvinced grin.

I wanted to tell him about a TV show interviewing American soldiers who had returned from a tour of duty in Afghanistan. How hard it was for them to readjust, and their friends and families didn't understand it. After a seven-month tour of duty on an old ship, I was still adjusting. But Charlie would never understand how hard it was and worry at this comparison.

My stomach growled. Embarrassed and to make it stop, I rubbed it.

The complaining was so loud Charlie overheard it and chuckled. "Behind you, there's a cooler with some drinks. The best pizza place on the East coast is in New Haven. Perfect halfway spot for lunch. I'll give the Yale grads a few points for that. Been around since the 1920s so hard to beat."

I drank an iced tea to quiet my babbling belly. Charlie surprised me again. He had graduated from Harvard, and Yale University was his nemesis.

"One short detour to stretch our legs." Charlie exited the freeway and parked the car at the Silver Sands State Park, which had an almost empty parking lot in November.

Charlie said, "I want to show you something." We walked along the boardwalk above the sand dunes and marsh to the waterfront. "Isn't it amazing here?"

"If it was warmer." A deep shiver traveled along my backbone through my thin leather jacket. That feeling is often described as if someone was walking across your grave. But that was nonsense. That shiver must be from the chilly air after leaving the red-hot car.

"I'm thinking about buying a getaway place in the Milford area," he said.

"Here? Why?" I didn't see any houses, and it was so far from Manhattan.

"The Hamptons is so overdone, and my ex is there. This is an easy drive. You could take the train here. Only ninety minutes from Grand Central."

"Right, I've heard that before. That's only if you live in Grand Central Station." Otherwise, add another thirty minutes or more. The recruiters who'd urged me to work for banks in Stamford, Connecticut, always said that.

"I'm not suggesting every weekend. There's an island over there with my name on it. It's practically calling me."

"Are you buying a place over there?" I took off my sunglasses for a better view of the small tree-covered island in the distance.

"Don't I wish. That's Charles Island. But it's part of a state park and not for sale. At low tide in the summer, you can walk over there. Search for buried treasure."

"Over there?"

"Yeah, Captain Kidd and his pirate crew stopped here in the seventeenth century. They say he hid plundered goods there before he and his crew were captured in Boston."

"Pirates?" No wonder my arm, near the tattoo, tingled in fear.

Charlie chuckled. "Can't you picture it? Johnny Depp sailing around with his merry band of raiders."

"But that's Hollywood. They're thieves, kidnappers, and murderers."

His laughter ended, but I turned, stumbled, and ran on the boardwalk. Straight back, as fast as my legs would carry me, to the safety of the parking lot and his car.

Footsteps echoed off the wooden walkway right behind me, but I couldn't stop and prayed it was only Charlie.

Chapter 8 ~ A Mystical Seaport

By the time we gained some mileage from the pirate hideout and exited the freeway into New Haven, I was starved. At Frank Pepe's popular pizzeria, we ordered the signature dish: a white clam pizza. And Charlie was right. It was delicious and better than many pies in New York City.

As we returned to his roadster after lunch, Charlie assured me we were over halfway to our mystery destination.

I decided to be more upbeat. "I'll drive awhile. If you think it's a good idea."

"I knew you'd come around." Charlie hugged me.

"This car is insured, right?"

"Would I take such a risk with an irreplaceable cargo of Kat?"

I giggled and repositioned the seat. "I'm not worth that much, but kind of you to say so."

Charlie cleared his throat. "A few things you must know. The roadster has an electric induction motor, which eliminates the need for a complicated transmission. It has just three gears, two forward and one for reverse. Shifting is manual." He pointed to the gearshift, and I rested my hand on it. "But there's no clutch."

"Weird. Okay." I sure wouldn't miss the clutch. "Should we set the GPS, so the chauffeur knows where we are going?" The car had an elaborate computer screen ready and waiting.

"No need. Besides, it will ruin the surprise. It's a straight shot, so we won't get lost. Unless we want to, that is." He leaned over and kissed my cheek.

But I ignored him to focus on controlling the fanciest, most expensive car I had ever driven.

He dictated some directions. "Just head back to Highway 85, head north, and hug the coast."

"We aren't going to Boston, are we?" No way was I driving that far or in a crowded city.

"Oh, no. Connecticut for a dinner party and one night."

"Dinner party? You didn't mention that."

"Part of the surprise. Abby packed an outfit for you."

"That Abby and you. Full of too many surprises." We had traded house keys years ago to help each other out. But sneaking inside for my clothes was never part of the deal. Tonight was a much bigger deal than I had assumed. "Do you work with these people?"

"Only one buddy from my old firm, Levittman, is coming. We still get together. The guys are bringing wives or girlfriends."

"Or both?"

He snickered. "Yeah, if they could manage it, they would."

"No doubt. Can't wait." I had never met anyone from Levittman who didn't overflow with arrogance.

"It really isn't that bad of a firm. I know you despise them. You're the only person I've heard of who nabbed a job interview and afterward told them flat out you had no wish to pursue it any further. Hell, everyone else would sacrifice their firstborn to work there. Getting an interview is high enough of a hurdle."

"Well, this isn't a job interview. I'll manage for one night."

"Kind of you, Kat. The food should be superb."

"That's the least they can do. I bet I know where we are going, Old Lyme. Fits the bill perfectly. Old, rich, and waspy."

"Nope, but not far from there. Trust me. You'll like it."

I hoped he was right, but I couldn't change it now.

~ ~ ~

After about an hour, we traded off again. Driving such an expensive car on unfamiliar roads and in heavy traffic required too much mental energy. I stretched my back and stiff legs from sitting inside the car for hours. This heavy traffic was why I hated long car rides.

The highway exit signs for the port town of Mystic and the Seaport Museum loomed closer. I figured we would pass it, but Charlie moved to the right lane and put on his right-turn signal.

I tried to form the words, "What? Not here. Please." But nothing came out.

"Surprise! Mystic, Connecticut, here we come."

"But it's the off-season and a big port. Why here?"

"Wait until you see where we are staying. I was texted a photo. You will love it!"

"I've been here before. Couldn't we stay somewhere else?"

"Kat, this is all arranged. We can't back out at the last minute. It will be fun. You'll see."

I contemplated how to convince him this was a bad idea. I didn't want to be in a town known for its port and ships.

"Did you stay here with your ex?"

"If you are referring to my husband Axel, who died, then yes."

"Sorry, I just think of him as an ex like mine. Bad memories?" He turned on his phone to find the address with GPS.

"No, not from that." I had never told Charlie that Axel planned to leave me before getting the cancerous death sentence. That revelation was humiliating and unnecessary. "Mystic is better in the summer when the weather is warmer."

As he drove through the town of Mystic, he ignored me, monitoring the GPS. "Did you know Mystic, the town and river, was named by the Pequot, a Native American tribe? *Missi-tuk* means a large river with winds and tides. Something about large waves."

"Wonderful. *Missi-tuk* to Mystic. Learn something every day." The vision of large waves gave me a stomach ache. But it could be from sitting still for so long.

"I can't wait to introduce you to some of my friends in Wyoming over Thanksgiving. I had a Native American babysitter and grew up with her kids. My best friend, Standing Horse, can't wait to say hello."

"Is his name really Standing Horse?" The unusual name drew my interest immediately.

"Yeah, most people call him Hoss, but I prefer to use his real name. More respectful. I still get sick thinking about what happened to his tribe. We practically stole their land and then killed so many off."

"Yeah, it was a sad time in our history."

"Did you know those high-end islands, Nantucket and Martha's Vineyard, used to be full of Native Americans? Today there isn't one single descendant left."

I nodded. "Terrible." What more could be said? I had seen sections of the Trail of Tears where Native Americans were forced to migrate. That brought me to tears for days.

Charlie said, "Standing Horse and his wife are having us over for a big party."

"Great." Meeting his family would be challenging enough.

"You'll like them. You are open to all sorts of people." Charlie patted my leg reassuringly.

I shifted in my seat to get comfortable. "What do you mean?"

"Hey, it's a good thing. That woman who brought you home on the motorcycle was pretty different."

"Yeah, I really like Anita." Rude pretentious people were the worst.

Charlie stopped at a security gate and mentioned our host, Jason Osborne, to the guard. The guard complimented his flashy new set of wheels and pointed out a parking spot.

Charlie unloaded his luggage from the trunk while I retrieved my small carpetbag from the back seat. He pulled his carry-on suitcase behind him and slung a garment bag over his shoulder. "Had to bring a suit for dinner and your dress."

"I wish you had told me what to bring." I had only packed a different shirt to go with the jeans I was wearing and a few toiletries and worried about what Abby had given him.

"I wanted it to be a surprise. This will be fun, Kat. Can you please enjoy it? For me?"

He took my carpetbag from me. "Is this from your cruise? Still caught in a time warp?"

"No, it was the first bag I found in my closet. Besides, this bag carries just enough for one night." I searched around again. "I don't see the hotel."

"That's because it isn't a hotel."

"No? Then what?" I stepped back, preparing for what I feared was the answer.

Charlie asked the parking attendant for the *Atlantic Dreams,* and he gestured toward the water.

"Oh, no." My feet sunk in my boots as if weighted down, and I dropped my bag. "I can't board another ship." An odd chant of my own, "It's too soon, too soon, too soon," echoed on a continual loop in my head.

"It's not a ship." He picked up my bag from the ground, swinging it around.

The "too soon" tune stopped in relief.

Charlie stood before me by the water where mega-sized motorboats were lined up along the dock.

He turned and smiled while balancing my bag on top of his suitcase. "This is a fricking fantastic yacht!"

My legs wobbled uncontrollably, grey spots floated in front of me, and the ground shifted.

Chapter 9 ~ My Horse Whisperer

Voices brought me back to Mystic, and I hoped they came from real people. Two men said something unintelligible to each other. I tried to open my eyes, but it was so pleasant in this hazy in-between state of semi-oblivion. Only one minute more, I promised myself.

"Maybe I should call an ambulance," a man said.

What the hell? To avoid an unwanted hospital visit, I opened my eyes and used my arms to sit up. This was unnecessary since I lay against Charlie's lap.

When I moved, Charlie propped me up. "Kat, are you all right?"

A man, wearing a preppy navy outfit, kneeled next to us on the cement walkway near the dock. I blinked to clear what felt like salty water from my vision, nodded, and opened my mouth. But no words came out.

The man handed me a plastic bottle of water, and I almost emptied it in one gulp.

"How are you feeling? Do you want to see a doctor?" Charlie held my hand with his face only inches from mine.

"No, I'm fine. Just thirsty." Memories of what just happened to me gradually returned.

"I wanted to surprise you. A special night on my friend Jason's yacht. He throws quite a shindig and planned this for weeks."

I looked over at the yacht and wanted to scream or run away. Instead, I swallowed the last of the water.

Charlie explained to the man crouched next to us. "That clam pizza for lunch was salty. I didn't realize she was so dehydrated."

"Me neither. I'm fine now," I said.

Charlie helped me stand, and I brushed off my pants. At least where I fell was dry and relatively clean.

To escape from the yacht, I snatched my overnight bag off the ground. I couldn't trigger another episode of navisphobia, my recently developed fear of boats and ships. I scurried through the parking lot back to Charlie's Tesla, desperate to return home.

Charlie trailed behind with his bag bumping on the asphalt and clicked open the doors. I threw my bag in the back seat and climbed into the passenger seat, ready to go.

He sat behind the wheel without starting the car. "What's wrong?" He shook out a tissue like a waiter with a napkin inside a high-class restaurant and handed it to me.

I accepted it and dabbed my eyes. "Just take me to Mystic's train station. We passed it on the way. You can stay overnight without me."

"Kat, please."

I shivered. "Really, I'm fine. You should stay after coming all this way. Hang out with your friends. Probably useful for your business deals."

He turned on the roadster's radio and heater but not the engine. "If that's what you want, but it's a long ride back. You really would enjoy this party tonight. And this isn't at all like your ship. No sails, just a motor, and not that big."

"Doesn't matter." I sat on my hands in an attempt to crush my overwhelming anxiety.

"All right, I'd rather be with you. I'll drive you home. We can do something else in the city."

The Rolling Stones song "Wild Horses" began, and he sang softly like a backup singer for Mick Jagger.

"Come on, Kat. Sing along with me some. You'll feel better. This is another one of our classic oldies."

I loved this tune and forced a smile but couldn't sing along.

He tilted his head back and closed his eyes. "A popular wedding song when I was in the band. I wonder how many marriages made it?"

I nodded. Many failed marriages only lasted about seven years.

When the news came on, he switched off the radio, took my hand, and kissed it. "Hell, I'm a Wyoming boy. My accent sneaks out whenever I'm with you. Back home, we don't give up without a fight."

"Fight? That's what I'm worried about."

He lifted his hands in surrender. "I don't mean fighting you. Fighting whatever it is you went through. Hell, or worse."

My voyage wasn't a daily hell, but sometimes uncomfortably close.

He patted my leg. "I won't give up without trying. Can we take one last look from shore and ask them some questions?"

Unconvinced but willing to try, I got out of the car. We left our luggage locked inside the Tesla. He put his arm around my shoulder, and we walked over to the super-sized yacht together. I stopped about three feet from the gangway, unable to go an inch further and past my imaginary line. Before me, the *Atlantic Dreams*, the size of a house, floated while tied to the dock.

Charlie grabbed my hand. "See, it isn't so scary docked here like this. No masts or sails. Just an oversized motorboat."

"But isn't it going somewhere?"

"Where? Like the Caribbean for one night? Afraid not." He chuckled.

"Are you sure it will stay docked until tomorrow?"

Charlie motioned for a uniformed crew member to approach and repeated my question.

The crew member said, "Yes, sir. As far as I know, we shall remain docked. The owner wants to take her north tomorrow afternoon with a few of his friends."

"Hear that, Kat? Totally fine. Just a hotel that happens to be tied to the shore. What could be safer than that?"

Lots of things like my apartment or a hotel in town, but I didn't argue.

The uniformed young man said, "Sir, let us know if you require any assistance with your luggage."

"Later. It's inside the car. We are still making a decision." Charlie had taken charge and was letting me take my time.

The crew member shrugged and walked away. He assumed I was a city slicker, but I couldn't help it. Ten to one he had never sailed on a real ship under extreme conditions. Unless they'd been on ocean-crossing vessels for months and faced real danger. Working on a luxury yacht that puttered along the coast didn't quite qualify.

I turned to Charlie. "Sorry. I can't. I'll find a hotel nearby and see you later. Or you can go to the dinner party and sleep at the hotel with me."

"Just one short night. Certainly not seven months at sea. We're here for less than twenty-four hours. There isn't time to go anywhere, even if they wanted to."

"I know. It's silly to worry, but that gangplank and being on the water again makes me nervous. It's a real thing called navisphobia. After all those months, I can't walk up that."

"Is that all?"

I nodded, wondering if it could be any worse.

"You've heard me talk about working with horses back home in Wyoming, right?"

I nodded again. I had some of my own in Texas, and we had shared stories.

His green eyes sparkled magically in the sunlight. "Those song lyrics about wild horses gave me an idea. Once, we had a fire inside the barn. The horses panicked, but we got them all out by covering their eyes. Are you game to try it?"

"I guess so."

He took my scarf and tied it around my eyes, blindfolding me.

"I'm crouching down right in front of you. Climb on my back."

His back touched my knees. "I'm too heavy. I might hurt you."

He sighed in exasperation. "I may not work out like before, but I can handle it."

I climbed on his back, and he stood, struggling. He leaned to one side and then the other, adjusting my weight.

I bit my lip. If Charlie falls, I fall. With my arms wrapped around his chest, I couldn't remove my scarf.

He took one firm step and then another. "No problem at all." His voice was energetic and upbeat.

After about ten steps, he stopped. "We made it, Kat."

I slid down from his back and pulled off my scarf. I seized

the railing so tight my hands ached while focused on the gangway and water below. My stomach still churned, but I lightened my hold. I was on board. If my ridiculous boat phobia was gone, this whole trip was worthwhile.

The crew member who gave me the bottled water approached with an amused smile plastered across his face. "That sure was a different way to board."

I glared back. All phobias, not just navisphobia, weren't laughing matters.

He asked Charlie a few questions and signed us in. We were the first to arrive, but the others should show up soon. At least a crowd didn't hang around to leer at our piggyback boarding style.

A female crew member, wearing a navy sailor outfit, escorted us to our cabin. We followed her, but I peeked back at the gangway. I planned to practice boarding and disembarking a few times on my own before we left.

Charlie said, "I hope you don't mind we are sharing a cabin. I know you haven't been up to … well, anything yet. But they know we've been dating, so it was weird to ask for two rooms."

I took his hand and smiled. "I am thrilled to be in your cabin."

He kissed me. In anticipation of what lay ahead, I wished I had the entire yacht to be alone with my horse whispering hero.

Chapter 10 ~ Life Back on Board

Our luxurious cabin had a king bed and the fanciest private bathroom I had ever seen on a ship. Upscale toiletries from La Mer were displayed on the counter.

"This is so ritzy." I longed to take a long soak in the spa bathtub.

"Better than your cabin on the ship?"

"Much better." This resembled nothing at all like my barebones cabin on the *Anne Kristine*. I had never explained how terribly basic it was without electricity or modern plumbing on board.

"Hell, I could live here for seven months and sail the seven seas with you anytime. Jason installed fast speed Wi-Fi and bragged how it's 'plain sailing' to stay connected."

Charlie jumped on the bed, kicked off his shoes, and leaned on his side. "Come here, Kat. Nice and comfy." Charlie stroked the bed and curled his index finger, gesturing for me to join him.

"In a minute." I stood in front of the mirror to comb my hair and look less harried. "Don't we need to socialize with your friends soon?"

"Jason estimated they will arrive in about an hour. Until then, the entire ship is ours."

"Yacht, not ship," I corrected him out of habit. Whenever I accidentally called the clipper ship a boat, I had been corrected. Vessel, ship, and schooner were permitted, but not boat. My secret name for it was a good-for-nothing half-sinking tub.

"Right." He saluted.

"And we aren't alone. Don't forget the crew."

He patted the pillow next to him. "Yes, but they aren't right here."

Undressing in front of him made me nervous, but I couldn't think of any other excuses. After pulling the curtain across the window for privacy and still dressed, I slid into bed next to him. He kissed me gently and then intensely, reaching under my sweater. I flicked off the light on the nightstand. Carefully hidden in almost complete darkness, I snuggled up against him, happy for the warmth and comfort.

Kissing him with his body right next to mine felt right and surprisingly marvelous. Just as we started to undress each other and I pulled off my pants, a loud rap sounded on the door.

"Hey, Charlie. Where's my DJ?" The sharp rap turned into a pounding.

"Damn. That's Jason. He's early." Charlie kissed me and turned on the bedside lamp.

I pulled the blanket over me to hide.

Charlie opened the door a crack. "Hey, Jason. I need a few minutes."

"What for?" Jason said. "Ah, gotcha. Is she here? That mystery woman you've been waiting on forever?"

"Yeah, she's here." Charlie's voice was gruff.

"When do I meet her?"

Jason reminded me of a kid who always got everything he wanted instantly.

"Soon, bro. She's busy now. I'll be out in ten."

"All right, bud. Don't let me stand here in the way." Jason laughed.

Charlie shut the door, and the lock clicked. He sat on the bed next to me and put his hand on my shoulder. "So, where were we?"

He kissed me again.

But knowing I would soon be judged by Jason and his moneyed friends, I lost my nerve and pulled away. "You need to go, Charlie. He's waiting."

"Let him wait," he said, kissing my neck and lifting the bottom of my sweater.

"No, I can't do it on a timer like this. I'm not a three-minute egg. Later, after the party, okay?"

"All right, you win. I'll start up the music and be back in a few. You look tired. Why don't you just relax?"

He didn't need to ask me twice. The cotton sheets were ultra-buttery and soft, and I snuggled underneath, not wanting to waste another second.

~ ~ ~

"Hey, sleeping beauty. Time to rise."

I turned over, still wearing my sweater and underwear. Charlie had changed into a suit.

"I fell asleep?"

"You sure did. Even snored some."

"Oh no."

"It was soft and cute. I barely heard a thing."

I sat up, registering how much he had dressed up. "That fancy?"

"Afraid so. I shaved again."

"I can't believe I slept through all that."

"Hey, that's what this weekend is for. R and R with me."

"Sounds perfect except for being on the water." And Charlie never relaxed for long.

He sat on the bed next to me and played with my messy hair trying to straighten it. An impossible task to accomplish without a wide-tooth comb.

"I thought you missed the ship and the ocean."

"Nope. I endured enough days at sea to last a lifetime."

"So, I guess a seven-night cruise in the Caribbean for your birthday next year isn't a fab idea?"

I stared at him, wondering if he was insane. "Do you enjoy torturing me or something?"

"No, Kat. Believe it or not, I only want the best for you."

He handed me a bottle of water, took a small orange container out of his jacket pocket, and shook out a pill into his palm. "You should take this. Very routine and above board. It might help you."

I stared at the white pill in his palm and shook. "Help with what?"

"Anxiety. Since you refuse to see a doctor, this might help reduce stress. Heck, I read somewhere most dogs in America take meds for anxiety."

"But I'm not a dog."

"No. You are much more valuable to me than any animal, or anyone else for that matter. I only want to help you recover,

Kat."

"I just need some time. I'll be fine without drugs."

"You will, but this might speed things up. It's helped me. Perfectly legal." He handed me a standard orange prescription bottle for Charles Richmond.

"Why do you take this?"

"For stress."

"I'm shocked, Charlie. You really need this?"

"Yeah, I stress out sometimes. About my job, clients, the news. Especially about you and our relationship."

Charlie always seemed so stable and in control. "I'm sorry. But I can't." I dropped his evil pill back into the ominous container and handed it back. I considered telling him how my brother Keith died of a drug overdose. Except I needed more time to explain what happened.

"Kat, millions take them every single day."

"I know, and that's their business. Remember Jefferson Airplane's warning about what pills can do in "White Rabbit"?"

His smile turned into a grimace. "That's just made-up lyrics. Not real life."

I looked away, wishing I were back home and alone.

"Okay, I get it. Forget I mentioned it. I better return to the guys and the music. I'll leave you to get ready." He tapped my leg goodbye, walked to the door, and looked back. "When we go to Wyoming for Thanksgiving, my band is reuniting to take us down memory lane. You're going to love the brass."

"Brass?"

"Horns. You know, the sax and trumpet. My buddy Benny is the best trombone player ever."

"That sounds amazing."

"Definitely. I've got to go. Come join us soon. The outfit Abby sent along is hanging inside the closet. You're so lucky to have such a great friend as your neighbor. She packed some dressy shoes, too."

"Wonderful." Abby had overstepped our unspoken boundaries. I marched to the closet to inspect my outfit.

"I almost forgot." He handed me a red velvet box. My

heart pounded, flooding with anxiety that this might be a diamond ring.

To my relief, I fingered a more casual gold necklace with a black and white stone charm. "Oh. This is beautiful."

"Moss agate. A special quartz from Wyoming and the wild Laramie river. Mother went shopping with me last time I was home and suggested it for you."

"That's kind of her."

He latched the necklace around my neck. "I hope you're not disappointed. Diamonds another time."

"I like this much more. The stone resembles little black flowers and fossils." I stood on my toes to match his height and kissed him.

"Mother is so eager to meet you at Thanksgiving. Everyone back home can't wait."

"Me too." I swallowed hard. In a few weeks, I'd meet his family of rough, tough cowboys living on a real working ranch. My anxiety kicked back in, but one of his pills would never be the answer.

Charlie kissed my cheek. "I'll be inside the Grand Salon. Just ask the crew if you can't find it."

~ ~ ~

The Armani cocktail dress Abby selected from my closet was the only upscale designer clothing I owned. A giveaway from a friend that I'd only worn once. After gaining some weight during the past few months, it was hard to zip up, but I had a little room to breathe and move.

But my sleek black look was ruined with an ugly reminder. The ornate tattoo circling my right arm was impossible to hide without sleeves, and I didn't have a scarf or sweater to conceal it.

When my mom saw my unwanted souvenir tattoo last summer, she gasped. My dad's jaw dropped in alarm. After that, I kept it hidden. Charlie would be shocked and humiliated in front of his business colleagues and friends.

My leather jacket was the only way to hide it. The mirror practically screamed that this was a huge mistake, but I was out of options.

I whispered, "Sorry, Giorgio," to my reflection and went in search of Charlie.

Inside the yacht's Grand Salon, I accepted a fancy blue cocktail called 'The Mystique' from a crew member-turned-waiter. This mysterious drink reminded me of the Caribbean. Customized drink recipes, typical for weddings, were now standard items at small dinner parties. All this need for an extra wow factor seemed extreme.

The ultrarich and influential crowd was dressed up. I would have fit in better without the leather jacket, but it was edgy and hip. Except at my age, it made me look desperate.

Regrettably, the booze didn't help me recapture that elusive, I-don't-care attitude. All I could focus on was the lost opportunity to show Charlie my repulsive tattoo in private.

I hummed along to the music, sipped my cocktail for courage, and watched Charlie from behind, delaying the inevitable. Finally, I strolled over to Charlie, who was busy chatting with two identically dressed businessmen.

Before I could get his attention, a woman squealed and rushed up to me. "Kat. Kat Jensen?"

The stylish dark-haired woman embraced me while I held my vibrant cocktail away from her expensive, fuchsia-colored dress and gold shawl.

She stood back. "I can't believe it's you, Kat."

I smiled back at her familiar face, trying to remember her name.

She smiled. "Desi. Desiree. I'm Greg Overton's daughter. We met at his house on the Upper East Side last year. I recognize that Armani."

"Oh, Desi, of course. What a fantastic surprise. So wonderful to see you."

"When was it? November last year? You left soon after for the grand voyage."

"I did. For a lot longer than I'd planned on."

"Papa told me. I want to hear all about it. He was truly heartbroken when you left."

"Who was heartbroken?" Charlie asked.

"Oh, Charlie, thrilled to see you. Long story." They

exchanged standard French-style air kisses on each cheek.

"Do you know, Kat?" she asked him.

"I should hope so. She's my girlfriend."

"How, how wonderful. Steve is over there." Desi acted flustered and motioned toward her husband. "You must say hello."

Her husband was the person I should have listened to last year. As an experienced sailor, Steve had tried to convince me to stick to a modern luxury cruise ship and stop looking for a genuine sailing ship.

I was introduced to Jason, our host, and his fiancé, Lacy. Their buddy, Wyatt, mentioned that his date was on her way.

Jason was friendly but overbearing. He pulled me to the side, explaining how he had looked forward to meeting me. Jason was taller than me but shorter than the other men. He pressed on with his relentless questioning. His inquires dived deep, so I kept backing away from him.

Desi said, "Kat and I will return momentarily." She dragged me away, and I would have gone anywhere with her to avoid Jason's inquisition.

"Oh my God! You're dating Charlie?" Desi asked, clearly in shock.

"Yeah. Is that a bad thing?"

"Oh, no. Charlie is a sweetheart. Known him for years. He worked with Steve at Levittman. Knew his ex-wife too. But not to worry, she's not showing up here. Not tonight."

"That's a relief. Charlie really hates her."

"Few people like her. From the start, she was a vindictive bitch."

Desi's loudmouth husband Steve was lecturing on about price-earnings ratios, debt covenants, and a slew of other boring Wall Street high finance subjects with the guys.

Desi apologized and shook her head, resigned to Steve's tirades. "Boring work discussions never end. But it pays for a beautiful home in Old Greenwich. Dull compared to the city but right on the water and ideal for the kids. You must stop by tomorrow on your way back to the city."

She gave me a business card with her contact information.

"Please email me your info. Come up for a girls' weekend. I'd love it. Steve goes out sailing most weekends. The nanny can keep an eye on the kids while we play."

"That sounds amazing."

Desi was good-natured and fun to be around. So even with the long commute north, I would do it. But I'd take the train, not a car. Later, I would invite her to spend some time with Abby and me in the city.

We caught up about the past year quickly. I explained some generalities about settling in again. Desi went over her life with the kids, Steve, and her passion project, an animal welfare charity.

Desi nodded toward Lacy and another woman. "See that woman over there?"

"Which one?"

"Heather in the obscenely tight green dress with the slit up to her you-know-what. She's here with Wyatt, but he's gay. Not a big deal to me either way. But Wyatt is covering for somebody."

The tall brunette did look stunning. "Is she trying to win an ugly three-sizes-too-small dress contest?"

"Oh, believe me. That and more. She's a complete phony. And she is probably having an affair with Jason."

"You think so? But why —"

Just when I expected the juicy details, a waiter interrupted and rang a bell to herd all eight of us to the dining table. On the way, I was introduced to the scandalous Heather. She acted nervous but not surprising if she was playing around.

I was sandwiched in between Charlie and Steve. Heather was bookended by Steve and Wyatt. If Jason planned to sit next to her at his dinner party, he'd struck out.

"Are you cold?" Charlie pointed at my leather jacket.

"No. I'm fine." I was hot but tried to hide it.

The waiters delivered our appetizer plates filled with Kumamoto oysters on the half-shell flown in from Japan that day. Jason must have allocated an unlimited party budget. A deliciously rare white wine was served with them.

Quickly, I dabbed my forehead with my napkin. Charlie

asked, "Why don't you take off your coat? Men wear them, but you don't need to."

"Umm. Well. I can't."

"Is your dress ripped?"

"No, it's not that." I lowered my voice, hoping no one else would overhear. "I have a tattoo on my arm."

"A tattoo? From your cruise?"

"Yes. Not so loud, please."

He threw his head back and laughed. "Well, so what? Celebrities are covered head to toe." He pulled at my jacket to help me take it off.

"Don't say I didn't warn you." I pulled off my leather jacket. The unwanted disfigurement was on my right arm next to Steve.

"Whoa. That's something." Steve touched the ornate braided design. "From your grand voyage to ports unknown?"

Charlie leaned around, almost dipping his tie into the oyster juice on his plate.

"Yeah. An unwanted souvenir," I said, trying not to care.

Know-it-all Steve said, "Kat got drunk or crazy or both while cruising around."

"None of the above actually. Wasn't my idea." I exhaled to let off some steam and with it some anger.

I smiled as the waiter replaced the oysters with our main course, a lobster tail.

"Kat, let me see," Charlie said while the others around the table stared at us.

I swiveled around in my seat to let him examine the intricate three-inch band around my arm.

He touched it. On instinct, I jerked my arm back.

Charlie pulled his hand away. "Does it hurt?"

"No, I just don't like it. It's embarrassing."

"It's undeniably unique. But nowadays with lasers —"

"Nope. I tried. The dermatologist said it won't work."

"Who cares? It's only a tattoo."

"Right." I struggled to put my jacket back on.

Charlie patted my arm. "Don't bother. It's not a big deal. Really."

"Yeah, Kat." Steve must have overheard our discussion. "It's a form of artwork appreciated by someone in a jungle somewhere."

In the Dutch East Indies over a hundred years ago, I wanted to add.

Desi approached and offered me her sparkly gold shawl. "You can wear this if you want, Kat. But I wouldn't worry about it. Your tattoo is bold and daring." She bent down and whispered, "Mine is a small flower. I'll show you later."

I thanked her for the shawl, wrapping it around my shoulders to hide my tattoo. "This design signals protection, spiritualism, and fertility," I said to her.

"Fertility?" Steve and Charlie said in unison.

I grinned. I was past the age of childbearing.

Steve laughed, but Charlie appeared hurt.

The ship vibrated, and an engine rumbled.

"Are we moving? Leaving port?" I got up in a flash, stumbling and knocking over my chair, and scrambled to get to the gangway and back onshore.

Chapter 11 ~ *The Call of the Sea*

From the deck, the lights of Mystic winked goodbye and teased me as if saying, "I fooled you." Our yacht, *Atlantic Dreams*, was at least ten feet from the pier, so I couldn't jump.

"No, no, no," I said, unable to stop.

I clenched the railing, digging my nails into the polished wood. I closed my eyes, bowed my head, and whispered my all too familiar prayer to Salacia, the goddess of salt water. She provided calmness and tranquility across all global waterways. Her husband, King Neptune, was the wild, unpredictable one.

Charlie touched my shoulder. "What's wrong?"

"Wait." I finished my prayer to return to terra firma.

"Are you praying to God? I thought you were agnostic."

"This is different. Not a god, a goddess, and she helps sometimes."

His scrutiny unnerved me. I put my hand on his chest to push him away.

"I'm not ready for this. I can't go to sea again. You lied! You said we were staying in port."

"I thought so, but Jason wanted to take us out in the harbor for a few hours."

"Yeah, right." I swore under my breath to never believe another word he had to say.

I searched through my purse for my phone, but I'd left it charging inside our cabin. "Can I borrow your phone?"

Charlie handed it to me, but it was password protected.

Annoyed, I passed it back, demanding he turn it on.

"What do you want to see?" He asked.

"The date. Today's date."

He unlocked his phone and pressed it into my hands. "I have no secrets. Read whatever you want."

The calendar showed Nov 2017 in red, and a 12 was in a shaded-red box. I sighed in relief. Today was still November 12, 2017. He had an all-day event, "Kat in Mystic," with the port's address.

"Great. Thanks." I returned his phone and immediately grabbed the railing with both hands while I craned my neck, watching as Mystic disappeared from sight. My heart pounded as if it would explode and rip open my dress.

A crew member stopped by and asked if we needed any assistance.

I stared in disbelief. "Yes, we must go back. I can't do this."

Charlie and the crew member appeared confused.

"This is just a short excursion around Fishers Island and back to Mystic," the crew member said.

"I don't care if we are going to the moon. We must sail back. Now."

"I shall communicate your concerns to the captain."

"You? No, never mind. I'll go talk to him."

The crew member was probably used to clients who were wealthy eccentrics and trained to accommodate their weird peccadillos. "This way, please."

I followed the crew member up several flights of stairs, with Charlie trailing behind. Before letting us into the bridge and mission control, he asked us to wait.

"You're shaking." Charlie put his arm around me while we were alone and kissed my hair.

I let him hold me and tried to control my nerves. I had to gather my strength. Most captains were complex and demanding, and I couldn't let this one win.

~ ~ ~

During our introductions, Captain Willem spoke with an unusual accent.

"Are you from Scandinavia?" I asked.

"No, the Netherlands. What you call Holland."

"I'm aware of that. I've been there a couple of times."

He smiled with wrinkles crisscrossing around his eyes. Few Americans include the Netherlands in their European itinerary. Many got the Danes and the Dutch mixed up, but the languages had few words in common.

The pilothouse was filled with sophisticated equipment. Radar, GPS, radios, and other navigational devices were crammed into every empty crevice and on the counters.

While the captain spoke to Charlie and me, his first mate took over. Captain Willem looked as if he was fond of eating well. His formal white shirt and uniform were stretched to the max over his protruding belly.

Inside the cramped space, we were surrounded by computer screens, which reminded me of being on a Wall Street trading floor.

"I understand you wish to return to Mystic. Why?" Captain Willem stared at me for a moment and then monitored his navigational screens.

"I'm concerned. So far from port. This could be dangerous." He appraised me as if I was a complete fool.

"Few vessels are on the water, and the weather forecast is calm." I stood so close to him, I smelled sausages and onions on his breath. But luckily, no beer or alcohol. "In this area, the coast guard is less than fifteen minutes away."

"Yes, but the weather can change in a flash. What if the equipment stops working? How do you monitor our position then?"

Captain Willem scratched his head, sparsely covered with grey hair. "If we have a power emergency." He pointed to a few backup computers and mentioned the generators.

"I mean no power period. Can you use a sextant to calculate latitude? And the chronometer for longitude? Where are these instruments? In the dark, they could be hard to find. You need candles and gas lamps ready."

Captain Willem chuckled. "Here's something better." He reached into a drawer, pulled out a couple of flashlights, and gestured to some fire extinguishers in the corner.

"And this is one of our EPIRBs." He pointed at an orange-colored piece of equipment, frowned, and spoke directly to Charlie, ignoring me. "An emergency position-indicating radio beacon. If in distress, we would use it to alert SAR."

"SAR?" I asked.

"Search and rescue. But tonight, the waters are calm, and this yacht is extremely seaworthy. There's a ton of other backup safety procedures, but it would take too much time to explain now. Hell, there are more dangers on land." He waved toward the shore where I wanted to be.

"All okay now?" Charlie was completely satisfied, but I still wanted to return to Mystic.

"Excuse me a moment." The captain spoke to the first mate and monitored the computer screens. After a few minutes, he asked me, "Why the concern?"

"I, well, I —"

Charlie interrupted, putting his hand on my back. "Kat was on a sailing ship for seven months. From Denmark all the way to Hong Kong. She learned all about life at sea."

Captain Willem narrowed his eyes. "Which ship?"

Charlie's hand against my back pressed me to explain what he couldn't. "An old Danish clipper ship, the *Anne Kristine*. Unlikely you've heard of her." I rattled off the closest comparison, somehow etched permanently inside my brain. "A square-rigged three-master similar to the American clipper *Flying Cloud*."

The captain said, "Impressive. Seven months. Quite a voyage."

I nodded. Only someone in the know would understand. "I'm still readjusting to life on land."

He said, "The *Flying Cloud* was one of the best designs with a flat hull. Flew at a clip but still stable with ample capacity. I would love to see photos of the *Anne Kristine*."

Charlie knew the answer and didn't hesitate. "She doesn't have any. Electronic malfunctions onboard. Apparently, they weren't as prepared as this ship." He motioned to the yacht's supply of flashlights and auxiliary equipment.

The captain stared at me. I wanted to quiz him about other potential emergencies but couldn't think of how to phrase it without sounding unbalanced.

"My third great-grandfather was a captain in the Dutch navy. Never met him, of course, but you'd appreciate this." The captain pulled out a book and insisted I take it. "Not the same edition used by captains back then."

When I reached for it, Desi's shawl slid to the floor. I held his new, pristine book, *The American Practical Navigator,* recalling the similar but much older version on board the clipper ship. That copy was ragged after daily use to calculate the ship's location.

The captain swooped up my shawl and stared at the ornate design of my tattoo before handing it to me. "Proud to say the book is still in print. Written back in the 1700s by the American Nathaniel Bowditch."

"Impressive." Charlie inspected the book. But he wasn't a sailor, so the handbook would be meaningless to him. "Shall we be going, Kat? I'm sure Captain Willem has other important things to do."

I nodded. "Thank you for your time, sir."

He scrutinized my arm, where the tattoo was now safely hidden. "Anytime, Miss Jensen."

~ ~ ~

Back outside on the deck with Charlie, I stared across the dark water at the outline of Fishers Island. Desi joined us and tried to convince me to return to the salon. They were all waiting for us. She sent Steve to coax us inside, but I couldn't abandon my post, and Charlie wouldn't leave me.

"Come on, Kat. Aren't you cold? Let's go back inside." Charlie urged, bored with the view.

"You go. I'll be there in a few minutes."

He sighed and touched my hand, still firmly attached to the railing. "Find anything out there? A sea monster like the kraken?" He crowed in delight at the memory of one of my goodbye gifts. The rum bottle's label had a sketch of a mythical and notorious sea creature from the deep.

"Sure, go on and laugh."

"What are you so worried about?"

"I'm not worried. I'm busy monitoring things."

"Can't you monitor from inside the dining salon? Don't you hear the music? We could be dancing." He sang along to the upbeat music, "Time of My Life" from the movie *Dirty Dancing,* playing inside.

I regarded him for a second before returning to monitor what might still be a dire situation ahead of us in Long Island Sound. "No, sorry. I must stay here. We may go too far and be unable to return."

"Kat, come here." His arms opened to embrace me, but I shook my head.

Unstoppable, Charlie moved behind me and wrapped his arms around me, giving me a bear hug from behind. "You're cold. If you insist on staying out here, I'll grab your coat."

He rubbed his mouth against my ear. "Don't stare so hard. Krakens are all imaginary."

"Charlie, that's the problem. They aren't. I saw one fished up from the deep and it … never mind."

"Oh, Kat." He meant to reassure me, but I knew he didn't believe me.

"Forget it. This is why we can't have real conversations. You don't believe anything I say."

"I do. I promise. If you saw one, you did. You certainly had the opportunity. But you are safe here with me."

He kissed my neck and hair. "I read a fascinating book about a sailor while you were gone."

I listened with only half an ear since scanning the water and horizon for danger required intense concentration.

"I loved part of it and thought of you. Here's a quote: '*And the lone seaman, all the night, sails astonished among stars.*'"

"What book?" Overhead, the stars were lackluster and too dim to help with my surveillance.

"Robert Louis Stevenson's diary, *In the South Seas*. About his voyage from San Francisco to the South Pacific in the late 1800s. He also experienced dangerous moments on the water like you did."

"Yeah." I knew he wanted to know more but now wasn't the time or place.

The crew member who led us to the bridge reappeared. "The captain asked us to inform you that we are now returning to Mystic."

"Excellent news. Kat, let's go back inside."

The faint lights of Mystic, Connecticut's shoreline beckoned reassuringly. Nothing looked out of the ordinary, and I loosened my grip. Exhausted from my intense focus, I let go of the railing and took Charlie's hand.

~ ~ ~

We rejoined the gang, all still seated at the dinner table. Our dinner plates remained, but the others had moved on to a trio of desserts. I washed down a few bites of lobster, savoring the expensive wine.

Jason asked me, "Everything okay and above board?"

I hesitated. Did Jason want a complete status report?

Fortunately, Charlie came to my rescue. "Kat knows a lot about ships. She was inquiring with the captain about safety. Checking on lifeboats and life vests in case of an emergency. Things like that."

Jason laughed. "Charlie told me you're an internal auditor. Ours are always worrying about the lights going out, and where's the emergency exit? Don't they realize we just switch on the backup generators and keep on trading? An auditor for life, huh?"

I grimaced. "I suppose so." He should appreciate auditors and their attempts to keep him and his firm out of trouble.

Lacy must have more sense since she glared and acted irritated at Jason's flippant rudeness. I nodded a thank you to her. Even if I wasn't respected or well-paid, my audit work was usually rewarding.

"Captain Willem went through the regs with me when I hired him." Jason's tone was condescending. "Commercial vessels of this size face a maritime alphabet soup of laws more involved than our overly complicated banking mess. If you can't sleep, I'm sure he will loan you the book of SOLAS which stands for *Safety of Life at Sea*."

I acted like I understood. All those new procedures were not standard or in effect when I was on the clipper ship. I couldn't handle being at the mercy of turbulent waves again.

Heather and Wyatt excelled at faking a romance and were dancing up a storm. The feel-good tune, "Dancing in the Moonlight," began. Charlie asked me to dance, and I readily agreed to escape from the table and feeling foolish.

Chapter 12 ~ *When a No Sounds Like a Yes*

I gazed at Charlie, sleeping beside me. After worrying about me, he'd overindulged and celebrated with what he said were our "just desserts." On top of the sugar rush, he'd overdone it by tasting an assortment of rare bottles of cognac and unique whiskeys. Jason had insisted they all had to be taste-tested at least once. I begged off, but agreeable Charlie complied.

When it neared midnight and the bewitching hour, Desi and Lacy made their apologies and went to bed. But not Heather, and I hesitated, unsure if I should abandon her. She bounced from acting like a ditz to being mysterious and astute.

Heather and I joined the guys on the deck. We admired the stars high overhead and the lights from Mystic. When a crew member removed the hot tub cover, steam rose in the chilly air.

"Care to join us, Kat?" Jason swayed and sat down to pull off his shoes. Charlie looked uncomfortable.

The modern-day cauldron on the deck was inviting. With my tattoo no longer a secret, I was tempted. "I didn't bring a bathing suit."

"Wear your underwear like Heather," Wyatt said.

Heather had stripped down into her black lingerie, an impromptu sexy bikini, looking at ease and camera ready. Perhaps she was glad to be out of her tight dress. At that exact moment, I knew I was in the way. After saying goodnight, I retreated alone back to our cabin.

When Charlie reappeared hours later, I woke up briefly. I was amazed he'd found his way back after all that booze. He'd had trouble undressing, but I played dead, not wanting to be bothered, and he slid into bed.

When Charlie turned over, he pulled the covers to wrap up inside them. Chilled, I got up and put on the complimentary bathrobe. I sat in the chair, wondering what happened after I left.

Our first night together, since I had left on the cruise almost a year ago, was a major disappointment. But at least he'd seen my tattoo and didn't freak out. The timing worked in my favor, so I was a fool to fret. Some people had so many tattoos they had lost count.

Six a.m. was early for a weekend, but I ached to escape from the yacht. This was a convenient opportunity to start jogging and get back in shape. I slipped into a long-sleeved T-shirt and stretch pants. Just in case, I jammed a ten-dollar bill inside my tennis shoes.

I hurried down the gangplank to solid ground. On the dock, I studied Jason's yacht and how it bobbed slightly in the water. To prove I could do this, I ran up and down, boarding and disembarking several times.

My navisphobia was truly gone. Time would only tell if this applied to all types of ships. But this was significant progress. Each time I stepped back on board, I gained strength and more control.

At a small coffee shop, I bought a cup of coffee to go. As I sipped, I wandered up and down the docks daring the assortment of ships to threaten me somehow. *Atlantic Dreams*, our yacht, was still quiet, with only some crew wandering about.

Aimless, I wandered into a small park with a jogging path. To ease into this exercise routine, I planned to start with a fast-paced walk. Next time, I would transition into a more challenging jog back home in nearby Central Park.

"Good morning." A man's voice boomed through the quiet. Captain Willem was out of uniform and wore a casual outfit.

"Morning. How are you?" I wanted to avoid any mention of last night and my unfounded fears.

"I'm fine. Can I walk with you?" the captain asked.

I nodded even though I preferred to be alone.

"I dreamed about my ancestor last night. The one who experienced firsthand the glorious clipper ship era. He wrote his family some vivid letters and diary entries. During that time, the maritime trade controlled the world. I wish I had experienced it myself."

I stopped to dispel that romantic idea. "Not that special.

Period movies and TV shows make it appealing and romantic. Those days were filled with poverty, disease, and dirt. Nasty smells were everywhere. Some people lived like animals."

"Is today that much better? Twenty-five percent of the population lives without electricity. Cancer still isn't curable, not to mention all the new and stronger diseases out there. Millions of kids die every year since their parents can't afford treatment or from poverty."

"Aren't you full of morning cheer, Captain."

"You know what I mean. Going back two hundred years doesn't sound so bad. Our environment is doomed. Don't get me started. We can't see the stars with all the light pollution."

"I'm aware that our future doesn't look rosy. But back then, it would have been much worse. At least today, there is some hope. Possibly, people will figure things out."

He stopped and flung out his arms out in frustration, "In one hundred years, the air and water will be completely poisoned. The whole human race might be wiped out. Sorry to be so pessimistic, Miss Jensen."

I cringed at his formality. Being a widow, I was technically Mrs. Jensen, and my maiden name was Carlson. "You can call me Kat." I looked at the water, realizing how so many people took the environment for granted. "I try not to think about it. But I try to be kind to my fellow humans and animals to leave a smaller footprint." I stopped and lifted my foot to emphasize my point.

He scowled. "More must be done and fast. By corporations and government."

We continued our brisk power walk. The captain's breathing was more labored than mine. A woman jogger stopped near us, leaned down, and picked up a plastic bottle left on the trail. She stuck it inside a plastic bag she was carrying and resumed her run as if nothing had happened.

"That was odd," I said, stopping to let him catch his breath.

"Garbage cleaners. The Swedes started it. Tourists throw trash everywhere. Who can keep up?"

"Well, at least some of us are trying."

He made a grunt, acknowledging that some people cared.

"So, Captain Willem, where are you sailing next? To another port?"

"Jason Osborne is paying me to show off his new toy. We are sailing to Newport, Rhode Island, and docking there."

"Then what?" I was curious about the modern-day life of a sea captain.

"I drive home to the wife. Look for local Thanksgiving charters. *Atlantic Dreams*, at least, puts a turkey on the table. I freelance. A captain for hire, and jobs are scarce in the winter."

"My job is like that too. I'm an independent contractor and an auditor in New York City. Nothing to do with water, except for my daily shower and a swim at the gym sometimes."

He chuckled. "Kat, I want to hear more about your voyage on a real ship. These mega motorized yachts are merely expensive toys for rich folks."

I nodded. Buying one would cost a fortune, and every time you wanted to motor out, you needed a specialized crew.

The captain continued with his rant. "My Dutch sea captain ancestor would view *Atlantic Dreams* as a complete joke. Yacht is an old Dutch word that refers to a fast pirate ship. The Dutch navy used them back before the clippers to capture those pesky pirates."

"Pirates?" I repeated and crossed my arms, feeling a chill.

He said, "Duty calls. I must return to my post. Come by the bridge in an hour. I have a business proposition for you."

After escaping from the captain, I wanted to run. But this was more of a slow jog. I wondered what his business idea was about. Helping out as part of the crew was out of the question. My head cleared, and I focused on the path and my breathing.

Running, or any form of aerobic exercise, supposedly grows new cells inside the brain. Those brand-new cells improve your memory, generate new ideas, and deal with new situations. If I could double those cells and create a surplus, this short jog was worth it.

Five minutes later, my side ached, signaling how out of shape I was. I wanted to achieve that state of flow, the runner's high when you lose time and place. To reach that goal, I had to continue running for at least twenty minutes, but it was time to meet Charlie. At least I'd had some time away from the yacht to decompress.

~ ~ ~

"You're up early." Steve sat down next to me inside the empty dining salon, interrupting my thoughts about the captain.

Steve put his overloaded plate of food and coffee on the table next to me. "Where's Charlie?" I asked.

"He's out in search of a supercharger. Another challenge with a Tesla. Did you wear him out last night?"

"Me? I'm sure he'll be fighting a hangover all day. Were you guys trying to kill him?"

Steve frowned. "No breakfast, Kat?"

I had my usual cup of steaming coffee with milk and ignored the elaborate breakfast buffet. "I prefer brunch."

"Another one of those who won't accept breakfast is the most important meal."

"Thank you, Steve. Now I've been told one million and one times."

"We aim to please. I can tell you need someone with a firm hand."

"Apparently, you aren't up on the latest. Dr. Oz says it's better to fast at least twelve hours. That means skipping a meal, and he suggests breakfast."

"Does he now?"

"Yeah, studies show it prevents Alzheimer's and other diseases, helps your gut, and might add some quality years to your life."

He pursed his lips as if ready to argue.

"Google it if you don't believe me."

He pulled out his phone. "I just might before I devour the rest of this." His plate was filled to the rim with eggs, sausage, bacon, and pastries.

"Is Desi on her way?" I asked him.

"You just missed her. Emergency with the nanny, so she

left early. She will text you."

A sleepy Heather arrived and stood behind us. She tapped Steve on the shoulder. Not so much of a pat but more of a caress. Steve dropped his phone on the table and smiled. Perhaps Desi was wrong. Heather was having an affair with Steve, not Jason. I clenched my teeth and tried to ignore them.

Heather stood between us and then bent down from the waist, so her derrière stuck out. She whispered something secretive in his ear.

Steve said, "Yep. Got it. In a half-hour or so." I expected him to pat her on the ass and tell her to scamper off when she left for the buffet.

When Wyatt and Jason arrived, the three men talked about some rich but clueless clients. They wanted desperately to unload some slow-moving junk stocks from their portfolio.

"You guys in sales are such schemers, I said. "You'd dress up wastewater with some pink food color and convince an innocent customer to drink it."

"You would?" Heather asked, glancing in my direction. Even at this early hour and after a late night, she was to-die-for gorgeous without having to try. Her long hair glistened, and her skin was practically luminescent.

"Why sure. Seems like sweet pink lemonade to me." Jason sneered as if I were a fool.

They switched topics to reminisce about a recent boys-only jaunt to Vegas. Something about snorting cocaine off a hooker's tits.

I wanted to scream. How demeaning and deadly. I watched Heather for a sane reaction, but she leaned in for more.

I left the room but ran into Charlie, who convinced me to rejoin the group.

"Ladies, I could use your help." Jason's voice boomed. His request came out more like a command.

"With what, Jason?" Heather asked in her sickening sugar-sweet voice. If it had anything to do with cocaine, I was out the door and off the yacht.

"Renaming my yacht. I need a female perspective for my

female vessel." Jason flipped through pages in a book. Heather wore a low-cut sweater and leaned over to look.

I wanted to escape from this nonsense. Wyatt seemed untroubled, while Steve and Jason ogled Heather. I looked at Charlie, but he didn't make eye contact with me.

"Why don't you ask your fiancé?" I suggested to Jason.

Lacy should be here to observe this. Walking down the aisle with Jason might be a huge mistake.

Jason ignored me. "She left with Desi. Endless wedding prep. So, unless we count the two female crew members, you and Heather are the only two women on board."

"I have no opinion. This is stupid. Heather, what do —"

Charlie, the peacemaker, interrupted me. "Why bother? *Atlantic Dreams* is apropos and as good a name as any."

"Nah. My yacht, my name." Jason watched Heather as if he owned her too.

I stared at him and his blatant rudeness. How long does he plan to continue with a fiancée and a girlfriend?

Jason sneered and stared at me. "At least I'm not going for a name like the one a notorious Saudi Prince selected."

"What was that one?" I couldn't help but ask.

"*Tits.* Serviced by two tenders, *Nipple I* and *Nipple II*."

"That's awful." Heather didn't use her usual coy accent. She covered her mouth with her hand as if dumbstruck.

"The rumor is he recently renamed it *Hashtag Me Too*," Charlie said.

"Are you serious?" Wyatt said.

Charlie laughed. "No, and Jason, you are never serious either. Full of WASP-y bullshit." He play-punched Jason's arm.

"How about *Hedge Your Dreams* or *Hedge Fun?* Excellent names, since cash bonuses from my hedge fund paid for it," Jason said with an evil twinkle in his eye.

"Can you do that? Rename it?" Charlie asked.

"Absolutely. I can do whatever I want. Even scuttle it." Jason glowed with pride at his new possession and looked at us as if we were under his control too.

"What?" I asked, shocked at the waste.

"Just kidding. I'm no fool. Worth too much even with the insurance," Jason said. "To rename it, I just break a bottle of champagne across the prow. Heather, will you do me the honor?"

"Sure, babe. When?"

"Next time when we are all back on board." Jason assumed another yacht adventure with Heather, and the rest of us was a sure thing. Except there would be no next time for me.

I marched to the buffet for a final coffee refill. I had ten minutes before it was time to meet Captain Willem. While I was curious, an ominous message from my gut insisted this was a bad idea. I nibbled on a banana to settle my stomach.

If only Desi were still here, or Lacy. There is safety in numbers, especially for women, and I didn't want to drag Charlie into this.

"Kat, that's the coolest tattoo ever. Can I see it up close?" Heather asked.

"Nope. Sorry."

"Oh, please. I'll show you mine." Of course, a beautiful woman with skin that angels would envy would ruin it with a tattoo.

Before I could respond that this was completely unnecessary, she slid into the chair next to me. Using the tablecloth as a cover, she pulled down her second-skin pants and a narrow strip of her panties to show me.

"Can you see it?"

I saw a glimpse of pink and wings and took a sip of coffee. "Cute butterfly."

"It's Tinker Bell. Take another look."

I lifted the tablecloth to appease her. "Didn't she wear green like Peter Pan?"

"Could be, but I love pink."

The edges were disintegrating. "Looks like you're losing part of Tinker's wing."

"Shoot. That hot tub last night." She stared at it in dismay.

I turned green with envy matching Tinker Bell's green, not pink, colored dress. Hot water and vigorous scrubbing did nothing against mine. "Well, if you find some magic pixie dust, sprinkle it in my direction."

"Sure. Now can I please see your tatt?"

"All right. Will you do me a favor afterward?"

Heather nodded and looked excited, continuing her usual I'm-game-for-anything attitude. Lucky for her, my plan was less painful than getting permanently inked and wouldn't take much time. I was doing Desi and Lacy a favor by dragging her away from their men.

Inside the narrow corridor, I rolled up my sleeve to show her. She oohed and aahed politely.

Quickly, I led the way to the bridge and Captain Willem.

Heather followed right along, speaking to me from behind. She was either desperate for female friends or excessively chatty. "I overheard you're a CPA. An internal auditor."

"Yeah. I am." I turned around, wondering if someone had connected me to Jackson or Melville Consulting. "How'd you hear about that?" Not even Charlie knew the name of my boss or company.

"One of those jerks called you a certified public asshole. Stands for CPA."

"Heard that a few hundred times. But thanks, you've made my day, Heather." That old line from the Broadway show, *The Producers,* and the movie version was so overused. "Let me guess. Did Jason say this?"

She snickered. "Nah, Steve. He's just envious he's not a CPA. The unlicensed jerk."

I was astonished at how aggressive she came across. "From what I've heard, Steve has done pretty well for himself. Rare for a lowly CPA to hit that sky-high pay scale."

She shrugged. "How did you meet them? Did you work with them?"

"Nope. I went on a bad blind date with Charlie about a year ago. Met Desi and Steve through her dad. He's a well-known architect. Why?"

"Stop for a sec." Her voice was agitated and nervous.

I paused. We would be late, and like kings, maritime

captains expected obedience on their vessels at all times.

She batted her long eyelashes. "With all this talk about money, do you think they are doing something illegal?"

"Illegal? Hell, if I know. There are tons of complicated rules on Wall Street which tastes like vinegar to businessmen. And you have greed and the aggressive quest for money. Think of that as the oil to keep the money machine running. And we all know oil and vinegar don't mix very well."

Heather frowned and chewed her lip as if she'd swallowed some of my bitter salad dressing based on the often-seen recipe for failure.

"Why are you so concerned? I thought you worked in advertising."

Heather said, "I do. I'm an admin assistant. But my uncle got in trouble once. It devastated his family and ours."

Her personal financial problem confession was believable. "Sorry about that. If they ask you to do any trades or favors, anything that doesn't sit well inside your gut, say hell no." I almost told her to stop dating these rich bastards, especially if they are engaged or married. But I needed her help.

"Thanks. I'll keep that in mind." Her smile was lopsided and more of a grimace.

Despite all the negatives about Heather, I felt a pang of sorrow. I hoped for her sake, it was a false signal, and my concern was unnecessary.

Chapter 13 ~ A Paranormal Proposal

Captain Willem greeted us with his eyebrows raised in surprise at seeing pretty Heather with me. I introduced him, and he was agape at her natural beauty like the rest of us. If she dressed less sexy, the women on board might warm up to her.

He shook hands with her and looked at me like I was an idiot. "Fifteen minutes late. Your Captain Mikkel Madsen wouldn't approve."

My jaw dropped in surprise. How did this small-town yacht captain find out the name of the captain on my clipper ship?

Captain Willem asked his first mate to show Heather some of their instruments and assured them we would return shortly. I wanted her to refuse and come with me, but she missed my signals.

Reluctantly, I followed Captain Willem down the hall. Perhaps he would show me a ship register, like the one Jason had, that mentioned the *Anne Kristine* clipper ship. It might say what happened to the passengers, crew, and officers after I left.

He opened a door and motioned for me to go inside. "Not as luxurious as your cabin. Nowadays, passengers are given the very best. Not like it was back in the good old days when being a captain commanded real respect."

His cabin was well-lit and orderly. He sat at his desk, pulling up an extra chair. "You should sit."

I slumped down in the seat, and he handed me a packet of frayed and worn brown envelopes.

I untied the red ribbon and opened one envelope. The straggly faded writing was difficult to read. To illuminate it, I moved the desk lamp closer. "This isn't in English. I can't read it."

"Oh, that's right. Allow me to read you some excerpts." He explained that these letters were sent home to the Netherlands from his third great-grandfather. He'd been a high-level captain for the Dutch Royal navy stationed in the Dutch East Indies, now known as Indonesia.

He took the letters and read one, stumbling along as he translated from Dutch to English. The first letter was filled with dull comments about the ship and the weather. Bored, I pulled out my phone to fight the monotony and also send him a message.

Captain Willem frowned. "Okay. I'm jumping into the awesome stuff."

"Please do. I promised Charlie to be back in fifteen minutes. We must leave soon."

"You only allotted such little time to listen to my fantastical tale?"

I frowned. "I thought this was a business deal."

"Just wait." Captain Willem smirked and flipped through more letters. "Ah, here it is. He mentions an American woman he'd met in the Dutch East Indies in the spring of 1863. The crew fished her out of the water and hoisted her on board. Practically naked and out of breath, she had begged for their help. Pirates were pillaging the clipper ship anchored across the harbor in a cove from whence she had swum."

I swallowed hard and struggled to remain calm.

"What do you make of that?" He kneeled down with his face just inches from mine.

"A fantastical tale, as you said. I should be going." I pressed against the table to stand.

"Wait. There's more." He put his hand on my shoulder, pressing me back down.

"Thanks, but I've heard enough."

"You must hear it. I do apologize, and it's not pleasant. I will summarize the highlights."

My gut screamed to leave, but I sat as if in a trance.

The captain droned on with his translation. "This American woman was on board your clipper ship, the *Anne Kristine*, captained by Mikkel Madsen. Her name was coincidentally Katrine, similar to yours. After his crew of soldiers subdued and killed the pirates on her ship, they escorted her back."

I swallowed hard, remembering that terrifying night. "Glad it turned out well." I made another move to escape.

"Wait! Here is where the plot thickens. While in port, she was kidnapped by natives. Retaliation for the death of a thieving pirate onboard the *Anne Kristine*. An extensive search of the island was undertaken by the Dutch navy and militia. Later, she showed up at the harbor alone and on horseback. The tribe's territory was discovered about that same time, but the Dutch wanted vengeance. Natives were interrogated and tortured. A speedy trial took place, and the leaders were —"

"Enough." My voice shook despite my efforts to stay calm. "What does this have to do with me? I must go."

"Here is why you should care." He shoved in my face a letter with a drawing identical to my tattoo.

"What does that mean? Those types of tattoos are popular in Indonesia."

"This is an exact replica of your tattoo. After witnessing it, he sketched it. Sufficient proof to me that you are that American woman. He further explained in his letters that her actions were odd and eccentric. He even speculated that she, or should I say you, were from another time."

"What? That's ridiculous! That woman, whoever she was, lived over a hundred years ago. She has nothing to do with me. My voyage, the cruise, was a reenactment. All make-believe."

I stood, losing my balance as if in a turbulent storm even though the yacht was anchored and barely moving. To escape, I would crawl if necessary. I reached for the door handle, but the captain slammed his hand against the door, forcing it to shut.

"Kat, I don't mean to scare you. And I don't wish for you to relive it."

"What is it you want from me?" My words came out as a cry for help.

"Men like Jason Osborne and all the self-indulgent others like him will pay exorbitant sums of money for experiences like that."

"To be kidnapped by locals in Indonesia?" Now it was my turn to laugh. I turned to study him. "If they are that gutsy, they can fly there and wander around in a jungle. Book a scuba diving vacation on Sipadan Island in Malaysia, wave lots of money around, and they might get kidnapped in a flash."

"Not like that." He used such force that I had to wipe some of his spit from my cheek.

"Did you hear that over six hundred people agreed to pay north of 200k to go to the moon on Branson's Virgin Galactic? And it's not operational yet. What the two of us could offer would be just as unique."

"That's insane! I'm not interested."

"National Geographic Expeditions sells tours to take you to another time. What do we care if the ultra-rich want to play around and be stranded on a god-forsaken island like Tom Hanks in *Cast Away*?"

"Yeah, right, and hang out with a ball named Wilson?"

"Hell, yes. People want to test themselves with this insane survival shit! It's everywhere. We've got to move fast and cash in now."

He let go of the door, and with about a foot clearance, I slid out.

"You're clearly nuts," I muttered.

Behind me, he said, "Kat Jensen or whoever you are. I will not be ignored and lose out. I'll be in touch."

Heather was gone, and I ran downstairs to escape from his voice and the memories. This situation was so strange and terrifying. Finally, someone believed me but for all the wrong reasons.

I turned the corner so fast, I bumped into one of the crew. I mumbled an apology but didn't stop.

Heather rested against the railing facing the water and was talking on the phone. I walked toward her to apologize, but why should I? She didn't stay with me and disappeared with another guy.

What if she had overheard the captain and wanted in on his get-rich-quick scheme? She didn't act like the super-rich, and money can change everything. Particularly if it sounded low-risk and problem-free.

Heather's voice was strange without her usual seductive kitten tone. As I neared, I couldn't resist listening in.

Heather said, "Yeah, it's all working out. I'll be back in Manhattan and can brief you in a few hours." This sophisticated voice wasn't the Heather I knew.

She hung up and turned, appearing distressed. "Kat, you're back. I couldn't find you and had a call. Sorry." Her Heather-sounding voice was back to normal.

I nodded, not wanting to explain, but now it was her turn. Another mystery, except whatever her game was, I didn't care. I hurried inside the dining room to drag Charlie as far away from here as possible.

"What the hell happened?" I asked.

A strange woman wearing a white blouse and skirt was connecting an IV to Wyatt's arm. Jason sat next to Wyatt and was already hooked up. A bag of greenish-yellow fluid hung from a metal rod. A blue plastic sheet covered his injection site.

Heather banged into the back of me when I stopped so suddenly. She staggered back and apologized.

Charlie tapped me on the shoulder. "We're up next. If you want to, Kat."

"Up for what?"

"An anti-hangover shot filled with an herb and vitamin mix," Charlie said.

"Two at a time. You and Charlie. Then Heather and Steve," Jason said, still running the show. "I had Nurse Steph come here to get us going again this morning. I feel better already."

"An IV? Nope. Not for me." I shook my head.

Charlie looked disappointed. "Drip bars are all the rage now."

The nurse handed me a brochure and recited the company line. "These vitamin infusions are really popular and by appointment only. We only offer onsite concierge services for our best clients."

The brochure advertised infusion drips to combat colds,

migraines, jetlag, and hangovers on top of dehydration and ordinary fatigue. But this marketing push didn't change my mind one iota. No one was poking me with a needle. "Whatever happened to drinking OJ and taking vitamins?"

Heather might be game to try this, but her face was expressionless.

"Kat, you are so old school and behind the times," Jason said.

Now was the time to use my pre-planned excuse. "I really need to head home. Job search and all that."

"Job search?" Steve asked. "We might need someone in audit at Levittman."

"Thanks, but I have some promising leads." I lied, but Levittman was the last place I'd work.

Steve rolled his eyes as if I were a complete loser.

Jason said, "Kat, I'll pay you to not join my company. Another audit is the last thing we need."

I shrugged. The idea was mutual, but it didn't make changing jobs any easier. So many positions were found through personal contacts and the grapevine.

Wyatt said, "Heather, are you in for an IV? There's time, right?" He sounded desperate, as if his life would be ruined without it.

Heather didn't smile but answered in her girly I'm-game-for-anything voice. "Sure thing, babe."

I stared at them. Their strange relationship made no sense.

"You won't regret it. YOLO!" Jason said.

All the others but me echoed, "YOLO."

"What does YOLO mean?" I whispered into Charlie's ear.

"You only live once." Everyone around overheard him and stared at me.

Steve said, "Poor Kat, she's got an excuse. She went AWOL for a year and lived life to the fullest. Dangerously. Who else, without any nautical skills, would head out on an old clipper ship for seven months?"

I didn't make eye contact but listened to their comments which included, "Not me. Hell no. What the fuck."

Only Heather was in awe, commenting with a series of

wows.

Steve's words reminded me of the threats from Captain Willem, and I pressed Charlie to not linger further.

We made our polite farewells to everyone. Steve followed us to our cabin while chatting with his best bud Charlie.

Charlie asked him, "Are you joining them on their sail north?"

"Yeah, accompanying Jason on this tub to Newport. Getting a lift in his helicopter back to Greenwich later tonight. I'm not a fan of puttering around with motors. I prefer the canvas like your girl."

Canvas meant sails, and I was unsure if Charlie knew this nautical term. "I guess she did or used to." Charlie put his arm around me, squeezing too tightly.

I slid under his arm into the cabin to change clothes in the bathroom. With the door ajar, I eavesdropped on their conversation.

Steve said, "Did Kat tell you I warned her not to go? Way back before she booked her voyage and bobbed around lost in the seven seas. Could have avoided that sailor initiation rite with a tattoo. Cool in a macho sort of way if you are into that."

"Missed out on that story. Kat has so many secrets. She shares stuff slowly." Charlie frowned and never liked to be in the dark. "Something to ask about on the long drive home."

"You're not the only one with a marked woman." Steve's tone was mocking. "Desi got herself a small rose on her hip. At least it's discreet."

Charlie laughed, and the door slammed, signaling Steve had left. We gathered our belongings and strolled to the gangway. The crew insisted on carrying our bags off the yacht. I strutted down the gangplank, proud that my phobia was conquered.

Heather stood by the railing watching us, and I felt a tinge of regret. "Charlie, should we offer Heather a lift to the city?"

"Nah, she's sailing north with Wyatt and the rest. A party girl, that one."

After all, Heather was an adult, and the crew was available if something went wrong. We had not become best buddies and didn't bother exchanging contact information. She acted so desperate for an adventure with friends who could throw oodles of cash in her direction.

When I took one last glimpse, Steve stood next to her. We waved goodbye once more. I hoped Heather wasn't messing around with Steve. A sharp pain in my stomach reflected how Desi would feel if she was wrong about Heather's real boyfriend.

Chapter 14 ~ Uncoupling in Connecticut

"Shall I drive, Charlie?" His face was pale, and his usual healthy appetite was absent this morning. Conceivably, if you were that hungover, shooting up a vitamin IV might be beneficial.

"Kind of you. I thought you didn't like to drive that much."

"I don't. But I did a lot of driving over the summer. Made a solo trip to California from Texas and then north to Oregon to visit some friends."

"If you had told me, I could have joined you."

"Well, it was all last minute. My parents had a vacation planned. Texas was heating up in July, and my brother's car was sitting there."

"Still. Why didn't you ask me?"

"I thought about it. You were busy working in London and then at your family's ranch."

"We could have juggled that around and met in Wyoming."

"Oh, yeah, a minor detour." I wanted to lighten his mood. "My brother's old car needed work. The convertible top fell to shreds, and then the transmission had to be replaced. Adding extra weeks for repairs."

"Another excellent reason to buy a new car like this one."

I nodded but would never do that. A car in Manhattan was one more hassle, not to mention the unnecessary expense.

"Who'd you visit out there?"

"A college roommate from Texas lives in L.A. and former work friends in Marin County, across from San Francisco. Since I was so far north, I went to see a longtime friend in Oregon. We were exchange students in Denmark for a year."

"That's a long drive. Were you lonely?"

"Sometimes. From Texas to California, I-10 felt like it would never end. The Pacific Coast Highway route north was spectacular."

"After so much time on that ship, I figured you would

want to be around people."

"The ship was full of people. I was only alone inside my cabin and whenever off the ship, escorted or guarded. When I wasn't … well, it could be dangerous. So, I needed some time on my own."

"If you hated your cruise so much, why didn't you just leave?"

"I tried to, but I had to see it through to the end." I turned the music up to drown him out, consoled by Katy Perry's encouraging song "Roar," a battle cry for women everywhere.

Charlie turned the volume down to talk. "You aren't the type to put up with something you hate for seven hours, much less seven months."

"We've talked about this enough. Whatever. Now the lioness is back."

Charlie cleared his throat. "I didn't realize until last night that Desi Smith's dad is the world-famous architect and your friend Greg Overton. Are you still in touch with him?"

"We traded emails, and I met him once. He has a new girlfriend. All for the best."

"Well, that's a relief. I thought I had more competition."

I glared at him and back at the road.

"Just one brief stop before Manhattan. I'll direct you." He sang along while I hummed to the music.

I replayed in my mind what Captain Willem had said about Indonesia. His desire to recreate time travel trips was scary. No one would enjoy something like that. Even if people thought they would, once they arrived back in time, they would regret it.

How would the captain set it up? The travel agency that booked it went out of business. Before I resurfaced in Hong Kong, the staff decommissioned Max, their computer, with too much AI for its own good. They assured me this would never happen again. Captain Willem's get-rich-quick scheme would never work. He should stick to ferrying around rich investment guys with overpriced yachts.

Charlie interrupted my brainstorming on how to resolve the problems with Captain Willem. "Exit up ahead. It's not much farther."

I didn't bother asking why we were stopping, but it had better be short. I followed a series of rights and lefts, zigzagging through the wooded suburbs. "Next time we go to Connecticut, we should come earlier in October when the trees are busting out with fall colors. Did you know I love pumpkins?"

Charlie grinned. "I figured that out."

"Besides the coffees, I love pumpkin smoothies. Ever tried pumpkin ravioli?"

"Nope. But I love pumpkin pie. Mom makes them for Thanksgiving."

"I'm not fond of pumpkin pie the regular way. But throw it into the blender with ice cream, and it's delish." I smacked my lips for emphasis.

"Silly girl. Turn right here."

A sign announced something, but I didn't have time to read it. I drove up a long driveway through a park setting filled with evergreens.

"Is this it?" A white colonial building with green shutters at the end of the driveway resembled a historic and chic bed-and-breakfast inn.

"Yeah. Park over there in the visitor spot."

A sign said, "Welcome to Green Pines." Smaller words underneath mentioned, "Rest, relaxation and therapy."

"Are we visiting a friend of yours?" I didn't remember hearing about anyone sick. His family lived in Wyoming.

Charlie didn't respond right away. "We need to go inside to see someone."

"Fine. Go see your friend. I'll wait here."

"No, Kat. You're coming with me. You need help. I keep trying, but you shut down. These people are the best."

"What people?"

"They're therapists. We go inside and chat with them for couple therapy. Then we'll go home."

Fiddling with the electric lock, I locked and unlocked the door, listening to the clicks. "Nope. Let's go."

"One short hour, Kat. If we don't go inside soon, we'll

miss our appointment. It's a miracle they squeezed us in."

I shook my head with such force that my hair fell out of the plastic clip. "We aren't a real couple."

"Yes, we are, and I want us to be one. Please. Do this for me. I need some help here."

There was no upside here. "I just need more time. Without useless talk."

"I love you, Kat."

"You do?"

"What do you think? How many guys would wait for their girlfriend to come back from a vacation that goes on for seven long months instead of two? And when you finally reappeared, you immediately left for Texas, and that stretched out to California and Oregon."

He touched my arm gently, but I instinctively pulled away. "Come on, Kat. I've been here waiting for you for close to a year."

"Oh, all right. But I must get back to work on my job search. After one hour, we leave. Okay?"

"Deal."

I started my phone's timer and confirmed it was counting down. Inside the Green Pines, shades of brown had taken over. The interior was furnished like some sort of lodge, and people wandered around as if on vacation.

Charlie signed us in at the counter while I sat on an overstuffed sofa in the waiting room. Signs said cheesy things like, "Reach your highest potential," and "Don't give up on your dreams."

I skimmed through some sections of yesterday's Sunday New York Times and found the book review, my favorite part. Charlie opened up the sports section.

I said, "I can't believe we are doing couple therapy. We aren't even engaged."

"He's one of the best."

"Best what?"

"Therapist. A well-known pro."

"Well, I'm not paying for this."

"This is on me." Charlie patted my leg to reassure me.

Ten minutes later, we were introduced to Dr. Price, a chubby dark-haired man. He had fifty minutes left.

~ ~ ~

After five minutes of the doctor's steady prodding, we had brought him up to speed with a mini-life story about both of us. I wished I could give him a copy of my resume to speed this up. He seemed primarily interested in me, but I kept turning the story toward Charlie.

"Did Charlie tell you his name isn't really Charles Richmond?"

The doctor narrowed his eyes.

"Yep. True story. Tell him, Charlie."

Charlie glared at me.

"Hey, this was your idea," I said.

I tried to read the description of an oversized purple handbook ominously labeled *DSM-5* on Dr. Price's desk. This took extra concentration since the text was upside down.

With my prodding, Charlie explained how his rich uncle suggested he change his name. Travis Rich wouldn't sound sophisticated enough for a job on Wall Street. So he became Charles Richmond.

DSM-5 stood for the fifth edition of the *Diagnostic and Statistical Manual of Mental Disorders* published by the American Psychiatric Association. Mystery solved, but utterly useless unless I hurled it at someone.

The doctor tapped his pen on his notepad and got my attention. "Now, Kathryn, tell me about your seven-month voyage."

"What do you want to know?" I gazed at my phone, wanting to send a clear message that I was bored. Forty long minutes still remained.

"Did you enjoy it?"

"Not particularly."

"Why did you choose to take such a long vacation?"

"Well, it was only supposed to be a few months. Unavoidable changes to the itinerary. The ship's captain had specific reasons, so ask him."

"How is your relationship with Charlie? Level of

intimacy?"

I squirmed and focused on my jeans. I never spoke about my sex life with anyone.

Dr. Price repeated his question, but I waited for him to move on to another less invasive question.

Apparently, Charlie had no such inhibition. "Well, Doc, that's one of our problems. We've been on a half dozen dates, but she pushes me away with a slew of excuses. Usually, to watch the same old movies over and over."

"What about yesterday on the ship? Your friend Jason interrupted us. I waited for you last night. You were out drinking yourself into oblivion."

"All right. Agreed. My fault. But after our dates, Kat doesn't invite me in. And it's not like we didn't … you know, weren't more active before she left."

"I didn't want to because …" They both stared at me, waiting. "I was ashamed."

"Of what?" Dr. Price asked.

"My disfigurement." I lifted my sleeve high enough to show Dr. Price my marked arm. A doctor should understand.

Charlie pushed his hair back. "So what? Millions are covered with them nowadays. You had a wild night, got drunk, and did what thousands of sailors before you did. Next day regrets."

"I didn't get drunk. I was kidnapped … forced against my will. Every time I see it, I am reminded. It isn't as painful as it once was. I am improving."

"Jesus, Kat. I'm so sorry. Were you, uh, —?" Charlie looked like he didn't want an answer.

"Raped? No." My words were forced and full of pain.

"I was going to ask if you were assaulted or hurt," Charlie said.

"Let's just say being held hostage wasn't my idea of a fun time."

Dr. Price interrupted our bickering. "No one should ever say or imply that situation was pleasurable. Nevertheless, it's helpful for those afflicted to talk it over. I'm assuming you reported this to the proper authorities where it occurred."

"Yeah, it was reported. The men in charge had a quick trial and everything."

Charlie said, "Kat, I'm so sorry."

"Now you have heard about my sordid past. Still sure you want to introduce me to your mama for Thanksgiving? I'm damaged goods." I sniffled and pulled a tissue from a well-stuffed box on the doctor's desk.

"I don't care about the past. Only our future together." Charlie spoke slowly as if weighing each word.

"You say that now, but."

"But what?" Charlie's voice was sympathetic, but his pity would be unbearable.

Our relationship, like me, was permanently damaged. "I don't believe you."

Dr. Price resumed control since things had gone from bad to worse. Divorce proceedings loomed ahead, even without an engagement. Less than half an hour remained. I could make it.

"Let's shift the conversation back to your extended trip, Kathryn. You must have acquired some friends while being gone so long. A voyage on an old ship would be difficult."

"Yes, it was, and I did. I think about the crew and passengers sometimes, but I try not to." After my discussion with Captain Willem about Timor Island, vivid memories had resurfaced.

"Are you still in touch with any of them?" Dr. Price pressed on, sticking his nose everywhere.

"No. Not anymore."

Dr. Price's eyes widened. "No emails or posts on social media? Or old-fashioned letters?" He gestured to some unopened envelopes.

A strange-looking paperweight sat on the corner of his desk near me. I fought back the urge to pick it up. "Nope."

"Why not? If you miss them, it would be normal to stay in contact."

"Well, I don't try because …" I leaned forward to examine the paperweight. The wooden mount said, "Keep it under wraps." A small brown object was covered with a thick piece of plastic wrap and sealed in polyurethane.

"Are you afraid Charlie would be upset?"

"No." I shook my head for emphasis.

"Kathryn, help us understand. Why did you cut off all contact?" The doctor's voice softened, but his questions hurt as if drawing blood.

"Because …"

The doctor lowered his reading glasses, and Charlie scrutinized me.

I leaned forward to pick up the unusual paperweight. After a sharp inhale, I said, "Because they are all dead. Are we done with that question?"

"Dead?" Charlie repeated in disbelief. "Not just the captain, but everyone?"

I nodded but wished I could swallow back my words. I had gone too far.

Dr. Price put his hands in the prayer position and held them to his lips. After a short break, he continued his slow, methodical inquisition while Charlie peppered me with rapid-fire questions. An actual police interrogation might be smoother.

Their nonstop questions picked away at me. "How did they die? Did the ship sink? When? Why? Where exactly?"

I turned over the paperweight in my hands, tempted to throw it at the wall in anger. But that would make the situation veer into an unfixable problem. The brown object resembled a walnut, and Dr. Price, the shrink, sees nutty patients all day. Disgusted, I put the paperweight back on his desk with a thud.

With the interrogation heating up, I debated proclaiming my innocence by pleading the fifth. People in trouble do this all on time on TV crime shows. Or they demand a lawyer. This was a voluntary doctor's appointment, and I had privileges and rights. But what were they exactly? On top of all that, I didn't kill anyone or cause anyone's death. So, what did I have to fear?

"I'm not sure exactly how they died. When I got back home, I knew. Figured it out."

Finally, the fifty minutes were up. My phone alarm played

the beginning notes from the song "Imagine." They glared at the sound coming from my lap, but I didn't apologize for the interruption.

I switched off the alarm, stood, and picked up my shoulder bag. "Thank you. Our time is up. Dr. Price must have another nut, I mean patient, waiting."

Charlie and the doctor sat still.

"Ready, Charlie? We agreed on one hour."

Dr. Price cleared his throat. "Kathryn, under these unusual circumstances. I must urge you to stay here longer. We can discuss this more and delve into the truth."

"That was the truth. There isn't any more to delve into. I never heard exactly what happened to them."

"The mind can deceive you. Particular when trauma is involved."

"Regrettably, I still remember everything. Every single day, and I wish I couldn't. I don't want to know what happened to the people on that ship."

Charlie and Dr. Price stared at each other as if they were trying to transmit a secret message that I couldn't decode.

"Like I said. I got off the ship in Hong Kong, flew home, and can't contact them. They might still be alive, but I doubt it."

Charlie stood and put his hand on my shoulder. "Kat, the doctor is right. Sit down a minute. Let's talk this through. You could stay the night here, and I'll pick you up tomorrow. You can talk to Dr. Price some more and be back home healthy and strong."

"I am healthy and strong. You're the one hungover, not me."

"Your overnight bag is in the car, so it's easy to stay tonight."

"What? I can't stay here. My new job is important. We just arrested a drug trafficker who heads up a major drug cartel. Tomorrow morning the long weekend ends, and I'm due back at the office." As soon as the words were out, I regretted them.

The doctor jotted something down. "You did what?"

KAREN STENSGAARD

"I can't tell you any more about that. Sensitive info. I'm under an NDA – a nondisclosure agreement."

The doctor flipped a page in his notebook, furiously writing notes. I wished he wouldn't, but objecting might dig me into a deeper hole and make things worse.

"Kat, you said you were quitting. You can call in your resignation from here," Charlie said.

"I changed my mind. Yesterday I realized that it's a pretty decent job. Friday sucked, but that was a weird day. I promised Jackson a month and —"

"What? Are you working for Jackson Chow, who does special investigations?"

I hesitated, fearing how angry Jackson would be when he learned his name was discussed openly. "You know Jackson?"

"I hired him."

"Why?" Jackson took on diverse under-the-radar projects. Why would Charlie or his company hire someone like Jackson?

"To find you. Your assistant Mel recommended him to Abby. Jackson took my twenty grand and came up empty. Never found you or your ship. His excuse was that some people just don't want to be found."

Charlie stood ready for action. The mention of Jackson made him tense and combative. "Dr. Price, while you prepare the forms, I will grab her overnight bag."

"Charlie, don't you dare."

"Yes, Kat. It's for the best. You'll end up thanking me."

This time he'd gone too far. There was no way I could stay here overnight, and I needed a private place to figure out what to do.

"Fine. Is there a restroom I can use first?"

Chapter 15 ~ An Uber-Scape

Alone, for the moment, I sat inside the bathroom stall farthest from the door and considered my options. The ladies room appeared escape-proof, with bars on the window and an alarm sticker. My overnight bag was in Charlie's car, but luckily, I had my shoulder bag and never took off my jacket.

I left the restroom, determined to find a discreet way out of the clinic. Some employees lingered in the hallway. To give my wanderings more of a purpose, I took out my phone and held it to my ear, pretending I was getting instructions on where to go. I spoke to an imaginary doctor on the phone as if we were best friends. And we were. An imagined Siri voice came to my rescue.

I opened a door marked "Exit" and trotted down the stairs with my hand bouncing against the railing. In the basement with a flimsy excuse ready, I held my breath and opened an unmarked door. The hallway was lit but unrenovated, and the ceilings were supported with old wooden beams.

Footsteps neared, and I slipped into a small closet to hide. After the footsteps faded, I opened another door, revealing a large storage room filled with wooden racks of paper goods and cleaning products.

Despair hit when I didn't see a way out. A hint of light came from behind a wooden rack filled with boxes. Behind the storage rack, I climbed a small stairway toward what I hoped was an exit. From the top rung, I surveyed the parking area and a loading zone at the back of the building.

The pleasing scent of fresh air and freedom made me want to scream out in joy. After confirming that no one was watching, I scampered out, dodging the boxes and packages. A clump of evergreen trees wasn't too far away, and I ran toward it.

When I reached the cover of the trees, I scanned the clinic for possible pursuers. By exiting out the back, I was on my way without anyone noticing. I clicked on my phone, praying that my service would work here in the woods.

One power bar for phone service must do the trick. After opening my Uber app, I requested a pick-up and listed a train station as my destination.

Within a minute, an Uber driver in the area was on their way. I hated to leave my hideaway, but I had to meet the Uber. I ran through the woods toward what I hoped was the road. But I had veered off course according to the phone's map, so I ran the other way.

Without any trees for camouflage near the road, I stayed low in a ditch. I was nearly out of breath but muttered a brief "Hells bells," to release some tension.

A small black Mini Cooper drove up, possibly my ride. A well-paid doctor wouldn't cruise around in a low-cost car.

At the side of the road, with little to lose, I waved the vehicle down. The car stopped, and I stared at the unusual automobile. Two long white stripes followed the length of the black Mini.

Slowly, the passenger side window went down. Encouraged, I stepped closer, ready to get out of here. The driver, a young woman with long dark hair, peered at me. "You requested an Uber?"

"Yep, I did." I opened the door and jumped into the back seat.

She said, "Just to confirm —"

My labored breathing made it difficult to talk, but I interrupted her. "Can we just leave?"

"Sure thing."

The car sped down the road, and my breath slowed in response. Calmer, I explained, "I put in for the Stamford station. But any nearby with trains for Manhattan will do."

She snickered. "They all go there. So you didn't like Green Pines?"

"Nah. Not for me. Couple therapy was a complete time waster. I opted out of that and our couple-dom. He can keep it."

"I probably would too. I'm Zhila Mehregan, and this is my skunk-mobile." She patted the steering wheel and peeked back at me, smiling.

The car did resemble a little skunk. "Glad to meet you, Shelia."

"Not Sheila, but almost. Z-H-I-L-A. Pronounced Zhee-la. Persian for joy."

"Cool. A name with meaning. I could use some joy right about now." I snickered. Then I stopped remembering where I was and scanned behind us, still rattled.

"I'm Kat Jensen, short for Kathryn. Cute little car. Smells like food inside here."

"Sorry. I just ate a burger." She lowered the car's windows a few inches. "I try to keep it clean. Does your boyfriend happen to drive a red-hot sports car?"

I slunk down in my seat. "Yep, a Tesla."

"Hate to tell you, but he's behind us."

"Shoot. Whatever you do, don't stop." I scrolled through the texts on my phone. "He's texting me."

"Don't answer, please! That happened last month with another passenger. The guy went cuckoo and ran the poor skunk off the road. We ran over a huge rock, and underneath there was so much damage."

"Never want to speak to him again."

"I will slow down so Mr. Fancy Pants in his fancy car can pass by." She handed me a scarf. "Put this on. It's a hijab to cover your blonde hair. He won't recognize you."

Slumped down, I pushed my hair under the fabric, sat up, and glanced around.

She eyed me from the rearview mirror and laughed.

"This isn't disrespectful to the Muslim community, is it?"

"Oh no, all's fair in love and war in my book. By the way, you put it on sideways."

I readjusted it carefully to keep my hair hidden. "Is he still behind us? I'm afraid to look."

"Yep, but he is getting ready to pass us. Just look to the right, and it'll be fine."

With a whoosh and way over the speed limit, he passed us. I asked, "How much farther is the train station?"

"A few more miles to Stamford. The big one."

"I know that place too well. Too many hours waiting

there for long commutes to attend meetings at a miserable Swiss bank. Charlie might be waiting for me there."

"Yuck! Well, if he is, I'll take you to another station."

"Terrific. But don't you need to wear this hijab?" Her head was bare, and I hated to mess things up, especially something religious.

"Not around you. That's why I like driving for Uber. A taste of freedom. Sometimes I become bored out of my skull at home."

"Are you a Muslim?"

"Yeah. My parents are from Persia, but I was born here. I do my prayers every day but only wear my hijab around family. My husband is cool about it, but he's afraid of his parents. They don't like the skunk, but I couldn't sit idle and wait around. He's a doctor. Not the kind you saw at the clinic. He works in the E.R. at a hospital in the Bronx. In training to be a heart surgeon."

"Wow. How challenging for both of you." I was uncomfortable telling my life story to inquisitive taxi drivers or passengers on a plane. It wasn't worth the effort. However, her chitchat relieved my stress.

Zhila turned into the train station's lot. Charlie's car was double-parked, blocking a handicapped spot.

"Is he handicapped?" She asked.

"Only in the brain."

We howled in unison, instantly reducing my stress level further.

"That's a flashy car. He must be rich."

"One would think so, but he spends it all. Perpetually broke. A $250,000 car he'd like to buy but has no need for."

She whistled at the cost. "Oh, brother. Sorry."

"His problem." I lacked the energy to talk about him. "I have another idea." I made a brief call to Desi, and she was thrilled with the change of plans. "New destination. Old Greenwich."

Zhila guided the skunk to the next exit.

"I'm not in a hurry to go home anyway. I'd planned to do another job search but decided to stick it out another week."

"Job hunting, that's the worst." Zhila's voice was full of sympathy. "I'm so lucky my husband can pay the bills while I write poetry. And do the Uber thing when I am restless after hours trapped behind my laptop."

She drove on, and we chatted about my job. I lamented about how hard it could be for women and internal auditors in the wild world of finance.

Zhila said, "I thought everyone in finance and Wall Street had it made."

"If you're young, an Ivy League grad, and have built high-powered connections. But I don't fit those qualifications. Some companies don't want anyone over 50, and I'm getting close. Everyone seems to want young moderns to attract more millennials in their 20s and 30s."

"But why?"

"They are usually better with computers, considered more flexible to new ideas, and not stuck in their ways like an old dog. Since they are newer to the workforce, they're often cheaper."

"Some of the older crowd haven't learned how to send texts," Zhila said.

"Yeah, but how hard is that? It takes five minutes to learn how. Even my mom sends texts. Training employees would reduce so many major cutbacks and having to hire new staff."

"You're so right. Spend a little time. Uber was simple to learn. Can't you sue, though? Here in America, it's so common."

"Sure. Age discrimination lawsuits are always an option. It's a slow, costly process. You need documented proof, not just a series of problems. Most companies employ high-priced attorneys and can wait it out. Anyone over 60 runs out of cash or time."

"That sucks, to be stuck in the muck and out of luck."

I giggled at her weird rhyming verse. Pure poetry like that is hard to beat.

We cruised up to a stop at the security gates to register with the guard outside Desi's subdivision. While we were stopped, I switched to the front passenger seat but kept wearing her hijab.

"Can I buy this from you? If you don't need it." I could use another disguise and offered her a twenty-dollar bill.

"That old thing? Consider it yours and keep your money." She pressed the twenty back in my hands.

"One of these days, I'd like to see what's left of ancient Persia. Now I have something to wear."

After having so much fun chatting with Zhila, I didn't want the ride to end. I considered hiring her to drive me to Manhattan to keep our conversation going. But the added cost and the idea of running into Charlie outside my apartment stopped me.

While we waited for Desi to authorize our entry, Zhila shared advice on traveling to Muslim countries. "Whatever you do, don't go to the Middle East during Ramadan. It's the worst. Honestly. All day you can't eat, drink, or have sex. People are angry until they can pig out at sundown. Totally sucks!"

I put my hands up in surrender. "Promise. Marrakesh is on my list but I won't go then." I was curious about how they monitored the sex part.

"You are making me hungry. Moroccan food sure is delish! Tagines filled with couscous and olives in the medina. Yum." She smacked her lips.

Desi gave the guard permission to let us inside, and the gates swung open to her magical kingdom.

Zhila's little skunk-mobile crept past blocks of sumptuous McMansions.

"You have some serious friends with money." Zhila was impressed, but to me, it was a gilded cage.

"Most of my so-called rich friends spend it all and are in debt up to their eyeballs. Her dad is super-rich."

"Well, it's been fun having you onboard, Kat."

"You're awesome. Fan-uber-tastic!"

She chuckled and handed me her business card." For your next adventure in the wilds of Connecticut."

I wanted to laugh, but this was still too close to comfort.

She asked, "You won't tell anyone, will you?"

"What?" Was this a mistake or another trick?

Zhila said, "My stories about sneaking pizza and burgers during Ramadan."

"Oh, that. Me? The person who escaped from the Green Pines Clinic?"

She slammed the steering wheel with her hand in jest. "Yeah. Who'd believe you anyway?"

"Exactly! Nothing to fear from me."

Desi exited her Mediterranean-style McMansion holding hands with a kid in a Halloween costume and the leash for a yellow Labrador retriever. I stepped out of the skunk-mobile glad to see Desi's welcoming face, and waved goodbye to Zhila.

"Kat, is that you?" Desi asked.

"Yeah, it's me." I laughed and took off the hijab stuffing it in my bag for later.

The little boy said, "Mommy, who is that strange lady?"

I lifted my hands up, forming claws like a cat, ready to grab him.

The dog barked in excitement while the kid took decisive action. The pipsqueak punched my leg with tremendous power for a little kid.

I moaned and massaged my injured knee. I shouldn't try to scare anyone wearing a superhero costume.

Desi calmed the runaway Lab and knelt next to him. "You mustn't hit people like that, Noah. Sorry, Kat. Are you hurt? Please forgive my little hellion."

"I'm fine. You're a strong guy, Noah. Or should I call you Batman?"

He nodded apologetically. "Must protect Gotham."

"Please do." He was a brave, altruistic guy we all needed around.

Desi smiled, grabbed the dog's leash, and escorted me inside her gray-marbled inner sanctum.

Chapter 16 ~ How the Other Few Live

During the house tour of Desi's dreamy Italian McMansion, her young daughter Justina trailed along, pointing objects of interest placed at her eye level.

My appetite returned, and I ate a tuna fish sandwich that their part-time cook left inside the fridge. I had counted at least four dining tables, but we sat on two bar stools at the kitchen counter.

When the kids took their afternoon nap, Desi had more time to chat. Goldie, her yellow lab, was rescued with only five minutes left at an animal shelter. The good-natured pooch lay near my feet, probably hoping for a nibble of my tuna fish. With permission from Desi, I granted this simple wish.

Desi cackled when I told her about my abrupt escape from the clinic. She agreed she would have done the same thing. "That's what we call an Irish exit. When you leave without saying cheerio, but it could have been badass and French. You leave and don't pay the bill."

"Pardon, Madame," using my best fake French accent. "My departure was French. Except, I'm sure they charged Charlie beaucoup bucks on our behalf. But his health care insurance must cover it."

Desi threw her head back and burst into gales of laughter. I couldn't help but join her. Besides, this was a free health benefit. Laughing was supposed to be great for almost everything.

"At least Charlie didn't take you to Séréné. If you need insurance, you can't afford it."

"What's Séréné?"

"A Swiss luxury treatment center to detox and destress in Connecticut. A mere $120,000 a month. Most of the ladies around here suffer from crippling ennui."

"Ennui? That sounds serious." Lyme disease, named after the nearby town of Old Lyme, started near here.

· "Nope. The ennui syndrome is plain old boredom. They need two young kids and a mega charity benefit to run. Not to mention a wayward, workaholic husband. Or a job like yours. Then there's no time to be bored."

I nodded. "I heard somewhere, 'An intelligent person is never bored.'"

"Absolutely." Desi put my empty plate in the sink and explained how the maid didn't like how she loaded the dishwasher.

She led such an opulent lifestyle with a chef, nanny, maid, gardener, and who knew who else. Money can't buy happiness, but it sure helped.

I bit my lip, remembering my money issues. At least I still had a job, but I'd never have this kind of wealth. My mind was made up. I'd give Jackson and Melville Consulting one more week.

"I should be going soon."

"Already? Please stay tonight, Kat. Even without your overnight bag. I have tons of stuff you can borrow. On second thought, keep it. I need to pare down. And it's a pleasure to hang out with you. What time do you need to be at work?"

"About 9 a.m. It's flexible."

"Wonderful. Steve takes the train, much faster than a car, so you can commute in with him."

"I hate to be any trouble."

"What trouble? We've got plenty of space, and our maid comes tomorrow morning. It's more trouble if you leave. This house has a NextGen."

"A what?"

"One of those separate mini-apartments popular with the younger crowd. You have your own small kitchen, separate entrance, etc. The kids will fight over it when they are teenagers."

"They're so lucky to have a mom like you."

She smiled at the compliment. "Sorry about the mess in the formal dining room. I had to use it for extra office space temporarily. I'm the co-chair for our annual charity benefit."

"Wow. Sounds complicated."

"I've been on committees for years, but this is intense. Easier to focus on the mega-donors who commit millions in one swoop."

She snapped her fingers as if commanding a million dollars was this easy and handed me a ritzy black-and-gold envelope.

I fumbled with the glossy paper. The invite stated, "Help your best friends." The inside of the card said, "Since they can't do it alone."

"Our annual benefit gala. At the Waldorf this year. For Goldie and all the others like her that aren't as lucky."

Goldie heard her name, and her tail banged against a table leg.

"So generous of you to plan such a big event. I want to rescue a cat or two once I get settled in with my new job."

"Purr-fect! So many cats and dogs need homes. People adopt springtime babies for the summer, and when school starts in September, they get abandoned. As though the poor dears could survive in the parks around here and in the city. They might as well dump them in the wilderness."

"How cruel."

"Yeah. The murderers rarely get caught. And, if they do, it's just a hand slap. Some of the animals are so far gone, the vets can't save them." Her eyes got misty. "What are you doing on Thursday?"

"Nothing but work."

"The gala doesn't start until seven. And it's at the Waldorf in Midtown, close to your apartment. I have some complimentary tickets, so, it won't cost you a thing. I'd love to see you there."

Prices to attend the gala ranged from a thousand dollars for a single ticket to fifty thousand for a table with extra freebies and special recognition.

"Is Charlie going?" The invite mentioned fine dining, music, and dancing. Seeing Charlie on the dance floor would be unbearable. Besides, this was way beyond my price range.

"Doubt it." She scanned the list of attendees. "Nope."

"I'd love to go, but I'm on a tight budget —"

"Forget about the cost. You can be my guest, and maybe help me out some."

"Okay. I'll try to be there."

"Perfect. Kat, I overheard something last night. But it can wait. You've been through a lot today."

"Tell me, please. It's better to know than be in the dark."

"All right. Last night I got a call from the nanny. Noah was upset and wouldn't sleep until he said good night to his father, so I went searching for Steve."

She went to the fridge and took out a bottle. "Wine? I know it's early."

"Sure."

She poured the Chardonnay into two crystal glasses. "I overheard some of the guys talking on the yacht. Jason complained about how someone wasn't right for their crowd. Not wealthy with a trust fund or a pedigree. The gang argued that she doesn't fit our wife's desired profile."

"I know I don't —"

Desi interrupted me. "Please, they are completely wrong. Charlie told Jason not to be a rube. When they didn't stop, Charlie said, 'Shut the fuck up.' He was pretty damn clear, and they apologized."

I inspected my short nails with a thin layer of clear polish. My do-it-yourself manicure didn't fit the profile either. But at least Charlie defended me.

Desi put her hand on my arm in a sympathetic gesture. "Kat, are you okay?"

An overwhelming sense of inadequacy overcame me inside her upscale multimillion-dollar home. "Thank you, Desi. I should really go now."

"Please stay. Ignore those idiots. You are so much more real than any of my other friends. Besides, they were high. I saw a glassine on the table."

"What's that?"

"One of those envelopes. The ones used for coke."

"Illegal drugs? Charlie, too?" Charlie looked awful this morning, and it probably wasn't just from the booze.

"I didn't see who was doing it, but there were a few white lines on a mirror, ready to go. Steve argues they need it to destress and can handle it on a rare occasion. He swore he won't do any speed-balling."

Still in shock, I said, "Speed-balling?"

"A cocaine and heroin mix. It's so risky. I wish Steve would stick to alcohol."

"Well, it's all over with Charlie. He isn't the guy I thought he was or could be." I almost told her about my brother Keith and his addiction issues. Except I wasn't prepared for another interrogation and didn't want to talk about his suicide.

"His loss. Plenty of nice guys don't want a rich bitch. I will introduce you to some sweethearts at the benefit on Thursday night."

I smiled weakly to conceal my discomfort. "Deal."

Desi was so upbeat and fun to be around. If she could find me a guy with her personality, sign me up.

She checked her watch. "Let's wake up the kids, or they will never sleep tonight. Do you like acting silly and dancing? My work on the benefit can wait."

~ ~ ~

After the kid's early dinner, we watched the movie *Mamma Mia* together before their bedtime. Our energetic dancing to Abba songs was exhausting.

"Please, Kat, tell us a story." Desi's adorable daughter Justina held my hand.

Her brother Noah chimed in. He sat on the second bed in his sister's pale pink bedroom.

"Is there a book I can read?" I hoped for a short story or a chapter.

"Read? We make them up, don't we kiddos?" Desi grinned. "How about one from your experiences at sea?"

So I complied and told them about a brave princess who escaped from an insane asylum. She went on to help rescue dogs like Goldie all over the world.

Justina fell asleep in a hurry. Little girls like her might grow up to make our world a more just and happier place.

Noah's bedroom was decorated like an underwater cave with blue walls and fish painted on the walls. Unsurprisingly, Noah requested a seagoing story.

Desi smiled. "Go for it. You're on a roll."

"Once upon a time, there was a girl named Kathryn, and she went on a long voyage."

"What kind of ship?" Noah had inherited Steve's tendency to get straight to the bottom of things.

"A big one with sails."

"Daddy likes those. See my collection?" He pointed to a shelf over his desk.

I walked over to see if one resembled the old clipper *Anne Kristine*. Some sailing ships were trapped, or perhaps protected was the better word, inside bottles. I selected the most similar model and handed it to him. "It looked like this."

Noah stared at it and then showed his mother while informing us, "She is a three-master." He referred to her three towering masts and sounded like an experienced seadog.

"So, now what?" His eyes widened.

Desi and I sat on his bed next to him.

"Well, this ship had only sails, no engines, and it approached some jagged and shallow reefs. When the wind died down, the captain grew concerned. A small island wasn't too far from the ship. He was angry at the second mate and the crew for not paying closer attention to the charts and the wind."

I paused, wondering if I should continue.

"Then what?" Noah, like his dad, wasn't about to waste time.

"He announced to everyone on board, 'The passengers should wait on the island. We will retrieve you later.'" I imitated the captain's stern Danish guttural accent.

I regretted not making up some stupid outer space Martian story, but it was too late to change now. To avoid another pushy demand from Noah, I continued.

"The crew launched the lifeboats into the water and threw a rope ladder over the side. Usually, the ship was docked in port, and they lowered the gangway. This was hard for the women in their long dresses."

"Kat, we need to say good night and sweet dreams soon." Desi appeared nervous.

I nodded, not wanting to give Noah a nightmare and glad

to end it. "Suddenly, the wind picked up, the sails were raised, and the danger ended. The ship sailed off toward the sunset looking for dolphins and whales."

That wasn't the actual ending on the island with the natives. But everyone deserves an upbeat Disneyesque happy ending once in a while. I chatted about how beautiful it was on board the ship.

After Noah permitted a quick goodnight kiss, Desi and I strolled back to the kitchen.

"Kat, those bedtime stories wasn't all made up, were they?"

"Not exactly." The truth about how it really was would be impossible for someone privileged like Desi to grasp.

"Your cruise vacation sounds incredibly hard."

"Sometimes it seems like a TV series I watched for months. At night when I can't sleep, it's especially vivid."

"How terrible for you, Kat. Well, think about the bright side. It's over, and you are back. Safe and still in one big, beautiful piece."

"I met a woman in Southampton, England, the first port of call. By then, I knew it was not for me, but I hung in there. She said, 'It could be worse. Instead of a clipper ship, it could have been a Viking longship.'"

"A longship?"

"Narrow long rowboats with sails manned by Scandinavian Vikings."

"Oh, of course."

"They discovered Iceland, Greenland, and Canada in those ships. Living onboard a barebones vessel like that would be much harder. She reminds me of you Desi. Really optimistic."

"The only way to be. The Vikings must have been savages with all that violence. I can't even watch *Game of Thrones*, the most popular TV show of all time."

Desi grinned, but I looked away in despair. "I never could watch it either."

She hugged me. "They say time heals. But I'm convinced it's really mother nature. She will take care of you if you let her."

"Sometimes, I wish she'd speed things up."

"You and me both."

We laughed even though I could have cried. My stories were real and not so happy.

Desi's phone rang, and she screened the caller before answering. "I've got to take this. It's Jim Steckler, my co-chair." After the call, she apologized for spending time reading emails and forwarded some to him.

"Jim is the best guy. Single and handsome. He works at Levitmann with Steve and calls himself a boring bond trader. But he's quite the opposite. A ton of fun."

Matchmaking made me nervous, especially with someone who worked for a bloodthirsty investment banking firm.

Desi kept on. "If I were single, I wouldn't hesitate. At the gala, I'll introduce you. Jim's a huge animal lover. He rescued a cat and two ferrets."

"I think I need a few more months."

"You don't need to marry him. If he's not your type, forget it."

She flicked open her photos on her phone. "Here is Jim over the summer. He visited us and played with the kids." Jim stood next to her kids with a wide smile. His face was brown from the sun, and he had dark hair and friendly eyes.

"Devilishly handsome but a complete angel." Desi sorted through color-coded folders, and paperwork piled on her desk.

"He really has a ferret? I've always wanted to play with one." In New Jersey, they were legal, but not in New York City.

"He's got two. They will melt your heart."

She pulled out some seating chart diagrams. "Jim and I must sit with some of the lead donors, but you can sit here. This is the table for singles, and I have one empty seat left. I'll place you next to some nice people and introduce you at the gala."

She pointed to a spot at a round table for eight. "I am officially writing Kat on this seat. In ink, so now it's yours."

"All right, I'll go. But what's the dress code?"

"Black tie. Tuxedos and all that. I've got plenty of outfits that desperately need a new home. After I call Jim back, we'll do some shopping upstairs."

I drank my iced tea and stared at the bare trees and a white gazebo on the grounds.

Desi called out. "Kat, Jim wants to say hello."

"To me? Why?"

"He's a super nice guy." She handed me the phone. "Just say hi."

After a few minutes of friendly chatting, Jim and I realized we both loved jazz and had a thing for foreign movies. We talked for so long that Desi put a glass of water in front of me.

Jim and I made plans to meet face-to-face on Thursday at the gala. We would see how it went before deciding whether to go on an actual date. He tentatively suggested the Village Vanguard for jazz and blues. I couldn't resist already ignoring my temporary rule to avoid the West Village after El Rey.

"I don't do blind dates anymore. I could fill a book about them." Jim joked around, closing with a fond au revoir.

I was reluctant as well. I had learned the hard way when I met Charlie on my worst date ever. The night ended with too much drama, and I set off down the road of life, turning down lanes where I didn't belong.

After I hung up, I reran our conversation in my head. Not wanting to end up as empty as my glass of water, I would give Jim and dating another try.

Chapter 17 ~ Mermaid Tails

Upstairs in a spare room devoted to her wardrobe, Desi selected a handful of evening dresses and dumped them on the guest bed. "You are doing me a huge favor. I need to declutter and would rather donate them to a friend."

I hesitated, but a year ago, she'd given me the beautiful black Armani now left behind in Charlie's car. I might never see it again.

She held up a long dress, more of a costume with a flared mermaid tail. The vibrant blue gown had shimmery green scales and white pearls around the scoop neckline. "This one practically has your name on it."

I touched the soft fabric. "I do like blue."

"Blue? This isn't just blue. It's lapis."

Desi zipped me in and murmured words of admiration. While the long gown was beautiful, it was tight at my knees and flared out like a tail to the floor.

"But who can walk in something like this?" Swimming around a ballroom at the gala wasn't an option.

"Walking's elementary, my dear." She giggled. "It fits you perfectly, like a second skin."

I hemmed and hawed, delaying a decision.

Desi, used to wearing ball gowns, fiddled with some of the scales and the hem. "Take a car there and the elevator to the ballroom. You stand around, sit for dinner, and dance some."

I tried on a few more dresses, but the underwater-colored mermaid costume outshone them all. "Perhaps the pale-yellow dress is better. It covers more and is easier to walk in."

My no-nonsense decision-maker shook her head defiantly. "Cover? What do you need to cover? These aren't dresses. They are evening gowns."

I covered my tattoo with my hand, wishing it would disappear.

"Oh, that." She inspected my badass tattoo. "It's not so bad. Not as intense as the one in the movie *The Girl with the*

Dragon Tattoo."

"I'm definitely thankful for that. The original title of that Swedish book translates to *Men Who Hate Women.* My arm reminds me of that hate."

"Get it removed."

"I tried, but it's hard to do because of how it was done."

"Just ignore it. You are like one of those cool, hip celebrities."

I nodded but could never pull off that attitude.

"Here's mine." She pulled down her stretch pants to show me a delicate, ladylike rose on her right hip. "Steve went insane when he saw it."

"That's small and cute. Sailors believe some tattoos can protect you. Superstitions rule when you are so far from land." I sat on the bed, and she joined me.

"What does a rose mean?"

I laughed. "Land. Lots of anchors and the North star. Some had tattoos of pigs and hens. Since those animals don't swim, they thought it would convince a god to help them if they were in a shipwreck." And by help, the sailors hoped to drown quickly and avoid suffering.

"Pigs? Really? But they can swim, can't they?"

"Yeah. They must have missed the crazy YouTube videos of swimming pigs."

Desi rummaged around inside her closet. "Here's a fab coat to go with it." She pulled out a furry white coat streaked with pale brown marks.

"Fur? I can't wear that."

"Would I wear real fur? It's fake. I'm buying only cloth and synthetic shoes and purses now."

I rubbed my hand on the soft, plush material.

"Just try it on. Please."

I admired the coat in the mirror. "You win. It's really nice. And better than my wool or puffy polyester coats. But I must insist. I'm only borrowing this."

"Whatever. I wouldn't be surprised if some of the ladies wear their dead animal coats. So cruel at a charity event for animals."

"It's so sad how minks and other animals are caged and treated." I had seen awful videos from PETA showing how they were skinned alive. The images made me sick for weeks and still bothered me. "Desi, I really want to reimburse you."

"Make a donation later when you are back on solid ground."

"I'm not that broke."

"You've been gone for a year and just started a new job. Save a few friendly felines when you're settled. Donate your birthday. Cash gifts like that help."

"My birthday? Love that idea."

She tapped my knee. "How about a cocktail?"

~ ~ ~

In her oversized kitchen as large as a studio apartment in Manhattan, Desi danced around while she shook a cocktail shaker. "You're going to absolutely love my lemon drops."

A jazzy radio station, courtesy of Alexa, played in the background. Goldie shadowed Desi everywhere food opportunities lurked.

Desi poured my cocktail into a martini glass. "I'm so glad you dropped by. Rare for my friends to stay longer than ten minutes."

She placed her drink masterpiece in front of me. I licked some of the salt off around the rim and took a sip.

"Oh, that's sugar. I thought it was salt."

"Part of my special recipe. I went to a cocktail class in New Orleans. Based on an old drink called a Crusta, from the 1860s, when the Civil War was raging. Heard it's the first sugar-rim cocktail. Those Southern women needed something sweet to survive."

"Yeah, I'm sure they did." But the last thing I wanted to think about was the nineteenth century. I knew firsthand things were hard.

"Did you like 'The Mystique' cocktail last night? I'm an amateur mixologist and created it for Jason."

"You did? That was delicious."

"It's a fun hobby but hard to find the time when managing Steve, the kids, and the house. Can you imagine getting paid to drink every day?"

I shook my head. Cocktails at parties with friends were fun. But boozing it up was a dangerous daily habit.

"I guess you drank a lot on your cruise. I sure did when we were on our honeymoon. I hated for it to end."

"Only at night, but not a lot. No one was permitted to drink alcohol during the day. The captain kept it locked up. The only exception might be a glass of champagne when leaving port. It wasn't a typical cruise."

She stared at me, and the Crusta lemon drop loosened my tongue. "The voyage was tough. Harder than anything I've ever done or probably ever will do. I may never recover fully."

"Oh, you will. Everyone says things like that. Childbirth with Noah almost killed me, but I did it again two years later with Justina. Women are stronger than we think."

I remembered the long days surrounded by water when I almost lost hope.

"Why didn't you leave? Disembark? Papa said he would have paid for you to come home, no matter how remote. Helicopters can land almost everywhere."

"It was nice of your dad to offer. I wanted to, but I promised a girlfriend I'd stay until we reached Hong Kong. I couldn't abandon her. And when we sailed into Victoria Harbour, it was really hard to say the final farewell."

Tears rolled down my cheeks. I sniffled and dabbed them with a napkin. "Sorry. Lately, there's been too many reminders. I get emotional."

She patted my arm. "It must have been so difficult. I can't imagine going somewhere alone for so long."

I swallowed the last of my cocktail for courage. "I was too impulsive in my quest for something unique and a bucket list-worthy trip. I should never have gone." Confessing my stupidity to a friend with an open mind was beneficial and soothing.

"Well, I'm so glad you're back. Now you can spend time with your American friends."

Desi insisted on making me a variation of the Crusta lemon drop. Initially, I declined since I hoped to get a solid night's sleep tonight. But she convinced me to try a tiny sip to give her my honest opinion.

She chatted while gathering the ingredients. "Kat, give yourself more time. After a vacation, I need a few weeks to get back in sync. Initially, I am thrilled to be home, especially if we went without the kids. But after a few days, I miss it. The biggest decision on vacation is what to do or eat. I'm tempted to book the next flight out. But you adjust, and the memory fades."

"Yeah, that's part of it. I'm getting back into my old work routine."

"What I would love to do is to unplug like you did for seven months. All this calling, texting, and emailing is insane. On top of that, we have all these social media sites to monitor. Hours wasted every day. But how did we manage without them?"

"It sure is more complicated now. Smart-phones are way smarter than me."

"Smarter than all of us combined, which is what's scary." A jazz melody was on the radio. "That's Thelonious Monk's 'Between the Devil and the Deep Blue Sea.' One of my favorites."

I listened and nodded.

Desi summed it up. "Lighthearted despite his dilemma. Keep it in perspective and work through it."

"Yeah, that's all we can do." I didn't want to think about devils, the deep blue sea, or omens from songwriters. "And where's that cocktail? Hand it over, or I'll hide your phone inside this mansion somewhere. It'll take you months to find it."

She laughed with me and filled our cocktail glasses so quickly they spilled over. I grabbed her cellphone just in time, saving it from drowning in her sugary escapist concoction.

Chapter 18 ~ A Girl's Best Friend

"No way! I don't care who she is and if she has five zillion followers on social media. It's not happening!" Desi hung up and turned off her phone, exhaling loudly in frustration.

I started to ask what happened but didn't want Desi to relive it. Besides, it didn't concern me. Stress and worry are like viruses that can spread quickly.

"I can't believe it. Again. Another celebrity got caught. A Hollywood big shot left her poor dog suffering inside a hot car for hours. To come clean, she wants to piggyback off our gala."

"Aren't celebrities beneficial? All that added publicity?"

"Exactly what their PR firm's reputation-laundering specialist wants me to believe. But I've been there before. They don't show up or donate anything. They expect us to pay for their name. We did it last year. Ever heard of Sean Brilliant?"

I shook my head.

"Our brilliant no show last year. Sean's star flamed out. Fine by me. Some celebrities don't contribute any of their personal wealth to their own foundations. It's ridiculous."

"That must be illegal." I made a mental note to ask Shantelle about it.

"Different laws for them." Desi grimaced. "After that call, I deserve another cocktail, but this will be a virgin variety. Too much to do tomorrow."

While she made another round of drinks, I unclasped my necklace and put it on the counter.

Desi picked it up. "From Charlie?"

I nodded.

She examined it under a bright light. "Nice. But not worth much."

"It's a unique stone from Wyoming. A sentimental gift."

Desi put the drinks on a silver tray. "Follow me. I want to show you something."

We entered her spacious living room with wall-to-ceiling

windows facing their backyard's waterfront views.

She removed a modern painting with clashing colors from the wall and tapped on a metal keypad. "I call this our *jolie laide*. A painting so ugly, I feel sorry for it. But it hides my personal portfolio of treasures."

The artwork was garish and not my style. Bold streaks of blues and greens were ruined by a bright orange triangle. Modernism was marred by an unsightly traffic cone.

She peered deep inside the wall safe, pulled out a velvet box, and handed it to me. An incredible ruby red necklace with thick diamonds sparkled inside.

"An Oscar Heyman. My latest. This is what you should get from Charlie."

"Me?" I shook my head.

Desi pulled out other jewelry boxes and put them on the coffee table. Her expensive collection of bracelets, rings, earrings, and necklaces embodied a rainbow of colors. Creamy pearls and diamonds offset the array of bright sapphires, emeralds, and aquamarines.

"Extract something valuable out of Charlie. You can always sell it later on."

I shook my head. "He can't afford it. His divorce settlement took most of it."

"Are you kidding me? He's killing it! Every month it's flowing in. Huge. Believe me, I pick up on this. If Charlie says he's broke, he's a tight-ass. His private equity firm wallows in millions of dollars, conceivably billions. Steven is aching to join him."

I stared in surprise. Charlie had talked about buying a car, but I had figured it was wishful thinking and way out of his price range.

"He's not a lowly investment banker on the sell-side anymore. Now he's on the buy-side at that super successful investment fund. He picks and chooses whatever he wants. Wooed all the time."

I knew his job paid more. But it wasn't like rolling dice, passing go, and collecting money on the Monopoly board. Charlie was a managing director at a top-tier private equity fund, and every day his results must be scrutinized. Hopefully, profits were higher than the day before.

There had to be days when it was blood red from losses. He logged long hours. When I first saw him after my long trip, Charlie blamed some gray hair on his new job with intense scrutiny and stress.

"I can't ask him for jewelry. I don't ever want to see him again."

"Tell Charlie to call me, and I will hint around. Then meet him for coffee, collect the gift, give him a quick kiss, and end it."

"I'll think about it." But in my heart, I couldn't be so devious. "Was that ruby necklace a birthday gift from Steve?"

"Heck, no. Just a surprise. My husband's real love is being out on the water, then the kids, and finally me."

I frowned. Steve's fascination with seafaring was weird. He didn't even own a boat.

"Don't worry, I've accepted it." She stood as though prepared to fight or defend herself. "He was probably as guilty as sin about something."

"Oh, no. What did he do?" But I regretted asking her since I didn't want an answer.

She shrugged. "Not sure this time. I see a hypnotist and a therapist, so it's been banished from my brain. Men are always up to something devious and naughty. At least now, I can stop ruminating over it."

Something outside clanked. I hurried to the wall-to-wall windows and gazed at the back deck and yard. The sun had set, so it was hard to see anything.

Desi said, "The neighborhood kids sometimes cross through backyards."

She fiddled with her phone, and the wireless speakers played Marilyn Monroe's "Diamonds Are A Girl's Best Friend." She swayed to the music, urging me to join her. We danced around the room, and I loosened up without anyone staring at us.

Desi laughed. "My theme song, and don't forget it."

"Yeah, but poor Marilyn. Things didn't end so well for

her."

"Diamonds won't buy happiness. But they sure as hell can pay some bills."

I picked up my glass. "I'll drink to that."

Desi checked her phone. "Got a text from Steve. Out sailing with the guys. Back late."

She sunk on the sofa, threw her head back against the pillow, and tapped on her phone. "I texted him an ultimatum to be home by midnight."

I had zero interest in getting into the middle of their fight. "Desi, I appreciate everything, but I really should leave. Tomorrow's a busy workday."

"Please stay. Steve will crawl home while you're asleep. And this time, he can't buy his way out with jewelry."

I still wanted to leave, but Desi wouldn't give up. "I can drive you to the station, so you'll get to work on time. I'm going to nuke some leftover lasagna for dinner. Please stay and share it with me."

The next song, Gloria Gaynor's anthem for women everywhere, "I Will Survive," urged me to stay. Desi swung her hips and sauntered back to the kitchen, and I checked my phone. I didn't want to, but it had become a compulsive habit again. I wasn't an official member of social media sites, but I still spied on my friends.

I had a slew of voice and text messages from Charlie. His last few texts begged me to respond, so I gave in and texted him. "I'm fine. With a friend. Don't need your kind of help!"

My phone's ringtone made me jump after I took it out of silent mode. I hesitated to answer the unknown number since it was most likely a robocall or a telemarketer. Then I figured why not and took the call.

My boss Jackson didn't waste time saying hello but jumped to the heart of the matter. "Everything all right?"

"Yeah. Why?"

"What the hell is going on? Charles Richmond called. He said you disappeared into the wild woods of Connecticut of all places."

"I got an Uber and left Charlie behind. I'm at a friend's

house in Connecticut and just texted him. And I will be at work tomorrow morning."

"Fine but call him back ASAP. He wants to report you as missing to the cops. A huge minus for the business and for you personally. Even with our mutual friend behind bars."

"Sure, I will as soon as we hang up. But tomorrow, you have to give me all the details about your search for me."

He sighed. "Client job. Strictly confidential."

"Don't hide behind that. This has to do with me. Why didn't you tell me during my job interview?"

"If I get his okay, I will. But not over the phone. And don't go wandering around in the woods up there. A sasquatch was observed near the Long Island Sound not long ago."

"A what?"

"Bigfoot. A guy you don't want to run into."

I was about to add this to my long list of worries when he laughed.

"You're deranged. You are aware of that, right boss man?"

"Yeah, just stay away from the water. No more disappearances on the high seas. See you tomorrow, bright and early."

Before I could say bye, a click sounded, and the line was dead. Jackson was always in a rush.

When I turned around, Desi was waiting. "Steve just called. He said Charlie is shitting bricks about you. He wants to call the police. You need to talk to him."

"I know, and I plan to straighten him out immediately."

Charlie answered on the first ring. "Thank God, Kat. I just got your text. I was beyond scared. Are you okay? I should never have suggested the therapy." His words were slurred, and he sounded as if he were thousands of miles away.

"It was more than a suggestion. You were leaving me there." Remembering it fired me up. "We are not a couple. Never were. I don't ever want to see you again."

"I'm sorry." He sniffled.

His words were meaningless. "Don't call the police or Jackson. My new job, working for him, is supposed to be confidential. I can't believe you hired him to find me."

"You were gone so long without a word. Not even an email. So, I asked Abby for help. She called your former assistant, and she contacted Jackson. But he never found you."

"Charlie, you can't bother my manager again or mention him to anyone. I will lose my job if you do. And you must stop following me around like a lost dog."

"You're safe. That's what matters. Staying at Desi and Steve's house?"

"Yeah. If you come over here, I'm leaving."

"Fine, I won't. I'll give you plenty of space." His words blurred together into one.

"Thanks." But his voice worried me. "Where are you?"

"I'm back on the yacht."

"Again? Why?"

"When I couldn't find you anywhere, I called Steve. So, here I am."

"Are you drunk?"

"A little, but I can handle it. I'm so relieved you're not hurt or lost somewhere."

He mispronounced the word relieved, so he wasn't just a little drunk. Someone on the yacht yelled and interrupted us.

"Be careful." I wanted to tell him to get off the yacht, but he wasn't my boyfriend anymore.

"Kind of you to care."

"I've got to go."

"Wait, please," he said.

"Sorry. I can't."

"All right." His voice sounded tight and high-pitched.

"Don't drive. And stay away from the water and railings, okay?"

Before he could respond, I hung up and glared at the weird painting hiding Desi's jewelry. How had my fun and romantic weekend getaway turned so ugly?

Chapter 19 ~ A Furry Best Friend

"Goldie, where are you?" I yelled into the darkness.

Doing Desi a quick favor by taking her dog out was a huge mistake. Her landscaped backyard had numerous hiding places with a gazebo, trees, and bushes before ending at the waterfront.

With urgent emails to respond to, Desi had asked for my help. Since we were bonding like sisters, why not?

The wind had picked up, and I regretted wandering around a strange place alone and in the dark. But how could I turn Desi down when she'd been such a great host and fed me such delicious lasagna?

She'd apologized about going too heavy on the onions and said the kids had refused to eat it. But it was delicious, even if the onions reminded me of El Rey.

Jackson's idiotic joke about a sasquatch running wild and the abundance of hiding spots didn't help. I wasn't sure what a sasquatch looked like. Probably similar to the imaginary Yeti, the infamous Abominable Snowman.

I walked further from the house, repeatedly shouting her name. Across the Sound, New York's Long Island was in view, but I stayed away from the waterfront.

Losing Goldie was partially my fault since I ran back inside to get my jacket and made a brief pit stop in the bathroom.

Tired of looking nearby, I ignored Jackson's screwy warnings and stomped toward the water. Some dogs were fond of the water, running along the beach, or swimming. A retriever's DNA was programmed to retrieve until exhausted, but no one had thrown anything.

The electric fence installed to keep Goldie away from her anti-dog neighbors must have stopped working. Desi assured me how Goldie had learned in a brief but painful way to stay on their property.

My throat ached from calling her name. Shivering, I stopped a few feet from the shore. To get warm, I strolled along the wooden boardwalk. "Where the hell are you, Goldie?"

I stared across the water, trying not to fret about Charlie and the rest of them on board the yacht. Perhaps I should try hypnosis like Desi to reduce my bucketload of stress to a more manageable pint-size. Except I feared what I might say under someone's control.

I cupped my hands around my mouth and yelled for Goldie one last time. She still didn't show. I had to give Desi the bad news and ask for help.

On my way back, something rustled near a cluster of evergreen bushes. As I got closer to the noise, I hesitated. I called her name again, and something moved in the bushes. But oddly, she didn't bark.

It could be a wild animal or a snake. I didn't want to surprise whatever lurked there and end up bitten and debated going back to the house for a flashlight.

I called out for Goldie, and the rustling increased. I squatted and pushed against the bushes to see if she was trapped. Perhaps she was playing hide-and-seek with me.

Retrievers were trained to work as service dogs, and they like people. Running away with no one else nearby didn't make any sense.

The branches were thick. They scratched my hands and jabbed at my arms through my jacket. If it was Goldie, she must be trapped. I fought against the branches and saw a flash of golden fur.

That was confirmation enough, and I wrestled my way into the bushes. My fingers felt Goldie's furry coat and a rope noose around her neck. A second rope was wrapped tightly around her nose. I wiggled my finger underneath to remove it, but it was too tight.

She shook all over from panic or excitement. The noose's knots were thick, and the rope was tied to the bush trapping her.

"Easy girl. Don't panic. I'm here."

Goldie was secured so tight that the noose dug into her neck. If the rope got much tighter, it could strangle her.

I needed a knife to cut the branches and her noose, but it would take time to get to the kitchen and back. She might panic and choke herself. The rope ends were tied deep into the bush, so I had to get her free immediately.

The bush didn't stand a chance. I quickly broke one branch and then another to get through while whispering reassuring words to calm Goldie.

My hands ached from the twisting and pulling, but I got closer. The knots were complicated. But I had spent countless tedious hours at sea and learned how to tie sailors' knots.

The knots loosened, and Goldie was freed from the bush. But the noose was still tight around her neck. She sat, and her tail thumped on the ground.

"Kat, Goldie," Desi yelled out.

I struggled with the noose. When Goldie heard her human mother, she pulled away and choked.

"Quiet, Desi!" I tried to calm Goldie. "Easy girl, one more minute."

At last, the second set of knots were loose. Goldie rubbed her wet nose against me as if to say thank you and ran toward Desi.

When I came out from under the mangled bushes, Desi stood there with Goldie jumping in joy. Goldie didn't seem to have suffered from any permanent damage. But like me, she wouldn't forget this anytime soon.

"What happened?" Desi asked.

I bent over to catch my breath, but bile grew inside my stomach. I turned back to the bushes and vomited some of the cocktails and lasagna.

"Kat, are you okay? Way too many onions in that lasagna. Sorry."

I shook my head, embarrassed by my distasteful reaction to stress. "The lasagna was delicious. I'm okay, just nerves. Let's go inside, and I'll tell you everything."

"Of course, I'm a terrible hostess." She put her arm around me, and the three of us headed back to the safety of her fortress-sized house.

~ ~ ~

After a stop in the bathroom to wash up and put ointment on my cut hands, I joined Desi in the kitchen.

She was, as expected, tense. "Can I fix you something else to drink or eat? But the bar is closed. No more cocktails."

"Not even a double whiskey?"

She shook her head, possibly fearing I meant it.

I grinned to show it was a joke. "Connecticut tap water is fine."

I explained what happened to Goldie and why I had severely pruned those bushes at the wrong time of year. We examined Goldie from head to foot under bright lights and agreed a visit to the vet could wait.

She repeated several times. "Who would do such a sick thing to a poor defenseless dog?"

"Your next-door neighbors who hate dogs?" I hated to accuse someone, but they met the three criteria for a crime, which included means, motive, and opportunity.

"No, they wouldn't. They may not be dog lovers, but they are wonderful neighbors. Besides, they went to their Caribbean winter home. We always watch their house while they're gone."

"Well, what if an unexpected guest moved in, and they forgot to tell you?"

From the downstairs guest room, we surveyed the neighbor's house. Other than the automatic nightlight out front, we didn't see any other lights or activity inside the house.

Desi asked, "Shall we go see? I have spare keys and the alarm code."

"We? No way. You should call the police."

"But what if it's nothing?"

"So what? You pay high taxes to live here. That includes police protection. I'm not going over there."

I followed her back to the kitchen, and she rummaged around inside a drawer, mumbling something about their keys. She said, "We could walk by and call the police if it looks odd."

"Don't even think about it. Whoever did this to Goldie

wasn't playing around. They might even be armed." I couldn't handle a repeat of Friday at the office.

She closed the drawer and held up a Gucci key ring.

"I'm serious. I'm calling the cops. Let them earn their pay." I grabbed Desi's arm to stop her from leaving.

I picked up her home phone, put it on speaker, and dialed 911. After I complained about how worried we were, the police agreed to send a patrol car to her neighbor's house. But tying up a dog wasn't a high-priority crime, so they probably wouldn't show up anytime soon.

"Desi, you've got to turn on your alarm. Also, put it on when you are at home."

"Well, I would, but it's broken." She explained the lengthy problems with their alarm company. Steve had agreed to fix it, but that was months ago.

"Don't wait. Do it yourself tomorrow morning. In the meantime, let's make sure things are secure."

She nodded.

With Goldie's unknown attackers out there, I tested the locks on all the windows and doors. Such a large house had too many points of entry. Lots of people maximized their outdoor views with minimal obstructions to access backyards. But all these popular open concept floor plans gave strangers and criminals open surveillance opportunities. A shiver traveled up and down my backbone. If someone saw Desi's expensive jewelry, they might return in force.

Her house highlighted the dangers of living in a McMansion compared to my more secure apartment with only one access point, the front door. The more I thought about my snug and protected apartment, the more I wanted to go home. But with criminals roaming around, I couldn't abandon her.

"What are you doing?" Desi sat on the floor in the living room, petting Goldie.

"I'm shutting these curtains. You can reopen them later."

"But why?"

"If anyone walks across the yard, they have an unblocked view inside your house."

"But almost no one ever does."

"Well, someone did about an hour ago, and they're still out there."

"Nonsense. Some bored kids played a cruel joke, and it got out of hand. They are long gone by now."

"Those knots practically strangled Goldie and were complicated. It took me a long time to untie her. That took some planning."

Desi pursed her lips and didn't respond.

"Why do you think they wanted to secure your dog so she couldn't bark? If I didn't find Goldie when I did …" I didn't want to scare Desi, but she needed to be extra careful.

"Okay, you win. How can I help?" She hesitated next to the curtains I had asked her to close. "My maid's going to freak when she sees this."

I shook my head in disappointment. Minor décor changes were better than finding our dead bodies. I motioned to the curtains near her, and we went through each room systematically. Later we turned on the TV but were unable to focus on anything.

"Any update from Steve?" I asked.

She had texted him several times without a reply. If it got much later, I was stuck here for the night.

Chapter 20 ~ Don't Be Stupid

When footsteps echoed from the front hall, we both jumped, still on edge. Her husband staggered inside. Relieved, Desi hugged him affectionately.

Steve eyed me and nodded. "What's the deal with the curtains?"

Desi described what happened to Goldie, the house next door, and the police.

Steve snatched the neighbor's keys from the kitchen counter. He strutted to the back door ignoring our arguments to stay here.

"You should at least take something," I said.

"Like what? One of my wife's cocktails?" He must have noticed the multiple sets of empty cocktail glasses in the sink.

"No, some protection – a knife."

Steve shrugged. "You've been sitting around on your ass unemployed and watching too many crime shows. That type of thing doesn't happen here in Old Greenwich."

His negative attitude zapped my desire to argue. Crime happens everywhere, and it's better to be prepared.

Desi and I put on our jackets and left Goldie in the house. We stood in the yard to monitor from a safe distance while Steve marched boldly on.

Steve opened the neighbor's door and staggered back.

Desi moaned, and I gasped.

Steve, the clown, waved at us.

"Not funny," I said to Desi.

A police car drove up and parked in front of the neighbor's house. Steve stopped outside the door, and all three of us hurried over to explain what had happened. The policeman said he'd do a walk-through and suggested that Desi and I wait at home.

About fifteen minutes later, Steve reappeared, tossed the keys back into the drawer, and slammed it shut.

"What happened?" Desi asked.

Steve ran his hand through his hair. "We didn't see

anything unusual or anyone. A complete waste of time. Happy?" He stared in my direction.

"You were so brave, honey." Desi kissed him.

"Nothing was out of the ordinary?" I couldn't believe it all went so well.

"A few dirty dishes in the kitchen, but otherwise it's fairly clean. Our neighbors often leave in a hurry for their flight."

"Did you search the entire house?" In such a short time, they either split up or ran through it.

"Just the main floor. Something about probable cause and privacy."

"What? That's ridiculous. If a criminal is over there, do you think they are going to be waiting downstairs to hand you a welcome cocktail?"

Steve glared at me. "The keys are inside the drawer. Play detective yourself, Kat. I'm exhausted." He frowned. "I suppose I'll see you in the morning. I leave early."

Feeling unwanted, I was determined to go home. "Now that you're back, Steve, I can go tonight. Thanks again for everything, Desi."

"Please stay. It's so late and dangerous to wait at the station for a train." Desi touched my arm to convince me while Steve shrugged, signaling he didn't care.

"I can call a cab or Zhila."

"What's a she-la? A new app?" She accented both syllables of Zhila's name.

I laughed. "Zhila is the Uber driver who brought me here. I highly recommend her." But it was late, and she was probably home with her husband or writing poetry.

Desi frowned. "Weirdos and homeless bums hang around in the dark corridors and by the tracks. Not worth the risk." Desi's warnings were valid. Taking a chance on getting robbed or raped wasn't worth it.

Desi escorted me to the spacious guest bedroom on the first floor. "Make yourself comfortable in your second home."

In the bathroom, she opened drawers and cabinets, pulled out a new toothbrush, and covered the counter with an assortment of sample-size toiletries. "Use any of this. Take them with you. I have plenty."

After she left, I gazed at my clothes, realizing I had to wear them tomorrow too. I searched the closet and dresser drawers for something else to wear. The idea of sleeping in the nude with a dog killer on the loose was nerve-racking.

Hoping Desi might still be up, I trudged upstairs to borrow a nightgown. Outside their closed bedroom door, I hesitated, not wanting to bother them.

Steve said, "I'm warning you. Stay out of it."

Desi screamed back. "She's my friend and one of the best."

"For what, two nights? I've known Charlie for years. You owe her nothing. Charlie should date someone with more class."

"She has tons of class. And integrity and honesty, which means much more."

"For god's sake, Desi. She went to the University of Texas. That isn't anything remotely similar to an Ivy League school. Her auditing job is with some small unknown consulting company. She's a nothing."

"No, she isn't. I won't give up on her."

"If that's how it's going to be, I'll be down the hall."

The door opened suddenly. I scrambled to hide, but there wasn't a corner or furniture to stand behind. I turned to escape, but Steve caught my arm.

His voice hissed in anger. "Fantastic! By snooping around, you got the message. Or should I repeat it?"

Speechless, I shook my head, pulled my arm away, and rushed downstairs.

Ten minutes later, after securing the entrances to my risky ground-floor bedroom, someone knocked at my door.

"Who's there?" My voice shook.

While I waited for an answer, I picked up the blow dryer, the only weapon I could find, and hid behind the door. The next chance I get, I'm buying a sharp metal nail file to carry inside my purse for protection.

"It's me. Desi. I brought Goldie."

"Why didn't you say so?" I flicked on the ceiling light,

put down the hairdryer, and pushed the extra security measure, an overstuffed chair, away to open the door.

Goldie bounded into my room, rubbing up against me. Desi held a dog bed. She chuckled at my makeshift toga from the top sheet and offered to bring me a nightgown. Then she stopped short. "What the hell? Did you build a fort?"

I had rearranged the furniture using a table and another chair to block entry through the window and door. "I heard something outside and blocked the entrances for extra protection. Please be careful until they find the wackos."

"You're right. I'm sorry about all this mess. Steve doesn't like Goldie in our bedroom, and I thought you would. She has much better ears than we do."

I took the large dog bed from her. "Sure. Thank you."

"Are you sure you don't want a nightgown? It will only take a sec."

"Nope, I'm fine." Holding my toga up, I bent down to pet Goldie's soft head.

"I'll leave my phone on. Call me if you get nervous or anything happens."

After I shut the door, Goldie stepped into her little bed on the floor. I desperately needed a goodnight's sleep before my early commute and the long work week ahead. I closed my eyes, counted to twenty in Danish to practice, and tried to ignore whoever might be lurking out in the dark.

When I rolled on my side, Goldie jumped up and nestled her warm body against mine. With her help, I drifted off to a safer place.

Chapter 21 ~ Commuting Aches and Pains

In my personal rule book, getting up at 5 a.m. should be illegal.

Desi stood in the kitchen wearing a robe and poured me a to-go cup of coffee. "I hope you don't mind. I'm exhausted. It's a short walk, and Steve will take you."

She handed me an overstuffed Saks Fifth Avenue shopping bag and a garment bag containing her long mermaid dress, which I promised to return.

"You're doing me a huge favor by taking these clothes. If you don't like them, just give them away."

"Thanks again. My friends love almost brand-new designer clothes." I sipped the strong coffee to kickstart my brain. "Don't forget to call the alarm company."

"Promise. And please just come to the charity event," Desi begged, hugging me goodbye.

"I will if I can." And I would. I had dreamed about meeting Jim and playing with his ferrets.

Steve appeared in a business suit, and Desi gave him an identical coffee to go.

"Ready," he said like a command.

Outside, a bright red roadster identical to Charlie's Tesla was parked in their circular driveway.

Steve said, "I drove it here. Nice wheels. Charlie took the train home."

I scrutinized the neighbor's house for anything unusual. I could have sworn the curtains moved slightly inside one of the upstairs windows. Steve was already six feet ahead of me, and he'd never believe me.

After almost spilling my coffee, I jogged to catch up to Steve. Like a pack mule, I was overloaded with my shoulder bag, the bulky shopping bag, and the garment bag slung over my shoulder. If I lost him, I would need to google the station to find it and be late.

"Steve, I know you think this is silly. Please keep an eye on your neighbor's house."

"You're right. Completely silly."

He didn't bother to look back at me and marched onward. I matched his fast pace but followed behind. During our powerwalk through Old Greenwich, I admired what I could see of the houses hidden behind privacy gates or foliage. But living in the burbs wasn't for me.

Steve stopped after hearing the bag repeatedly bang against my leg, accompanied by my moans. "My interfering wife." He took my cumbersome shopping bag. Steve carried a thin briefcase with a *Wall Street Journal* peeking out.

Steve said, "I commute with some buddies from work. So, we'll separate at the station."

Agreeing was no problem at all. After last night, enduring an hour plus to Grand Central with him was about as enticing as being at the clinic with Dr. Price.

"Charlie or someone else may tell you more about what happened on the yacht last night. Appreciate it if you don't tell Desi."

I hesitated, not wanting to keep secrets from Desi. "I'll try not to but —"

"Got it. You two are practically joined at the hip now. If you do, you'll stress her out. It was a minor situation. The yacht went aground. We were evacuated by the Coast Guard."

"What? Was Charlie onboard?"

"Yep. No one was hurt, but some serious damage to the hull. Not sure exactly what happened. Charlie and I didn't hang around. Jason fired the stupid-ass captain and will probably sue him for damages."

Inside, the station was filled with commuters headed to jobs in Manhattan. Steve handed me my bag and said, "I should apologize for what you overheard last night." After an awkward goodbye, he finally left.

I hurried to the crowded ticket machines and lined up. When it was my turn, I put the shopping bag down and juggled the garment bag on my arm. My purse slipped off my shoulder and fell upside down. Everything scattered when it hit the floor, and some fast-moving coins rolled away. I moved out of the way to let the next person buy their ticket and knelt to refill my handbag.

Someone tapped me on the shoulder, and a ticket was waved before me. Steve said, "Here, I bought you a ticket." He helped me to my feet, took my shopping bag, and waved his briefcase toward the stairs. "After you."

The platform was crowded. I hoped Steve's friends would show up, but he must have missed them with my delays.

Steve leaned toward me as a noisy train rolled to a stop. "Did you realize Charlie wants to marry you? I've advised him to secure an airtight prenup. Emailed him my lawyer's name and number."

"You needn't bother. I never want to see Charlie again. Since he spends every cent he makes, a prenup would benefit me, not him."

Steve said, "Famous last words. You need to pull yourself together. Ever considered electroshock or brain scans?"

Fear turned into anger. "I'm fine, Steve. If anyone needs help, Charlie does. I just want him to leave me alone."

He smirked as if enjoying our verbal boxing match. "We're cool, right?"

"Yeah, like Siberia."

~ ~ ~

My apartment was just as I left it, and I sighed in relief. I hurried past my faithful guard Giuseppe with a quick hello.

After changing clothes, I rode the subway uptown to Melville Consulting's new office in Morningside Heights, south of Harlem. The distance from my apartment was about the same as the office in the West Village. This route wasn't jam-packed since most commuters traveled downtown now.

These passengers, ordinary struggling people, were the opposite of this morning's Metro-North business people. These subway riders didn't live in McMansions, sail around on yachts, or ride in exorbitantly priced cars. I was with low-to-middle-class New Yorkers who wore inexpensive, casual clothes like me.

The air on the southbound train from Connecticut had been thick with expensive perfume and cologne. A scent that signaled prestige, winning, and control. The upper-class atmosphere had commanded, "Out of my way. I rule the world."

Here the air was filled with sweat, stained clothes, and unshowered bodies that asserted, "Another day, another hard-earned dollar, if I'm lucky."

A young black man, perhaps a student at Columbia University, sat next to me, reading a thick textbook. He might make it into the upper echelon with an Ivy League education. But without buckets of cash, most would only dream about it.

The previous few days had provided another brief look into how the one-percenters lived. Jason and his crowd didn't act that happy or content despite their opulent lifestyles. They needed drugs to relax and vitamin shots to chase away the resulting hangover.

The subway screeched to my stop. I was still unsure if this was the job for me. But I pushed onward, determined to give it another week.

Near the exit, a raggedy old woman sat on a piece of cardboard. She stared off into space without asking for help. I reached into a side pocket of my purse for a fast-food gift card and kneeled to hand it to her. She turned the plastic card over in her hands as though not recognizing it.

"A McDonald's gift card for five dollars." She could buy a cheap meal or trade it for cash.

She stared through clouded eyes. "God bless you, miss."

A shiver slid along my thirty-three vertebrae, and I struggled to stand. I recognized the old woman's unfocused eyes, possibly blurry from despair.

But this couldn't be. That poor woman lived in Southampton, England, my first port of call in 1862.

I wanted to ask her if we'd somehow met last year, but I couldn't formulate a logical-sounding question. I stood, brushing my hands against my jeans. She must merely resemble the other woman. As they say, we all have a twin somewhere.

At the top of the stairs, I rethought my decision to walk away without talking to her. But it was eerie. When I looked back, the old lady had vanished.

Chapter 22 ~ Swirls, Whirls, and Loops

I stopped to buy a cup of coffee at a bodega on Broadway near my new office. These small stores carried an extensive inventory in the small space allotted to them. A precursor to the 7-Eleven convenience stores, bodegas were now endangered by skyrocketing city rents.

I needed more caffeine after the long commute and difficult night and bought fruit cups for my breakfast-loving colleagues.

Our new office was a block east of the subway stop. The neighborhood became more residential as I neared the towering gothic Cathedral of St. John the Divine. With construction stalled at the two-thirds mark, it was also known as St. John the Unfinished. Nevertheless, it was a convenient place to pray or hide.

I buzzed the front door of a residential apartment building hidden behind scaffolding and construction permits. Anita answered.

After her prompt for the code word, I spat out the name of the infamous ship, "*Pequod.*" But how could I ignore this bad omen? The *Pequod* was rammed by the whale Moby Dick and sunk into oblivion.

The locks clicked open, and I climbed the narrow wooden stairs to the third floor.

Shantelle opened the door and hugged me. "Thrilled to see you!"

I handed her the bag filled with fruit cups and put my work bag and purse down while glancing around.

Anita said, "She's back! I knew you would, *chica.*" She took my hand and stared at me. "You look tired. Bad weekend?"

I nodded, but neither situation was permanent. "Yeah, missed you guys. I'm giving it another week. Where's Jackson?"

"He's at a meeting but will be back soon," Shantelle said.

We nibbled on our fruit, and they chatted about their

relatively routine weekends. In comparison, mine was overloaded with tasty morsels. However, I wasn't ready to share my dating misadventures, the runaway yacht party, or the dog rescue.

Our office was a century-old one-bedroom apartment similar to the last one, but larger. We unpacked the boxes and repositioned our three desks as they were in the Village.

In the kitchen, a table with seating for six doubled as our conference room. Our three desks, situated in the corner of the apartment's living room, faced the front door. Jackson's desk was inside the small bedroom, creating his private office.

The second-hand mismatched office furniture was worn but better than cheap veneer furniture. Unfortunately, the outdoor fire escape wasn't visible from our offices on this side of the floor.

When I exited the bathroom, something was burning. I ran toward the smoke with a glass of water to douse the flame.

Shantelle stopped me and swooped up the smoking container. A small stick of incense burned in a decorated bowl. She fanned the smoke with a large feather and strolled around our office.

"What's that?" I asked.

"A *palo santo* zodiac stick. It purifies the air."

I wrinkled my nose at the weird stench of citrus and pine. "But now it smells worse than before."

Anita was setting up her desk and laughed. "Hey, I'm with Kat. That stuff stinks. Sorry, Shantelle, it's the truth."

"You two will thank me later. Burning this bundle is called *saging*. Brings luck and positive energy. Reduces stress and builds concentration." Shantelle shrugged as if trying to shake off our negativity.

"All that by burning a stick? Does it work faster if I climb into the bowl with it?" I teased.

Shantelle shook her head in despair, frowning. "That's a sacred bowl."

Not wanting to offend her religious beliefs, I apologized. "Is that an African tradition?"

"No, Native American. My boyfriend introduced me to

it."

"Cool."

She asked me to stand still and slowly circled me while fanning me with the feather to coat me with the problem-solving smoke.

"Feeling better?" Shantelle said.

"Oh, yeah, I can use all the positivity you can send my way." I sniffed my clothes, not enamored of the odor. But any hint of good luck would wash off and disappear.

~ ~ ~

Jackson rushed into our office, spinning around like a whirling dervish. The others glared at him, but I stood in alarm, forgetting about his extraordinarily high energy level.

"Relax," he said, laughing at me. He turned to the others. "What's that stench?"

"Purifying the new office, Jackson," Shantelle said.

Jackson shook his head. "Lot of good that did last time." He leaned against the corner of my desk and read messages on his phone. "Give me ten minutes, Kat. We'll talk in my office."

Shantelle and Anita looked concerned about his formal summons and my fate. If he decided to fire me, I coached myself to be ready. I would say, "I quit," right before he dropped the ax. At least a one-week job wouldn't need to land on my resume.

I knocked on his door nine minutes later, and Jackson yelled to enter. He kept typing on his laptop. "One minute."

Too nervous to sit, I inspected the only decoration on the wall: a framed poster illustrating nine fingerprint patterns.

"Familiar with those?" Jackson asked while he got up and closed the door.

"Actually, I am. In high school, I took a pre-law enforcement course. We learned to dust and lift fingerprints with tape. Now I'm sure it's all done with digital scanners."

He appeared impressed. "Yep. All modern now. I trained the old way too. Still handy to know."

"I only knew about three types. Swirls, whirls, and loops. This poster has nine variations."

"Nothing stays simple. Sit down. Glad to see you got out of Connecticut in one piece." Jackson slid an envelope across the table to me. "I'm aware you want to quit. But hear me out first."

I opened the envelope and took out a check payable to me for fifty big ones. Shocked at the generous amount, I stumbled over what to say. Fifty thousand dollars would cover my expenses for months.

We were paid when projects were completed, and our secretive client must have been pleased with our work so far. Still squeezing hold of my paycheck, I thanked Jackson.

"An advance on Project Onion. Not bad for five days' work. But it's not always this lucrative. I added more for the stress on Friday. So, will you stay with us?"

I contemplated my malnourished and starving bank balance. "If I don't suffer through another Friday like that."

"Can't promise you that. We'll try." He leaned back in his chair, studying me so carefully I squirmed. "How was the therapy session? You want to take a break?"

"What?" I demanded.

"Heard you were enrolled in therapy. Then you got lost. Or disappeared."

I rolled my eyes. "Who said that?"

"A confidential client of mine."

"If you mean Charlie Richmond, forget it. Now, tell me everything."

"Sorry, Kat. No can do. Didn't get his permission yet."

"If you don't explain what happened, your investigation of me, I'm out of here." I stuffed my paycheck back inside the envelope and stood, hesitating in the hope he'd reconsider.

"All right. Sit down. Charles Richmond is an oddball." He scanned his phone for messages. "You could do much better."

"I plan to do just that. Now explain."

"He hired me to find you. When you were lost at sea on the way to Hong Kong. If you recall, I told you not to go back there."

I remembered, but that was irrelevant. "How did Charlie find you?"

"Through your assistant. Met her on that bank investigation when I met you. What's her name? Mel?"

I nodded, glad this meshed with Charlie's account.

"Mel called me. You were incommunicado. Not just with Mel, but also with the woman watching your apartment."

"Abby?"

"Yeah. So, I searched for you and your ship. We were concerned and rightly so. I feared you were at the bottom of Victoria Harbour."

He paused, but I waited to hear more.

"Mel mentioned you had a big fight at the airport and hated Charlie. He offered me cash upfront, and I was curious. You told me you planned to be gone for a few months. But seven?"

I shrugged. "Unexpected complications." Not quite the explanation he wanted, but telling him the truth about my voyage wasn't an option.

"A few months ago, I called Charlie. He owed me some out-of-pocket expenses. Said you were back, so I got in touch about the job."

That explained the email from Jackson out of the blue.

"Why did you run away yesterday?"

"We went to a short couple therapy meeting at a clinic in Connecticut. Then the plan changed to include spending the night there."

"How did Charlie know to call me?"

"I argued I couldn't stay since I had a job to go to today. Your name slipped out by accident. Only your first name and only once. Sorry."

"You violated your NDA. To be crystal clear, it means not disclosing anything at any time!"

"I know. I screwed up. Sorry." He glared at me. "I didn't tell the doctor your last name or the company's name. Nothing about El Rey or what we do. Charlie recognized your first name."

"But now Charlie and your therapist know." Jackson's eyes narrowed.

"So what? I'm an auditor doing numbers stuff. What you

promised me in our interview." My face heated up from anger. "No one else knows where our office is located. Or what we are doing."

"I see your point. But, and it's a huge but, you must keep my company and the rest of us out of your personal life. It's also off-limits for any counseling sessions."

"Fine. By the way, there will be no more counseling ever."

We stared at each other for a moment.

"So, you never did find me?" I wondered how hard he searched. But it was a complete waste of time. He'd never find me back then.

"Nope, I didn't. Charles didn't pay me that much, so I didn't spend that much time on it. Some people can disappear. Usually with the government's help or a ton of money. In this business, it's incredibly useful. You'll have to share how you managed to vanish from the face of the earth for seven months."

"Right. Long story. Another time."

"Fine. So, no more discussions with Charlie or anyone else. Deal?" He extended his hand.

"Deal." We shook hands like negotiating another strange business deal.

"I have a couple of jobs that are perfect for you. They don't involve drug lords or petty criminals. But despite all that, things can get hairy. They don't pay us to do nothing."

I swallowed my dread. He meant I might get scalped. If only he spoke standard English.

Jackson grinned and stood. "Not that bad, but you've got the idea. Let's take a half-hour break first."

Shantelle and Anita scrutinized me as I trudged back to my desk. I felt like I was wading through mud to reach the safety of my desk. Their gaze was so intent, I wondered if they would throw me a rope if I got stuck.

Releasing my death grip on the paycheck, I slipped it into my wallet. I snuck a glance at my work colleagues and the front door with longing, but first, I'd hear Jackson out.

Chapter 23 ~ Channeling Heidi and Pepi

When Jackson disappeared into the bathroom, Anita and Shantelle almost pounced on me.

"How'd it go?" Anita spoke so fast her words slurred together.

"I'm staying for the time being." I gave them my best confidence-building smile.

They both jumped up and hugged me.

Shanelle got emotional, and a joyful tear rolled down her cheek. "Thanks for being so brave. You won't regret it."

"Super fab times ahead, *chica*," Anita smirked, and we giggled.

"Hate to interrupt, ladies. We do have a business to run to keep the lights and heat on, etc." Jackson stood outside his office and motioned to me, so I hurried back in.

Multicolored folders lay on his desk, and he picked up an orange one. A well-used yellow legal pad had notes all over it. I attempted to read upside down but couldn't. No doubt he used a secret code for everything. Regardless, his writing style was too small for me to decipher.

"This job is for you and Shantelle. Need a legal eagle." Jackson called her, and Shantelle joined us with an upbeat bounce to her step.

He flipped through some printouts. "Got a banking fraud job in Shreveport, Louisiana, for the two of you."

"Where?" Shantelle asked.

"Northwest Louisiana, near Texas." I may not know a lot about Jackson's investigative techniques. But I grew up in Texas and visited the surrounding states on family road trips. "About two-hundred miles east of Dallas."

Jackson cocked his head and nodded. "Kat knows her geography. Even if it isn't a port of call. You need to examine the bank's files to look for phony documents. The client in Shreveport wants us to flush out a possible rotten egg or two. We need the legal and number side scoped out. Not a big paying gig. Short though, less than a week."

Shantelle smiled. "An ideal assignment for the two of us, but I can't leave town for a few weeks. My other clients need to be closed out. How about December?"

"Fine with me." I wasn't in a hurry to leave town. At least banks were incredibly safe with security guards. Unless they're the target of a bank robber. But if we avoid hanging around the tellers and the vault, we should be fine.

"All right. Mid-December it is." He handed Shantelle the folder and asked her to contact the manager and oversee the details.

"By the way, Shreveport is a port. On the Red River, but it looks like brown mud." I couldn't resist correcting him. Shantelle had mentioned Jackson was a member of Mensa, a group of people with extremely high IQs and geniuses. But she cautioned me to not say anything.

Jackson's mouth dropped open in surprise.

I beamed in pride at the idea of teaching a brainy Mensa something new. "It flows into the Atchafalaya River that feeds the Mississippi."

"Aren't you a wealth of nautical nitty-gritty? Well, stay off all those ships! And that includes riverboats. No Huckleberry Finn monkeying around. That's an order!"

Shantelle raised her eyebrows at Jackson's unusual warnings before leaving. I stayed behind and tried to keep calm.

Jackson pulled out a frayed and ominously colored red folder. "This job is solo. Has your name all over it."

"It does?" I fidgeted, imagining the worst. That blood-colored folder must have been passed around unwanted for years for a valid reason.

He must have noticed my concern. "Just an old folder that happens to be red. New client and job. I reuse them. Save a tree when I can."

"Oh, good."

"So, the job is this. A Danish woman needs help getting some art back from a Swiss bank. All you do is go to Denmark, meet her, fly to Zurich with her, review the paperwork, sign it, and you're done. A few days in

Copenhagen and Zurich for 25K plus expenses. Most of it is flying time. Catch up on some movies. Or even better, sleep." He pointed to my face. "Raccoon eyes."

I waved him off. I could cover my dark undereye circles, which were partially Jackson's fault, with makeup. "But I don't know anything about art. How would I evaluate it?"

"Don't need to. The client and the Swiss bank are in agreement. Just confirm with her and sign."

"But sign what? Legal documents? Isn't this more in line with Shantelle's skill set?"

"She could do this in her sleep. But our client doesn't trust lawyers and wants a neutral American. A plus if said person can speak Danish. You still do, don't you? And Shantelle can't leave town this month. I'm assuming you can."

I nodded. "But what if I sign something that I shouldn't?"

"The bank emails the encrypted docs here. Shantelle approves. Once you receive her written okay via email, you're done."

"I suppose I could." Leaving the country was at the bottom of my wish list.

"Why don't you call the client and discuss it?" He pushed the file that was so bright red, it almost flashed. "Her name is Inge Mortensen." He called her "Ing," mispronouncing her name.

"Ing-a."

He chuckled. "See? You're ideal for this job. The rest of us would mangle her name."

Anita and Shantelle had gone for lunch but left a note that they were bringing back pizzas to share. It was six hours later in Denmark, so I picked up the phone to find out more about this job. Inge might not like my Danish-American accent, sometimes called *Danglish*.

After a friendly chat with Inge, a grandmother living alone in Copenhagen without family available to help in Zurich, I accepted the job and genuinely wanted to assist her. The money was like the white frosting on a Danish pastry called a *kringle*: sweet but optional.

~ ~ ~

At lunchtime, my colleagues usually brought back takeout, or we took lunch in shifts to avoid leaving the office empty during work hours. Everything had to be locked up whenever we were out. Since we didn't want to hassle with a complete lock-up during the day, Shantelle, Anita, and I took turns leaving. Jackson, being the prime business lead generator, got to come and go as he wished.

When Shantelle and Anita reappeared carrying boxes of pizza and drinks, they were impressed at my announcement. In less than two weeks, I'd confirmed my first client assignment.

"You're brave to go solo," Shantelle said while Anita nodded in agreement.

"It's nothing," I assured them. "The client's a grandmother and wants someone to hold her hand at the bank in Zurich."

"And then we're off to Louisiana. Love that Cajun spice." Shantelle touched her stomach and smiled.

Anita frowned with envy. "We've got to do a job together. Travel somewhere like BFFs."

Jackson appeared in the doorway. "BFFs?"

"Best female friends," Anita said.

"I'm feeling excluded here," Jackson grinned, playing along.

"Sorry, you don't quite qualify," Shantelle said.

Jackson snagged a slice of pizza to go on his way out the door to some unknown location. We rarely asked since we usually got a vague answer.

"When are you leaving?" Anita asked.

"On Friday, if it's okay with Jackson. The bank in Zurich opens on Monday. I want to be back in the USA for Thanksgiving. That's my favorite holiday and I missed out last year."

"He'll approve that. The sooner the better, in his book. Always. We better set you up fast," Shantelle said.

"Thanks for offering, but I can make my own travel arrangements." I never bothered my assistant with making hotel or flight reservations.

"You betcha. This is a full-on do-it-yourselfer operation."
Anita laughed. "She's talking about something else."

"What?" I asked.

Shantelle looked at Anita. "Perhaps Jackson should explain this."

Anita asked her, "Why? We can tackle this. *No problema.* Kat, what's your stripper name?"

"Stripper?" I repeated in shock.

Shantelle smirked, hinting she was up to something. "She means your stage name."

"I don't have one. Never needed one." Whenever I had to make a speech before a crowd, I came down with a severe case of anxiety. Stripping would be a million times worse. Never happening, no matter what.

Anita slapped the table and burst out laughing, and Shantelle covered her mouth to conceal her laughter.

"What's so funny?" They were rude to act like this. I grabbed a can of sparkling water and debated leaving the office for more pleasant fresh air.

"That look on your face." Anita cackled so hard it was difficult to understand her. "And it's all pink."

"A stripper name is your pet's name and the street where you grew up on." Shantelle looked as if she was trying to stifle a laugh.

"Right." I sat at my desk and turned on my laptop, tired of this joke. "I don't want a stripper name. I already have lots of names with Kathryn and Kat Jensen plus my maiden name."

Anita stood behind me. "Nope. New names are required. Jackson says we've gotta do this."

Shantelle gave me a weird look but joined forces against me. "You need at least one alias. Ideally, two."

When I asked them for their aliases, they both grinned and refused since sharing them was on a need-to-know basis only.

After plenty of cajoling and brainstorming, we created two phony names based on my childhood pets and the streets where I lived. Heidi Montfort and Pepi Shalimar were officially introduced.

"I don't think Pepi is a girl's name," Shantelle said.

Anita agreed. "Yep, too much like Pepe, a nickname for José. And it's Puerto Rican slang for cocaine. They can't sound fake or strange, or you get remembered. The entire reason is to blend in or disappear."

"Jackson doesn't like it, but it's easier if you use names you will remember. Especially if the heat gets turned up. Any other pets on Shalimar?" Shantelle asked.

What heat? Copenhagen and Zurich were cold in November. "We had a Siamese cat named Kim."

"Kimberly Shalimar. Kim for short. Done!" Anita indicated that Shantelle should write that down.

Shantelle gave me a new look by rearranging my hair, swapping jackets, and adding scarves. Anita took some digital photos with her phone.

When we were done with the photoshoot, Anita said, "I'll send them to the guy who makes them. Ready for Friday before you leave."

The idea of sending fake information to someone unnerved me. "Are you sure this is legit, Shantelle?"

Anita took over when Shantelle mysteriously excused herself. "It's only for an emergency to confuse the bad guys. Completely routine for PIs like us."

Regardless of what other private eyes did, I would only use a passport and my official IDs in my real name. But if a harmless and fake ID kept my neck out of a tight spot and confused a criminal like El Rey, I'd chance it.

A few hours later, Jackson breezed back inside and asked me, "Code names all set up?"

"Yep, I'm Heidi Montfort and Kimberly Shalimar."

"Where'd you source those?" Jackson put his shoulder-bag briefcase down.

"My str… stage names." I couldn't say stripper. Imagining that was too bizarre.

He chuckled, and Anita and Shantelle joined him. Anita laughed so hard she had to sit down.

"What the hell?" I smiled at my silly names but became annoyed at being left out of the joke.

Shantelle finally broke the silence. "You passed. You are now officially one of us."

"Why? Because I have stripper names? What a dumb test."

"No, because you did it. Came up with phony names. We don't always get buy in. That means a lot, *chica*." Anita glowed with pride, but I felt like a fool.

I wondered who had been smart enough to refuse to play along. At least it wasn't mountain climbing or one of those other challenging team-building exercises I'd heard about.

Shantelle congratulated me. "We are going to miss having you around. When are you leaving again?"

"Friday night. I'll work a half-day."

Jackson said, "You're dedicated. No question about that."

That was par for the course since I took every job seriously.

"So, Kat. Back to biz. Every client job is called a project. They all get a unique code name like Project Onion. Steer clear of the client's name, location, or anything else that gives it away. Nothing connected to you like Heidi or Kim. Ideas?"

I glanced around the room and saw the pizza boxes from lunch. "How about Project Pepper?"

"Pepper?" Jackson raised his eyebrows.

I waved my hand at the leftover boxes and a plastic container of crushed red pepper flakes. "The Danish flag is a white cross on a red blood-stained battlefield. Has those same colors and its own name, *Dannebrog*."

"Aren't we full of tasty and historical tidbits today? Project Pepper it is."

I started writing a P for Pepper in large capitals on the front of the red folder, but he stopped me.

"Keep it here." Jackson pointed at his head with an extraordinary brain.

When you are a Mensa and not a mere mortal, it must be easy to remember everything. Next time I will create one with a long string of numbers to challenge them.

Shantelle said, "I checked the online ratings. Denmark is rated a level two because of some terrorism. Pretty benign considering most countries nowadays. Switzerland is top notch and a level one."

"Interesting. I thought both those countries were safer than our bathtubs at home." Jackson stroked his chin.

"What does that mean?" I asked.

"Part of our procedures. Some countries are dicey, and we factor that into the fees." Jackson read something on his phone and marched to his office.

Anita looked up from her paperwork. "Level fours are defined as 'do not travel.' Those are the ones to worry about, but really rare."

Shantelle said, "We monitor the warnings and advisories from the U.S. State Department. Sometimes from the U.K. and Australian governments. Equaldex tracks LGBT-related laws and rights."

I swallowed hard, processing the familiar ache deep inside my stomach. "Terrorist attacks in Denmark?"

"Nothing that serious. With lots of immigrants, they are careful. I signed you up for STEP. Smart traveler updates via email. Just steer clear of any large-scale protests or parades."

I nodded. That was obviously not part of my travel plans.

Anita yelled from the kitchen. "Hey guys, how about hitting the gym tomorrow? Brush up on self-defense."

"Works for me." I had taken self-defense courses before. Like target practice, it didn't hurt to brush up.

"Sorry, I made plans that I can't cancel," Shantelle said. "Next time."

"Jackson?" Anita said. "Even though Kat won't need it in fairy tale lands like Denmark or Switzerland, it never hurts."

"You bet. Prepare to get dirty and ripped, so wear comfortable old clothes. Our Kat will have more than just claws." Jackson stretched back in his chair, relishing the idea.

"A complete badass transformation!" Anita whooped and shook her fists above her head.

I smiled at how well today had gone. For the first time, I was ready to tackle tomorrow's challenges.

Chapter 24 ~ Finding Your Inner Goddess

From a corner table in our favorite French bistro, Darlene and Abby screamed "no" in unison, alarming the customers seated nearby. The usual noise level, approaching an ear-splitting decimal typical inside so many restaurants, stopped their cries from extending further.

I was surprised at their outburst after my travel update. I choked on my bite of a French baguette and downed my glass of water.

"How can you even consider going to Denmark again? Last time it was two months, and it ended up being seven." Abby almost yelled, which was so uncharacteristic of her.

"This isn't a vacation. It's my job, and I need the money. Besides, this is only a few days in Copenhagen and then Switzerland. I'm home in a week." I should never have mentioned it. Keeping secrets was always challenging.

The waiter interrupted to take our order. Abby and Darlene went with the three-course menu deal, but I opted for a healthier, low-calorie salad.

"What's up with that?" Darlene asked.

"Trying to lose some weight. For this job, I need to be in better shape." I was apprehensive about our upcoming workout. Anita seemed laid-back, but Jackson could be demanding, with my shortcomings reflected in his attitude.

"Why? Are you supposed to scale mountains in Denmark?" Darlene said, not missing a thing.

I chuckled, imagining my attempt to scale something high in Denmark like a church steeple.

"What's so funny?" Abby asked.

"Denmark doesn't have any mountains. You're thinking of Norway and Sweden. Denmark was created from glaciers. A glacial dump."

"A dump. Wonderful. At least, Danes are happy about it. The happiest country in the world. Way above the U.S.A." Darlene snickered at the irony of it.

"That's what they say. But it's contentment not jumping

up and down happiness. Most Danes rein in their expectations." I sipped my glass of French viognier, wanting to adopt a more Danish attitude.

"Not a bad idea," Abby said.

"Downright un-American to me." Darlene wouldn't settle for anything less than the best. "But I so much want to see Scandinavia. Shouldn't we go with Kat sometime, Abby? Get some of this happiness-contentment vibe and bring it back."

Abby didn't travel much but smiled at Darlene and me. "Perhaps. But not on a cruise ship. I would rather see the Norwegian fjords from dry land."

Before I committed to traipsing around Scandinavia with Darlene and Abby, I would test out a long weekend with them. Some friends were unreliable traveling companions, as I found out with Charlie.

"Shall we spend Thanksgiving together?" I suggested.

"What? I thought you were going to Wyoming with Charlie." Abby looked shocked.

"Yeah, what's going on in the romance department with that rich dude?" Darlene loved talking about sex and relationships. I was amazed this wasn't her first question.

I rolled my eyes. "It's over. Except I met another guy who I like." Now that I was single again, I had reminisced about the fun afternoon dancing with Frankie after target practice.

"Dirt! Tell us!" Darlene licked her lips as if ready to bite him.

I shook my head firmly. I hardly knew Frankie, and explaining how I met an NYPD detective would invite more NDA-prohibited questions. And Desi's friend Jim was just a short phone call and too iffy.

"But what happened with Charlie?" Abby moaned, unable to mask her despair.

"Our weekend together didn't work out. He's too untrustworthy. Better to move on."

Abby shook her head, disagreeing, but Darlene nodded. She dated and broke things off virtually every week.

The waiter served our food, and our conversation died off. When I saw their first course, I regretted ordering a healthy but boring salad. I stabbed the lettuce with my fork in frustration.

Darlene noticed. "Men are like lettuce. They wilt under pressure and are inedible after a week."

"My salad won't last an hour, but I can't switch guys as fast as you." I teased Darlene with her lightning-quick dating history.

"Don't you want to get married again?" Abby asked me. Perhaps she thought Charlie was my last shot for a happy ever after.

"Nope." I stabbed a rolling cherry tomato with my fork.

"Beware the dreaded S-word," Darlene warned.

"S as in single?" I asked.

"Modern-day spinster," Darlene hissed the S in spinster like a snake. She threw her head back and laughed.

"Being a wife isn't all that it's cracked up to be. Not ready to do that again."

"I second that." Darlene grinned. "Would you two like to become goddesses instead?"

"What?" Abby asked.

"I took a one-night class in Tribeca last week called 'Find Your Inner Goddess.' You are christened with a goddess name and everything."

"Why?" I asked.

"If you are a goddess, no one can mess with you. Unless you want them to." Darlene sipped her favorite, a glass of red Merlot. "For power, ladies. They tried to stick me with Athena, but I googled her. She was a virgin. As we all know, that would never work for me. So I need to go again. Come with me."

Darlene always came up with amusing things to do. "Cool. I'm in. Are you, Abby?"

"Why not?" Abby smirked.

"Are you still doing online dating?" I asked Darlene.

Darlene shook her head. "Not anymore. I'm in a swipe-free zone. Got a man in my life now. Did you girls start?"

Abby and I shook our heads. We were too chicken and old school.

Abby said, "I got some bad news about my neighbor Nathan today. His sister told me opioids were found in his system. Before he climbed into his bathtub and cut his wrists, he emailed her. Confessed that he couldn't continue anymore and closed out with a final sayonara. He loved all things Japanese."

The three of us were silent, contemplating such a sad ending. Darlene and I murmured words of shared sadness. The idea of being in such despair to end your life was devastating.

I wanted to share some good news and brag about helping to bring down a powerful narcotics trafficker. Except alluding to it would bring up questions I couldn't answer. Our waiter delivered our after-dinner drinks, and we sipped our amaretto coffees, still crestfallen.

"Kat, did you bring those photographs from your cruise?" Abby said.

"Yeah, do you still want to see them?" I feared their reaction might be like my parents and had kept them inside my bag. This time there would be no mention of any time travel. I rewrote that part of my history, and it was now etched on my brain. The voyage was all just a make-believe 1860 reenactment.

"Of course. Love to," Abby said.

Reluctantly, I put the worn envelope on the table. "These old-timey photographs are called daguerreotypes. We wore period clothes from 1860, part of the reenactment."

"Cool. Let's see them," Darlene said.

I pulled out the photo of me with the captain, passengers, and some of the crew and passed it around.

"Wow!" Abby said.

Darlene echoed Abby. "You really pulled this off. Crazy outfits and everything."

I nodded and pointed myself out, but that was unnecessary. The only other woman, Rosie, had dark hair.

"Too bad you couldn't use a regular camera or phone for better color photos," Abby said.

"Who are all these people?" Darlene asked.

I explained a bit about each person. The vivid memory of

life on the ship and seeing the gang every day returned.

"So, who were you together with?" As usual, Darlene dived into sex and romantic liaisons.

I indicated the captain. "And then ... well, with him. But very briefly." I reluctantly gestured to another man. "It got overly complicated."

"On a small ship? I'd say." Darlene scrutinized the photo. "What happened with the captain?"

"He had another girlfriend. A long-term relationship."

"Just like they say, a woman in every port," Darlene said.

Abby snatched the photo from Darlene to ogle them.

"A real love boat on the high seas. Love to hear more." Darlene scanned her phone and handed us a wad of cash for the bill. "Next time we hang out together. I'm meeting my man at a pop-up fashion show in the Village. I better scoot."

Abby flagged the waiter down to order a cognac and our bill. "After that revelation, I need something stronger."

Abby stared into space while she finished sipping her cognac. Now I regretted over-sharing. We left the restaurant and walked two blocks back to our apartment building in silence.

While we waited for the elevator, she spoke again. "I wish I could help you."

"With what?"

"To do the right thing,"

"What the hell is the right thing? Are you referring to Charlie again?"

"You need to give him a chance," Abby said.

"He isn't that great. You've been brainwashed."

"I hate all those people on that ship and especially the captain. He cut you off from everyone for months. They changed you." Her angry voice faded to despair.

"They didn't mean to. It wasn't their fault."

"Yeah, well, they were third-rate travel buddies. If you were the poster child for post-vacation bliss, no one would ever go anywhere."

As soon as the elevator doors opened, I said good night and retreated to my apartment. Our night out was supposed to be enjoyable and not end with an argument.

"I'm sorry, Kat. But it's true. Wait a sec. I have something for you."

~ ~ ~

Alone inside my apartment, I rotated the box in my hands, wondering what was inside. I sat at a kitchen barstool under the watchful eyes of Giuseppe. His life was so much less complicated.

Abby had declined to say who it was from, but it must be Charlie. Finally, curiosity got the better of me, and I ripped the ribbon and paper off the box. A gold and silver Apple wristwatch from an upscale jewelry store was inside. I emptied the contents, searching for a message, but it was either not included or lost.

Charlie had asked me about my missing watch, which needed batteries or maybe repairs. I wanted to save some money first. This watch was too extravagant, even if Charlie owed me big time.

A gadget like this required programming and could track my movements and might break Jackson's off-the-grid rules. My smartphone, even with the settings dumbed down by Jackson, worked just fine.

The message light blinked on my home phone, illuminating Giuseppe's right side and annoying both of us. I pushed play, figuring Charlie called about the watch, but an unexpected gruff voice made my heart pound.

"Kat, this is Captain Willem. I need the information. Now more than ever. Call me, or I'll be forced to drive down to see you." He rattled off a couple of phone numbers.

My shoes felt as if they were filled with lead weights, and I couldn't move. Even if I wanted to, I couldn't help the captain. Telling him anything was too risky. I recalled my carefully laid plans for the future. The time glitch was a make-believe game sworn never to be repeated or mentioned.

The second message was from Charlie. He asked me to call him and hoped I liked the gift.

The third was a repeat from Captain Willem. But this time, it was more ominous, with an edge to his voice and a clear threat with plans to go public.

How would he go public? Stand around in a public place like Central Park and make a speech? They do that at Speakers' Corner in London's Hyde Park but not here.

But what if he went to the police? I bit my lip, envisioning the worst. Jackson would go nuts at any unwanted publicity. I would lose my job and possibly my apartment. Giuseppe gazed in my direction, with his unfocused eyes appearing more upset than usual.

Prodded into action, I called him and left a voicemail. "Captain Willem, I would like to help you. But I have no clue what you are talking about. It's impossible to plan a trip back in time. Anyone in their right mind will tell you that. Sorry."

The phone rang as soon as I hung up. I answered on the first ring, intent on confronting the idiot blackmailer.

"Did you like the gift?" Charlie asked.

"The Apple watch is too much. I'm giving it to Abby."

"Please don't. Accept it as my apology."

"I can't."

"Never?"

In silence, I counted down the seconds until I could politely say goodbye and hang up.

"Will you listen to this song? Please, Kat," Charlie asked.

This was probably our last call, so I agreed and put the phone on speaker. I would miss his choice of music. The old Genesis number "Misunderstanding" sung by Charlie instead of Phil Collins played while I emptied the dishwasher.

When it ended, Charlie said, "We can straighten things out. I'm positive we can."

Lacking the energy to argue, I said, "Goodnight, Charlie," and hung up. A better song would have been Linda Ronstadt's "You're No Good."

I hoped an over-the-counter sleeping pill would silence the memory of the unrelenting yacht captain who had so rudely interrupted my life. Surely, when Captain Willem got my message, he'd realize his scheme would never work.

I drifted off, determined to get a good night's sleep, to survive tomorrow's intense round of self-defense training.

Chapter 25 ~ An Angel Investment

Wednesday was hump day, and like a camel's hump, it's stuck in the middle of the week. Even though this was only a four-day workweek, I wanted to celebrate. At day's end, I'd be halfway through my second week with Melville Consulting.

Jackson called a meeting inside the kitchen, multitasking as our conference room. He acted unusually upbeat, so I was suspicious.

The four of us sat around the table drinking coffee from Starbucks. We were dressed like college kids in jeans or sweats. If anyone looked at our faces closely, the wrinkles and lines courtesy of Father Time showed. Even with Anita's precise makeup, she couldn't hide them all.

Shantelle, prepared to cross *t*'s and dot *i*'s or write a brief, had a yellow legal pad ready. I brought a single sheet of paper folded pocket size, and Anita tapped encrypted notes into her smartphone.

Jackson said, "First off, things are going super. We all have projects in play, and Kat has a new client lined up. I'm beyond thrilled."

I smiled at the compliments but was eager to return to work.

Jackson wasn't in his usual rush, though. "This is a stellar team, covering all the bases. To get past legal mumbo jumbo, ask Shantelle. Police detective work, go to Anita. If it's numbers and forensic CPA analysis paralysis issues, call Kat."

Anita said, "And what is it you do, boss man?"

His eyes narrowed, but he laughed. "Someone has to run this group. Keep you in line. Like that TV show and movie *Charlie's Angels.* Except this operation is called Jackson's Angels."

"You must be kidding," I blurted out in surprise.

Anita acted annoyed while Shantelle narrowed her eyes as if scrutinizing fine print.

We were not actors in an imaginary P.I. crime game. It

took us years of study and on-the-job training to build our expertise.

Shantelle shook her head, looking disappointed. "Slippery slope, Jackson."

"All right, I apologize. You know what I mean. We all get along. None of us are dickheads. So why not revel in it for a few minutes?"

"Right. Anything else?" Anita asked.

"Can't I boast about us for a moment? We have all the skill sets necessary to take on any paying job that gets thrown at us."

In my humble, professional internal auditor's opinion, he was overestimating the range of our capabilities. However, I didn't want to be called a downer, or in my view, merely being realistic.

One thing was sure about Jackson. He must deliver excellent results since he had no trouble attracting clients willing to pay his high rates. I was terrible at the financial negotiation side, the main reason my small audit consulting business had folded.

"I called you here to announce something important. I want to share the company's wealth starting January first, based on future earnings. Kat, you have brokerage licenses besides a CPA. Can you investigate our options for opening a profit-sharing account? A 401(k) or whatever makes sense for a small four-person company."

Anita's slammed her hand on the table unexpectedly. "Extra money? I'll make the perfect angel, Charlie. I mean, Jackson."

We all chuckled.

"Sure, Jackson, Happy to do some research. My brokerage licenses are inactive since I'm no longer employed by a registered company. But I don't need them to do this. I'll report back soon."

Jackson grinned. "Shantelle, once we get some options, help Kat with the legal side."

Shantelle agreed, welcoming the added perk.

Employee retirement accounts usually had mandatory

periods for vesting, so it took time to cash out. If I didn't stay at least a year, I would receive nothing. But it was generous of Jackson to voluntarily do this.

Anita said, "One more thing. I don't like the new codename. Can't ever remember it."

"*Pequod i*ssues?" Jackson said. "All right. Starbucks without the final 's.' Easier?"

"Finally, something I can order without having to wail about it. Whale and wail, got it?" Anita made a karate chop motion followed by a mock bow.

"Kat, who or what is a Starbuck?" Shantelle asked.

"Starbuck was the second mate, right?" I asked Jackson.

He nodded. "How's it coming with the reading assignment?" Unfortunately, he recalled his bonehead mandate to read *Moby-Dick*, a book twice the length of the average novel.

Shantelle, Anita, and I looked at each other briefly. None of us could check that box off our to-do list.

I took a gentle stab at diplomacy. "We've been busy lately. On the list."

"Yeah, but at the bottom of the ocean too," Shantelle said.

Anita frowned, not bothering with an excuse.

Jackson stood in the doorway. "Your loss. None of you will learn how to dismember a whale."

We didn't hesitate to give Jackson our assessment of that task, yelling "gross, disgusting, and sick." Anita threw her plastic coffee lid at him, and we followed her lead, bombarding him.

He doubled over in laughter, raised his hands in surrender, and retreated to the safety of his office.

~ ~ ~

Shantelle and I met inside the conference room to eat our takeout lunches together, and we turned on the radio. Customarily, I worked through lunch and ate behind my computer. But today, I was in that rare situation when I was caught up.

I needed to deposit my much-needed paycheck at the bank, but I had pulled it out last night to admire it and left it at home. At least, it should be safe for a day on the kitchen counter under Giuseppe's watchful eye.

I had gathered information on retirement-plan options for Jackson. My flights to Denmark were booked and confirmed with my client Inge. I even downloaded information on hotels and restaurants in Copenhagen and Zurich.

I offered to help Shantelle and Anita with their projects, but they declined. Shantelle expected some legal documents soon, and Anita was also stuck in temporary project limbo.

Shantelle and I discussed the joys and some of the headaches of traveling. Despite not being home long, I welcomed some added distance from Captain Willem and Charlie.

Shantelle liked traveling and explained how we would be paired up for client projects. Job assignments for Anita and Jackson were more in the crime realm, usually within commuting distance of the city.

After a quick lunch, I flipped through Shantelle's magazine about the paranormal. She offered to do a tarot card reading, and I wavered for a moment but agreed. If the results were negative, I didn't have to believe them.

Shantelle reappeared like magic with a set of tarot cards and cleared the table.

Anita sat down to observe.

"Been doing this for a while?" I asked Shantelle.

"I'm not a psychic. This is just a hobby." She nodded to the magazine about the occult in front of me.

"I can loan you some back issues." She shuffled an oversized deck of cards and had me cut it several times.

"Learn my fate from a magazine? What's next?" Curiosity got the better of me, and I encouraged her to continue. "I didn't think lawyers believed in the supernatural."

Anita said, "It's no joke! Psychics are incredible. So many cases were dead. They find clues but don't get the credit that is their due. Jackson should use them more."

"Yeah, we should. The law is filled with gray areas, just like in the real world." A phone call interrupted her, but

Shantelle promised to return soon.

"How are Frankie and César doing?" I asked Anita now that we were alone. Since I was boyfriend-free, I mainly wanted to hear more about Frankie, the cute dancing Italian, but didn't want to let on.

"They're great. César's a workaholic. Frankie's on vacation and went to Disney."

"In Florida?"

"Sure thing. Frankie's a Magic Kingdom addict. Drags his wife and kids there every chance he gets."

"I thought he was single."

"Nah, he only acts like it. A real lover boy."

My idea of dating Frankie, the Italian stallion, went poof. All for the best, considering that a relationship with a guy working for the NYPD would be stressful.

"He might bring you something. Wait a sec, and I'll show you." Anita returned with a small statue of a mermaid with voluptuous flaming red hair. She handed it to me.

"Nice." I had seen it on her desk, but I hoped he didn't buy me one. I didn't want another dust-catching knickknack. My only exception was for Giuseppe, and he had a purpose and a job to do.

Anita said, "Frankie spends way too much money. It's valuable, so I keep it here. My neighbor's kids have sticky fingers."

Shantelle returned and shuffled the deck, turning over seven cards. Anita peered over my shoulder to see better.

"Those are lucky. Aren't they, Shantelle?" Anita said.

"Some are but others … well, it depends."

"What do they mean? Will I make it home tonight? Is El Rey still locked up?" I giggled, but Anita smacked me on the shoulder.

"What?" I asked Anita while rubbing my shoulder.

"Narco-traffickers are no joke. But, yes, our drug king is still locked up. Verified this morning."

Shantelle decoded the meaning behind the seven cards one by one. Three were fine, but four contained vague warnings that something terrible might happen when I least expected it.

When she was done, I thanked her for the tarot reading. But this new insight didn't change anything. After all, I couldn't stay home and hide under the bed.

Jackson waltzed in. "Pack up. Let's go, guys. Gym time."

I shut down my laptop and placed it inside the vault. "I forgot my gym clothes. Are jeans okay?" The sleeping pill had made me groggy this morning.

"Even better. Do you think perps care what you are wearing?" In a high-pitched female voice, Jackson asked with a chuckle, "Excuse me, can I change before you rob me?"

When I said *adios* to Shantelle, she said, "Try to enjoy it."

~ ~ ~

In the subway car, the three of us separated and didn't sit together. This precaution struck me as extreme, but Jackson was always secretive.

I wondered if Jackson had a wife or kids like Frankie. I had never asked, and presumably, he wouldn't like it if I did.

A local gym advertisement inside the subway reminded me how a healthy body equals a healthy mind. Unfortunately, I lacked both, but I'd get there.

Natural stress relief, mother nature, and trips to the gym would cure me. But first, I must get through this. I gazed at my soft stomach and adjusted my tight jeans from digging into my waist.

Anita sat across from me. During lunch, she had boasted about how she loved Brazilian jiu-jitsu and dabbled in medieval German swordsmanship. Both qualified as hardcore martial arts I'd never considered attempting.

I regretted being out of shape and clung to the hope they would go easy on me. Hells bells, surely they wouldn't want to injure their newest member and sole number cruncher?

Chapter 26 ~ Willful Power

Three hours later and post-workout, every slight movement on the subway ride home made me ache. My back hurt so much I couldn't sit. So, instead, I stood in the aisle and grabbed the metal bar for balance.

The word "again" repeated so many times by Jackson still echoed in my head. Grateful for a short two-block walk home from my closest station, I hobbled along while planning a muscle-relaxing soak in my bathtub.

Anita was a powerhouse fiend and tougher than Jackson. She flipped me so hard I temporarily saw stars and gasped for breath.

Outside my apartment building, I fumbled inside my shoulder bag for my keys. Unexpectedly, a hand landed on my shoulder, and a man said my name. Thinking it was a friend and too tired to do anything else, I forgot today's hard-earned training and turned around.

Captain Willem glared at me.

"What are you doing here?" I stepped back, but he seized my arm. I twisted desperately to use an escape move drilled into my head just an hour ago. But being over-exhausted, the training techniques and an opportune adrenaline rush were missing in action.

The captain was fast and muscular. He tightened his grip on my arm and pulled me away from my building. Fearing he might throw me inside his car, I dug in my heels while my legs screamed silently in agony.

"I got your worthless message. We need to talk. Now!"

I repeated my go-to response. "We did a reenactment of 1862 on that ship. It was all make-believe."

His angry red face was unavoidable and within inches of mine. "Let's resolve this."

"All right. There's a coffee shop one block up on Columbus."

We walked side by side with my arm in a vice. Outside the coffee shop, Captain Willem shook his head and pointed at the bar next door.

At a small table inside, I ordered a club soda, and he had a beer. I scanned the bar but didn't recognize anyone I knew who could help me. After a few deep breaths, I calmed down. A short, civilized discussion would end this.

Wrinkles crisscrossed his face, and his eyes darted around, making him appear deranged. "If you don't help me, I'll go see the newspapers."

"Like anyone would believe you. That woman would be 200 years old. Completely impossible and crazy. They will lock you up."

"Not me. You! Do you want to take a chance?"

"I already gave you the name of the travel agency that booked my cruise. That's all I have."

"They went out of business."

"So, you think I know how to book cruises on ships one hundred years ago?" I shook my head. Even if I could, I wouldn't.

He nodded, still convinced we could do it.

"Please, Captain Willem. Let's be logical. If people could go back in time, why would they go back for a vacation? Instead, they'd try to save someone's life. Prevent a shooting or a car accident. Stop a tragic death for a loved one. And if they could change the past, what would happen?"

He sipped his beer. "I never considered that aspect."

"Well, you should. It can't happen anyway. It's all just a weird coincidence that the woman in your ancestor's letter has a name similar to mine. Jensen is very common Danish surname."

"I don't believe you. No way am I giving up."

"But why?" I moaned despite sounding weak.

The captain sat back in his chair as though deflated. "I need money. You must have plenty to afford this fancy neighborhood."

"Money? What money? I'm broke. I took a year off from work after closing a failing business. I started a new job. This is only my second week. I'm an independent contractor like you without a fixed salary."

"You expect me to believe that with your rich friends? You silly bitch!" He stood anxious to leave. "Let's go."

On our way out of the bar, I figured our meeting was over. I would limp home alone.

But he grasped my arm again and paused for me to open the door to exit the bar. "I want to see for myself. I'm sure there's something upstairs to make up for my trouble. It's your fault that I lost my job."

"Mine? I had nothing to do with that. I wasn't even there."

"That fool Jason almost fell overboard. While I was trying to rescue him, we went aground. You poisoned their minds with worries about my seamanship like a witch. That's what you are."

I shook my head, not wanting to listen to his crazed accusations. If I hadn't been so exhausted, I might have twisted out of his grip and run away.

Captain Willem remembered where I lived and guided me back. We stopped in front of my building. He held my arm tighter, cutting off the circulation.

His chest pushed against my back, eager for me to open the door. I reached inside my purse for my keys. But I stopped when red danger signs flashed in my mind.

"Don't tell me you forgot your damn keys." His poisonous breath was hot against my ear.

My paycheck and Charlie's expensive watch were both out in the open on my kitchen counter. If he was this desperate, he'd steal them. Who knows what else he might try to do inside my apartment with only Giuseppe watching?

I searched around for someone I knew, or anyone, even a stranger, for help. But it was late, and no one was nearby. Captain Willem reached for my handbag, so I pulled out my key ring and dropped it to cause a delay.

I fumbled through the keys, intentionally trying the wrong ones. He was impatient and reached for them, so my stalling tactics would end.

"Kat, is that you?" Scott, a casual acquaintance who lived in my building, appeared.

Captain Willem tightened his grip.

Scott must have noticed my panicked expression. "Everything all right?"

"No, this man is bothering me. Call the police. Now."

Scott pulled his phone out of his pocket and started to dial 9-1-1.

Captain Willem let go of my arm. "You'll regret this, Kat."

I almost collapsed, but adrenaline and Scott kept me on my feet. We watched the captain stomp off from our building.

Scott said, "Shall I still call the police?"

"No, but I appreciate your help, Scott. Unfortunately, I know that annoying, rude man. He drank too much and gets like that."

"No problem. We're glad you're back in New York."

"Me too." A safe, modern building filled with friends was so worth it.

In the lobby, Scott said, "Abby told me about your around the world adventure. Did you meet him then?"

I could honestly say no, and begged off more questions, complaining about sheer exhaustion.

Scott, a tech employee at Google, was a complete gentleman. Although he lived on the second floor, and we didn't know each other very well, Scott escorted me to my apartment on the fourth floor.

Inside my locked apartment and out of harm's way, I greeted Giuseppe with a friendly head pat. My first paycheck in a year and the Apple watch were still on the kitchen counter where I'd left them. I tossed them into my handbag. Tomorrow I would give the fancy wristwatch to Abby and feed the check to my starving bank account.

My heartbeat returned to normal, and my stomach growled. Lunch was almost twelve hours ago, but I had no energy to cook. Buzzing inside a deliveryman or going down to meet him was too risky. I drank a beer while the microwave zapped a potato.

My home phone message light blinked, so I listened to another sad message from Charlie. He begged me to reconsider our Thanksgiving trip and accompany him merely as his friend. Needing a break, I ignored his requests to call him back.

I ate my baked potato, loaded with sour cream and salsa, while watching TV for some much-needed distraction. I was still keyed up, and my body ached even while brushing my teeth.

The tempting healing power of water won me over. After the bathtub was filled with lavender-scented bubbles, I soaked and brainstormed options to deal with Captain Willem. Jackson would go ballistic if this came out publicly.

If the captain went to the papers, they would think he was nuts and refuse to report it. But he could post idiotic stories online about me. A few might be popular, and their existence might pop up in online searches with my name. Any of these scenarios were terrible for my business prospects and Jackson's.

But who would believe me? Only one person came to mind who could help me. With a new game plan set for tomorrow morning, I sunk cautiously under the pinkish-white bubbles and apologized to my aging body for another brutal day.

Chapter 27 ~ The King is Loose

After a brief stop to deposit my paycheck, I arrived at the office faster than I expected. As planned, Jackson was the only one there. He buzzed me inside, looked surprised, and hurried back to his office.

After settling in, I knocked on his office door, ready to confess all about Captain Willem. Before Jackson shut his office door, I got a glimpse of the back of a brown-haired woman who must be a client. This was unusual since I'd never seen a client at our office.

Forced to wait around, I left the office to buy a sugary breakfast treat. Ten minutes later, I returned and walked down the hallway armed only with coffee and a donut. The mysterious woman who'd met with Jackson headed towards me on her way out.

"Heather? What are you doing here?" I barely recognized her. She wore old jeans and a baggy flannel shirt with her long brown hair jammed into a NY Mets baseball cap.

Heather looked around like she wanted to hide. Her face was clean of the heavy makeup she wore on the yacht. But her complexion still glistened with flawless ivory skin.

"Good morning." She stared at the floor, refusing to make eye contact. "Nice seeing you, Kat."

"Day off?" I couldn't imagine an advertising agency with such a casual dress code.

"Sort of. Sorry, I have to run."

Heather hurried to the stairwell, and I contemplated running after her. She'd acted nervous like a cornered animal. Perhaps she was in serious trouble and had hired Jackson. Or could her visit here be related to Captain Willem and his blackmail? Had he sent her to bully or charm Jackson?

After only a week, I was unfamiliar with the range of work that Jackson pursued and what he expected us to do. He often repeated how we were on a "need-to-know-only basis." Extracting details about him or his past client work was as easy as herding cats. But Heather's unexpected visit bothered me, so I had to know.

As soon as Jackson hung up the phone, I confronted him. "What was Heather doing here?"

"Who?"

"The woman you met with this morning. I just saw her leave."

"Hadley?"

"No, her name is Heather. She was on the yacht with me and Charlie this weekend." But then I remembered how her voice had changed when I overheard her on the phone. Even her tattoo looked fake. Heather must have been a phony name, but why?

Jackson turned away to dismiss me and stared at his computer.

"Why was Hadley here? Whoever she is."

He shook his head.

I put my coffee and donut bag on his desk and slumped down in the chair across from him. I pulled out the glazed chocolate donut and took a bite. "I'm not leaving until you tell me what's going on."

I licked sugary goo off my fingers, wishing I had picked up a napkin. But if I left to get one from the kitchen, Jackson might lock the door to his office and end our conversation.

Jackson frowned but stayed silent.

"Does this relate to any blackmail?" I asked, savoring the chocolate donut.

This piqued Jackson's interest. "Blackmail? No, it's a separate matter. She wanted some advice."

"About what?"

"None of your concern."

"Damn it, Jackson. This is serious. I'm being blackmailed, and she knows the guy. Heather-Hadley acted weird when she passed me in the hallway. If she is involved in this mess, I deserve to know."

I balled up my empty donut bag and threw it at him, but he ducked. Now I had his attention, and his laser-sharp eyes bored holes into my face. "Who is blackmailing you?"

The sugar sent me some energy, and I stood. "Never mind.

I'll work it out. Alone. Two can play this game of secrets."

He shook his head and frowned. "Kat, it doesn't work that way here. Sit down. You're part of my team. Tell me."

I sat back down, knowing I had some leverage. "Only if you tell me why Heather was here."

He narrowed his eyes. "Briefly. Fess up about this blackmail first."

Clearing my throat, I confessed to Jackson about Captain Willem. How I had met him on the yacht, his threatening phone calls, and intensified stalking. And how my attempt to talk some sense into him had failed miserably.

"What does he want?" Jackson asked.

His office door was wide open. Shantelle sat nearby and could listen in if she wanted to. I debated whether I should tell him in front of the others.

"He wants… He wants me to." My voice got scratchy, and I coughed. "Excuse me for a moment." Even though it was only 10 a.m., I went to the kitchen and took a can of Diet Coke from the refrigerator for extra caffeine.

Jackson followed me and shut the door to the kitchen and our conference room. He sat behind the table and encouraged me to sit and relax, but I couldn't.

I leaned against the kitchen counter and stared down at the gurgling can containing secret ingredients that supposedly originated in 1885 with coca leaves. When I was ready, I sat in the chair facing him.

Jackson listened intently while I explained about Captain Willem's ancestor. How he was a highly decorated captain in the Dutch navy based in the former Dutch East Indies. And how his old diary mentioned someone like me. And now he had a bonkers scheme to make money. "If I don't help him, he said he will go to the newspapers or the cops."

"But how would he make money?"

"By selling tickets to go on voyages. Not on your typical cruise but on extraordinary journeys back in time."

Jackson wrung his hands in an unusual display of what might be nerves. "Gotcha. I'll repeat this once. Then we won't speak of it again."

I clenched my fists under the table, preparing for the worst.

"He believes you time-traveled to the time of his ancestor and can help him repeat it. Wants to charge people an outrageous sum to do this and pocket it."

"Yep. I know it's crazy."

"Not that crazy. No wonder I couldn't find you."

"Sorry, Jackson. I'm not going into it. The travel agency went out of business, and their computer was deprogrammed."

"To stop this insanity, I'll need to talk to him. Give me his number and what you have on that travel agency. No sweat. I'll take care of it."

"Thanks, Jackson. You're a lifesaver." But the captain could try to convince him, and something might go wrong. "Promise me you won't help him. This whole reenactment idea, if it could happen, which it can't, is too dangerous."

"No argument here. I can't lose my A-number-one number sleuth. Putting your name in the papers, even if it's just the local NY rags, wouldn't be good for business. The cops would laugh him out of their office. Even if it were possible, they need a real crime."

An imaginary heavy weight fell from my shoulders, and I breathed easier. Jackson would fix this. Surprisingly, he didn't get angry or question my sanity. If Jackson could pull me out of this mess, I would work for him as long as he'd have me.

"Tell me about Hadley. She used Heather as a fake name for some reason."

"She joined us briefly. It didn't work out." He shuffled some papers around.

"Why not?"

"She didn't get on with the ladies."

Like most women, Shantelle and Anita didn't like her, but I had to know more. "And why was that? Come on. Jackson. We made a deal."

"Trust fund baby. Beautiful. Snobby. You know the type."

"Really? She claimed she was an admin assistant at an

advertising agency and came across as an insecure airhead."

He threw his head back and laughed. "She's anything but. That's an act. Like the bumbling Lieutenant Columbo in that old murder mystery TV show. It often comes in handy."

I sat transfixed while he brought me up to date on her undercover investigation into Wall Street insider trading. All her coyness and questions were to gather intel, and I had downright missed it. I swore to up my game and evade being trapped with the title, "worst operative ever."

~ ~ ~

During my lunch break, I called Desi and returned her frantic voicemail to get in touch. "Kat, we were burglarized last night. You were so right about the house next door."

"What? Are you okay?"

"We're fine. Last night Steve had a company dinner, and we were at a kid's birthday party. Thankfully, no one was home. We lost some art, and they tried to pry open the wall safe. Somehow, they must have seen me open it or knew about it. The only complete casualty was the hideous painting hiding it." She chuckled, not sorry about its demise.

"At least you're okay. Things can be replaced."

"They caught the culprits, and everything's in custody. Steve said he owes you a huge apology."

"Who did this?"

"A couple of local drug-addicted teenagers broke into the neighbor's house. Stashed their stolen loot upstairs and inside the garage. When the police came, they were loading up their dad's Range Rover and got arrested. No one was hurt."

"Wow. That's lucky. How's Goldie?"

"The vet said she's fine. She's still nervous, so I took her with us last night. The birthday boy got so attached to Goldie, he threw a fit when we left. But there's an upside. His parents are going to adopt a rescue dog. So, another pup gets a good home."

"Are you still going to the benefit tonight?" If she wasn't, that would be the ideal excuse to cancel.

"Yes, the show goes on. The babysitter will be here and is spending the night. I'm counting on seeing you this evening."

"I'll try."

"Please, Kat. I need you there. You'll enjoy it. Promise. I'll be at the Waldorf early and will send my car over for you."

After I hung up, I smiled. Quite possibly, I wasn't the worst sleuth after all.

~ ~ ~

That afternoon, Shantelle reminded me to plug my hotel information into their online database.

"I already did. But I'm not staying at a hotel. Inge suggested staying with her."

Jackson frowned. "What the hell? You can't stay with a client."

I shrunk down in my seat. "Why not? She has empty guest bedrooms in her house, and it's an upscale part of Copenhagen. I figured it would be easier and faster."

Shantelle said, "What if something happens or it's unsafe?"

"In Denmark? With a rich old lady?" Why were they worrying so much about nothing?

Jackson said, "Even if you know her, you can't get chummy like that. This is a business. Not an opportunity to sing kumbaya around a campfire."

"Fine. I'll tell her in person when I arrive."

Jackson shook his finger, warning me. "Put grandma's address in the system. If you disappear and we have to find you, at least we'll a starting point."

"Already in there." I followed the rules they bothered to tell me about.

"And if you so much as smell burnt toast, move your ass to quality hotel. Not some sort of hostel with shared bathrooms." Jackson grumbled about people who saved money to spend it on crap.

I ignored him to read a friendly text from Zhila. She invited me to a casual get-together at her place on Saturday night.

I texted back that I couldn't. However, if Zhila and the skunk were available, I could use a lift to JFK airport on

Friday. To circumvent being stuck in Jackson's cheapskate category, I insisted she bill me the undiscounted full fare.

A few minutes later, Zhila's messaged back a confirmation with a smiley face emoticon.

~ ~ ~

Jackson was on the phone and slammed his hand on his desk. "Shit!" He went through a long line of swear words. Some were in a foreign language, presumably Cantonese.

Anita and I hurried into his office to see what had happened, but he was still on the phone.

Shantelle stood behind us and dropped her briefcase in alarm. "I heard Jackson from all the way down the hall."

Jackson switched off his mobile phone and raised it above his head like a baseball, ready to throw it against the wall.

"El Rey got released an hour ago. Made the sky-high bail somehow. His accounts we IDed are still shut down, but he's getting money somewhere."

In frustration, we echoed his anger by cussing.

"Can't they just deport him?" I wanted him to disappear and be someone else's problem somewhere far away.

"He's Puerto Rican." Anita frowned and grunted in frustration.

"So what? He gets to live on a beautiful island."

"Where were you in history class?" Jackson asked, clearly frustrated. "Puerto Rico is one of our territories, and Puerto Ricans became citizens a hundred years ago."

"But still, Puerto Rico's not a state. Can't we send him back?" I implored Shantelle to think of something allowed legally.

Shantelle shook her head. "He's legally entitled to stay here. He could be extradited to another state or location within the U.S. to stand trial, but not deported."

A new Plan B immediately came to mind. "Will we get some more funds transfer and account data to sort through?" I could go through the Excel spreadsheets and accounts again, but I had already combed them so thoroughly.

"Our client is sending over more bank info tomorrow. We could use your help with that, Kat. But your flight ..." Jackson rubbed his hand through his hair in annoyance.

"Not until the evening. I can put in half a day."

"Great. Since El Rey is on the loose, stay home with the doors locked or be with others. He's likely hiding at one of his estates, but who the hell knows."

Anita and Shantelle looked unnerved, but all along, I had expected a snafu. Things never went as planned. Not in my professional experience anyway.

"That secretive client sure must be close to him. How does he or she get access to all this stuff?" I was dying to get the scoop.

"The how and the who is something none of you will ever know." Jackson pursed his lips and looked away. "I like my clients alive and healthy to pay our bills."

If our client was in danger, we must be in worse trouble. "Jackson, I was going to help out a friend this evening. She is running a high-priced charity event at the Waldorf. But if you want, I can skip it."

"That should be okay. Stay around people, but only ones you know. Don't roam the streets solo or take unnecessary chances. The Upper West Side, filled with expensive real estate, may lure you into believing it's secure. But it never is. Not fully."

I dragged out the all-too-familiar-computer spreadsheets and financial printouts. Spreading them across the large table inside the conference room, I searched for a missed clue. They had been scrutinized so many times, my eyes glazed over into a blur.

Shantelle walked in and looked over my shoulder. She inspected my messy color-coded lines and symbols that traced activity among the accounts.

"This is so dang frustrating." I twisted my hair into a knot in utter frustration.

"Try the Mozart effect," Shantelle said.

"What? The famous composer?"

She returned with her iPod, connected it to a wireless speaker, and played some classical music. "Mozart is proven to reduce stress and help creativity."

"Really?" This was a fascinating theory.

"Oh, yes. Doctors say it makes your brain smarter. Only briefly, though. While you are listening and for another fifteen minutes. Mozart's music reduces anxiety and boosts your immune system."

"Perfect. Mozart and his magic flute can unravel this mess." I welcomed the music, even if it didn't help. At home and when I had a private office, I usually had the radio on. But here, without much privacy, I hadn't bothered.

I circled and mapped some numbers that went nowhere, tore up the spreadsheets, and reprinted them. With new sheets spread out on the table, my colored pencils made heavy marks as I pressed hard for answers. "Come on, Wolfie. Help me out here."

"Who are you talking to?" Jackson had slid up behind me and reached into the fridge for a drink.

"I'm … no one." After this morning's time travel confession, if I told him I had asked Mozart for help, he'd be convinced I was cuckoo.

The next concerto started, and Jackson popped the tab on his Coke can. He cocked his head to listen. "Wolfie as in Wolfgang Amadeus Mozart?"

"Yeah, I'm asking a genius beyond the grave for help. But don't panic. I'm not expecting an answer."

"Did Shantelle put you up to this? Scientifically, it's not true. Any kind of music, even heavy metal from Metallica, helps. Listening to a good story or a walk outside can also do the trick."

I frowned, unsure who to believe, preferring the Mozart version.

Jackson laughed. "Whatever floats your boat, or should I say ship? *The Marriage of Figaro* is the only opera I've ever truly enjoyed."

He turned to leave but stopped. "Go home. Enjoy your fancy gala tonight. Tomorrow we will get new data to work through. Might make more sense."

"I suppose you're right. I don't want to let you down."

"Me? Us? No way. I was unsure how this would pan out.

So far, it's exceeded my expectations. You've worked for large multinational firms. This is about as different as it gets."

"But I had a small consulting firm with just one assistant."

"What, for a year or two?"

"Yeah."

He shrugged. My seven hundred days of struggling amounted to next to nothing. "Start fresh tomorrow. That's an order. I'm off to meet your friend in Warren, Rhode Island tonight."

"To see Captain Willem? But I don't know his address." Jackson might not find him after a long three-hour drive.

"Do I look like someone who needs that?"

"I suppose not. Best of luck, Jackson."

"Sheesh. This is nothing."

Somehow, I believed him. He didn't need addresses or luck. Jackson was trained to do this with his eyes closed or even blindfolded.

Chapter 28 ~ Dining with the Upper Crust

After a quick shower to rinse off the day's dirty news about El Rey, my mermaid costume refused to cooperate. A sign I couldn't ignore. I lacked the energy to fight with the gown or stand around all night at a ritzy gala.

My cell phone rang, and without hesitation, I answered Desi's call. Hopefully, the whole thing was called off.

"Please, you can't cancel. My co-chair Jim, the guy you talked to the other day, is MIA. He was in Philadelphia for business and should be back by now." Desi's voice was pinched tightly from stress. "And worst of all, my assistant has the flu."

"But won't others help you? I've been to some charity events, but nothing this upscale."

"All the other people on the committee just sit around expecting me to do everything. That's why I enlisted Jim for help."

"What kind of help?" I couldn't be a cocktail waitress dressed like a fish.

"For some minor tasks. Like giving out the prizes from the silent auctions." After a pause, Desi said, "I need a friend too. Steve has to work late tonight and canceled."

Her voice was way off-pitch, and I couldn't bear to hear her cry. "Okay, Desi. I'll be there." I seized the fancy costume by the tail, determined to squeeze into it.

Desi insisted on sending her car over to pick me up. Additional security would make Jackson happy. El Rey didn't know my name, where I lived, or what I looked like. So, all in all, I had nothing whatsoever to worry about.

~ ~ ~

Inside the Waldorf Hotel's grand ballroom for the charity ball, I finally found Desi. She was all smiles and at ease, as if she did this every night.

Like a child, I toddled slowly in my restrictive outfit, greeted her, and offered my help.

She cocked her head as if unsure what I meant. "Nothing

yet. Later with the auction. Mingle and relax. You are sitting at a table with some eligible men. I just wish Jim would arrive."

We were interrupted, and she introduced me to a well-dressed couple who could be on the cover of the upscale *Town & Country* magazine. When they realized I was unconnected to anyone or anything meaningful and couldn't help or entertain them, they ignored me.

My go-to answer to "what do you do" was consulting at a small firm. I would stay vague like the others who didn't work for a big-name company or need to promote an under-the-radar employer for sales and marketing purposes. Besides, ultrawealthy clients were notoriously bad about paying bills.

With one of Desi's signature cocktails, appropriately named 'Rescue Me,' I located my assigned table to see who I'd be spending hours with this evening. I didn't recognize any of the names, which was both good and bad news. All must be animal lovers, so at least we had something positive in common.

A man with a British accent smiled. "Shall we mix things up some?" He appeared to be about seventy years old with gray hair and an alluring smile. His eyes lit up at the idea of being mischievous.

"What a fantastic idea."

He picked up a nameplate for Ian Harker's place setting and held it in front of me. "I am the real Ian Harker. Promise." He nodded, tipped an imaginary hat, and chuckled.

I giggled and pointed to the one with my name. Ian switched his nameplate with Guillermo Rodriguez, who was supposed to be seated next to me.

The room was filled with well-dressed and well-to-do attendees. To my relief, my mermaid dress didn't look out of place and was a fashion trend. At least four other women limped around in fishtails, but none of us wore the exact same one.

I braided and twirled my hair into a casual bun behind my neck. Instantly, my hair fell about and lazed on my shoulders in a relaxed messy style. I shrugged and gave up the battle.

Almost all the ladies had flawless salon-finished hair. They had the time and money for a full day of beauty treatments. While I struggled to win the never-ending game of "follow the money and close the loopholes."

"Now, with our seating managed, shall we stroll around the perimeter to see the goodies up for auction?" Ian's British accent was charming, and that was a great suggestion. To help Desi, I should get prepared.

Rows of tables, placed along the edge of the grand room, held the donated items to be auctioned and fund the animal rescue organization. Most were being sold via a silent auction.

Auctions for other items would be bid on live via texts from phones. Donated dinners from upscale restaurants with thousand-dollar minimums were part of the live auction.

Ian jotted down bids for an assortment of items. I wanted to follow his lead, but I would be committed to anteing up the cash if I won. Regardless, I jotted my name down to start the bidding on a handmade work of art. An adorably unique clay teapot in the shape of a cat with an open mouth for the spout was irresistible.

I bravely bid on a few other items. Being the first to bid at the suggested starting amount was safe. They would most likely be snatched up by someone else. Possibly for thousands of dollars above my low bid.

I patted the clay cat farewell. I looked forward to the day my bank account reached a comfort zone to support Desi's charity and animals in need.

~ ~ ~

When the room was packed, and most of us had made the rounds several times to bid, Desi announced that we should take our seats. Ian and I made our way to our table.

Desi stopped at each table to say hello to her guests and confirm that everyone was getting introduced. She introduced me to a dark-haired Spaniard named Guillermo, who went by G and had arrived late, and moved him back to the seat next to me. We shook hands, and I asked him why he didn't use his full name.

He winced. "Most American mangle Guillermo. They

can't roll their r's. Please just call me G."

I nodded, not wanting to mispronounce it.

G received extra attention from Desi, and she emphasized his status as "her dear friend." But she wasn't subtle. To Desi, G was prime boyfriend material which I needed since Jim was still a no-show.

She leaned down to me. "Kat, Charlie is on his way. My misguided husband suggested he take his place. Steve's trying to make amends, I guess. But I realize it's over between you two."

I swallowed hard to suppress the anxiety in my dry throat.

Desi patted my shoulder. "He has an invite, so I can't bar him. I can ask him to leave if you want me to."

"No, I'll manage. I'm bound to run into Charlie eventually."

"There's my unstoppable girlfriend. If you change your mind, just tell me." She grinned down at me with a man sitting on both sides. "Isn't Ian a sweetheart? And G is such a charmer. Like Ricky Martin's older brother."

Ian grimaced, but he seemed pleased.

G rolled his eyes, unamused. How could someone not want to be related to the adorable pop singer Ricky Martin?

A young woman assigned to sit near me sat across the table intently chatting with the man next to her. Ian and I had switched other place cards around the dining table for the hell of it and put them together. If they knew, they might invite us to what might soon be their wedding.

G was stern and preoccupied compared to Ian and Charlie, but he oozed charm in a raw, manly way. His accent added to his mystique. G explained that he was from Argentina, and we both agreed on the beauty of Buenos Aires. I raved about the wonderfully good air there and snickered, but G didn't acknowledge my silly pun.

Waiters arrived with bottles of wine and dinner, so the need to make polite conversation subsided. I turned down more alcohol, knowing the two Desi-designed cocktails had already put me over my limit.

But G insisted, motioning for the waiter to fill my wine

glass. Absentmindedly, I neglected to drink enough water and sipped more wine, triggering another refill.

G informed me about how delightful the Pampas region of Argentina is during the springtime in South America. When a photographer arrived on his rounds to take photos of all the guests seated around the table, G excused himself.

I wondered if I should too. An unknown like me wasn't likely to end up in a newspaper or online. But as a precaution, I took my place card off the table.

After the photographer snapped a photo of Ian and me, he gave us a slip of paper. "It will be loaded on this Facebook site in a few hours. You can tag yourself."

I shook my head. "Nope. Thank you, but I'm not on it."

G returned and stood between Ian and me, listening in.

Ian said, "Facebook is overrated. Are you on Instagram? Everyone and their mother are on that one."

"Not anymore. Complete detoxed off all social media," I said.

"That's severe. Afraid of those Russian hackers?" G asked.

"Nope. Drug traffickers." I laughed to make it a joke. All those drinks had jarred loose the NDA locks on my tongue, throwing confidentiality to the wind.

"Are drug dealers pursuing you?" Ian smirked, assuming this was unlikely.

I shook my head while I chewed at my lower lip, resolving to stay quiet about my job. In a way, I might be hunted. El Rey was still on the loose. He lurked in the five boroughs of New York, or in the vast Tri-State area, with way too many hiding places. And even if the authorities found him, they couldn't keep him.

Chapter 29 ~ Saving Animals One Dance at a Time

When dessert was served, Desi came by again, working the tables as our supreme hostess. She looked pleased, and the drinks had loosened her up. She had worked so hard planning this event, and I was thrilled about her success.

Desi kneeled between G and me. Her full skirt created a plush circle of fabric on the floor around her. She explained how Jim was still missing and not returning her calls or texts. This was so unlike him. Then she dropped a bombshell. "Charlie is at a table over there."

I nodded, not wanting to make eye contact. G likely overheard and was curious since he turned to see where Charlie sat.

Desi said, "The committee suggested including an optional dinner date to bump up the donations for the restaurant dinner. Three single guys and three single women might get a luxurious meal at an upscale restaurant. Completely optional for the winning bidder. Beats online mystery dating. Interested?"

"What do you mean?"

"When we do the live auction for the six donated dinners, each of you will stand. People will bid on the dinner with a date. If they want to take someone else, that is up to the winner. But if not, you get to accompany them and enjoy a free and delicious meal."

"Get to?" It sounded more like being forced. "Can't you find someone else?"

Desi shook her head. "The committee says this often generates thousands of additional dollars. Often the winners take someone else, so it's just some added entertainment tonight."

G covered my hand with his. "I would. Why not? A delicious night out."

I shook my hand free. "Let G do it."

"Sorry, G. Three men jumped at it. Only one female spot is left."

G put his hand on his heart, play-acting an injury. "I understand. No offense taken." His phone vibrated in his hand again, so he made his excuses and left.

"Remember, Kat. The extra money goes to help those homeless mistreated animals. Keeps them alive another day to find a forever home."

This was a minor inconvenience and an easy way for me to help them. "All right. I will, for the sake of the poor animals."

"Great. We'll do this soon. Then music and dancing. So, stick around, okay? The silent auction is going well, but we need more to cover the rent for this place. Always so many expenses to put these things on." She stood and shook out her long skirt.

"Wait, Desi. What does G do?" He didn't volunteer much information beyond some vague healthcare business investments. G never bothered to inquire about my profession, a standard topic in money-centered New York City. Perhaps he didn't care since he wasn't an American.

"Some type of philanthropy. G isn't on Wall Street like most of the people here. Independently wealthy from what I understand."

"Must be nice," I murmured as I glanced around the room. As Mark Twain once said, "Lack of money is the root of all evil." And I didn't like being full of envy.

~ ~ ~

Live bidding for the restaurant dinners was announced. All six potential dates, including me, stood by our dinner tables, but the crowd urged us to stand on the stage.

I tiptoed along, limited to a short four-inch stride, in my mermaid dress. I stumbled on the steps to the stage, but a kind woman, who had also volunteered, grabbed my arm to keep me balanced.

They alternated men, then women, and I was the fourth one up. Each restaurant's meal for two had a starting bid of one thousand dollars. So far, the final bids were respectable.

The bidders were crazy to pay so much for a meal out with a stranger. But as Desi had explained, "Cheap entertainment while supporting animal rescue."

"Good cause," played on auto-repeat inside my head, along with the hope Ian or G would win. Otherwise, this was another awkward blind date.

My bid began, and I waved at the crowd. Ian promptly placed the minimum bid.

The auctioneer encouraged more bidders, chided the audience, and egged them on. Another guy I had never met bid more. Ian attempted again with two thousand, and I gave him my best smile. Then G bid five. Another man offered eight, and G surpassed it with an obscene bid of ten thousand. This topped the other dinners' auctions. If he won, I would need to study up on Argentina to have entertaining topics to discuss.

"Going, going —"

In the last second, a man yelled, "Twenty thousand."

Everyone looked to see who was so drunk and unbalanced as to double the current offer. Charlie stood with a broad smile plastered across his face. He bowed and nodded a greeting to me.

The unstoppable auctioneer tried again for twenty-one, but the room was at long last silent.

"Sold to the gentlemen in the back for twenty thousand dollars."

After a few minutes, some positives surfaced from Charlie's winning bid. I was spared from G and researching Argentina. But I would have preferred dinner with a complete stranger.

After the six restaurant dinner dates had been auctioned, we climbed down from the stage, and Desi helped me down the steps. "Looks like Charlie wants you back."

"Yeah, well, it won't work. At least, the food should be delicious, and the money helps animals in need."

"Absolutely." She touched my arm as a thank you before getting interrupted.

I slinked back to my table. G and Ian welcomed me back and lamented their loss.

G got another phone call and left again, swearing this was

the last time.

I chatted with Ian about his British ancestors and what little I knew about mine until I felt a tap on my back.

Charlie said, "So, Kat. We'll have a fantastic meal at One if by Land, Two if by Sea. I've wanted to take you there forever." He eased his way into G's empty chair.

"I hope so. You sure spent a lot of money."

"All for two first-class causes. For the animals and to be with you. You look beautiful tonight. Like the mermaid on that beer label. Remember?"

"This dress wasn't my idea. A loaner from Desi. It's terrible to walk in." After a dry-cleaning, Desi would get it back.

"Tough life being a mermaid?"

I frowned. "Yeah, life on land isn't effortless for them either."

"Since Wyoming is canceled, how about dinner next week?"

"I'm going to Europe."

"London?"

"Nope. Copenhagen and Zurich."

"Denmark? Didn't you get enough?"

"I was only in Copenhagen for a few days last year. The ship stopped at lots of ports before arriving in Hong Kong, remember?"

G reappeared after taking urgent phone call number four. Or perhaps it was number five at this point. His line of work must be terribly demanding. But if he was so wealthy, why didn't he delegate more? G didn't interrupt Charlie to reclaim his seat but hovered nearby.

"It's just so sudden," Charlie said.

"This is not a vacation. It's for my job. That's why they call work, work."

"So Jackson appreciates you?"

"Yeah. He's great." I wished Charlie would stop mentioning Jackson's name. When we were alone, I would remind him again.

"Glad to hear it. I know how desperately you wanted to

work again."

"Want to? I have to. I'm not like all the ladies here who spend their days eating lunch in top-end restaurants and shopping on Madison Avenue. Or your rich friends who can afford to play on yachts and drive flamboyant cars." I clutched my evening bag to leave for some privacy inside the women's restroom. That was the only place where Charlie wouldn't follow me. "Excuse me."

G stood aside, and I shuffled away. This mermaid outfit might work well underwater, but on land, it was ridiculous.

A high load of alcohol raced through my system. After the punishing gym workout yesterday, coupled with getting used to the daily work grind, I was exhausted. The DJ's dance music blared, and after an hour of dancing, I'd head home.

~ ~ ~

The contemporary dance songs were a welcome change from Charlie's old rock classics. Ian invited me to dance, and I adapted some slow mermaid moves for Taylor Swift's "Enchanted." The lyrics were about meeting someone new like Ian.

When the music stopped, Ian excused himself and strolled to our assigned table. Maroon 5's pop number "Sugar" started. Charlie bowed low and took my hand. "My sincere apologies, Kat. About everything. Shall we?"

I shook my head. "This tune is so silly."

"Maybe to some. But I like it."

"Nah, you like the classics. The Doors, The Eagles, Journey."

"You think you know me inside out, but you don't. I'm not all sugar and sweetness." Charlie sang some of the lyrics. "Let's just dance."

"You don't know me either. Things happened while I was gone that I haven't told anyone about."

Charlie shrugged. "I don't need to know. Unless you want to tell me."

"After our fight, I didn't plan to see you ever again."

"And now, here we are together. I don't want to fight with you ever again."

"If you knew what happened to me, you wouldn't just walk away. You would run."

"From my mermaid who gave up her legs for love?" He beamed. "Never!"

He stopped talking and let me focus on just dancing. When the song ended, I scurried back to my table, ending our pointless conversation. Ian was out dancing, and G was at another table, so I was tempted to leave. But I would be polite and say goodnight to them first.

I glanced around and saw Charlie sitting alone. A nagging uneasiness told me Charlie might get snagged in Heather's insider trading investigation. I could keep it vague and warn him. Charlie observed me approach him.

"Can we talk somewhere privately?" I asked.

The DJ switched the music to an oldie, Billy Idol's "White Wedding."

"Finally, some real music. Let's dance. Tell me all about it." Charlie took my hand, led me back to the dance floor, and kissed me on the cheek. "I knew you would come around."

I shook my head, but he didn't notice.

Before I could share my carefully rehearsed warning, he asked, "Did I ever tell you the happiest day of my life?"

"No."

"The day we met. That blind date at that overpriced Mexican joint. Yeah, it's weird, but I knew then."

"That's sick. Sad, actually."

"Come here, I'll show you sick." He hugged me, but I jabbed him with my elbow to push him away. "Space. Yes, I remember."

I nodded and wanted to stop dancing. But I'd soldier on to the end of the song.

"What's your best day? So far, of course," he asked.

"The day I came home from Hong Kong. When the plane landed at JFK."

"My second happiest day. The day you came back."

I needed to transition this conversation into his job and the dangers of Wall Street with all the rules and regulations, including severe penalties for violating them. But he took my invitation to dance completely wrong.

"I knew we'd get back together. Best 20K I ever spent."

As if he had bought me like a stock or trading deal. I stopped dancing and wanted to slap him, but not at Desi's charity event or in front of all these people. "We are not getting back together. Not ever. I'm sorry your happiest days revolved around me. You can go to hell or wherever you want!"

I retreated back to my table in defeat. At least I had tried to help Charlie evade possible legal trouble. Now it was up to him.

At the table, G was arguing with Ian about how bigshot Wall Streeters, including men like Charlie, were ruining the environment. Ian, the diplomat, was no match for G, who threw out statistics on speculative oil and gas companies. G argued these "destroyers of the environment" got easy financing from "the money guys at investment firms."

My all-time favorite song, "Imagine" by John Lennon, began. I couldn't help but sing along to the music wishing for a better world. G put his hand on his heart, begging for a dance. I nodded to be polite, but my feet ached from wearing high heels.

G held me tight and moved so slowly it was barely a dance. My nose almost touched his jacket, which reeked of tobacco. He must have been sneaking smokes during his frequent phone call escapes. He crunched on some mints to conceal his bad breath.

G said, "Looks like your rich boy is abandoning you." He turned so I could witness Charlie walking out. G put his hand on the back of my head as if to console me. "Disappointed?"

I shook my head to get free of his hand, "No, relieved."

G moved his hand possessively to my neck. "That's my girl."

The DJ announced that the following number was the last song for the night. The predictable tune, "Last Dance" by Donna Summer, blared.

G stood still and clenched his fists, apparently not a fan of disco. He fumed and swore, insisting they switch to another song that would meet his approval.

Appropriate or not, I swayed to the music, more than ready to call it a night and slink home.

Ian interrupted G and took over the last dance, smirking. After G stomped off, Ian said, "Had to rescue you from G. He's such a muggle."

I giggled. "What's that?"

He threw his head back, laughing. "Per the rules of Harry Potter-mania, a muggle is someone without magical abilities. But in Britain, it also refers to a foolish person."

I wondered what Ian meant. G was condescending but stupid? If anyone qualified to be a muggle, I did for still being here.

I caught G staring at me. Gradually, I danced around to face the opposite direction.

Since Ian didn't win the bid, I was thankful Charlie had outbid G. However, Charlie would have the devil of a time scheduling it.

Chapter 30 ~ *Rain is Really No Big Deal*

As usual late on a Saturday night, taxis were in short supply. A misty rain fell, ruining what should have been a short commute home. Even the alternatives, Uber and Lyft, were booked up. So typical when they were needed the most.

Subways ran twenty-four hours, seven days a week, but it was a long walk coupled with a subway transfer to get home which would be a challenge in my dress. And with Jackson's warnings about El Rey, I should wait and weather the drizzle.

Ian insisted on accompanying me since his apartment was located in the West 90s, north of my place. I enjoyed his irreverent humor, and he didn't act like he'd insist on a post-party nightcap.

A black limo pulled up, and a man I didn't recognize climbed out. "Kat Jensen?"

"Yes?" A twinge inside my gut made me regret answering this dark-haired stranger.

The back seat window scrolled down, and G stuck his head out. "Can I offer you a ride home?"

Ian nodded in agreement. He appeared as ready as I was to escape the cold rain. I scurried as fast as my tight skirt would allow. The classic limo would have ample space for all of us.

The man who called my name opened the door, G slid over, and I ducked my head, climbing inside, carefully to not tear Desi's expensive gown. A third man, the driver, who looked like their brother, glanced back at me.

The door slammed shut with a bang. Inside the dark leather interior, I looked at G. "What about Ian? I thought we were both invited."

"He'll get another car," G said.

"I hope so." I stared out the back window at Ian, who was bent over as though picking something up from the sidewalk. I considered demanding we stop to wait for Ian. But the car had already pulled into traffic, and Ian disappeared from sight.

"Your purse, please." G said as if a command.

"My purse?"

"Just a precaution. My guys insist on this now. I promised them."

Reluctantly, I handed my fragile bag over. G passed my bag through the open partition to the trickster in the passenger seat next to the driver. They were carrying their security procedures way too far. A limo was definitely not an airplane.

Angry at my rash decision to get into this car, I fumed while I watched wet Midtown Manhattan slide by.

The man in the front seat said, "Clean," and tossed my elegant evening bag back to G.

I snatched my contaminated bag from him. Clean before their grubby hands went through it. My pocket-sized bag carried next to nothing. Whatever they were concerned about was ridiculous. I opened it up, relieved to confirm that my credit card and cash were still intact. I was getting out at the next stoplight.

"You don't have a weapon on you, do you?" G chuckled. "Not that it would fit inside your tight dress."

"On me?"

Before I could react, G pressed and patted his hands along the outside and inside of my coat. "Sincere apologies, but I've been shot before."

"What the hell?" I asked. If he pawed at me once more, I would slap him. Despite my intense training with Jackson and Anita, I had failed to react yet again. Too much alcohol and exhaustion were my only defenses. "I want out. Right here is fine."

G laughed while I flicked the handle on the door. Surprisingly, the door swung wide open. We were in the left lane, but his driver didn't stop. Instead, he sped up.

The pavement was a blur outside the door, and I hesitated. A cabbie in the right-hand lane next to us slammed down on his horn, warning me to reconsider.

G pushed my hand away, jerked the door shut, and yelled something in Spanish to the two men in the front seat. Angry clicks signaled the limo's automatic door locks.

In disbelief, I tried the door again, but it refused to open.

My heart pounded harder with my escape route cut off. My intuition told me G wasn't just an animal-loving friend of Desi's, but someone much more dangerous.

But my imagination often gets carried away. I had spent hours sitting next to G, hearing about his lifelong love of animals. Perhaps G was a businessman with enemies who shoot first and exit as soon as possible.

G opened the minibar, took out a bottle, and twisted off the top to take a sip. I monitored him and the scary road ahead, regretting the increasing distance from the safety of the Waldorf-Astoria.

"Thirsty?" he asked. "Where are my manners?"

I shook my head. But he didn't notice or care and took out another drink, opened it, and handed it to me.

The bottle of Mike's hard pink lemonade, filled with alcohol and sugar, was ice cold. I shivered. I had reached my alcohol limit hours ago, so I gave it back.

"No drink?"

I swallowed my panic to fake a state of calmness. "Too much sugar. Thirty-two grams to be precise."

He pulled out a zero-calorie bottle of water and dropped it in my lap. "We aim to please."

Luckily the cap was sealed, or I would have ignored it. I drank greedily, soothing my parched throat.

"That place for the benefit was a dump. Desi could have done much better. No wonder they're closing for a two-year renovation."

"They are?" I took another sip, grateful for plain water, the water of life, and a conversation that wasn't so sinister.

"Yeah, into condos and hotels like the Plaza. For more money. Nothing stays the same."

I mumbled vague words of agreement.

He turned to face me. "I could use a smart woman like you on my team. Loaded with exclusive benefits."

Career coaches, recruiters, and former managers had urged me to network and always keep my job options open. But working for a guy like this was out of the question. I would prefer to ask my parents for help or move.

To be polite while trapped in his limo, I asked, "What kind of job?"

"Bookkeeping, money transfer, and accounting stuff for my pharmaceutical biz."

Analyzing his accounts and money transfer was what I just did to identify El Rey's accounts. Could G be El Rey? But El Rey's real name was supposed to be Esteban Miguel Rodriguez, and the odds were entirely against it. I was confused and speechless.

"How about it? You're a numbers gal, and I need one." He tapped my leg much too casually.

Was G seriously offering me a job? I was vague tonight about my consulting work. A job interview, like the dozen recently, I could deal with. "With benefits like getting searched and manhandled? Sure. Sign me up."

"I apologized about that. We must be careful. You should be too."

"Yeah, big mistake getting inside this car." I should have jumped out, rolled on the asphalt, and prayed that I would escape being flattened by the taxi and other cars. Jackson and Anita would be so disappointed I wasn't more physically assertive after all their training.

"I'm serious. I checked you out. You're an excellent fit with my family operation."

Were my colleagues at work all wrong? Is his name Guillermo and not Esteban Miguel? Or that might be an alias like my two new ones, Heidi Montfort and Kim Shalimar, that were just a dumb joke.

I could ask him flat out, but then he'd know I was on to him. It was safer to play dumb. Despite this sensible plan, based on solid rationale, sweat poured down my back. But I couldn't take off my coat. An escape might still be doable.

Even if he wasn't our drug lord, I should confirm G's business involved narcotics trafficking. "Why would I fit in? Is it because my brother OD'ed?"

He hesitated, finished his pink lemonade, and tossed the empty container back into the minibar. "Your brother?"

"Yeah. My only sibling had a drug addiction."

"I didn't know. Sorry about that." He tapped his leg impatiently and stared out the window before looking back at me. "Can't win them all. It's not addicting if you are smart. Want to sample some?"

"No way." Holy hell, G could be El Rey. If he is, what a twisted turn on the roulette wheel of life. I tried to plan my next move, but I was trapped and abandoned by Lady Luck.

Desi's smiling introduction to G replayed along with a vision of her innocent young children in Connecticut. "Don't you realize that babies with mothers that use are addicts from day one?"

"We start them early. More business for the rest of us." He grinned at his sick humor.

I would appeal to his heart if he had one. "Those poor babies cry uncontrollably and suffer from tremors and diarrhea. There's so many now. They even named it NAS for neonatal abstinence syndrome."

"And to beat it, they take prescription opioids expensive doctors prescribe from Big Pharma."

"Only to fight back against the drugs you sell. Babies must be weaned off it with morphine or methadone."

"Basta. I've heard enough." A passing light flashed, illuminating his teeth which were bared like an angry dog. I leaned away from him and clenched my teeth to avoid provoking him further.

I was a lousy gambler. Slot machines ate my cash in a hurry. Debating with someone so unreasonable and demented was a waste of time. Similar to being stuck in a Vegas casino, I chose to withdraw. I still had some dignity left inside my pocket and would hang on to it as long as I could.

"They should make alcohol and tobacco illegal. The real killers." He lit a cigarette and exhaled in my direction. "This is what's going to kill me and you. Secondhand smoke."

"Yeah, thanks." I faked a cough back at Mr. Esteban Miguel or Guillermo Rodriguez. Ultimately, his name didn't matter since he was a diabolical monster. I was eager to head back to my office tonight despite being dressed like this. I would help Shantelle bury him and his accounts under a load of legal judgments.

The limo cut through Central Park to the Upper West Side and my home. "You can let me off right here. I can walk home."

"Walk at this time of night? My *madre* would never forgive me. What's your address?"

After so many lectures on privacy from Jackson and the others at work, I knew not to volunteer any personal information to him or his mother. "No need. Just drop me right here. Anywhere is fine."

We neared the mega movie complex a block from my apartment. I had spent countless nights there in the dark, disappearing into another world on the screen. But now, I wasn't merely watching a movie. I was trapped in a crime thriller. Someone always died in those films, often the femme fatale.

G shook his head. "Aren't you inviting Paolo and me inside to —"

"No." I slid open the glass window barrier and told the driver. "Please stop, right —"

G yelled something in Spanish and slammed the dividing window shut. He might have severed my index finger if I hadn't pulled my hand away. I had to reason with him. Keep him calm with whatever it took.

"My apartment's a big mess, and I'm exhausted. You must be super busy too. How about next week?" We zoomed up Broadway but stopped at the light on 70th Street, a few blocks north of my apartment. "What about right here? Please, this is fine." I pulled on the door handle, but it was still locked.

"I decide when and where you get out." G's Spanish accent came out stronger, along with his anger.

Now I really was trapped like a character in a crime thriller without a clue how it would end. Jackson had talked about destroying El Rey's drug empire by running a chainsaw across his coffin. At the time, I had shuddered, but now it didn't sound half bad.

Broadway traffic was oddly heavy at what must have been approaching midnight and the ominous witching hour when I preferred to be in bed. I regretted not bringing my cell phone or wearing a watch. Charlie's Apple watch would have come in handy, but I had to focus on the present. Jackson would want every single detail about this evening.

Paolo reopened the interior window and swiveled around to face us. "Sir, the West Side Highway is backed up. An accident. We'll take Broadway north."

G rubbed his head in annoyance and said something to Paolo in Spanish. Even drug lords must accept they are powerless to control traffic.

G must have asked Paolo to turn on the radio since Dolly Parton was singing her heart out with "Jolene."

"You like country music?" G's question was more of a statement, so I bit my lip to avoid saying something dumb.

I strived to remain rational, focused, clever, and agreeable. "Yeah, it's okay."

Paolo opened our dividing barrier again and mercifully turned down Dolly's laments about Jolene.

"César is on the phone," Paolo said.

"Not now. I'll call him from home." G didn't just speak. He barked.

"Yes, sir." Paolo slid the window closed again.

G's phone rang, and he pulled it out of his pocket and answered. But the ringing blared from his briefcase on the floor. He fumbled around to find the other phone, but he was too late, and it stopped ringing.

"Damn. I need to talk to you without all these dumbass interruptions."

Right when he said "interruptions," his phone, still in his hand, rang again.

"What?" He screamed so loud I shook. "You did the Narcan? And a second dose? Then get the hell out of there. I don't care who the asshole is!"

While still on the phone, G took another bottle of hard lemonade out of the minibar and handed it to me, signaling to open it for him.

I untwisted the metal cap for him. G, accustomed to having people at his beck and call, took it without pausing his phone conversation. "What the hell? If he was fool enough to inject his neck … Leave now. *Rápido.*"

He took a plastic container of water, dropped it in my lap, and rubbed his forehead. "Then dump him in that side area. End of story." G hung up and started scrolling through his email and texts. "Idiots. Like I can do something about a situation in Kensington on the phone."

"In London?" I remembered that trendy, upscale neighborhood fondly.

"No, Philly-Delphia. Too bad and why Jim was a no-show. Another Wall Street idiot but an animal lover."

My Jim? The ferret-lover and friendly guy I was supposed to meet at the gala? To eliminate a blind date debacle, after a cursory face-to-face meeting, we had tentatively scheduled a date for jazz at the Village Vanguard. G must be referring to another Jim.

G clicked off his phone and tossed it inside his briefcase.

To relax, I took some deep breaths and tried to figure out a Plan C or D. Perhaps I should lie, agree to take the job, and turn him down later. This could still be a weird coincidence and a misunderstanding with a different drug dealer.

"Now, Kat. As you see, I have enough problems without you poking your snout into my bank biz. You must stop immediately. Tell your idiotic boss, I said so. Or you won't live long enough to regret it."

I stared at him in shock. The few doubts still flapping around inside my brain flew away so fast that I was left with a painful headache from their claws.

"No more wasting time. Who in the hell hired you?"

"What do you mean?' The client behind Project Onion could be anyone. Only Jackson knew, and he might risk dying to keep that information secret.

"Come on. I know you work for that scum bucket Jackson. Nosing around in my business."

Hearing Jackson's name, I froze in fear. G is undoubtedly El Rey, the king of the North American narcotics cartels. My body shrunk down as though it was melting.

"What? I can't fricking hear you." He seethed in anger,

and the air grew warmer.

"I don't know. He wouldn't tell me." My body shook uncontrollably.

"Damn him." He touched my shoulder as if sympathetic. "All right. Give me a clue, and you're out of here. Come on. What's the name of the job?"

"O … Orion." At least I'd kept the codeword "onion" secret. For whatever that was worth.

"Hell, I like that one. Celestial, but useless." G continued on with his rampage. "Tell Jackson to go after the goddamned Colombians and Dominicans. They cut heroin with tons of fentanyl, creating something much more deadly. And now we've got the doozy drug, carfentanil aka *wildnil*. So strong it's used to put elephants down. My product is pharmacy safe in comparison."

I searched inwardly for a credible response but came up empty. All opiates were deadly in my book.

G didn't appear to notice and continued his verbal rampage. "Did you hear about *Santa Muerte*? Saint Death to *gringos*?"

I dug my short nails into my legs to focus on the ache and stay calm. "No." That one word was a shaky effort, but he didn't seem to notice. Stressing people out was no doubt one of his special talents if he didn't kill them first.

"Bad batch of heroin other gangs brought in. As soon as that shit hit, hundreds OD'ed on it. Those that didn't die wished they had. They screamed in pain and scratched their skin clear to the bone."

I shuddered at the nauseating image. At least Keith didn't go through all that. But what if he had? My parents never shared his autopsy results with me.

"My business is the same as what funded your President Roosevelt's start in life. His grandfather's company made millions on opium. Back when a million meant something." He slapped his thighs for emphasis, and the size and strength of his hands made me swallow so hard it hurt.

To calm him, I tried to keep the conversation going despite already knowing the answer. "Which Roosevelt?"

"FDR, the crippled one. Those Asian trading companies pushed their opium on the Chinese for their overrated tea. Even fought wars over it. The Ivy Leagues sure didn't turn their noses up at the money."

Comparing himself to a president and schools like Columbia University was going way too far. I had worked as an auditor for a British bank that built their business on selling opium to the Chinese. But that was over 150 years ago.

"That's nothing new. Today it's a major health issue and must stop."

"Blame the greedy bastard drug companies and Big Pharma. Squeezing out the little guys. I'm a businessman and a minor player. Doctors get you addicted to prescription drugs by practically shoving them down your throat!"

"I took prescription Vicodin once, but I never got addicted." With two herniated discs in my back, I had experienced sciatica nerve pain along my right leg. I popped Vicodin pills, all prescribed by doctors for months. Luckily, I never got hooked and stopped taking them when the nerve pain disappeared.

He stared at me, waiting for more personal information that I'd never share voluntarily.

"Tell me something I don't know." I regretted my unagreeable quip.

He shot back a response. "Did you know most overdoses are by white males between 33 and 55? Just like Jim, that rich, overprivileged guy. They can afford the drugs and chase the high. I keep telling them to back off. Everything in moderation."

I shrugged, unwilling to give him a single millimeter. Please let it not be my Jim, I prayed silently.

"I told you and Ian at dinner. I'm on the board of an indie company looking for an addiction cure. We hired an Italian medical researcher last week. He costs way too much."

And to think I had been fooled and admired him a few hours ago. "Great plan. Get them addiction-free so they can get addicted again."

"Shoot, girl. I've got the antidote, naloxone, right here in the car. I force training down everyone's throat. Even you can get it from a pharmacy. I'll show you."

G flicked on the light, pulled something out of the backseat pocket, ripped off its foil covering, and forced it into my hands. "I bought a shitload of this. I don't want my customers OD'ing. What kind of businessman would I be without any customers? If people start OD'ing, we give it to them. Right, Paolo?"

G slid the window open and barked something at Paolo in Spanish. Paolo said, *"Sí,"* followed by an obedient, "Yes, sir."

I read the label out loud, "Narcan nasal spray 4 mg," and returned it.

"Keep it. Maybe you can help someone. Just insert and spray into one nostril. That should do the trick. If they're OD'ing from opioids. Won't work for a heart attack."

He demonstrated with his fingers how I would inject the spray. "We also stock the more expensive prefilled syringes. Goes right through clothes into the upper arm, or …" He patted his leg. "But the spray is the easiest. Usually works in a few minutes."

"Okay, thank you." My words spilled out before I realized he didn't deserve any thanks. He was evil and an enemy who caused so much pain and death. But I would go to a training class to learn how to help people from overdosing with this antidote.

"They may still die, but you've bought them some time. Narcan is harmless. Cops won't hold you responsible if it doesn't work."

Now it made sense. G only tried this last-ditch effort to keep his customers alive and paying since he wouldn't be prosecuted.

He reached across me, and I held my breath and froze, afraid to move. G snatched my sequined evening bag off my lap and unzipped it to slip inside the nasal spray. "Now, you're ready. Courtesy of your great friend G."

I took my overstuffed bag back but didn't respond.

He said, "I'm one of the good guys. What do you call those people that help everyone?"

I had no clue what he meant and stared at him blankly.

He patted my thigh. *"Un buen samaritano como yo."*

I understood some Spanish and pushed his hand away. He could save a billion people, but he'd never be a Good Samaritan to me.

"What they need to do is set up safe houses. For lifesaving, in case someone OD's. They are everywhere but this idiotic country."

"So, let me get this straight. Places where people can legally use drugs with built-in babysitters, so they don't —"

"Die. Get high but stay alive. Like booze. You can drink legally at a bar and get a ride home. Sometimes free."

Would that even work? I was tired of arguing with him and thinking about this. Alcohol had addiction issues but comparing it to opioids was pointless. He wanted to legitimize it, like medical marijuana, to make more money.

"What now?" He tapped his fingers on the armrest by the window. "What else is in your bag?"

Dolly Parton's greatest hits album was still twanging along. The theme song for the movie *9 to 5* grated on me. Working got me into this mess, and my workday was often closer to 9 a.m. to 9 p.m.

"Nothing much." I shifted in my seat to shelter my purse underneath me.

"Hand it over."

Impatient with the wait, G turned on the overhead light and pushed me away to steal my bag. He sighed in apparent frustration, unzipped it, and stuck his fat fingers inside, pulling out my credit card and lifeline home. He put on his reading glasses. "Kathryn Jensen. That Jackson. Didn't he warn you to never use your real name? You won't last long in this business."

I wrongly assumed I didn't need an alias tonight. Besides, it would have been wasted. Desi knew me and had introduced me using my real name. What unbelievably lousy luck! He must have known who we were, and when he heard my name, my fate was sealed.

"How can I convince you to join us? I have zero ego. We

treat everyone with respect. I'll make sure it's only for the aboveboard legal crap."

I didn't say anything. Not only was G in control physically, now he held my evening bag with everything I had besides the clothes on my back.

"I started out as a bartender. Worked hard, and here I am. Whenever I can't outsmart my rivals, I hire them. How much is that loser paying you?"

I paused, unsure of what to say. My job lacked a regular paycheck, but he doesn't need to know this.

"Don't tell me he doesn't pay you." His tone was rude and arrogant, with such hatred for Jackson.

"He does, but it's based on the job and the client. My pay varies."

"Then what's the problem? Every week you'll get plenty of clean cash. Guaranteed."

I shook my head.

His voice softened. "Give it a try. What's the harm?"

"But … you haven't seen my resume. You might be disappointed."

"Resume?" He laughed. "Don't need that paper shit. I can tell you're smart. I'll pay you ten times what Jackson's paying you. Hell, name your price. Can't be anything near the cost of our new Italian doctor-scientist."

My brain paused, my gut signaled a yes, but my heart won. "Sorry. I can't." The Dolly CD finally came to a merciful end, but it was replaced with Neil Diamond. His classic "Forever in Blue Jeans" distracted me with my wardrobe predicament.

"Mark my words, you'll change your mind. Beg me for a job. But the sweet deal I've offered expires…" He glanced at his Rolex, "by midnight on Friday. You have twenty-four hours to think it over."

"Fine. Give me your card with a phone number. I'll call you."

"A number? Trying to trick me? No, I'll call you."

G fumbled inside my purse and pulled out the fifty dollars in cash I had shoved inside for emergencies and the cab ride home.

"Big spender. Only fifty?" He pocketed the bills. "Your contribution for gasoline."

I swore under my breath since this made it even harder to get home. But my credit card gave me hope.

"Lipstick, of course." He unscrewed the lid and pressed the brownish lip gloss against my lips. "Dark red would suit you better." He tossed it back inside my bag. "Forgot your phone?"

"I didn't bring it." I'd left my phone on the kitchen counter charging under Giuseppe's vigilant guard duty. All for the best, since G would have searched through my texts and emails and probably stolen it.

He didn't open the tiny inside pocket where I had zipped my house keys. Losing them would be a pain since I'd need to change my locks. I could bother Abby or the building superintendent to get inside, but it was so late.

"No protection? Nothing going on with the smartass who outbid me tonight?"

I shook my head at the thought of Charlie. "We broke up." His apartment was less than ten blocks from mine. If only I had been friendlier and shared a cab with him.

Looking out the window, keys and a boyfriend meant next to nothing. The traffic still crawled along, and this limo ride felt like it would never end. We were leaving my familiar turf and the borough of Manhattan. A bridge carried us over the Harlem River into the Bronx.

"You look so nervous. Here's just the thing." He pulled out a small plastic bag with something white inside. He wet his pinky finger, stuck it inside, and removed his finger coated with white powder. It resembled powdered milk, but that was naïve wishful thinking. He extended his frosted finger toward me. "Take a tiny taste. For courage."

I shook my head. "No, I can't."

"What am I going to do with you?" His tongue flicked against his snowy white finger until it was brown again. Then he reached into his briefcase and pulled out a handgun.

I gasped, drew my legs up under me, and formed a ball,

getting as small as possible. He wants to break me, and I couldn't let that happen. Reluctantly, I retreated into a dark but familiar zone.

Mentally, I tried to conjure up the advice from Anita and Jackson during the self-defense training. They had said, "Stay calm. Don't panic. Focus on what's happening. Avoid dwelling on the what if. It makes things worse. Search for a strategy. There's always something."

G waved the gun around to torture me while laughing. "Sorry. Not what I was looking for."

After what felt like an eternity but was probably less than a minute, G put his pistol back in his briefcase. He took out something small, wrapped in shiny plastic. He stuffed it into my swollen evening bag and smacked his lips. "Another small gift from G. Keep yourself STD-free. Don't want my female friends to suffer."

He flung my evening bag back at me, repacked with the Narcan and the shiny thing, but minus my cash, and clicked the light off.

I was so nervous I shook. When I opened my mouth to thank G, words refused to form. Now I was trapped in silence, not just his limo.

He laughed and wrapped his hand around my shaking wrist, holding it firmly. He scolded me and commanded that I sit more like a normal person. Slowly, I uncurled from my protective ball and put my feet back on the floorboard.

G scooched over next to me when "Sweet Caroline" began playing. He held my arm and sang along, yelling the refrain, and commanded me to join him. Gratefully, the darkness and his enthusiastic baritone drowned me out.

"Kiss me."

I leaned away, but his lips touched mine, and his tongue forced my lips open. I guess this wasn't pleasurable since he stopped, said something unintelligible in Spanish, and cupped my chin in his hand.

For the first time, I realized how a small rodent felt when toyed with by a cat. Mice were typically trapped until the cat grew tired of them. Like me, their prey had two options: death or freedom.

"What am I going to do with you?" He stared at me. "Take your coat off."

"No." My voice came from deep inside my throat, weak and muffled.

"Fine. I'll rip it off you."

Slowly, I took my coat off, using it to cover my lap.

"Throw it over there." He pressed against me, pushed the coat to the floor, and put one of his hands on my crotch. He rubbed his lips against my cheek, whispering, "*Qué bonita*."

After this ordeal, I was anything but pretty. The knots inside my stomach moved upwards to my throat, strangling me. At least there was one plus to dressing like a mermaid. My second-skin gown was so tight he couldn't move it or touch my body buried under the slippery fabric.

"Take your dress off."

Images of Jim, my brother Keith, and my former apartment neighbor Nathan flashed before me in the dark. All dead because of illegal narcotic empires like G's. "No, I can't. Kill me if you want to. I don't care."

He grasped hold of my neck and lifted my head about an inch. "I have another idea." He unbuttoned his shirt, complaining he was hot. Next, he unzipped his pants and pulled them down on his thighs to show off his self-proclaimed oversized male attributes.

I looked away and heard a trio of familiar male voices. From somewhere in the next world, Jim, Keith, and Nathan yelled, "Don't look. Get the hell out. Now!"

"Over here." He pushed my face toward his groin and turned the light on.

Besides what I expected all along, I saw an unusual orange-and-black butterfly tattooed on his right hip.

The nasty smell of sweat and cigarettes overwhelmed me. A wave of nausea pushed its way from my stomach upward. My insides caved in and heaved, throwing up the drinks and food from the gala all over his lap.

The colorful pile of vomit on his bare skin was so unexpected and indescribable that I froze, transfixed. The red bits of tomatoes and strawberries blended in with shades of green from the salad and spinach dip. A freaky homemade Christmas-colored decoration covered his ornament.

"Ow! *Maldita puta!* Dammit, bitch." After pushing me away, he snatched my furry coat, still technically on loan from Desi, and wiped the vomit from his groin and pants. "*Asqueroso!*" He added what must be the English translation. "Fricking disgusting!"

G zipped his pants up and slammed his left hand on the glass panel while yelling at the driver to pull over. I wiped my mouth with the back of my hand, still feeling sick. The Neil Diamond number "I Am I Said" mingled with my sniffling while tears rolled down my cheeks. He kept complaining, alternating between "*Madre de Dios*" and "Mother of God" several times.

Outside, a sign advertised the Bronx Zoo. G yelled to his two goons in the front seat. "Pull over. Here! Where it's good and dark."

He yanked my hair, so I faced him. "If I overhear anything on the police radio, you're dead. I've got friends everywhere. Got that, *puta*?"

I nodded, shocked that I was alive and relatively intact.

"And tell Jackson, he has forty-eight hours to schedule a one-on-one with me. He'll want to hear about some strategic business changes." A menacing chuckle followed.

The door locks clicked, reminding me of the sound of a prison cell opening on a TV show. But after trying to open the door so often, I was still in denial and fumbled with the handle.

G groaned and reached around me to open my door while the car slowed down. "They say cats have nine lives. You'll need them!"

Before I could react, I fell forward from the kick on my butt. I landed hard on my hands and knees, facing the wet asphalt road, and yelled out in surprise.

My coat, flung from the car, slid off my back into the street. I stayed down and convulsed again. But my stomach was empty, although still filled to the brim with fear.

Chapter 31 ~ Not on the Tourist Top Ten List

Something silver flew over my head, landing nearby in the weeds. It must have been my sequined purse. Ignoring my aching knees, I stood and flexed my wrists, relieved they weren't broken. I rescued my molested evening bag, still containing my keys and the Narcan. A fast search confirmed my credit card and cash were gone.

I rescued my coat from the road and shook it. My dress and coat were ruined, but this outfit was destined for the trash. Even if they were cleaned and repaired, this evening's memories couldn't be undone.

Another car was parked about forty or fifty feet away in the same direction as G's departing limo. Maybe they would help me. I limped toward the car, but then I stopped. What if it was G?

The car's brake lights were mirrored in the wet road. I tried to decipher the plates, but my vision was blurred, and they were too far away. While I was great at numbers, my ability to judge distances was awful. Besides, I hadn't noticed his license plate number.

The mermaid skirt had ripped during my clumsy but successful attempt at preventing a nose-dive. This made walking easier but might scare anyone from stopping.

The familiar-looking sedan backed up and narrowed the gap between us. I turned and ran to keep my distance, grateful that my fight-or-flight hormones had kicked in. But I could never outrun a car, even in reverse. I scanned the area, begging for another car or truck, even a motorbike, to appear on this deserted road. About a quarter-mile away, I saw some lights and heard traffic.

Behind me, brakes screeched, and a door opened, but I refused to stop and ran. The dress made it too difficult, so I reached down and ripped the skirt's slit higher to run faster. But I was so out of shape, my sides screamed in pain after a short distance.

The hum from the car's engine closed the gap behind me.

Someone who sounded like Paolo yelled, "Come back here. Please, now."

Another man, presumably G, said something in Spanish, but I didn't understand the words.

Paolo said, "*Lo siento.* Sorry Kat. We have your credit card. And money. Let us drive you home. *No problema.*"

Were they insane? Getting back into that car again was the last thing I would ever do. They could wave a million dollars in my direction, and it still wouldn't work. My jog turned into a full-out sprint, hampered only by my ridiculous dress and shoes. I considered removing my high heels but running barefoot on glass, or other sharp objects, was too dangerous.

A nondescript white sedan, but not a limo, turned down the small street. This motorist must be a modern-day knight ready to swoop me up, like a damsel in distress. He would drive me home without asking bothersome questions or having bizarre expectations. From then on, we would be best friends forever. Hells bells, we might even get married, just like in the fairy tales.

But apparently, he didn't share the same fantasy. As the white car neared, the driver didn't slow down. I panicked, ready to gamble all. While I ran into the street, I waved my arms as if drowning. The white sedan slowed but moved into the left lane to avoid me and sped up, leaving me behind. At least my reluctant knight did one good deed. They scared off G's lumbering deathtrap.

Nervous about being alone, I jogged along the dark road to the intersection. The land on either side of the road was empty, with construction equipment behind barbed wire. Weeds grew through the cracks in worn-down slabs. Broken glass and garbage were scattered along the crumbling concrete from what once was a sidewalk. But this was a welcoming sign. I was returning to civilization and the mess humans leave behind.

People call New York City the city that never sleeps. But they must be referring to Manhattan and not the Bronx. From the sight of these old decrepit buildings, this part of town never truly woke up. A chill ran down my spine. I hoped this didn't mean someone was watching me from a hiding place behind the worn facades.

At the intersection with a streetlight, cars passed by, and I tried to flag one down, but no one stopped. No doubt worried about dealing with an insane woman or a druggie on a semi-deserted road in the middle of the night. Here, in the worst imaginable part of town, I wouldn't stop either.

Conceivably, no one would. Without any money or a credit card, I couldn't pay them a cent. At this hour, it was unlikely anyone would drive me more than a few miles. I had no idea where the nearest subway station was located. But even in the Bronx, there must be several nearby.

The few shops and large warehouses were closed. Anita's gripe session yesterday focused on how people complained about her neighborhood, the Bronx. Here, in front of me, was why those comments still had merit. This place was downright scary.

I debated standing in the road, but the cars were speeding along. The drivers could be drunk or high and hit me. Topping off this night with a visit to the hospital or the morgue wasn't worth it.

I tried to flag a car down a few more times and considered searching for a safe place to wait for daylight. Inside my molested purse, I double-checked the inside pocket, hoping I was somehow mistaken. If only my lifeline, the credit card, were still there, but my hopes were dashed.

Inside the lining of my evening bag, I touched a small plastic bag. I held it under the streetlight to examine the baggie and its contents. The bag was filled with white powder, which must be cocaine, G's narcotic of choice. A goodbye gift that would transform me into an addict and his desperate customer. The coke was probably worth enough to pay for a ride home, but I could never trade it for money.

This small and squishy bag represented evil, pain, and death. I'd seen my brother handle these baggies, but he always acted embarrassed and tried to conceal it. To my dying day, I'd regret not saying something and pushing him harder into rehab.

I tossed the baggie on the ground. But what if someone found it in the morning, or a dog ate it? They could die, and it would be my fault.

Trained to do the right thing, I picked it up, tore it open, and shook the contents to disperse them into the air. Unfortunately, most of the cocaine landed on my coat and the pitiful remains of the mermaid tail. I shoved the empty baggie into my purse to dispose of later.

His other two parting gifts were still intact, and I debated throwing them out. But I couldn't be a litterbug. The condom didn't bother me, and the Narcan might save a life.

A compact car approached, and I waved my bag to flag them down, but they sped up and passed by. A second dark grey sedan slowed. Emboldened, I stepped into the road full of hope that this was a genuine white knight, just slightly discolored. The motorist stopped, but a sudden flashing light show from the car's rooftop disoriented me.

Unprepared for what must be an unmarked police car, I stepped back to take my chances and wait for another ride. I scanned the area, desperate to find a direction to run for cover and await the sunrise.

But I was indecisive and slow to react. The driver climbed out of the car and rushed toward me.

Chapter 32 ~ A Persian Prince

Sitting on a hard plastic chair inside an overcrowded hospital waiting room was weirdly comforting. Despite the clientele surrounding me, the complete opposite of the uber-wealthy types at the charity ball, I felt safe.

Sandwiched between people with varying degrees of severe health issues, judging from their vacant stares and occasional moans, I reassessed my injuries.

On the way here, I had difficulty speaking to the undercover cop who'd picked me up in his unmarked car. I had submitted my purse for another search upon his request. He'd pulled out the empty baggie, condom, and Narcan, complaining about how I was killing myself.

Then he dropped me here, inside the E.R. of the closest hospital in the Bronx. Luckily, I wasn't charged with anything or arrested. Thanks to my lightning-smart action to trash the illegal white powder.

Without my voice or an I.D., I was registered as Jane Doe. The hospital staff viewed me suspiciously following my escorted police arrival. My half-drowned mermaid appearance didn't help matters. Everyone in the E.R. was probably convinced I was a dope addict turned hooker. My mermaid's tail slit reached my upper thigh. The only consolation was knowing that wearing a bikini was more revealing.

When my voice returned, I insisted I was A-okay. But why would anyone take the word of a bedraggled, possibly strung-out coke addict without an I.D.? My real name was on the tip of my tongue, but I didn't dare tell them who I really was or about G. He might find me or hear about it on a police radio. I had to talk to Jackson or Anita first.

Coming up with a phony name should be simple, but there were suddenly too many confusing options. I gave them one but forget what name I made up and switched to another. All the while, I was careful to sidestep using my new fake names, Heidi Montfort and Kimberly Shalimar. After trying three variations, the overworked hospital staff gave up.

They wanted a real name and especially proof of insurance so someone would foot what might be an outrageously high bill. Shantelle had mumbled something about medical and dental, but my medical cards were still pending. Convincing the staff that I had coverage required my real name.

From the looks of it, this hospital admitted all the uninsured. Critical arrivals, people with gunshot and stabbing wounds, got first priority and were rushed through. If you were not in the immediate danger of dying, you sweated it out inside the waiting room.

After my name and the sign-in fiasco at the front desk, they wouldn't let me use their phone for a local call. I promised to be out of their way soon, but the admittance clerks and nurses still refused. I was afraid to sneak out and run into G or someone else equally dangerous.

I considered begging to borrow some money. But if using the phone was a no-go, they would think the cash was for drugs. A measly twenty was a fortune and would bring me to a subway stop and get me home.

On the way to the women's bathroom, I forced down what felt like a gallon of water from the grimy fountain. In the bathroom, I washed off my smeared makeup and gargled soapy water. I finger-combed my wild hair and pulled it into a loose knot.

My parched lips welcomed some lip gloss. My dress and coat were sponged off with a paper towel. I still looked terrible but slightly less deranged. More importantly, I left the bathroom armed with a new life-saving plan to return home.

I strolled back to the nurse's area and rested against the counter. A statuette of Ariel, the mermaid, and Triton, an underwater god, struck me as out of place. But a hero rescue would come in handy, and Ariel's carefree smirk encouraged me to try.

When the clerk glanced up, it was now or never.

"I desperately need some cash to get home. My evening bag needs a wash, but it's valuable with a designer label." I deposited my sequined evening bag on the countertop for inspection. "Are you interested?"

The plus-sized front-desk attendant, with dark circles under her eyes, pursed her lips and stared at my dirty purse.

I delivered my best, most professional smile. "How about twenty dollars?"

Her sudden facial language delivered the short answer. "Take that nasty thing off my counter and return to your seat."

I rescued my glittery bag, which had seen better days just a few hours ago.

The desk clerk spritzed her work surface and me with disinfectant. She wiped the counter down angrily as if my poor defenseless bag had deposited a life-threatening virus.

I stepped back a few feet, wiping my disinfected hands on my beat-up mermaid tail. Slowly, I inched along the long counter, hoping to ask a different clerk or nurse who had a heart. But when I made eye contact, they quickly looked away in disgust. To them, I was stooping lower than low to sell a grimy bag for a twenty-dollar fix.

At the end of the countertop, I had a clear view of their shared desktops. A colorful array of knickknacks surprised me. Disney-themed memorabilia littered their workspace. Not just Ariel-the-mermaid, but Minnie Mouse, Snow White, Cinderella, Tinker Bell, and Elsa from Frozen were lined up. As though they waited for an organized parade through Neverland. The statues were so familiar, but I couldn't recall seeing them in the kid's rooms at Desi's house.

As soon as I reached my seat, an older nurse summoned "Jane Doe," but kept her distance. Obediently, I followed her to an empty examination room without a phone to help me.

To get comfortable for what might be a long wait, I curled up on the exam table. My dirty coat and the protective paper sheet covered me. Against my strict instructions to remain alert, I dozed off. I woke with a nudge on my shoulder, returning me to my Bronx hospital nightmare.

A man said, "Jane! Jane Doe! Can you wake up? Open your eyes."

His voice was alarming, so I sat up and blinked at a

blinding flashlight. The dark-haired man wrapped in a white haze smiled with ultra-white teeth, and I shrunk back in alarm.

"How are you feeling?" He put his stethoscope on my chest and throbbing heart. My beats weren't at their usual steady pace since medical exams were always unnerving.

"I'm okay. This is all a terrible mistake. I just need to go home and get some sleep. Tomorrow, I mean today, is a really busy workday."

"First, we must do a medical screening exam. It's the law."

That was news to me, and I swallowed hard, hoping I would pass. "Okay. I had some alcoholic drinks tonight. But I never ever use drugs!"

The doctor put the stethoscope on my chest and asked me to breathe in and out. "Well, your heartbeat and vitals are fine. Why are you here in the E.R.?"

"I was at a charity ball at the Waldorf Hotel and got a ride home. Or so I thought. The guy got angry and drove me up here. He took all my cash and a credit card. I just need to borrow a phone or some cash to return home."

His brow furrowed. "The paperwork says you refused to speak or complete any paperwork with the detective who brought you here. We all know Jane Doe is not your real name."

I stared down at my hands. "My name is … but …" I read his nametag. "I can't say anything more, Dr. Mehregan. It's too dangerous."

He pulled a chair next to me and sat down. His eyebrows arched higher as if curious, and his name was unusual but so familiar.

I almost patted my head when I remembered, but this would be a dangerous action in front of any doctor assigned to judge my well-being. "Are you by chance, Zhila's husband? She's an Uber driver and said her husband is an E.R. doctor."

He hesitated, understandably nervous that somehow I had learned his wife's name.

"She's not in any danger. I would explain more, but it's

complicated. I really like her. She's driving me to JFK later today. That's why I must get back to Manhattan as soon as possible."

He blinked a few times. Zhila had complained about how he practically lived in the E.R. and ran on fumes from permanent exhaustion.

"I love her car. The skunk-mobile." If he was Zhila's husband, I had to convince him.

His eyes lit up, and he cracked a smile. "I've heard about you. Isn't your name Kat? Something like that? She invited you over for Saturday."

"Yeah, she did. I wanted to come, but I have a business trip. Can you please not put my name in your records? It would be a huge favor."

He nodded and jotted something on the paperwork. "Okay, Jane Doe. I'm discharging you."

I slid off the examination table and stood to prove how healthy I was and take action. "Thank you so much. I just want to go home and sleep. I guess Zhila isn't taking customers now. I'm temporarily broke."

He shook his head. "Nah. She's sleeping. But I can loan you some cash. Wait here. My wallet is inside a locker."

"I will pay you back. I mean, Zhila. Can I borrow a phone for one short call? It's really critical. Almost life and death."

He nodded, and I trailed behind him down a hallway, getting farther from the waiting room and into a small office. He pointed to the desk with a phone. "Nothing foolish like calling overseas?"

"Oh, no. A short local call. Promise."

When the doctor left to get some cash, I called Jackson's emergency number. Fortunately, I had followed my coworkers' instructions and memorized the information. Numbers were as simple as one-two-three for me to recall. But I never thought I would use it.

Jackson answered on the second ring. "What the … this better be damn good."

Despite his snarl, I was so relieved to hear a familiar voice I almost wept. Somehow, I got across where I was and that I needed help without disclosing anything confidential. Their standard procedures when using unsecured phone lines had been drilled into my brain by my new colleagues.

"ETA is about thirty minutes. Lay low near the E.R. I'll find you." He clicked off, and I hung up, unable to move, staring at the desk and phone.

Despite's Jackson's reassurance and his rescue plan, my body shook uncontrollably, and I sunk down in the chair.

The door opened in the haze, and I saw a body covered in white, standing in the foggy doorway. "Kat, a policeman is inquiring about you at the front desk. There's still some time to avoid him. Here's the cash."

I struggled to focus on the man, who must be Dr. Mehregan. My vision was so blurred, I couldn't see anything clearly. My head felt like a balloon that, if untethered, would float away. I stared at the doctor and the doorway. Any minute, I expected the cops with G or his henchman to walk in and grab me.

"Did something happen?" The shadow of a man squatted before me, and I felt his breath on my face. "Don't go into shock on me now, Jane Doe."

Hearing my alias, I shook my head to lose the sense of foreboding that took me hostage for a few minutes. I stood ready to go. "Sorry. I'm fine, Doctor. Thanks, but I don't need the money after all."

"Take it anyway, Miss Jane Doe." He pressed a few twenties into my hand.

"A friend is coming to pick me up. Over by the E.R. entrance." I had lost all sense of direction. "Can I get there and avoid that policeman?"

Dr. Mehregan opened the door, glanced both in directions, and stood in the hallway blocking the view from the front desk area. "Go that way." He pointed to the right. "Down the back stairs and out the emergency doors to the street. The alarms posted won't sound. Taxis park there, and the E.R. entrance is right around the corner. Be careful."

I was about to leave when I realized Jackson would be furious about my failure to gather more intel. "Did you happen to see what he looked like?"

"Yeah, I've met that cop. Name's César. He's usually here with his Italian sidekick. I forgot the other guy's name, but we call him Mr. Disney. He brings the women gifts from there all the time."

I swallowed hard, recalling Anita's gift from Frankie and how similar it was to the statues at the front desk. Frankie could be Mr. Disney, and César might be here looking for me. After being so wrong about El Rey, I couldn't screw up again. I racked my brain for a distinguishing characteristic for confirmation. "Is César on the heavy side?"

"Not obese yet. But he is at risk for a whole host of issues."

"Please, whatever you do, don't tell him I was here."

He nodded, and I touched his arm in appreciation while mumbling a sincerely gracious farewell. There was no mistaking: this doctor was my white knight.

Chapter 33 ~ Special Undercover Vehicle

My boss and hero, wearing a strange hippie disguise, drove out of the hospital parking lot in a flash. He swerved, narrowly avoiding a man who stepped out dangerously close to his right front bumper. Somehow, despite the long-haired wig, Jackson drove with finesse.

I gained a new appreciation, even envy, for how cool Jackson reacted under pressure. In all probability, the CIA lost one of their best operatives when he quit. Somehow Jackson had found me lurking near the E.R. within seconds. Before I'd even registered how he'd found me, I was inside his old nondescript SUV, and we were headed out of the parking lot.

Jackson handed me a big bottle of Gatorade. "You must be thirsty. Drink some electrolytes."

I drank heavily, ignoring the calorie or sugar count.

"So, Kat. What the hell happened?"

I paused, unsure how to begin. "I'm … a lot. For one, I met El Rey. A terrible accident. I mean a coincidence. But he, G, threw me out, and César ... Anita's friend showed up. He's a cop. Mr. Disney is Frankie, and —"

"Stop! Drink, take deep breaths, and start from the beginning. Slowly. Unless I should do something. Is anyone at risk of dying right this second?"

"No, I don't think so." I drank the rest of the tangy Gatorade, reconsidering. How should I know what G and his henchmen might be doing right this instant? But Jackson must mean something life-threatening that he could stop.

Jackson pulled over at a gas station and parked near a streetlight.

"Sorry. I'm better now."

"Being up close to a criminal can do a number on your system."

"Yeah, it sure can. It did." I shivered at the way he made this sound like a frequent occurrence.

"Start from the beginning. When you left the office today."

So, I told him about attending the benefit, meeting our evil drug czar, and ending up in the Bronx. I briefed Jackson on how he tried to recruit me and was irate about our investigation. And how he had demanded our top-secret client's name, which I didn't know.

Jackson occasionally laughed or swore but urged me to continue my story while it was fresh, and I could remember.

We took a brief break to use the restrooms at the gas station. When I hesitated, in fear at the flimsy door and lowlifes hanging around, Jackson stood guard outside the bathroom door.

Jackson bought a large coffee to go, but I was so wired that I was beyond the need for any caffeine. On the way out, I spent some of Dr. Mehregan's cash to buy two bottles of water and a couple of chocolate bars.

Back inside his SUV, Jackson pulled off his hippie wig and tossed it on the console between us. "Itches like a mother."

Quickly, I concluded updating Jackson. When I added my theory about how Anita's NYPD buddies named César and Frankie were probably helping El Rey, Jackson stopped me. He called Anita and instructed her to follow up on her friends who might be crooked cops.

I skipped confessing the sex part and vomiting. This was just too embarrassing to mention and didn't change anything. "The last thing G said was a threat. You have forty-eight hours to contact him. Something about his business changes."

"Shit. I've been ready to meet mano a mano for years. If he has the balls to show up without a loaded gun and his thugs."

"He pushed hard for the client's name. I'm glad you never told me."

"Yep. Same here. If it's of any consolation, they also have a personal vendetta against him. Like you and your brother."

I was surprised he remembered my confession about my brother Keith's drug issues and overdose when we met in Hong Kong years ago.

Jackson started the car and drove out to the main road.

"Where are we going?" I asked as he drove south toward Manhattan.

"Your place. Unless you'd rather not."

"No, that's great. But shouldn't I report this to the police? To someone you trust. Kidnapping is illegal." I preferred to go home, rip off what was left of this miserable outfit, and take a long, hot shower. But legal issues from delaying an official report gnawed at me. My stomach, even with some chocolate inside, wouldn't let me forget it.

"Kidnapping is illegal and a federal offense across state lines. The reason he let you out here in New York State. But he has two witnesses in the front seat of the limo that will say whatever he wants. How many will side with you?"

"Ian. He saw me leave."

"But from what you said, Ian saw you enter his limo voluntarily. Holy crap, you danced with the guy and sat next to him all night. People at the Waldorf can testify to that."

"Right but —"

"If you want to report it, you can. I'll turn around and drop you near a police precinct. But this, we, never happened. I didn't pick you up or take you anywhere. My involvement and Melville Consulting must stay out of it."

"But you did —" Tears blurred my vision from these added complications.

"Sorry. I can't be brought into this. I thought you understood this when you joined up. Our client investigations must stay private and confidential. If you were physically injured, then it gets complicated. Things usually get reported. Otherwise, everyone learns to work things out. On their own terms."

"So, if I report it, I lose my job. If I stay silent, I let him get away with it."

"In this situation, he will anyway. But there are better ways to get payback. Channel that frustration to fight him. You'll find a way. Hell, he wants to hire you. That opens up an entire realm of possibilities."

"I doubt he would now. He was seriously angry."

"Shit, don't worry about that. Use your anger to fuel your

desire to put him away. Legally."

I stared out the window at the gas station's outdoor ice storage unit and considered my options.

Jackson rapped his thumb on the steering wheel, a signal his patience was running out. "See this from a cop's point of view. You weren't physically harmed. You have no one to witness that you wanted out of the car. You only complained to El Rey and his buddy Paolo. Did you demand that the driver pull over and let you out? Do you get their names? First and last?"

"I tried to get out. I asked the guy driving. He might not speak much English. I don't know his name or Paolo's last name." What a fool I was. I didn't even ask.

"He might admit you wanted out. Sadly, when you got out of the limo, you fell. Tripped on your long dress or something. He'll call that an accident. He came back to apologize. But you were so drugged up or drunk, you ran away and got hysterical. And then there's Jane Doe and the E.R. visit. Good luck explaining that. How seriously do you think the cops will take that report?"

I visualized the scenario. The police would write down my complaint, laugh after I left, and toss it into a file cabinet, which might as well be the garbage. "What would you do in my situation?"

"Me? That should be obvious by now. Remember tonight, learn from it, and fight harder to bring him down. Petty accusations without proof won't do it. You need more, much more."

"It's so unfair." Tears streamed down my face, and I wiped them away with my coat's dirty sleeve.

"Hey, that's the way the game is played. You'll catch on. This was a tough first job." He started the car. "Ready? Decision?"

"Yeah. I'm exhausted. No police report." I wished my brain had an on/off switch so I could stop thinking for a while. He drove on a major road with little traffic at this time in the morning. "I know why you call this Project Onion. Getting close and cutting into a drug trafficker can make you cry."

He chuckled. "I was eating a burger and onion rings when the phone rang and got this gig. Been waiting a long time. Opioids are white. White onions were inside the rings."

"So, no real meaning." I regretted wasting time trying to decipher who was hidden behind the codeword onion.

"Afraid I'm not that creative." He chuckled. "My project names can't mess with Melville or *Moby-Dick*."

"Are we going to my place?" I would go anywhere, even the moon, with Jackson in his old SUV.

"Yep. I don't think you need a safe house. Did you tell him your address?"

"No, he asked, but I didn't. My address is —"

"I know where you live. He might know that by now. I'll secure it first."

"Oh, Jackson." I stared out the window as we drove across the bridge back to my familiar and much-loved Manhattan. But my sense of well-being didn't improve. "This world is a real mess. Sometimes I hate it. Life can be unbearably cruel."

"This is all we have. The world isn't cruel. But people can be. Avoid them. Find the good ones out there."

I smiled and thought about the friends I enjoy being around.

"I hate psychobabble. But here goes nothing." Jackson cleared his throat. "Don't expect too much. Sometimes you get beaten down in life. This job does it. But stay strong. Try to keep doing the right thing. We'll get through it as a team. Okay?"

"Yeah. Helpful babble. Appreciate it." I sent him an appreciative smile, but he concentrated on the road ahead.

As we passed the exit from the West Side Highway for our office, a clue from the near-disastrous sex scene somehow floated to the surface of my half-submerged brain. "We should stop at the office. I think I can connect the other accounts."

"Now? No way. You need rest, and I certainly do. Your flight is in what … twenty hours?" He pointed to the clock on the dashboard.

"Yeah. Sorry about this. I ruined your night."

"Shit, you got into this working for me. We're a team,

remember?"

"Yeah, but I'm the weakest link."

"No way. You've already proven yourself with the accounts in just one week."

"Next month, I'm going to take the New York State PI exam. Shantelle said she'd help me."

"Why? I have to take the darn test since I run the company."

"It might help me to learn more about this business."

"But you, of all people. You have so many already." He counted my licenses listed on my resume on his fingers. I had a CPA, Certified Fraud Examiner, Certified Anti-Money Laundering Specialist, Certified Internal Auditor, Certified Bank Auditor, and three stock brokerage licenses.

He continued trying to convince me. "It's a pain. Every two years, they make you retake it."

"Can't be as bad as the CPA exam." For my own peace of mind, I must be more prepared. The private investigator's license might help.

"All about criminal and penal procedural law. Stuff that will put you to sleep. But if you want to, I won't stop you."

"I just wish this whole night never happened." Regret and despair stabbed at my skin, and I rubbed my arms for some relief.

"Well, it did. Tomorrow we'll talk about it. Work it to our advantage. Besides, I needed a break from Fortnite."

"What's that?"

"My addiction." He tapped the palm of his hand on the SUV's steering wheel for emphasis.

I wondered if that was slang for an illegal drug. Please don't let Jackson, my lifeline and boss, be an addict.

"Don't tell me you haven't heard of Fortnite."

Embarrassed, I stayed silent. The name was vaguely familiar, but another druggie confession would destroy me.

"Fortnite's an e-sport. A shooter-survival video game. Millions play, and I'm one of the best. Minecraft is another big one."

"I can't face another computer at night after sitting behind one all day. Isn't that all make-believe?" His hobby was a time-waster, but I wouldn't insult his preferred way to unwind.

"Yeah, but there's big prize money for the best player. I've got an edge over most of the yahoos. I'm trained. Done it IRL."

Hearing about shootouts, even imagined, was the last thing I needed. Jackson's in-real-life experience shooting firearms should reduce my fears. But my stomach complained to the contrary.

Jackson didn't mention seeing Captain Willem. Maybe he didn't find him or didn't bother so he could play the Fortnite video game. After G, his threat wasn't such a big deal. Besides, I was leaving the country tomorrow.

"Another thing. G, I mean El Rey, took a call from someone. Probably his dealer in Philadelphia. They talked about a guy named Jim, who might have OD'ed."

I hated to speculate, but Jackson would know what to do. "I think that guy was my girlfriend's co-chair for her benefit. He never showed up and was in a desolate place called Kensington near Philly. But he might still be alive, and —"

"Kensington? Ground zero for druggies. The largest open-air market on the East Coast. If he went there to get high, he's a serious user."

"His family may be searching for him. Can I tell my girlfriend and let her report it to the police?"

"Nope. It raises too many questions. If it's him, the authorities will find him and tell his family."

"But he might be alive and need help."

"And if he is, they'll send him to the hospital. All's good, right?"

"But what if he's dead? They might not be notified for days. His wallet could have been stolen."

"So what? Trust me. If he's dead, he won't mind."

I couldn't believe Jackson lacked an essential empathy gene. "Because it's so wrong. His family should —" I was about to mention his cat and the ferrets starving to death when he cut me off.

"If you call her, what will you say? By the way, your buddy G is one of America's most-wanted narcotic traffickers? And even if you don't delve into the details, she'll wonder. The cops certainly will. Everything you told me, and more, will be forced out and dissected. When El Rey hears, your next joy ride won't end by falling on your knees. If this guy OD'ed, it's too late anyway."

"But Jackson." I stretched his name out into additional syllables. "She is my friend."

"Some friend. She introduced you to El Rey, the head of a major drug cartel. He could have killed you." He snapped his fingers as if it could have happened that fast.

I shook in fright, and he apologized. "If you stay quiet, I'll call my buddy in DEA. Tell him I got a tip from a snitch. That keeps you and El Rey out of it. Agreed?"

"Yes." I sniffed away the onset of tears, unable to do more for poor Jim.

"Deal. What's the guy's name?"

"Jim, short for James. Last name, Steckler. He works at Levittman, where her husband works. My friend's name is Desiree Overton Smith, and her husband is Steve Smith. I can write this all down for you on a notepad or in your phone's notes."

"Rule number one: nothing in writing. Use your memory muscle. I don't want or need his full-blown bio or all these peoples' names. Just his name. Jim Steckler. I'll remember."

We arrived at my apartment, and he found a prime parking spot right out front. Jackson promised to make the DEA call from my apartment.

He had monitored the rearview mirror and all around while he drove. "An upside here, Kat. No one's following us."

I grinned in relief but avoided speculating on what would have happened if we had been followed.

Chapter 34 ~ Hunkering Down

Inside my apartment, Jackson went into what could best be described as "commando mode."

After he had searched all the rooms and windows, he fired questions at me. "Anything else but the front door and these windows? Other access points?"

"No. Wait! There's a fire escape in my office, but it ..."

He didn't wait to learn how it's only accessible from inside the building. Or how in all the years I've lived here, no one had ever used the fire escape.

He climbed out the window onto the fire escape and nearly flew down the four flights to the ground floor and storage area. In one of those super-fast New York minutes, he climbed back inside and locked the window.

Once he was satisfied that my apartment was clean and unwanted visitor-free, I got his permission to move about freely. I went straight to my bedroom, tore off what was left of my dress, washed my face, and threw on a thick robe. My clock radio forced me to accept it was after 3 a.m. But with all the commotion, I was nervous about taking a shower and reluctant to go to sleep.

When I walked back into the living room, Jackson was on the phone with his DEA buddy, asking him about Jim. He'd taken me up on the offer and was drinking a beer.

Exhaustion set in, and I was ready to push him out the door once he hung up. But Jackson sat on my sofa and fiddled with the Tiffany-style lamp on the side table. He pulled the chain, repeatedly turning the light on and off. The flickering light, a spooky signal, was unnerving.

"Did you know Philly's Kensington has more OD's than anywhere else in the country? The drug bosses are largely Puerto Ricans called *bichote*, big shots. No wonder El Rey is in deep there. Like I said, one of the busiest open-air markets for dope. What they call the Badlands."

I shook my head, not wanting to picture the smiling face of Jim from the photo dying there.

He slammed his hand on a decorative pillow. "To stop it, my buddy told me the city had residents install blue light bulbs. What Philly does. They make it a little harder to find a vein. But that stops no one. They snort it instead."

I sunk down in the chair across from him. We were fighting a losing battle.

"Your buddy fits the OD profile if he's white, affluent, and forty plus. Likely started innocently with a pain prescription."

Shrugging my shoulders, I remembered the photo Desi had shown me of Jim with her kids. His wide grin lit up a healthy-looking face.

Jackson shared more news. "My guy said some of the charities to help the homeless regularly cross the Delaware River from New Jersey. They bring addicts food, clothes, blankets, and tents. Stuffed animals and even Teddy bears for Christ's sake. Everything they need to camp out in the Badlands and keep right on using. Sam bitched about it. Forget I said that."

I nodded. Jackson presumably meant the name Sam. "Completely forgotten."

"My buddy says they provide three meals a day. Delivered right to the door of their campsite. If they didn't make it so effortless, the druggies would get hungry or cold and move on. So now, most refuse to go to rehab. They might as well buy drugs and hand them out."

"G said he wants them to use in moderation. Keep them using but not addicted."

"G? That asshole. Don't get me started on that. He gave you Narcan, the OD reversal antidote. Keeps them alive and kicking to come back and buy. This is so effing hopeless." His voice was low, weighted down from despair.

"We'll arrest him again. I promise. I'm not giving up." I was optimistic but exhausted. If I didn't get some sleep, I wouldn't be able to fight back in a few hours. "Thanks for rescuing me." I stood ready to walk him to the front door. Since he was so skilled at reading people, he must be getting the message.

"Whoa. Stop with that. I would need to thank you. All this back and forth isn't part of the job. You flushed him out. Now we know much more about him."

I froze, recalling how something like this could happen again. The idea of quitting flashed before me, but I pushed it away. "All right. Good night. See you tomorrow."

"It is tomorrow." He snatched the throw blanket from my sofa and shook it out. "Do you have another pillow?"

"Are you sleeping here?"

"Yeah, Queens just adds more hours. Besides, this couch is plenty comfortable and beats the floor. You're safe from me. Promise."

"Wouldn't you prefer the guest room?" He must have seen my spare bed covered with boxes during his comprehensive inspection.

"Nah. This is fine. Don't want to bother moving those boxes. Better here in the center, by the windows and all.

"But I'm on the fourth floor."

"I am well aware of that."

The image of a nutjob rappelling off the building from the courtyard to reach my apartment made me smile.

"Never underestimate him. Or any of them. Promise me that." Jackson was suddenly serious.

"Okay. I promise."

"What's the deal with all these boxes and suitcases in your guest room? Planning to move?"

"No, just some emergency supplies."

"For what?"

"Well, if something happens. Or if I must leave in a hurry."

"I poked around. Looked inside for security reasons. That's a shitload of soap, freeze-dried food, and water."

I nodded, knowing this was weird. I had a detailed emergency list and prep supplies in case of a sudden evacuation. Clean clothes, canned food, water, purification tablets, sunscreen, mosquito repellent, medical supplies, and toiletries were carefully packed in those boxes. But they were stored in the guest room, so I often forgot about them.

"Well, if we need to board Noah's ark, we're ready." In a few seconds, he ridiculed weeks of hard work.

Being ready for a worst-case scenario was no laughing matter. "That's my plan." I even stocked a smaller emergency box at my parent's house in Texas. Mom bitched that I had become a hoarder, but I had my reasons.

Jackson said, "My parents did the same thing. You should have seen their basement. A major fallout shelter with months of supplies. But you know what?"

"What?" I didn't really want to know, but I humored him and braced for another lecture.

"Never needed any of it. When my folks downsized to a condo a few years ago, my sisters and I convinced them to let it all go. And I'm an ex-CIA guy who excels at pre-planning."

Jackson wanted me to admit it was overkill, but I couldn't. Being prepared with those supplies kept me sane and helped me sleep.

"I'm setting the alarm for eight. There's time for four hours of shut-eye. Try to sleep. If not for your sake, for your friend Jim. Busy workday ahead."

"Yes, sir." As dirty as I was, a hot shower must wait. I had to regain my strength to find G's bank account loopholes and fight back. Kick him below the belt, where it hurts, in the financial underbelly. Not just for Keith and Nathan, but now for Jim's sake.

As soon as my head hit the pillow, I drifted off. Falling asleep never felt so good.

Chapter 35 ~ Capturing the Butterfly

When Jackson and I arrived at the office, we regrouped with Anita and Shantelle inside the conference room. After the coffee maker stopped dripping, I poured myself another big cup. Jackson adeptly brewed coffee in my kitchen this morning, but I needed a gallon of caffeine to function today.

Surprisingly, I had seized a few hours of uninterrupted sleep. My bedroom curtains were thick and blocked all outside light, so without an alarm, I could sleep through a sunny day.

I had pursued a decorating scheme suggested by Hypnos, the god of sleep. He lived in an underground cave that blocked all light and sound. Not easy to emulate when you live in the middle of a noisy city. Hypnos had placed sleep-inducing plants outside his cave while I made do with lavender-infused sprays and oils.

Jackson and I took turns explaining to Shantelle and Anita my chance meeting with El Rey and the ill-fated limo ride.

Anita argued that she needed more proof before believing her buddies César and Frankie were part of any drug czar's operation. But an investigation was in play.

They were amazed when I explained how, according to El Rey, it was all merely business. He wanted to increase profits to the bottom line and be a bigshot in pharma. Addiction, pain, and death weren't his problems.

Jackson pulled something out of his pocket and slid it across the table to me. I hoped for another hefty paycheck, but it was a small black device. "Sorry, I should have given this to you before."

"You forgot?" Shantelle said harshly.

Anita frowned, and Jackson shifted in his seat.

"I was wondering why you didn't use the Jackson in the limo. What in the flipping heck happened?" Anita rapped him on the arm but not in jest.

"What's a Jackson?" I asked.

Jackson glared. "Yeah, I screwed up. Happens rarely. But this time, I simply forgot."

"God, Jackson. You paid so much for them, and all the setup time." This was the first time I had seen Shantelle so irate.

She patted my hand in sympathy. "We call them little Jacksons. You know how your cell phone can pinpoint your locations? Retailers use it all the time to track your shopping. Well, we disabled that on our phones, but if there is an emergency, like last night, you push this button. A deceptively small, but invaluable, device tells us you need help."

"You mean that's a tracking tool?"

Jackson smiled. "You got it. It's extremely accurate. Cell towers only cover 160 feet. GPS locations drop it to sixteen feet. With Bluetooth, it's down to inches. If you are moving, it follows you."

"G, I mean El Rey, would have found it. He examined everything inside my purse and even frisked me in his car."

"You? In that tight dress? Sheesh. Bigger ass than I thought," Jackson said.

At first, I thought he was insulting the size of my butt, but he meant our mutual enemy. "That reminds me; I need to cancel my credit card. He took that and my cash."

Anita clenched her fists, ready to punch someone. "Holy crap! What a complete pile of —"

I interrupted her to avoid more untranslatable obscenities in Spanish. "Yeah, he's a real winner."

Shantelle said, "If he's offering you a job, he must be extremely nervous about his accounts and your indepth analysis. Well done, Kat."

"Damn straight." Anita beamed from excitement, and her gold hoop earrings sparkled.

Jackson even broke out of the norm with a wide grin. "You should accept his job offer."

"Hey, trying to get rid of me already?" I tried to smile, but last night was still multicolored and too lifelike.

"Just briefly." Jackson looked resolute, and I wanted to punch him.

Anita nodded, agreeing with Jackson.

Shantelle appeared horrified at the idea. "Much too

dangerous. Even with the tracking device."

My body grew cold and stiff from panic. "I can nail him from the safety of this office. I have some new code words worth pursuing."

"Why not? Give it a shot." Jackson couldn't mask his disappointment.

"I will, but I've got to leave here by 2 p.m. for my flight. Unless I should try to delay the job in Europe."

Jackson pursed his lips while considering his decision. "Call your client in Denmark and ask her. We might nab El Rey while you're gone, or he gets off easy for a few days."

~ ~ ~

Half an hour later, the familiar spreadsheets were open on my laptop, and printouts covered our conference table. I spread some around the edge of the room in piles on the floor using colorful Post-it notes to keep track.

I tried every variation of G and Guillermo I could think of, but nothing meshed. Anita came in for coffee and peered at the reports over my shoulder.

"It's still not working, Anita." But I refused to give up.

"You think Guillermo is the answer?"

"That's all I have."

"But way too obvious. If he uses Guillermo publicly instead of Esteban, why would he reuse it for his account?"

"You're right. Does Guillermo mean something else in English?"

"It's William in English. Try that. Sorry, got to do my own computer crap." She moved toward the door. "But if you need help, just yell."

Just my bad luck to run into another William. Willem was the Dutch version. I plugged "William" and "Willie" into the formulas in my spreadsheet to see if they helped, but they were all a no-go.

I stretched my head back and put Visine in my aching eyes. My neck was stiff, and I rolled it from side to side. Human beings were not designed for staring at rows of tiny numbers in computer files for hours.

Shantelle came in and sat down next to me.

"This is so frustrating. Nothing works." I hated to whine.

"Well, I'm surprised you are even here after what you went through last night."

I looked at her sympathetic brown eyes, glad they weren't green like the Excel spreadsheet files. They reminded me of a soothing cup of hot chocolate.

"Yeah, it was awful. There is something else I didn't tell Jackson. He wanted to have sex, but my fancy dress was so tight it wouldn't come off. Then, he wanted …" I couldn't say it and pointed to my crotch.

Shantelle touched my hand, and her eyes widened in alarm.

"Oh, that's it." His tattoo, the orange-and-black butterfly, was a monarch. I hurried out to ask Anita.

We googled the monarch butterfly and translated it into Spanish, *Mariposa Monarca*. I plugged the English, Spanish, and variations of both into my computer.

Anita stood over me and watched. The computer program ran, and some positive matches appeared.

"Anita, it's working." I jumped up, letting the computer run and do its thing.

"Fabulous!" Anita sprang in the air, matching my excitement.

"Amazing." Shantelle joined us and watched the screen. "Sad about those butterflies. If their habitats and food supply don't rebound, they are destined for extinction."

That was our desire for all drug traffickers but not for innocent butterflies. "Why is that happening?" I asked.

Shantelle sat down on the corner of the table. "Monarchs only eat milkweed, and there isn't much left. Herbicides and development are killing them. Those butterflies migrate thousands of miles from the United States or Canada to Mexico and back. So, like a truck stop along a highway, milkweed needs to be available. They estimate the monarch's population dropped by 90 percent during the past twenty years."

"Wow. How terrible." G must care about them with that tattoo.

Anita said, "Swarms of monarchs still make it to Mexico every year. But my cousins in Mexico are worried. Every year they see less and less. Why did you think of the monarch as a clue?"

"A tattoo. El Rey had it here." I pointed to my hip where his butterfly was located.

"You saw that there?" Anita blinked in disbelief.

So, I spelled out what had happened in as few words as possible.

"Whew, girl. That's intense," Anita said.

"Yeah, it was awful. But then I threw up and —"

Jackson listened in from the doorway and interrupted me. "You threw up? Are you sick?" He clenched his fists and tensed up.

"Not now. Last night."

"When?" Jackson glanced around, confused. This didn't fit in with my chain of events with G.

I shook my head, not willing to go there. Some personal details should be permitted to stay private from your supervisor, especially when it happens to be a man.

"She's tough and better now. Believe me." Anita patted my shoulder, stared at Jackson like a protective sister, and refocused on the computer screen. "You got some matches, Kat. Put me to work."

I printed several copies of the report, highlighted activity to research, and we got down to business.

~ ~ ~

With Anita's help, I had evaluated the results and made a list of how the money flowed from one account to another. Our analysis implicated another group of well-known banks.

Jackson and Shanelle joined us to go over the data and my notes. Our secret client had provided the original information for us to use. This person or group might work for El Rey, and if he or she could identify them, their life was in danger.

Jackson scanned the list and groaned. "Don't all these banks follow basic anti-money laundering procedures? They might as well unlock their doors and publish a sign 'Hide Your Illegal Money Here.'"

KAREN STENSGAARD

The results were embarrassing. Most banks had offices in the United States and were heavily regulated.

But Jackson didn't dwell on their negligence. "Shantelle, call this into your contacts at FinCEN. Try another person this time. Let's hope they do a better job with it."

Jackson referred to the U.S. government's Financial Crimes Enforcement Network, nicknamed FinCEN, a division of the U.S. Treasury. I had never spoken to anyone working there before, so I let Shantelle take the lead. Being a lawyer, she knew how best to coordinate with them.

"On second thought, we should follow up with the banks directly. Can you reach out to their internal auditors by phone, not email?" Jackson asked me.

"Sure. I'll make some calls." Some auditors would be thrilled to dig into this. But the lazy, complacent ones would rue the day they answered my call. Besides irritating senior management, who often preferred to look the other way, this meant additional audit work for resources they didn't possess. "But you realize this will lead to a firestorm of questions and formal requests."

"You're right. Skip it." He frowned at being powerless.

"Lots of these transactions were less than the $10,000 threshold set by the Bank Secrecy Act. So they are harder to catch." Internal auditors often shouldered the blame for anything that went wrong when they didn't set the rules.

"Millions of suspicious activity reports were filed last year. Not just by banks but also other businesses that process cash. Any out-of-the-norm activity for the account should require a SAR filing with FinCEN. Most of these transfers were small but as a group they add up," Shantelle said.

Our computer reports clearly told me that. "You're right. Their computer systems should have flagged them, and their auditors should have pointed out surveillance issues."

"I wonder how many of those SARs led back to our man. Who in the hell screwed this shit up?" Jackson stretched out his arms and acted as if he wanted to grab El Rey around the neck and strangle him.

"Who cares? To hell and damnation with effing protocols.

Nail their asses." Anita smirked as if ready to personally evict them from their high-priced bank buildings. "You can't trust anyone anymore. What I know for sure."

"I disagree, dearie," Shantelle said. "We've got to work with them. But don't worry. I'll investigate the why."

The Melville business phone rang. Shantelle answered and handed me the phone. "Kat, it's your client in Denmark."

I picked up the phone in the conference room and spoke with Inge in a mix of Danish and English. After hanging up, I said, "I've got to go. Inge has already arranged meetings with the Zurich bank."

"What was that with those names and years?" Jackson asked.

"Oh, that was for my grandparents. She wants to see if we happen to be related. Doubtful, since my grandparents weren't from Denmark. Two were Swedish immigrants, and another came from old Bohemia."

"And you just do that? Give her confidential personal info over the phone?" Jackson shook his head in disbelief.

"She's into genealogy. What's the harm? I don't use their names or birthdates for passwords or anything."

"Doesn't matter. Our man G acted pretty nice at the Waldorf. Otherwise you wouldn't have jumped into his limo."

Jackson's insults hurt. "Ian was going with me."

"Don't be so sure that ride wasn't prearranged. Ian could be another flunky working for G."

"I seriously doubt that. Sorry. It won't happen again."

"Did you eliminate all your social media accounts? If I google you, you better come up blank."

My nod didn't convince him. He said, "Shantelle, can you double-check?"

"I already did last week. It's all good, boss. Kathryn and Kat Jensen are gone."

An eerie feeling draped over me after hearing a lawyer confirm that my online presence had been wiped out. My back shuddered, reminding me of the old superstition that this signaled someone had walked across my grave. As though, all of a sudden, I didn't exist anymore.

Chapter 36 ~ Goodbye Crystals

Now that the account transfers were figured out, our conference table was covered with takeout Chinese food, paper plates, and drinks. Eventually, G's team would redo the account codes and open new accounts. Still, for the moment, I was proud of my efforts and our progress.

"Have you been in touch with your girlfriend?" Shantelle asked. "The lady who introduced you to El Rey?"

"Desi? Oh no. I don't want to see her again. Bad reminder." I swallowed some of my hot and sour soup before it got cold. Keeping my distance was safer for her and her family.

"Big mistake. Stay in the loop. Learn about him, his friends, and where he hangs out. Anything and everything." Anita's dark brown eyes grew wide in excitement.

"No, no, no." I coughed, choking on my soup. "He's evil and could have killed me. He warned me not to tell the police." I had done precisely that. "To him, I'm dead already."

"He just wanted to scare you. We would set it up carefully. Protect you. Listen in and monitor 24/7. Perfectly safe." Anita took a serving of beef with broccoli and rice. She sprinkled on top some red pepper flakes leftover from our pizza lunch on Tuesday.

I dropped my plastic spoon in my bowl and stared at Anita, dumbstruck. I doubted I would ever feel completely safe while he was on the loose. If I did what they asked, I would end up dead while they watched.

"What about your buddy, his guy, César? And Frankie the flirt? How are they doing? Living *la vida loca?* Spending *mucho dinero* courtesy of El Rey?"

"Hey, *lo siento, chica.* I've said I'm sorry. What three times already? César is being watched so closely, when he sneezes or farts, I hear about it. Ariel is inside my drawer under lockdown. The little mermaid is evidence and can't swim away."

The others snickered, but I couldn't. Unable to stomach

anything red-hot or spicy, I drizzled soy sauce on white rice with steamed veggies.

"Keep following César." I hated to harp on it, but he had to be the leak. Someone gave El Rey our office address last week. Why I had to be the one to figure this out was beyond me and my job description.

"What about Frankie?" I asked Anita.

"He won't be in Disney's Fantasyland much longer. Might be his last hurrah with the kids for a long while." Anita nodded, but she looked like someone who'd been stabbed in the back but survived.

Jackson grabbed another eggroll, dipped it into the spicy mustard sauce, and changed the subject. "Kat, if you gave it a try as his accountant for a week or so, it could save tons of lives."

I shook my head, tempted to put my hands over my ears.

"I'm not asking you to sell your soul for personal reasons. Lie to him, get close, learn just enough, and put him out of biz permanently." Jackson held his eggroll midair, waiting for my response.

"You make it sound so simple. But I've never worked for the CIA or the NYPD. I didn't obtain years of super-sleuth undercover training."

I took a big sip of sparkling water and glared at them. "So, when El Rey or his hired help find out I'm a mole, I'm on my knees begging." In a desperate voice to drive the point home, I said, "Please don't kill me. Don't I get one final call? Oh, and thirty minutes for someone to show up and rescue me?"

"Come on. It could work." Jackson would never back down.

"Yeah. Could is the operative word. Not will." I was surrounded by people with a death wish. "Didn't Faustus sell his soul to the devil for information and magic? And then he lost the magic, his soul, and his life to devils. Not quite my long term career plan."

"Think about how much we could do with your intel. Last year, we lost more lives from drug overdoses than from gun violence or HIV at its peak." Shantelle, the sensible one, surprised me by moving over to their side.

"Doesn't sound like much of deal to me. Forget about my soul, this is my life. A real true breathing life in exchange for finding out how and where he pushes his millions around."

"You might learn more than that – people, names, places, how he moves product. Everything," Anita said.

"Great. Then the reason to kill me moves from the second floor to a sky-high penthouse on the fiftieth floor."

"If you are in any danger, just say so. We'll pull you out." Jackson made the whole far-fetched idea sound so darn easy.

"Yeah, but in the meantime, they may figure it out and push me over the edge. Falling that high —"

"First off. You must believe." Anita reminded me of a motivational speech from her idol Oprah.

"Yeah, well, sorry. After Thursday night's limo ride, I don't believe in much of anything except fear and danger." My internal audit training to find a solution to problems kicked in. "Why don't I just fake my death, and then you all go in and figure this out?"

Jackson shook his head. "What, you think he'd show up at your funeral? Come on. You fascinate him with your number magic, but that won't happen. If we try to visit his operation, there could be three very real funerals."

I stared at my flimsy paper plate, unable to finish my rice dish, wishing it were time to leave. All this talk about dying was killing me.

"Don't decide now. Think about it while you're gone next week. We would never want you to be alone with him. Ever." Shantelle utilized her smooth legal counseling voice.

"We can position it like this. You quit your job here and say you're desperate. You need quick cash for an emergency so you agree to work for him. Then you rip the whole damn thing apart from the inside out. Besides El Rey, we dive into the whole cartel. All contacts in the business, not just his employees. Who would suspect an accountant and a woman?" Jackson danced around like a feisty Yorkie, anxious to nibble on my leg.

"Shall I remind you? I am a forensic auditor, not an

accountant. And, to answer your question, Esteban Miguel Guillermo Rodriguez, that's who."

I could tell they were disappointed by my reaction. "All right. I'll think about it. Satisfied? But I'm not contacting Desi. She has to reach out first. This could be dangerous for her too." That image of dancing with her two kids was something I didn't want to see obliterated by G.

Somehow our discussion must have sent Desi a weird subliminal message. My personal phone buzzed with a call from her. I left the room to keep the call private and undissected.

After a brief greeting, Desi got right to the point. "G messengered over your credit card and a very generous check. A donation to the cause in your name."

"He did what?"

"He said you dropped your Visa card in his limo. He wants me to messenger it over to you."

All I was focused on was G and the donation. "I mean the check."

"I knew you'd be surprised. I texted you a photo of it. Another much-needed donation to help homeless animals."

I paused, unsure of what to say.

Desi asked, "You still there?"

"Yeah, sorry. Just distracted here at work."

"Sorry to bother you. But G insisted I call and convey his sincere apologies. He was vague about why. What happened?"

"I got out in a hurry. But I'm fine." I touched my bruised knee, a painful reminder.

"G asked me for your cell phone number and home address. But I stalled him. Apparently, he wants to send you flowers and everything."

"Please, Desi. Whatever you do, don't give him my number or address or anything."

"Oh?"

"I'm leaving on a business trip so flowers will die. And you can destroy my credit card. I canceled it already."

This logical explanation satisfied her, and we agreed to

talk later. Perhaps by then, I wouldn't shake with terror at the sound of G's name.

After hanging up, I printed the photo of the cashier's check from G and handed it to Shantelle. "I just got this from Desi. Here's another bank that El Rey uses."

Shantelle read the bank's name out loud. "Wait, your name is in the reference field."

I nodded, unable to ignore it. "An apology."

Shantelle jumped up and showed it to Anita and Jackson.

"A contribution for fifty grand? Shit. This changes everything." Jackson licked his lips.

Anita squeezed my shoulder. "He must be in love."

"Doubtful. Just sorry about kicking me out and nearly killing me near the Bronx Zoo. My chances were better with one of their poisonous snakes."

"What? You said you were pushed out of the car. Didn't the car stop?" Jackson said.

"Not completely, and it was more of a kick." I showed them my bruised palms. "My knees are scraped up and hurt too."

"Did something happen to bring this on?" Jackson fired back.

"He snorted something white, probably cocaine. He must be the type who gets mean when drunk or stoned. Now he has some regrets."

"I still think he's after you. The narco king got hit by Cupid's arrow." Anita danced around, kissing the air and acting silly. "If only Cupid had shot him with real bullets."

I shook my head. "I'm not his type. He has a thing for Dolly Parton. Besides, I never want to see him again. His bank accounts are the only things of his that I'm ever touching." I grimaced at the memory of his unzipped pants. "Is that altogether one-hundred percent clear?"

I hesitated, letting this sink in, and was met with a chorus of yeses from all three colleagues, followed by "Kat," "Madame," or "Sir." Finally, it had sunk in.

"All right. Forget it. It could be dangerous." Jackson accepted defeat, but he was a gracious loser and leaned back with a grin. "All three of you have that rare quality I seek."

"What's that, *hombre*?" Anita asked, as curious as the rest of us.

"Grit. You all carry around a shitload of grit." Jackson raised his bottle of beer in a toast. He scraped and shredded the label with his thumb, which must be a nervous habit, and continued on. "Whatever you ladies want to call it. Bravery, backbone, *cojones*. Shoot, the three of you have so much, we could sell the excess. But don't. Keep it."

I smiled, pleased to get another compliment from a manager who wouldn't say this if he didn't believe it. To celebrate, I raised my plastic bottle of lime-flavored sparkling water, secretly wishing it was a glass of champagne. "To our next job together."

"To teamwork." Shantelle grinned and raised her fruit smoothie.

"There's nothing, and no one we can't stop," Jackson said, holding up a bottle of beer. Drinking beer during work hours was unusual, but Jackson rationalized that one beer wouldn't hurt on a Friday afternoon.

Like Jackson, Anita held up her bottle of beer. She mentioned a study by some Scandinavians who drink regularly to boost their creativity and problem-solving skills.

I laughed. "That might be worth trying. But not until I've finished my work here, and I'm safely at the airport. Now, leave so I can finish."

With less than an hour remaining, I organized and labeled my file folders to sort out the various statements and reports. Color-coded Post-it notes with arrows and letters from A to Z explained how they all flowed together. My colleagues needed to be able to follow my logic and understand this while I was in Europe.

While I worked, I thought about how strange it was to be an employee here. A year ago, Jackson had floated the idea of a job offer with his investigative company before I left for my cruise and followed up when I got back.

Since he had never seen my resume, I figured it was a long shot. When I finally got in touch, Jackson gave me a much-needed boost when he raved about my expertise and said he didn't regret waiting. Despite everything that happened with G, aka El Rey, I enjoyed working with them.

When I handed over the files, Shantelle handed me a small box. "A small goodbye gift."

Inside, I found a silver necklace with three small unpolished stones dangling from the chain. I recognized the purple one since amethysts are my birthstone.

"I made this for you," Shantelle said.

"Wow. So unexpected and kind of you."

"The amethyst promotes peace and protection. The blue one is a mineral called kyanite, which sends positive vibes and connects you with helpful spirits. The clear quartz crystal gives you energy." She helped fasten it around my neck.

"Beautiful, I feel better already. I love it." I gave her a brief hug.

She acted embarrassed. "The others chipped in to buy the stones."

"Thank you all. Couldn't wish for a better team." I didn't believe in magical gems or spirits, but a pretty necklace couldn't hurt.

Anita went to the refrigerator and placed a paper bag in front of me. "For you. I wanted to loan you my Walther PPK. The firearm 007 liked to use. But going on a plane without a permit won't fly." She cackled at her joke.

I pulled out a cold glass flask labeled Kombucha. "What's this?"

Anita grinned. "Fermented tea. Naturally carbonated with a tiny bit of alcohol so one won't hurt."

Shantelle said, "It's filled with probiotics to improve gut health, immunity, and digestion. Excellent for your long ride to the airport."

I wondered how such a small drink could do so much.

Anita said, "Chinese people call it the tea of immortality."

"I'm not sure if I want to live forever." But I thanked her for being so thoughtful and took a sip.

Jackson left his office to join us, looked at the bottle, and raised his eyebrows.

Anita stared at Jackson. "I had to give Kat something special. Like Q did for James Bond."

I asked her, "Is this a Q-created secret drink for me?"

She nodded with a goofy grin.

I laughed. "Well, call me when you finish making a portable invisibility suit, Madame Q."

She chuckled. "Sure. Might be ready when you're back. Then I'll retire with all that money flowing in." She looked over at Jackson.

He said, "You invent that, and we are all going to reap mega rewards. But a week later, you'd all be bored out of your skulls, begging for your jobs back."

Anita punched his arm. "You know me too well, *Señor J.C.*"

I grinned. But a mother lode of money could fight off boredom for months.

"Can you bring us back a small Danish pastry? *Por favor*?" Anita smiled.

"They might be stale and inedible. I'm flying back from Zurich. How about one of their pretzels or some chocolate?"

"Sure thing. But I was hoping for a world-famous Danish." Anita grinned.

"Next time. I've got to hurry to make my flight. See you next week sometime. I'll be in touch."

Jackson swung his jacket over his shoulder. "I'll walk you out." Over his shoulder, he said to Anita and Shantelle, "See you ladies, Monday. Start your weekend."

Chapter 37 ~ Whale-Sized Worries

Outside, while I finished my Kombucha drink, Jackson scanned the streets for our drug lord or whoever else haunted him. "I'll drive you home. We need to chat."

A few blocks away, we found his SUV with paper attached to his windshield. He'd parked about a foot into a restricted yellow zone. He ripped the ticket off his windshield and crammed it into his pocket. "Don't they know we're the good guys?"

"Apparently not." And with his secrecy, they never would.

He drove southbound on Broadway toward my apartment. The subway was faster, but I got a few more valuable morsels of information when we were alone.

"El Rey's throwing money around to find you and apologize. Jeez, he's nuttier than a Kind bar."

I smirked at the empty wrappers of Kind nut bars littering the floor of his SUV.

"Which airport and who's driving you?"

"JFK and an Uber driver named Zhila."

A frown crossed his face.

"She's a friend."

"Cancel. I'll drop you. I live in Queens, close to JFK."

"Not necessary, but thanks. Zhila is completely trustworthy." Besides, she's cheerful and inspiring, two positive personality traits I sorely needed.

"So, Jackson lives in Queens," I repeated this rare piece of personal intel.

"Ozone Park. A sneaky name. The ozone refers to fresh air, not a noxious chemical. The breeze off Jamaica Bay kept it malaria-free." When Jackson opened up, he was a wealth of fascinating information. "But don't tell anyone. It's crowded enough."

"You like living there?"

"What's not to like? Home to John Gotti and the Gambino crime family. Another of my favorite novelists, Jack Kerouac, lived there. A total melting pot, and full of Asians, so I blend right in."

"Cool." Some weekend, I should drag Abby out there for lunch and scope it out. Accidentally running into Jackson and seeing his reaction would be an added thrill.

"Are you meeting with El Rey before his 48-hour deadline?"

"Yep. But it's doubtful he'll show. You don't need to stress about the Looney Tunes Captain Willem anymore. I met him last night and got things arranged."

"You never said anything. I assumed you couldn't find him."

"Shoot, I'd find that guy blindfolded. Last night your focus and memory had to be on El Rey. Not a shitty seaman. Damn, that came out wrong."

I nodded. "What happened?"

"I got confirmation. The captain successfully shipped out this morning from Mystic."

"Shipped out?" I asked.

"Departed. Floated away. Whatever you call it. The *Charles W. Morgan* set sail at 1100 hours."

In nautical lingo, that was 11 a.m. Captain Willem was well on his way by now. "Where's he going?"

"South America. A long journey on a genuine whaleship. I hope someone brought a copy of *Moby-Dick* for when he wakes up."

"A real whaling ship? Oh my god, those ships are treacherous."

"Before he starts marketing voyages to customers and ripping them off, he should experience a real one firsthand."

"But Jackson, whaling ships are at sea for years."

"Even better. Don't go soft on me. The blowhard needed a readjustment." Jackson chuckled. "More wind in his sails to carry him far away. One less problem for us to track."

"But … he could die." Working on a whaler was the worst job at sea. I wouldn't want anyone to go through that, except someone named Esteban Miguel Guillermo Rodriguez.

"He'll be home in a few months. After he's seen the light

or shore, he'll leave you alone."

"I hope you're right."

"He sure was a whack job. All those sea days must have …" Jackson stopped at a traffic light and twirled his finger in a circle, signaling that Captain Willem was bonkers. "Far and away over-salted and weathered to his core. Was the captain on your ship that unbalanced? All those days bobbing around must shake the gray matter upstairs."

"Absolutely not. My captain was highly skilled and a gentleman most of the time." My voice trailed off, remembering.

"Great. Willem threw back enough whiskeys to drown. He'd never find Moby Dick."

~ ~ ~

Back inside my apartment, Jackson ran through another security inspection. I argued that he could skip this ordeal since I was leaving soon and pointed to Giuseppe, my faithful guard dog.

But Jackson's knitted brow told me this was no joke. "I know your first solo job overseas isn't what you had in mind. But this is a useful break. You're safer in Europe for a few days."

I couldn't help but frown. In less than a week, I would be back to worrying.

He pulled out of his jacket pocket a piece of paper and tossed it on the kitchen counter. "Hardship pay for last night. A small advance on this new client."

I held another generous paycheck and mumbled a thank you. At this rate, my financial worries would end soon. But depositing it must wait until I return.

Jackson chuckled when he saw me fold the paycheck and stick it under Giuseppe's bottom.

I frowned. "Giuseppe the Gargoyle is honest and low maintenance. A wonderful roommate."

"I bet. At least he's quiet and won't violate my NDA. Forgot to ask you this morning. Don't you have a house cat on the prowl?"

"Xena, but she died from mammary cancer. There's her

cremains." I pointed to the bronze-colored container with an embossed paw print.

Jackson nodded politely. "Sorry, Kat and cat."

"If I don't travel so much in the future, I plan to adopt another cat. Or maybe two, so they can keep each other company."

"Go for it. Nice apartment." He scanned the living room. "Easy to entice someone to cat-sit when you're gone."

Jackson's mention of gone reminded me how close I came last night. The risk still loomed over me with G free on bail.

"If something happens to me, will you remind my parents to mix my cremains with Xena's? I want us to be scattered together. Somewhere along the Hudson River, where it's legal."

"Sure thing," Jackson said, "But, first off, this job's a project, and it isn't dangerous. If I called it Operation Onion or Pepper, like the CIA, then it's serious fan-hitting shit. And second, you will most likely outlive me."

He slung his bag of paperwork and secretive stuff, like onion rings, over his shoulder to leave. "Give Inge my regards. Remember to refer to her not by name with us but as Project Pepper in any public discussions, calls, or emails. When you wrap up, ask her for referrals. And if you come across a valid lead, give them a company card. But be discreet and selective. That keeps us afloat."

I agreed but was insulted. I knew firsthand how consulting works. One job leads to another, or you starve and shut down. My unsuccessful consulting business had only lasted a few years, and I lost money from day one. Monthly bank statements still reminded me that my savings account may never recover.

"Don't look so glum. He will be locked up or on to something new when you're back. We've got that connection to César and Frankie, thanks to you."

I prayed he was right. But, just in case, I put on the deadbolt as soon as he left.

While I switched into a sweatshirt and casual stretch pants for the overnighter in the sky, I repeated some of his practical parting advice. "Stay alert. Keep moving. Repeat." Of course, he'd sprinkled in a few F-bombs.

I zipped up my overloaded carry-on bag and called my parents. When they both got on the phone, I updated them on my business trip.

"Denmark? Not there again," Dad said in a worried voice.

"A straightforward assignment, so I won't be gone long. Promise. I'll see you in San Antonio for Christmas as planned."

"We are so eager to finally meet Charles in December," Mom said.

"Well, about that … we broke up."

"Aren't you going to Wyoming for Thanksgiving to meet his family?" My dad sounded confused.

"Nope. That's off. I meant to tell you, but things have been so busy lately with my new job."

"We really like Charlie. He called us while you were gone. He spent a lot of time and money looking for your ship," Dad said.

"Why didn't you tell me? I just found out about this."

"After you got home, we were so relieved, it didn't matter. Axel's been gone for a while now. Another relationship is a way to move on." Mom was always practical and often unemotional.

I had never confessed how Axel planned to leave me for his former girlfriend in Denmark, except cancer cut short his plans. If they knew the truth about their son-in-law, they wouldn't pressure me to find another husband. But I hated to mention this and be subject to their disappointment and pity.

"Why don't you wait a week or two and reconsider bringing him here for Christmas? We wanted to meet him and force-feed him tamales on Christmas eve." Dad chuckled about the unusual San Antonio tradition to eat Tex-Mex tamales that night.

"Charlie isn't trustworthy. I can't —"

Dad broke in. "Some people argue that everything is forgivable. But it's your decision."

I simmered at a low boil, refusing to go into details about

my personal relationships.

"Have a nice trip." Mom knew to back off from unnecessary confrontations.

I hung up, trying to forget about Charlie. I should have told them about my new Thanksgiving plans with Abby.

I grabbed my briefcase and carry-on bag and stopped to chat with Abby. She still had a spare key to my apartment, but I preferred to say goodbye in person.

She leaned against her door, looking tired.

"I'll be back by Wednesday for Thanksgiving. We'll have fun."

"I'm not counting on it. It feels like you are going to war or something." Abby made eye contact but didn't smile. I couldn't really blame her when my past two trips had stretched out unexpectedly.

"Not war, just a job. Thanksgiving is my favorite holiday. I refuse to miss it again this year."

"I gave Charlie the watch back. He's really sorry about whatever it was he did."

"Thanks. I'll explain more when I'm back. I've got to hurry."

We hugged, and she wished me the best, reassuring me that all would be fine here at home. But I sensed her disappointment.

Chapter 38 ~ Do the Kind Thing

On the street outside my apartment building, I checked the time. Zhila and her skunk-mobile should be here by now, so I texted her.

Someone touched my shoulder and said my name. I swung around, and my hands formed fists, ready to strike even with my phone in one hand.

"Whoa." Charlie moved back to a safer distance. "Are you okay?"

"I'm fine. You surprised me." I took a deep breath to slow my thundering heartbeat and reminded myself how much safer it would be in Europe.

After I lowered my fists, Charlie approached slowly. "Heard you're headed to the airport. I've got a car on standby."

"I don't need a lift. Where's your red-hot number?" His impossible-not-to-see red roadster was missing.

"In the shop, I'm afraid. Jason borrowed it last night while I was at the gala. A fender bender costs an insane amount to repair. So, you were right. An SUV is more practical, and I can rent one."

I wouldn't harp on how I was right. "At least no one was hurt. Why aren't you at the office?"

"I should be, to focus on keeping my job especially when I can't keep a girlfriend. I wanted to see you and thought we could chat on the way to the airport."

"Well, you thought wrong. Again." That comment was uncharacteristically cruel. "A car is on the way."

"Can I keep you company until it comes? Or is there already someone else? That guy Ian or the Spanish guy?"

A chill raced down my back at the memory of G. "No, there isn't anyone else. I don't want anyone right now. Is that clear enough?"

"Jeez. Sorry I mentioned it. But can you promise me one week won't turn into two months or more?"

"This is work. But I plan to be back next week."

"I can't bear it if you disappear again. Last time, I calculated down to the hour how long you were away." He looked away as though embarrassed.

"You did?" I had never bothered to figure that out. His weird comment was creepy, like a stalker.

My phone beeped with a text from Zhila. She apologized for some traffic delays and would arrive in about five minutes.

"You know Kat, when we danced last night, you said things happened to you. Things that you don't want me to know about. Well, I have some embarrassing things in my past to tell you too."

"While I was gone?"

"No. Long before, when I was eleven, and for a couple of years."

I stepped back with my luggage. "Stop! Don't you dare do a true confession thing here on the sidewalk. I can't deal with that now." Riding with him down a bumpy road into his childhood would be painful. My current load of mental stress couldn't process more gut-wrenching memories.

"When you return, I'll tell you. You deserve to know. This was buried deep inside my head for years."

In desperation, I stood on my tiptoes looking for Zhila's skunk-mobile. But only a taxicab headed our direction.

Charlie said, "I tried to be stoic. A tough Wyoming cowboy that takes shit from no one."

I was touched by his desire to share his past. Charlie wasn't much of an actor, so this must have been incredibly painful. His confession had piqued my curiosity, but it must wait.

Charlie stepped closer. "Getting some professional counseling helped me and might help you, too."

I stepped back to a safer distance. "Counseling might work for some. But I can't relive my past or deal with all those invasive questions. My plan is to make peace with it and move on."

"I'm sorry. Taking you to that clinic was a huge mistake."

"I need space to breathe and to be free, not stifled."

"When did I ever try to stifle you? I only suggested

counseling. They suggested staying overnight, not me." Charlie blinked rapidly and looked upset.

"You … you just do. By being here. Hovering around."

"Fine. I'll stand back." He stepped back about a foot. "Better?"

I nodded. "When I was gone for so long, I had to adjust and blend in like a chameleon. I had to wear the right thing, say the right thing, and do the right thing. Not make any mistakes. I can't do that anymore. I must ... I need freedom."

"Sure. Be free. I won't try to make you do anything. Our relationship isn't a prison."

"I can't be what you want. A regular girlfriend to follow your lead and decisions. Someone else, like Abby, would be better for you."

He frowned. "You are officially anointed the prime decision-maker." He bowed. "Your wish is my command."

I giggled but doubted this would last. Charlie was too accustomed to calling the shots. "Are you going to Wyoming for Thanksgiving?"

"No. I decided not to go solo. I volunteered to go to our London office next week. So we will both be in Europe. Can I call you?"

"Sorry. I'm going to be awfully busy." With the client's project, travel schedule, and bank meetings, there would be limited free time to juggle his calls.

"I'll be busy as well. Going to empathy and mindfulness training, if you can believe that. I'm spearheading the rollout in the U.S. How not to insult or mistreat the fairer sex. That Harvey Weinstein idiot."

"For getting caught or for what he did?"

"What do you think? I have three sisters. Don't you think I know how to treat them? And want them treated fairly?"

"Just verifying. You can't blame me. I don't work with you."

"Personally, I don't think I need it. But there are plenty of bozos who say awful things about women. If taking a course will help change them, then the entire world should." With every word, Charlie's voice grew louder in anger.

"And, as we know, people don't like to change."

"Particularly men in power. That old saying about what you learned in kindergarten holds true."

I nodded, remembering some mischief in my Montessori preschool.

Charlie looked toward the park and back at me. "Sometimes, emotions run rampant and out of control. Regrets follow."

A car honked, and Zhila waved from the skunk-mobile.

"My ride is here."

"In that? I remember that car from Connecticut."

"Yeah, my getaway driver."

Once Zhila popped the trunk, Charlie insisted on hoisting my suitcase inside.

"Have a productive trip. Enjoy yourself this time. You deserve it. When you are back and up for it, we can book that restaurant. I can explain some more. You might even forgive me."

Doubtful, but I didn't want to be rude.

With Zhila double-parked and blocking the one-lane road, impatient motorists would soon line up behind her.

Charlie opened his arms, offering his usual bear hug. My stiff body shrunk back to keep my distance, but I felt him pull at my coat pocket.

I reached inside and pulled out the watch I'd returned to Abby. The valuable wristwatch was unwrapped without the protective box.

I held it out to him, but he stepped back, refusing. "If you don't want it, I'll give it to one of my sisters. But I bought it for you, and you need one."

While I deliberated, Charlie leaned over and introduced himself to Zhila. They shook hands and chatted like old buddies. A cab came up from behind and honked, interrupting him.

To get going, I said, "Oh, all right. Since you keep insisting. Thank you for the watch."

I climbed into the skunk-mobile's front seat, smelled onions, and quickly found the source. Leftover wrappers from a Big Mac burger were on the floorboard. Overcome by the reminder of Project Onion, I unrolled the window to air out the car.

Charlie leaned in and smiled, appreciating the gesture that had nothing to do with him. "Bye then. When you're back, maybe we can catch a movie. We've always talked about it."

I nodded in a noncommittal way, unwilling to promise him anything.

Charlie stood back on the sidewalk, waved, and looked sad.

Zhila put her car into gear and drove toward Central Park. The idea of Charlie getting caught up in Heather's insider trading investigation net haunted me. With his psychological issues, he might veer off and take an irreversible action like my neighbor Nathan. I couldn't let that happen.

"Stop!"

Zhila slammed on the brakes, and the cab's horn behind us blared while I opened the door to jump out.

"I'm sorry, Zhila. Can you circle the block and pick me up? I should warn him about something." Jackson would disapprove, but I could tiptoe around the details to avoid violating the NDA.

I ran toward Charlie, yelling his name. He turned and jogged toward me.

"I only have a few minutes." A man walked by, and I leaned in to keep my words confidential. "Be careful at work. Don't do anything shady. Nothing in any gray areas. There's a big investigation going on into insider trading. If you get caught up in that mess, it could ruin your career."

He took my hands in his but shrugged as if unconcerned.

"This is serious. You could lose your job. Even go to jail. But you can't tell anyone or mention me. I shouldn't even be telling you. If you do, I'll never speak to you again."

"I promise I won't breathe a word. You know, Kat, risks surround me every single day. Except I control the narrative and always stay on the right side of the law."

"What in the hell does that mean? If illegal activities are happening at your firm, by management or your colleagues, they could blame you. Even set you up. Then you might get barred from the securities industry or end up in jail. Take your pick."

He shook his head as though my dire predictions were impossible. My naïve optimistic Wyoming boy had never been circled by desperate Wall Street sharks in a feeding frenzy to survive.

"I'm dead serious about this. I can't tell you more. Please don't bring this up in an email or anything."

"Steve was right. Said to be here to say *au revoir.* How you're worth fighting for."

"Desi's husband said that?"

"Yeah, and more. Old Stevie urged me to patch things up with you."

I narrowed my eyes, convinced Charlie was exaggerating. "He did?"

"Steve said, 'She's sharp, a hard worker, and not bad to look at. So, don't fool around and lose her again.'"

I shook my head in disbelief. Maybe helping Desi out at the gala and my warnings about the thieves brought him around.

"Come on, I promise it's true. After this long week, I could use a supportive hug goodbye. Truce?"

"Why not? But Charlie, you must keep this, what I told you, between us."

Zhila was back, and the car idled in the middle of the street.

Charlie held me tight and kissed my cheek. "That and more. I'm counting the hours and minutes again."

Somehow that didn't make me feel better. But it would be so much worse if I returned and Charlie was jobless, arrested, and facing a court date with possible jail time.

Chapter 39 ~ A Tiger in My Tank

Back inside the skunk-mobile, Zhila drove toward the street's dead-end at picturesque Central Park.

Zhila said, "Just to make sure, you need JFK airport, also known as Idlewild? I like that old name better." With three airports used by New Yorkers, sometimes people went to the wrong airport and missed their flights.

"You bet. Onwards to Idlewild. Just not too wild. Things have been insane lately. Did you hear how I met your husband early this morning?"

"Yeah, the hubby said, 'Your friend's exciting and sure to inspire some zany poetry.' I'm dying to get the details."

The scent of onions had dissipated, so I rolled up the window. I exhaled slowly, wanting to keep most of what happened with El Rey confidential. But I needed some advice, and sometimes you should take a chance. "Last night I met this guy from Argentina, and he offered me a ride home. But he took my money and dropped me in the Bronx. I'd left my phone at home. One of my worst nights ever."

"Sounds terrible." Zhila said. "Is Charlie the guy who chased us in Connecticut?"

"Yeah, that's Charlie. He's apologized so many times. A real glutton for punishment. I don't know why he bothers. I'm ordinary looking and not much fun to be around."

"Don't say that. You are a lovely girl when you smile, and you have so much going for you."

"I don't believe in happy endings. I was married before."

Zhila smoothly changed lanes to pass a double-parked car. "What happened?"

"He died but was going to divorce me." I kept my voice emotionless as if I were talking about the weather. "He got cancer and that ended it. Eternally, if you know what I mean."

While she quietly processed this, I rambled on. "Your husband, the doctor, is a keeper. You've got that happy-ever-after thing going. Good for you." But I regretted being so cynical, like an overripe bitter lemon.

"You never know. Marriage doesn't come with a guarantee. Romance books don't all pursue that kind of ending anymore. Often it is happy-for-now instead of happily-ever-after."

"Well, that's smart. Everything is for now."

"Truer words were never spoken, girlfriend."

Before agreeing to share the gritty details about last night, I convinced her to tell me her top-secret pen name. Once I got on the internet, I would order her self-published book, which she referred to as "her baby." Her no-nonsense approach to life and her kind of poetry was smack dab what I needed.

While we passed over the Queensboro bridge and left Manhattan behind, I explained things using an imaginary friend's predicament to tiptoe around Melville Consulting's menacing NDA. And how my friend's company wanted her to meet with a kingpin dope trafficker.

Zhila pursed her lips. "I don't see any other option. You, I mean your friend, must go after that drug czar. Do what they suggest."

My entire body tensed up at the idea of meeting El Rey again.

The skunk-mobile scooted around a slow-moving truck in the right lane. Zhila's response, like her driving, was calm and no-nonsense.

Deep down, I knew she was right, but it scared me. "Doing this would be so dangerous for her."

"Danger is all around us. For crying out loud, driving to the airport is risky. I love that saying. And most accidents occur inside bathrooms. Did you know that?"

"No, but I'm not surprised."

"I know the stats. I'm a mathematician and a quantitative analyst."

"What? You said you're a poet." Was she lying to me? Could she be part of El Rey's shady team?

"Relax, I am a poet. Math and poetry have a lot in common. Mathematics is useful to count syllables, analyze word patterns, and create rhythm."

"But why aren't you a quant during the day and a poet a

night? Those jobs are in huge demand. You could be —"

"Making a killing with beaucoup bucks in the bank? Like you, I didn't want to get my bones picked clean by the vultures on Wall Street. No, thanks."

"You continue to amaze me, Zhila."

"But Kat, back to your friend's dilemma. She has a fantastic opportunity. Most of us will never get to do that."

"Do what?" This annoying how-lucky-I-was talk made things worse.

"Something extraordinary. Be a kick-ass woman warrior. Put a big-shot narcotics trafficker behind bars. Help the good guys fight the opioid epidemic on behalf of so many people."

"She hasn't ruled it out yet." I stared out the window, ready to escape from all this pressure. Being around complete strangers next week would be a welcome break.

Zhila said, "I met some Muslim women this week. They've started wearing their hijabs again. That piece of cloth on your head makes you a target, but they do it bravely. Not because of their religion, but to peacefully protest the surge in Islamophobia in freedom-loving America."

"But why?" I asked.

"To stand against all these threats and to fight off prejudice in a nonviolent way. They travel all over the globe to meet and greet non-Muslims. Show them who we are and that we aren't threatening. Sometimes they even go solo."

"How incredibly brave."

"I'm planning to join them next month. Albert Einstein once said something about how the world is dangerous. Not because people are evil, but because people do nothing about it."

"Nobel prize-winning Einstein. That's deep."

"Yeah. So, here's what I'm trying to say to you. You can be a *shirzan* like us and fight back. *Shirzan* is a Persian word for a lioness and a strong woman." She put the car's blinker on to change lanes. "Sorry about the lecture."

"No need to apologize. I know what you mean." But now I had another danger to brood over. An anti-Islam nut might attack Zhila.

"One last piece of advice and I'll stop." Zhila was energized and rolling along on more than just the four wheels of the skunk-mobile.

"Go for it." I looked out the window.

"Don't shut yourself off."

"What do you mean?"

"That guy, Charlie. He may be a complete Mr. Wrong. But he doesn't seem so bad. When you talk about him, it's clear he infuriates you. But you care, and there's a strong connection between you. I sensed it."

I recalled his stressed look when we said goodbye. "Yeah, that's the trouble with Charlie. He can be sweet one moment. Then he drives me crazy and almost over the edge."

"Things are never perfect. My husband and I have strong personalities. But it's better to disagree with someone on occasion than get stuck with a wimp."

"If you know someone I could introduce him to, just say the word." Charlie weighed me down like an oversized piece of luggage that refused to fit inside an airplane's overhead compartment.

"That goes for you too, kid. Be more open to new people."

"Okay, Mom. I sure will."

Zhila gripped the wheel and passed cars with drivers likely unfamiliar with the airport. "Turn up the radio, will you? It's Friday. The best day of the week. Pure magic and optimism are in sync."

U2's song "Beautiful Day" blared from the car's small but powerful speakers. We sang along, determined to enjoy another day and live life to the fullest.

Zhila weaved through the departure lanes at JFK and stopped at the curb outside my terminal. Despite lugging my carry-on out of her trunk, I felt lighter. The heavy burden from last night had slipped off my shoulders.

Zhila gave me a quick farewell hug. "You are the captain of your own ship. It's your life, and we may only have this one. Stand tall."

I nodded, kissed her cheek, and promised to let her know my return flight information. Before she could refuse, I stuck an envelope on the dashboard. I'd gathered a wad of twenties to repay her husband. Tucked inside, my thank you note suggested that she take her kind and understanding husband out for a fancy dinner. An impartial lionhearted friend like Zhila was priceless.

Chapter 40 ~ Welcome Back Resilience

After airport security, I debated two options. I could head to the upscale airport lounge reserved for business class travelers for a drink, or I could shop inside the duty-free stores. My index finger went through the enlarged moth hole in my cashmere scarf. To avoid looking unpresentable to my new client for the next four days, shopping won.

With a new scarf around my neck, I found a seat at my departure gate. I scanned my phone one last time for messages. A text from Desi begged me to get in touch as soon as possible.

> Kat: Hey!
> Desi: Hi, Kat. Thanks again for your help last night!
> Kat: Sure.

I couldn't help but be polite, but no way would I offer to do it again.

> Desi: Can we get together this weekend?
> Kat: Nope. At the airport. Going to Europe. Back next week.
> Desi: Ugh. Already?
> Kat: Yep. Work trip.
> Desi: I have awful news.
> Kat: What?
> Desi: OMG. Jim died. I knew something was wrong.

At least she knew, but this final confirmation about Jim was what I had feared.

> Desi: My heart is broken.
> Kat: Your co-chair Jim? How?
> Desi: Not sure. He died in Philly. His parents saw him in the morgue.

My stomach was in knots, and I dropped my phone in surprise.

> Desi: Police found his work ID. No wallet.
> Kat: OMG
> Desi: His exec manager told Steve. So unbelievable. I'm totally numb.
> Kat: Why don't we talk, not text?

Desi: Can't talk now. Will cry. Text better.

Kat: I'm so sorry. Poor Jim.

Desi: RIP. He was in a car accident years ago. In tremendous pain, but he kept going. Now he's pain-free.

Kat: Yes, at least that.

The only upside was still a complete downside. But this explained Jim's drug addiction. When his prescription was cut off, he turned to illegal, dangerous opioids.

Desi: Funeral's Monday, I think.

Kat: Oh, so sorry. Back Wednesday.

Desi: You never got to meet him. Please don't stay gone for months this time!

Kat: Nope. Not even a week.

Desi: Put Saturday, December 9, on your calendar.

Kat: For?

Desi: Our holiday party here. Stay the night! Our alarm is fixed. G will be here too.

A shiver flew down my spine. I whispered, "Hells bells and buckets of blood." But if I withdrew from my friends and life, he'd win.

Kat: Maybe

Desi: 🌚

I debated what to do in silence. A social gathering was the ideal neutral place to meet El Rey one last time. My friends and colleagues would protect me, and I could get some intel. G's brutal disregard for Jim last night gnawed at me. Like Zhila's lioness, I should fight back and rip El Rey to shreds.

Kat: Okay, I will be there. Thanks!

Desi: Purr-fect. Miss you, ♥ Desi

Kat: Me too. Take care. XO, 🐱

I wasn't a frequent emoji user, but the smiling cat face with heart-shaped eyes fit me. In despair, I turned off my phone, unwilling to deal with more bad news. Jim died in such a terrible way, all alone and in a dangerous part of town. At least Desi and his family knew what happened, and his pets were rescued.

I glanced down at my small carry-on bag. This consulting job was like carrying around an impossibly heavy suitcase full of secrets. I was forced to lug an invisible weight everywhere I went. Was it worth keeping secrets when it might hurt someone I care about? Next week after this job ended, I'd decide.

An excited family of four, waiting to board my flight, sat nearby. They chatted about their upcoming vacation of a lifetime to Denmark. Tomorrow they planned to visit Tivoli Gardens, open and decorated for the Christmas season. I envied their joy and fearlessness.

The flight attendants announced business-class travelers could board the plane. I stood determined to take on whatever got thrown in my direction. After all, Dorothy made it to Oz and back, so I could too.

Lined up with my fellow priority-boarding travelers, I fingered my new necklace. I would miss the office and my colleagues next week. The purple protecting stone reminded me of Shantelle, and the upbeat blue one had Anita's name on it. The no-nonsense quartz was just like Jackson. Despite everything that went wrong, in the end, I did something right by accepting that job and sticking with it.

Herman Melville's most famous novel, *Moby-Dick*, about a life-threatening voyage and quest for a massive whale, was unsuccessful during his lifetime. To pay mounting bills, he switched midstream to work as a customs house inspector. That novel became his masterpiece and a much-loved classic. Proof that things can change when you least expect it, and like Melville, I would adapt.

The excitement of boarding a plane, meeting new people, and diving into a fun adventure beckoned. I strutted down the jetway, ready to rule like a *shirzan,* making Zhila proud. I clutched my boarding pass along with a hefty dose of optimism tightly.

~ ~ ~

The End

~ ~ ~

About the Author

Karen Stensgaard is the author of two novels, *Aquavit* and *Blueness*, part of the Aquamarine Sea series. She is a member of The Author's Guild, the largest and oldest organization supporting working writers. Currently, she lives in Philadelphia with her husband and two rescue cats.

Karen grew up in San Antonio and spent a year in Denmark as a foreign exchange student. After completing her MBA, Karen moved to San Francisco and worked for the Federal Reserve Bank as an examiner and Bank of America as an internal audit consultant.

Seeking new challenges, Karen relocated to New York City to join PricewaterhouseCoopers and held senior internal audit positions at various financial firms. Over the years, she obtained many professional and brokerage licenses, including a CPA, and a Certified Internal Auditor, Fraud Examiner, and Anti-Money Laundering Specialist designation. Her work experience and licenses came in handy while writing this novel!

Ways to Connect on Social Media

 My website & blog: karenstensgaard.com

 Facebook Author Page: Karen Stensgaard, Novelist or @karenjstensgaard *

 Twitter: @ThisKarensKind *

 Instagram: KarenStensgaard

 Pinterest: KarenStensgaard
With a Project Onion photo album

 LinkedIn: KarenStensgaard *

 Goodreads: KarenStensgaard *

 YouTube: KarenStensgaard
With a Project Onion song playlist

 Amazon: KarenStensgaard *

*   Includes my blog feed

Q&A with the Author

You were an internal auditor and consultant for financial firms on Wall Street for many years. Any truth to the story?

Some nuggets of truth about auditing, money laundering, opioids, Narcan, goddesses, and ships are scattered throughout. But if you left your skeptical self behind on page one, that was the best plan. All of the characters and situations were dreamed up with the help of my muse, Madeline.

I did run a few hypothetical situations by some police officers but not with lawyers or anyone from the CIA. The beauty of writing fiction, as opposed to something official like an audit report, is dreaming things up. I hope it came across as possible, but it's not probable. At least, I hope not for poor Kat!

How did you research the drug trafficking and opioid crisis?

I did most of my research by reading and watching documentaries about the drug crisis. Unfortunately, my new hometown of Philadelphia has been in the news and is a hot spot. I also attended a half-day class the city offered to learn more about the opioid issue and how to use Narcan. I have an emergency pack ready but haven't administered it yet. Like Kat, if the situation comes up, I would like to help someone in need.

What's it like to publish a book?

Self-publishing is a challenge. I try to write stories that entertain but still make sense and possibly educate you on a current issue. While writing and researching news and situations, I also study the craft of writing to create a better story. Since I am a do-it-yourself author, with only a professional editor and proofreader's paid assistance, writing often gets sidetracked. Without a big-name publisher or marketing team, positive online reviews and sharing my books with friends really help spread the word.

What's next?

Project Pepper is the next book in the new Melville Consulting series. Kat gets into hot, spicy trouble while completing her next client job in Europe. I hope you enjoyed *Project Onion* without any onion-induced tears and want to read the next one!

Do you want to add anything else?

I'd like to thank my friends and family who have read the drafts. A writing workshop and another critique group provided helpful feedback. With so many people to mention, I won't drag it out, but I do appreciate the help.

Also, I realize that *Project Onion* might not be your kind of story. Many popular best-selling books don't grab my attention either. Luckily, there are plenty of great books to read, not to mention live theater, movies, and TV shows which provide so many fantastic stories. I'm honored you spent time on mine.

Book Club Discussion Topics - Spoiler Alert!

1. Our in-over-her head auditor Kat Jensen makes decisions but often changes her mind. Which one stood out to you as a huge mistake and why?

2. Kat has a wide range of friends and colleagues in this story. Who was your favorite, and what did they do or say to win you over?

3. Should Kat have refused to take on her next assignment, code name Project Pepper, and quit working for Melville Consulting?

4. When Kat warned Charlie about Heather's investigation, she probably broke her nondisclosure agreement. Should she have done this?

5. The abuse of opioids and addiction continues to be a serious global crisis. What's your opinion, and do you have any ideas to help solve it?